"IT'S OKAY, LUKE."

She gave him a level stare. "You don't owe me an explanation. You moved on with your life without me. I obviously complicated things for you by coming back."

"You did complicate things," he admitted. "But you also forced me out of this rut I've been living in."

She blinked. "Really?"

He nodded as a slow smile curved his mouth. "You made me start thinking about everything I want out of life. Everything I can still maybe have."

Swallowing the lump in her throat, Grace opened her mouth to say something, but Luke leaned forward, silencing her with his mouth before she could form any words...

~MISTLETOE~
ON MAIN
STREET

Book 1
in the Briar Creek Series

OLIVIA MILES

FOREVER

NEW YORK   BOSTON

Copyright © 2014 by Megan Leavell
Excerpt from *A Match Made on Main Street* Copyright © 2014 by Megan Leavell

All rights reserved. In accordance with the U.S. Copyright Act of 1976, the scanning, uploading, and electronic sharing of any part of this book without the permission of the publisher constitute unlawful piracy and theft of the author's intellectual property. If you would like to use material from the book (other than for review purposes), prior written permission must be obtained by contacting the publisher at permissions@hbgusa.com. Thank you for your support of the author's rights.

Forever
Hachette Book Group
237 Park Avenue
New York, NY 10017

www.HachetteBookGroup.com

Printed in the United States of America

First Edition: September 2014
10 9 8 7 6 5 4 3 2 1

OPM

Forever is an imprint of Grand Central Publishing.
The Forever name and logo are trademarks of Hachette Book Group, Inc.

The Hachette Speakers Bureau provides a wide range of authors for speaking events. To find out more, go to www.hachettespeakersbureau.com or call (866) 376-6591.

The publisher is not responsible for websites (or their content) that are not owned by the publisher.

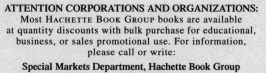

For Avery Grace, with love.

Acknowledgments

I would foremost like to thank my editor, Latoya Smith, for reading this manuscript, finding something special in it, and opening a whole new set of doors to me. I'm eternally grateful to you and the wonderful team at Grand Central Publishing for this amazing opportunity.

Thank you to my family for their love, support, and encouragement, and for believing in me at times when I'd stopped believing in myself.

Thank you to my husband for sharing this experience and for celebrating with me along the way. Special thanks to my beautiful daughter, Avery, who inspired the character of Sophie in this book and who keeps the magic of Christmas alive.

I am fortunate to have shared this journey with my oldest friend and critique partner, writer Natalie Charles. It's been a long road, and it's been even more special traveling it together.

Thank you as well to writer Victoria James, for her ongoing support and generosity. One of the best things to have come from this entire experience has been finding your friendship.

I am so grateful to all my friends and extended family who have cheered me on and supported me over the years. I'm blessed to have such wonderful people in my life.

And last but certainly not least, thank you to my readers for making all of this possible.

MISTLETOE ON MAIN STREET

CHAPTER 1

Pretty as a postcard.

As much as she wished to deny it, Grace Madison knew that nothing could top Vermont at Christmastime. Drawing to a stop as the snow-dusted road rounded a bend, she stared at the bridge in the near distance, her lips pursed with displeasure. Snow was falling slow and steady, neatly covering the slanted roof in a white blanket. Someone had hung a wreath complete with a red velvet bow just above the arched opening, and icicles gave a natural picot edging to the red-hued truss.

With a sigh, Grace pressed on the accelerator and drove across the bridge, over the frozen water below, and into her childhood home of Briar Creek. The hand-painted sign to the side of the road welcomed her, boasting of a population the size of her city block in Manhattan.

Make that her *old* city block in Manhattan, she corrected herself.

She continued down the familiar path, turning onto Mountain Road as the sun began to dip over the Green

Mountains. Grace flicked on her windshield wipers and fumbled for her headlights, cursing herself for not having learned the way around her rental car when she'd first picked it up. She scrambled with the gadgets around the steering wheel, smiling in grim satisfaction when the warm yellow glow illuminated the vast stretch of road before her. It was times like this when she remembered why she truly did prefer city life. This was the first time she had driven a car in...well, longer than she should probably admit. She and Derek never kept a car in the city—when they needed to go somewhere, they just hailed a cab.

Derek. No need to think about him now. With thinning lips Grace reached over and snapped off the radio and the depressing reminders of its melodies, but as silence encroached and left her alone with her darkening thoughts she abruptly flipped it back on, desperate to find a station that wasn't bleating Christmas carols with limited interruption. Surely there must be a talk radio station somewhere. Something that wasn't a painful reminder of how lonely this Christmas was going to be for her.

Her windshield wipers were in overdrive, in a vain attempt to keep up with the swiftly falling flurries. Wind swirled the flakes, stirring them up from the road in front of her, blinding her path. She slowed her pace to a near crawl, wrapping her hands tighter around the steering wheel, and squinted through the pellets beating against the windshield.

Her tires skidded on a patch of ice, causing her heart to drop into her stomach, and she eased off the gas, fumbling for control until the car came to an abrupt stop.

Grace opened her eyes and looked around. She was staring at a wall of snow as high as the hood of her car.

The woods around her were eerily quiet, and the only sound to be heard was the thumping of her own heart.

She swore under her breath. She not only had to figure a way to get the car on the road again but, unfortunately, she also still had to continue the drive. As if this trip wasn't bad enough already.

She checked herself quickly. She was not dead, or even injured, save the pinch mark on her arm where she managed to convince herself she really was still here. The impact had been comically soft, leading to nothing but complete aggravation about a trip that was already stressful enough. The ear-piercing scream she had released as the nose of the car collided with the snow pile had obviously been an overreaction—fortunately, no one was around to hear it. That also meant there was no one around to help, either.

The snow had turned heavy and wet, so that the flakes no longer flurried in the wind but instead created a dense blanket on the hood of the car. Gritting her teeth, Grace slid the transmission into reverse and gently pressed the gas pedal. When nothing happened, she gave it a little more force, wincing at the sound of her spinning tires. She clenched her hands around the steering wheel, feeling the panic squeeze her chest, and tried again. Nothing.

Without giving it any thought, Grace whipped off her seat belt and pushed open the car door. The wind howled around her, whipping her long, chestnut-brown hair across her face. The stretch of road before her was depressingly barren. The sun was starting to disappear over the mountains in the distance. It would be dark before long, and this old back road hadn't seen a plow all day. By nightfall, it wouldn't even be granted the light from a streetlamp.

Quickly, Grace walked to the front of the car, pressed her palms against the edge of the hood, and gave it a hard push, grunting at the effort. Four more attempts left her exhausted and upset. It was time to call for help. For not the first time today, she wished that Derek was here. This never would have happened if he had been driving.

Foolishness! She climbed back into the car, turning up the radio for company as she searched for her cell phone. It wasn't that she wanted Derek here—after all, they were over. Finished. She'd given back the ring; they had ended on good, if chilly, terms. No, she didn't want Derek here, not rationally speaking. She just wanted the things that Derek could provide, or at least, once had. Security, stability, safety. Comfort and joy. *Good tidings of comfort and*—Oh, that blasted Christmas carol!

Grace flicked off the radio and kept it that way. The last thing she needed right now was to get worked up. She had promised her mother she would arrive in time for dinner, and the last thing she owed anyone in her family was a frown by way of greeting. It would defeat the whole purpose of coming home at all.

She sighed again as she rummaged through her overstuffed handbag, still in search of her phone. Finding it buried beneath two candy bar wrappers and a receipt for the Christmas gifts tucked into her bags, she scrolled through the list of her family members until she found her youngest sister's number.

"Hello?" Jane's voice was barely audible above the clanking of pots. In the background, Grace could make out her mother's voice, followed by that of her middle sister, Anna. No doubt they were gathered in the warm, cozy kitchen right now, hovering around the big island that anchored the family home, squabbling over which side dish they should make, or who would cover the dessert. She imagined her little niece, Sophie, watching a classic holiday movie or making out her list for Santa.

Grace hesitated as she considered the gift she had bought Sophie for Christmas. She had no firsthand experience with four-year-olds, and Jane was forever raving about how quickly children changed. The last time Grace had seen her had been in the spring, and the time before that was when Sophie was only a year old when Jane and Adam had visited New York for a long weekend. She had been startled by how different Sophie looked nine months ago, and reminded of how much she had missed by staying away all these years.

Well, all the more reason to chin up and make this Christmas count. It was time to start making up for lost time. Time to stop wallowing in her own sorrow.

"Hey there—"

"Where are you?" Jane hissed through the crackling connection.

Grace frowned. "What kind of greeting is that?" She considered turning the car around right then and there. She could be back in the city by midnight, tucked into her bed with a bowl of her favorite Thai delivery and one of those feel-good Christmas movies that they played by the dozen this time of year. But then she remembered that she wasn't exactly feeling the holiday cheer this year. And that she was stuck in a rental car on a snow embankment on one of Briar Creek's most remote roads. And that she no longer had her own bed or her own apartment to hide in. All of her possessions that weren't locked in a storage unit in Brooklyn, New York, were crammed into four bags in the trunk of this car. *Damn it.*

"Sorry," Jane said. "I didn't mean it like that. I'm just...stressed. You know how it is."

Yes, Grace did. This time of year always brought out a hyper, frenzied side to their mother, who would be fretting for weeks in advance over table arrangements and menus, who would stand twenty feet back from the porch and scrutinize the pine garland with narrowed concentration, until her three daughters would shiver with cold, finally rolling their eyes and retreating inside to the warmth of the fire while their father stood patiently awaiting her suggestions, adjusting the garland to her satisfaction with an amused twitch of his lips.

Kathleen Madison was hailed the "Christmas Queen" of Briar Creek. Their house won the Holiday House contest twelve years in a row, until Kathleen deemed it in poor taste to continue, graciously stepping aside to accept the role of judge. "Let's give another family a chance," she had whispered to the girls, suggesting that no one else in town even stood a chance so long as the Madisons were entered.

A freelance decorator, Kathleen saw Christmas as her biggest opportunity of the year. The interior of the Madison home was always finely detailed with a porcelain Christmas village in the bay window, and an antique train set looping around the spectacular Douglas fir that the family selected together each year at the tree farm. Twice the Madisons' tree had appeared on the front page of the *Briar Creek Gazette*. Their annual cards were each laboriously calligraphied by Kathleen's own hand, and she approached her holiday baking with the rigor typically reserved for army drills. Every neighbor, friend, and teacher looked forward to Kathleen's homemade gift basket; the annual Christmas bazaar relied on her to deliver. And she always did.

"Are you still coming?" Jane asked, trepidation dripping from her words.

"Of course I'm still coming!" Grace squinted through the falling snow, searching for a sign of headlights.

Seeing nothing, she fell back against the headrest, considering Jane's insinuation. She couldn't blame her sister for being skeptical. With the exception of that painful spring morning nine months ago, Grace had managed to stay clear of her hometown and the memories it held. Five years had passed since she'd first left home—not knowing at the time it would be for good—and each year that stretched successfully distanced her further from her past, until eventually her life was tied to New York, not the sleepy New England town. And definitely not to anyone in it.

"I told you I would be there by dinner," she added, furrowing her brow through the whiteout. She flicked her windshield wipers a notch higher. It was no use.

"I just wanted to be sure..." Jane trailed off as the connection began to crackle. "I didn't know if you had changed your mind at the last minute because of...well, you know."

"If you're referring to the person we shall not name, you have nothing to worry about. I've avoided him for years, and I plan to avoid him for the next week, too." Grace swallowed hard. It could be done. She'd stay at the house, reading books, baking cookies, and trying not to think about the proximity of her first love. Her first heartbreak. Or everything else she had lost recently. "Besides, I'm not even sure why you're giving this any thought," she added with more conviction than she felt. "He and I are ancient history."

There was a pause on the other end of the line. "If you say so," Jane said softly.

Grace bit down on her lip, knowing it would be useless to try to defend herself. Jane knew her too well; Grace couldn't hide from her. Everyone in the family knew the reason why she had left Briar Creek and stayed away. It was all because of the man whose name they had promised never to say aloud in her presence. The man who could cause Grace's stomach to twist, her blood to still, and her heart to break all over again, just by mere mention.

She had changed her mind about this trip at least a dozen times, but in the end she knew there was no way around it. There was no telling what would prevail in Briar Creek while she was here. The wounds it would open. The scars it would sear. Her life was crumbling enough as it was—she couldn't risk any more upset.

Things were bleak. She'd managed not to think about it now for, oh—she checked the clock—seventeen minutes. Well, that was two minutes more than the last time she'd stumbled into her darkening thoughts. Her relationship wasn't the only thing that was over. Her career was rapidly unraveling as well.

She firmed her mouth. She couldn't think about any of this right now.

She slammed her foot on the accelerator, whimpering as the wheels ground deeper into the snow.

"Well, before you get here there's something I wanted to talk about—"

Grace almost managed to laugh. Now was hardly the

time to settle in for a long chat. "Can we discuss this later, Jane? I'm sort of stuck in a snowbank here."

"What?" Jane's voice was shrill, and Grace pulled the phone away from her ear, bringing it back in time to hear her sister say, "Should I call the police?"

"Relax," she said, giving the pedal everything she had in her. "I'm fine. I just slid off the road and now I can't get this," she pressed on the gas once more, knowing it was pointless, but still hoping, "stupid car to move!"

"But you're okay?" came Jane's urgent reply, and Grace instantly regretted worrying her. With everything their family had been through in the past year, she knew all of them were feeling sensitive.

"Yes, I'm fine. We've been talking for minutes, haven't we?" Grace put the car in park and trained her eye on the rearview mirror. "I just...I need you to come and get me. I'm going to have to call for a tow." From the distance, Grace thought she detected the sudden glow of a car making its way through the darkness. She perked up, sitting straighter in her seat, watching intently as the headlights grow closer. Sure enough, the SUV slowed and then pulled to a stop in front of her. She bit back a smile as she began gathering her belongings, ready to make a swift getaway.

"Never mind, Jane," she said quickly. "Someone just pulled up."

"Oh, good," Jane gushed. "So you'll be here soon?"

"I'll hitch a ride into town, but I might need you to meet me there." She could wait in her father's bookstore if need be—the thought of it brightened her. There was one silver lining to coming back to Briar Creek, at least. Main Street Books always had a way of making her forget her troubles.

"Okay. If I don't hear from you, I'll assume you're on your way."

Grace disconnected the call, musing over their casual comfort at the mere notion of hitching a ride with a stranger. She would never consider such a thing elsewhere, if the opportunity was even granted. Things were different in these parts, though. If someone saw a car pulled over in Briar Creek, they'd stop and lend a hand. If the same situation happened in New York, they'd just keep on going.

A tapping at her window startled her and she quickly crammed empty coffee cups and evidence from an indulgent stop at a fast-food joint somewhere near the Vermont border into their bags. Smiling apologetically, she shifted to face the window, her breath locking in her chest when she saw Luke Hastings's equally shocked face peering back at her.

She stared at him, not blinking, clutching a grease-stained paper bag to her heaving chest. *This day keeps getting better and better.* She had barely skidded past the town line, and she was already running into the one man she had hoped to avoid. Forever.

The lights from his black Range Rover beamed strong, and Grace noticed with a heaviness in her heart that he hadn't lost his looks since she'd last seen him. If anything, his features had hardened into something more manly and strong. The fine lines around his dark blue eyes gave him character, and their deep-set intensity gave her the same rush it always had. *Damn him.*

Grace held his gaze, knowing she was trapped. She was at his mercy now. He could walk away, refuse to help, drive off and leave her stranded on this unlit mountain road. In a snowstorm. No man would do that, not even Luke. But oh, she bitterly wished he would.

For not the first time she found miserable irony in the fact that Luke was, and always had been, a gentleman.

Grace rolled down the window with the press of her finger. "What the hell are you doing here?" she demanded.

An inquisitive smirk passed over Luke's rugged features. "Shouldn't I be the one asking you that?"

"I'm here for Christmas," she said tightly.

"Christmas isn't for another week," he said gruffly.

"So, it's still my town."

He lifted an eyebrow. "Is it?"

Grace looked away. "You can be on your way, Luke. I just got off the phone with Jane; she can come and get me." Her face burned as she fumbled in her handbag for her cell phone, blindly reaching for wherever it had landed.

Luke assessed the situation with a frown. "Looks like you've gotten yourself into a bit of a jam." He studied her. "Are you hurt?"

Grace pinched her lips and shifted her gaze from his scrutiny, but her eyes kept flitting back. Despite the winter chill that nipped at her nose and fingers, she felt overheated and stifled. "I'm fine, thank you. Everything is just…fine." And it was, or it would be, when he left. When he turned his back and walked away, like he had all those years ago.

A hint of a smile passed over his lips. "Really."

"Yes, really!" With that, Grace raised the window, feeling a moment of relief for the thin glass that separated her from…from the man whose name was never to be mentioned. She knit her brow and turned to glare at the steering wheel. Clenching her teeth, she pulled the car into reverse and hit the accelerator at full throttle. The tires spun loudly, but the car didn't move.

Heart pounding, she stared despondently at the dashboard for a few seconds before shifting her eyes to Luke's penetrating gaze. The corner of his mouth twitched, those blue eyes sparked, and Grace dragged a deep sigh, digging her nails into her palms.

He pointed his finger toward the car handle, gesturing for her to unlock it. His intense stare fused with hers, hooded by the point of his brow. His full lips spread thin, giving insight into his displeasure.

Well, the feeling was mutual, Grace thought with a huff. Tearing her attention from him, she unlocked the door. An icy cold wind whipped her in the face as she pushed open the door.

"What were you doing driving on this road in these conditions?" Luke demanded as she climbed out of the car. His dark hair spilled over his forehead, slick with snow. "You should have taken Oak or South Main."

Grace yanked away his half-hearted gesture to help her, and he let his hand fall at his side. She narrowed her eyes at the smirk that curled at those irresistible lips. The lips she had known as well as her own. Every line, every curve, every taste. She squared her shoulders and met his eye stonily. "Well, I took Mountain Road, okay? Besides, I could say the same thing to you!"

Luke tipped his head. "Not really. I live off Mountain Road. And I have four-wheel drive."

Grace bristled. She hadn't even thought to take South Main, even though it would have been a straight shot into town. Somehow, subconsciously, she had driven herself in the direction of the one person she hoped to avoid. The little part of her that longed for something that could never be had overruled all rational thought. And now, well, she supposed she'd gotten what she'd wanted. She was standing here, staring into the face of the man she hadn't seen, with the exception of that one, fleeting time she'd rather forget, in five years.

"I meant driving in the snow. At...this hour." She motioned to the darkness all around them.

She watched as Luke fought off a smile. A sheen of amusement lit his eyes. He made a show of checking his watch. "It's five o'clock," he said. "And my place is just down that way, as you'll remember." The grin finally got the better of him.

"Well." Grace inhaled sharply, the cold air slicing her lungs, and looked away. The snow was coming down in heavy, thick flakes. The hood of her car had already collected at least an inch, and her hair felt wet and heavy against her gray wool coat. *Perfect snowman weather,* she couldn't help thinking. If she were feeling the Christmas spirit, that is—and she wasn't. She most certainly wasn't.

"What are you doing out here?" he asked.

"I told you. I'm on my way home."

His jaw hardened. "Thought you said you were never coming back to Briar Creek."

She glared at him. That was only half the story, and he knew it. "Jane asked me to come home," she explained. "With everything that's happened recently, I couldn't exactly say no."

Luke nodded slowly. "I suppose not." He looked to the ground, shoving his hands in his pockets. "I didn't know you were coming."

"That's a surprise. Word usually travels fast around here." She folded her arms across her chest defensively, eyeing him through the falling snow.

He narrowed his gaze. After a beat, he murmured, "Yes. Yes, it usually does."

With a sigh he broke her stare and wandered over to inspect the collision site. She waited to see if he would find amusement in her predicament, but he didn't seem to be in the mood for laughs. The realization disappointed her, all at once reminding her of what they once had and no longer did. Standing here with the one person who knew her best, alone in the dark, on this cold mountain road, she had never felt more alone.

"Well," Luke said, bending down to inspect the situation more closely. "It doesn't look like you're going to get it out of this bank on your own."

"I'll call for a tow truck then," she said, rummaging through her bag and inadvertently setting a candy bar wrapper loose. She watched it whip through the wind, somewhere in the direction of the woods, and she could practically see Luke chuckling from her periphery. Finding her phone, she furiously tapped the number for information and waited. Nothing. Her breath caught in her chest as she pulled the phone from her ear and glanced at the screen. Connection lost. Of course.

She eyed Luke furtively, feeling her anger burn as a twinkle of enjoyment flashed through his blue eyes. Was this so easy for him? Did he not feel anything?

"No connection?"

"I had one a minute ago…" She exhaled deeply, and then rolled back her shoulders to fix her gaze on him. A rumble of something dangerous passed through her stomach as she studied his face. Would he ever not have this effect on her? "If you don't mind going into town for a tow, I'll just wait inside the car." She paused, gritting her teeth as she hesitated on her next words. "Thank you."

He looked at her like she was half crazy. "You think I'm going to go for help and leave you out here?"

She shrugged. "Why not? You've done worse to me."

A flash of exasperation crossed his rugged features. He rubbed a hand over his tense jaw, his eyes sharp as steel. Grace knew that look, knew it all too well. She'd made him angry. *Well, good.*

"Get in my car," he ordered, jutting his chin in the direction of his big black vehicle. "It's freezing out here."

Grace tried to suppress the shiver that was building deep within her. She'd be damned if she let him see how cold she was in her simple wool peacoat. She planted her feet to the ground, but it was no use. She shuddered, then inwardly cursed as Luke's expression softened.

"Here, take my scarf." He started walking toward her, but she reflexively took a step back. He stopped, his shoulders slumping. "Grace. Take the scarf."

Grace lifted her chin, her lips thinning. She glanced at him out of the corner of her eye, and her heart panged. There he was. Her sweet love. Luke Hastings. The love of her life. The man who had chased her through the icy waters of the creek in the heat of summer. The man who had taken her to bed in cool, cotton sheets. The man who had kissed her until she wept, the man who had held her until she couldn't breathe. The man whose smile could warm her heart, and whose frown could stop it. The man who represented every part of her past, and who was supposed to have held every moment of her future. The man no one since had ever been able to live up to.

"Fine," she muttered, reaching out to take the navy scarf. As she tied it around her neck, she subtly breathed into the fabric, closing her eyes to familiarity of the musky scent. She fingered the fringe at the bottom, knowing she had never seen Luke wear this scarf in all the years they were together.

She wondered when he had gotten it. She wondered if his wife had bought it for him.

"Your bags in the trunk?" Luke asked, and Grace nodded. Without another word, he popped the trunk and pulled out two large bags. He carried them low at his sides to his car and then returned for the second round. "You never did pack light," he grumbled as he brushed past her.

Grace hung back as he loaded her belongings, and glanced despairingly at her rental car, which was obviously not going anywhere on its own. "Should have listened to my gut," she whispered to herself. *Shouldn't have come here at all.*

"You coming or not?" Luke called with obvious impatience.

Grace closed her eyes, shaking her head in the negative even as she began walking toward the glow of his taillights. Each crunch of snow under her boots brought her one step closer to the part of her she had tried to deny since the day she left this town for good. Each inch closer to Luke's world took her further out of the one she had built for herself.

She reached the passenger door and yanked it open. If she stepped inside this car—Luke's car—there would be no going back. She paused, her breath coming in ragged spurts. She wiped a strand of cold, wet hair from her forehead. Inside the car, Luke was watching her expectantly, the heat from the vents felt almost suffocating against the crisp evening air.

With one last breath for courage, she climbed inside and left the safety of her world behind with a slam of the door. Like it or not, she was back in Briar Creek. And so far, it was going even worse than expected.

CHAPTER 2

The car was too quiet for his liking. Luke glanced sidelong at Grace, finding her pushed up against the passenger door, staring sadly out the window. His chest constricted at the familiar sight of her profile, the lift of her chin. He fought off a grin. She was still the same girl he'd fallen in love with nearly fifteen years ago. Still willful and proud.

He felt his lips thin. Proud to a fault, that's what she was. He was never good at dealing with her when she was like this—petulant. Stubborn. Impossible. There had been a time when he'd found this quality in her endearing, but that was a long time ago.

Grace's chestnut-colored hair hung in thick wet clumps at her shoulders and she combed her fingers through the matted tresses, flashing Luke back to all those summers spent splashing in Cedar Lake, the way she'd climb out of the water in that little red bikini, her long hair dripping down onto his face as she leaned him back on the warm sand, bending forward for a kiss.

She turned her bright green eyes on him, forcing him to look away.

"Music?" he suggested abruptly.

She shrugged. "Sure." She leaned in to inspect the dashboard, finally finding the switch to the radio. A well-known Christmas carol burst out at maximum volume, startling her enough to jump. She laughed to cover her surprise and he grinned. He'd forgotten the sound of her laugh. Forgotten how much he liked it.

"Sorry," he said, turning the dial. "I was listening to a rock station before I found you stranded on the side of the road."

"Sure you were," Grace bantered, then frowned. "You know, I wasn't *stranded* on the—" She stopped herself, laughing under her breath. "Thanks for the ride."

"Anytime." Luke managed a smile. It felt good. Too good. Like old times, almost.

He stiffened. Those times were better forgotten. Something he should have learned by now.

Tearing his gaze back to the stretch of road in front of him, he gripped the steering wheel. He'd gotten used to life without Grace in it. After the initial pain had worn off, he'd moved on with his life, and he almost appreciated her absence from the town she'd abandoned. The town he still called home. Living here without her around meant he could go about his day without any reminders. It meant temptation never surfaced. It meant guilt could be kept at bay, a niggling sensation in the recesses of his mind.

It meant he didn't have to work so hard to try not to think of her. It meant he could forget her. In theory.

Without a word, Grace turned the knob to a classical station, and the music settled into the background. She leaned back into her seat and extended her hands to the vents, splaying her fingers.

So she really had been cold—he *knew* it. Just like he knew she would never admit it. She'd rather get frostbite than let him help her.

The realization saddened him. There was once a time when all she ever wanted was his help. When she turned to him for everything, and he granted her every wish because he just couldn't say no to her. Then it all went off course.

"How long are you staying?" Luke asked, even though he wasn't sure he wanted to know, wasn't sure which response would be worse. The snow was falling harder now, but the four-wheel drive of his SUV had no problem on these back roads. Soon they'd be in town, and Grace would slide through his grip again. He swallowed hard.

It was better that way.

"Just through the holiday," Grace replied.

He nodded pensively, angry with himself for the disappointment that tugged at his chest. "New Year's?"

"God, no!" she scoffed.

"Figured as much," he said flatly. She hadn't changed—not one bit. And shame on the part of him that wished she had.

"I have to get back to New York soon. I'm only here through Christmas day."

"I'm surprised no one mentioned it," he mused as a sneaking suspicion took hold. In Briar Creek, word tended to travel fast, sometimes too fast. People around town must have known that Grace was visiting but made a point not to mention it to him.

Luke frowned. He'd have to have a chat with his sisters

to see how deep the secret went. Forcing a smile to lighten the mood, he said, "It's not often that best-selling author Grace Madison *graces* us with her presence."

"Ha!" The one syllable word was sharp with hurt, spoken with such bitterness, that Luke was startled enough to pull his eyes from the road.

She stared ahead, her eyes flat, her mouth a thin line. His own frown deepened. The old Grace would have rolled her eyes, chuckled at his attempt at a corny pun, but he'd obviously hit a nerve.

He'd seen the reviews of her latest book—he followed her career more closely than he should—and he was aware of a fair bit of criticism, but surely that wouldn't have her so distressed? The Grace he knew would have narrowed her eyes to the naysayers, taking enjoyment in proving them wrong. But the woman sitting beside him looked dejected and lost.

"I was back last spring," she offered and Luke nodded. They both knew why she had come back then.

"I'm sorry," he said, lowering his voice. "About your father."

He glanced at her quickly. She nodded, briefly meeting his eyes before her lids drooped. Her full, pink lips were pulled into a polite smile typically reserved for condolences.

"I paid my respects to your family," he continued, looking back to the road. "I hope I did the right thing by staying away from the funeral."

He held his breath, waiting for her response. According to chatter around town, Grace was in and out of Briar Creek in less than thirty-six hours. She'd stayed with her youngest sister, Jane, while Anna had moved in temporarily with their mother. She didn't reach out to him, and he didn't go looking for her. After hours of contemplation, he had decided the best thing he could do was to lay low and go about his life in Briar Creek. She knew where to find him; she would seek him out if she wanted to see him.

And she obviously hadn't.

A part of him feared the message it would send if he didn't attend the funeral. It would confirm every negative thought she held for him. It would cement him as that guy she thought him to be—the guy he knew he wasn't. The guy she thought had moved on from her, the guy who had thrown away every memory they shared, every bond they had formed.

She couldn't have been more wrong.

He'd sent a card, but it felt callous, cowardly even, to show support from such a distance. He wanted to be there for her, for all of the Madisons, showing them that he understood. Loss was something he was all too familiar with. He knew how it felt to grieve, to mourn. If Grace hated him the way she claimed to, wasn't it better to stay away? Had he done the right thing? He wasn't so sure.

After a pause she said, "You did."

He tried not to feel the sting of her words. So there it was. He wasn't sure what he had expected her to say, or what he even wanted her to say, but he knew what she should have said. She should have said that he had every right to be there, more than most in town.

How dare she think it was okay to deprive him of saying goodbye?

It had killed him not to attend Ray Madison's services. The man had been like a father to him since his own had died when he was only ten. Not long into his courtship with Grace, Ray had taken him under his wing, gently introducing him to the types of hobbies his own dad never had the chance to share. In the Madisons' garage, Ray had constructed a large workbench, where he tinkered with all sorts of things: from dollhouses when the girls were young to birdhouses and even some attempts at furniture. He'd sit out there for hours, and every so often Luke would join him. Ray would grin and hand him a sheet of sand-paper, sometimes a drill, and guide him through the next steps of whatever project was on hand. Once Luke got a handle on things, he'd set to work, eyes narrowed in con-centration. Ray spoke sometimes of his life, of his days in the classroom teaching, of the bookshop he ran by the time Luke had come around. Other times they wouldn't speak at all, but somehow the silence was companionable, and the hours always flew by.

Thinking back on those times now, Luke felt his chest ache. It still didn't seem possible that Ray was gone. He'd died way too early. That seemed to be a theme around these parts, he thought as a bitter taste filled his mouth.

"He was a good man."

"He was the best," Grace said quietly, and immedi-ately Luke regretted saying anything. It was too soon. Too fresh. He knew better than anyone how long the mourning period could be. "You meant a lot to him," she continued, surprising him slightly.

Luke managed a sad smile, feeling touched at the gen-erosity in her statement. "Well, the feeling was mutual."

"Sometimes I was almost jealous of you," Grace admitted.

"Jealous of me?" Luke darted his gaze to her, but she

was staring out the window, her attention focused well beyond the confines of the car.

"Oh, you know. Three daughters." She sighed. "He'd never admit it, but I'm sure he always wanted a son. You were like the one he never had."

"Oh, now. He adored you girls."

Grace smiled, seeming satisfied with the reassurance. "You're right."

They lapsed into silence as they turned into town—the decorations serving as an easy distraction. Luke scowled as they wound through the streets. The snow was letting up and the wonderland was in full view, made even more spectacular by the fresh blanket of whiteness that lent an almost eerie hush to the quaint storefronts. Each tree was wrapped in twinkling lights, each lamppost in pine garland and red velvet ribbon. A life-size depiction of Santa and his reindeer flew over the town square. Each shop window was decked out for the annual window display contest, and they didn't stop at wreaths or holly or a simple candle in the window.

They didn't stop until there was nearly a power outage, he thought, grimacing.

"Oh, well, look at this," Grace mumbled with clear disdain.

Luke looked at her quizzically. "I thought you loved this type of thing."

"That's my mother you're thinking of, not me," she corrected him.

"I seem to recall you getting pretty fixated on winning that igloo-building contest one year. You even drew up blueprints." He grinned at the memory of Grace bent over the table in his mother's kitchen, her eyes earnest and stoic when she informed him exactly how they were going to win. He always loved her determination—the way she could set her mind to something and see it through to completion. The way she stayed focused, and didn't let anyone sway her resolve.

He supposed that's why she'd gone so far in life at such a young age. Why Briar Creek could never be enough for her.

"Well," Grace huffed. "That was a long time ago."

"I guess I figured you came back for Christmas seeking this out. All this . . . spirit."

"I don't exactly have much Christmas spirit this year," she replied tersely.

"Then what do you know," he said with a small chuckle. "We have something in common, after all."

Grace looked at him. "You don't feel up for it this year either?"

Not this year. Not last. Luke fixed his eyes on the road, pulling to a stop at the intersection. "Nope," he said simply. It didn't seem like the time or place to elaborate.

After a long pause, Grace said quietly, "We have more in common than our lack of Christmas spirit, you know." *A lot more,* came the unspoken words.

Luke took a long, hard look into the depths of her large, green eyes, hating the shadow of hurt that passed through them. "I know," he said, holding her gaze until he began to feel something he shouldn't. It felt too familiar to be here with her like this. After all these years, he'd figured he was safe, that they would feel like strangers when they met again. Instead it felt like old times, and the ease of their conversation only solidified the depth of their connection. It felt like the past five years had never happened—

He gripped the steering wheel until his knuckles turned white. He couldn't think that way. It wouldn't be fair. Or right.

"I'm sorry about Helen," Grace said, as if reading his thoughts.

He ground his teeth. The sound of Grace's voice uttering his wife's name felt wrong...awkward. It felt like a betrayal, even now, after all this time.

"I know you probably don't believe me," Grace continued, "but I am truly sorry. No one deserves to die that young."

Nope, they didn't. Luke took a hard right down the next street. Chuck's Auto Service was at the end of the block. Their time together was nearing its end. Although, he thought grimly, he supposed their time had ended long before tonight. "You staying at your mom's?" he asked.

"Yep."

"I'll let Chuck know you need a tow and then I'll drop you off."

"Just drop me off at the bookstore," she told him.

Luke froze. "The bookstore?"

Grace gestured toward the next intersection. "If you bring me over to Main Street Books, I can call Jane from there. It won't take long for her to come and get me. I'll call Chuck while I wait."

He nodded slowly, focusing on the road as his mind reeled. Didn't she know? Hadn't someone told her? Obviously not.

"It's probably not open right now," he lied.

"Well, it's worth a try. Besides, it's not even five thirty, as you were so quick to point out earlier."

"Most places in town close early around this time of the year. Maybe you don't remember—"

"You're going to miss the turn!" she cried out, and reluctantly he turned the wheel, easing off the accelerator until the car crept to a stop in front of Main Street Books. The front windows were dark, a stark contrast from the sparkling storefronts that lined Main Street, and the light that had once illuminated the front stoop was off. He could barely make out the brass letters of the sign; only a few obvious books haphazardly arranged in the display case gave insight to its purpose.

"Closed. See." That was all he would say on the subject.

Grace was already unfastening her seat belt, and as she reached for the door handle and began to climb out, Luke scrambled to do the same. Sooner or later she was going to find out about her father's bookstore, but he didn't want to be here when that happened. She blamed him for enough already.

"Maybe they closed early today. There's a key hidden," she said, bending down to lift a pot that in the spring might have held flowers but was now covered with snow.

He held his breath and waited, wondering what she would think when she went inside, saw its current state.

"No key!" she exclaimed to his relief. She stood, frowning, staring at the pot. "It used to be there. I'm sure of it!"

Luke anxiously glanced through the glass panes in the door, to the stacks of books beyond. He had to get her away from this place. This wasn't the way for her to find out.

"Ah, well, let me drive you home," he suggested, forcing a casual grin and hoping she didn't sense the eagerness in his tone. He thrust his hands in his pockets, turning his back to shield himself from the howling wind that cut through his coat.

"That desperate to get away from me, huh?" She shot him a disapproving look and brushed past him to a large paned window, cupping her hands on either side of her face as she pressed her nose to the glass. The interior of the store was dark, the light from the iron streetlamp was dim, and Luke doubted very much she would see anything inside other than a few shadows. He hoped not, at least.

He shifted his weight on his feet as she searched under another empty pot, traced her finger over the top of the chipped and fading door frame, and jiggled the door handle one more time. With mounting unease, his gaze roamed from Main Street Books to the equally dark storefront adjacent to it.

He closed his eyes quickly, steeling himself against the biting wind, against the pain that was lodged in some deep, untouchable part of him. This was a street full of memories. Full of possibilities now gone. They shouldn't be here.

"We should get going. Chuck's going to be heading out soon, and you don't want your car stuck on the road overnight. There's no telling how much more snow we're expecting."

Grace lazily turned to face him, and he was struck at the disappointment in her eyes. She looked tired, deflated, and for a moment he forgot where they were. He'd seen that look once before, the last time he'd seen her. She stood there, the glow of the sun reflecting off her hair, her eyes full of hope, her lips still parted from their kiss, and he'd watched in agonizingly slow motion as the light left her face and her smile faded, until the girl he had known, the girl he had loved, was lost.

Catching the empty storefront in his peripheral vision, he stiffened and began to turn back to the car. "It's late. We should go."

Grace glanced wistfully back at the shop, finally giving a defeated shrug. "Well, I guess I'll just have to wait until tomorrow."

Luke watched warily as she maneuvered her way over the snowbanks that had gathered near the curb, pausing now and then to look over her shoulder. Her dad's bookstore meant everything to her. He could still remember finding her there after school, so engrossed in whatever book she was reading that she usually wouldn't even notice he had come in. Ray would often be roaming the aisles, shelving books or going through inventory lists, humming some tune. Grace would always claim he embarrassed her with his singing, but Luke knew better. She was a daddy's girl, and Ray could do no wrong. It wasn't only because of her love for books that Grace spent so much time here; it was because this was the one place she could have that special time with her father, away from the rest of the family. It was their place. A room full of happy times. And now it was gone. Just like Ray himself.

Luke cursed under his breath. It would kill her to know that the shop was closed, not just for the night, but for good. This place meant more to her than four walls and a roof. More to her than anyone, other than himself, could really understand.

He forced a grin. "Shops around here close early during the holiday season. This isn't the big city, Honeybee."

His pulse skipped at the ease of his words, the slip of his tongue. Silence stretched as he chastised himself. He had no business calling her that; he should have been more in control.

"I haven't been your Honeybee in a very long time," she said coolly as she climbed back into the car. The anger in her tone cut him straight to the bone. Any warmth in their unexpected reunion turned suddenly cold, serving as a reminder of how deep their history went. Their bond might be permanent, but it had severed a long time ago.

He set his jaw. "Force of habit."

"Don't let it happen again," she said curtly.

Oh, I don't intend to. Luke slid into the driver's seat and slammed the door shut. He wasn't sure which was worse: feeling like she was still the girl who knew him inside out, or feeling like she was a total stranger. That he meant nothing to her anymore.

But Grace Madison could never be nothing to him. And that was just the problem.

CHAPTER 3

Honeybee!

Grace stared out the window, shielding her face with the damp clumps of her hair, and watched the town, lit up and sparkling, whirr by.

She blinked rapidly, hoping Luke couldn't see how greatly he had shaken her. It was a nickname he'd come up with when they were kids, when she'd been cast in the role of a big, fat, yellow-striped bumblebee for the town's summer dance festival. She was twelve years old and all the other girls were playing beautiful flowers or butterflies, but not she. While they were gracefully floating around in gauzy, pastel-hued chiffon dresses, she was stuffing herself into a padded black and yellow leotard, her face hot with humiliation. Before it was her turn to go onstage, she'd hidden behind a group of hydrangea bushes at the far end of the park that was hosting the event and wept off all the makeup her mother had so carefully applied.

Luke was the stagehand back then, since his mother ran the dance studio, and when he'd found her crying he'd wiped at her tears and vowed he would never again allow his mother to cast the most beautiful girl in Briar Creek as the ugly duckling. And Grace knew then and there that he was the one.

It would take him two years to start looking at her as something other than his friend, but he still hadn't forgotten his first impression, and by then she almost didn't mind his little term of endearment.

Honeybee. She hadn't thought of that nickname in years, and she certainly hadn't expected to hear it again. Ever. But now she had and she couldn't deny the part of her that liked it entirely too much.

This was exactly why she should never have come back here.

Luke drummed his fingers against the steering wheel, his eyes focused on the road ahead. How many times had she sat next to him like this, lapsing into easy silence as they swerved through town, or laughing as they sang along to the radio? Now, his presence felt oddly unfamiliar to her, his body larger than she remembered, and even though he was right there, close enough to reach out and touch like she once so casually could, he felt further away from her than ever.

She shook her head and stared out the window, as the lights from town fell dim behind her and the road turned dark. She should have stayed put in town, camped out in the diner or Anna's café until Jane arrived. It would have been the sensible thing to do.

But then, when was she ever levelheaded when it came to Luke Hastings? The guy had crawled under her skin and stayed there, and try as she might, she couldn't shake him from the part of her heart that still yearned for him, and everything else that might have been.

"You can drop me off at the edge of the road," she told him, her tone decidedly clipped. If she let him see how easily he had gotten to her, she wouldn't stand a chance of getting through this trip in one piece. As far as Luke knew, she was over him the day he broke her heart, and she'd never looked back since. Best to let him keep on thinking that. If he had any idea how long the pain had lingered...

She rolled her shoulders against the seat back. She didn't want his pity. He didn't deserve her love. He didn't deserve any part of her.

"Afraid to be seen with me?"

His banter had succeeded in disarming her, and she gave a small smile. "You know how it is in that house. Two sisters and a mother. If they saw you dropping me off, I'd never hear the end of it."

"Would that be such a bad thing?" He slid her a glance and she lowered her eyes.

"Yes," she said firmly.

She grew quiet, returning her gaze to the window. Luke knew how her family worked, having known them as well as his own—it was what had made their breakup extra hard, on her at least. She knew her parents expected her to settle down with Luke, live close by, and stop over for Sunday dinners. Instead, she'd spent the last five years hiding out in New York City, licking her wounds and willing herself to forget the man who was so much a part of her, so ingrained in every ounce of her life, that there seemed no other way than to turn her back on her old life—the life she shared with him—completely.

She'd been so busy hiding from the man she had loved and lost, she had ended up losing the one she loved even more. Her father.

She glared at Luke from the corner of her eye. She'd missed so much.

A few minutes had elapsed when they turned down the winding road that led to her family home. Pine trees bent under the weight of snow, and many of the yards showed evidence of a day spent building snowmen. Christmas trees were centered proudly in the front windows, twinkling and inviting.

Grace bit her lip. She could just imagine what her mother would say about their subtle attempts. Surely comments would be made about the mismatched lights, the uneven distribution of the ornaments. While festive, the selection was understated to say the least. It would be nothing compared to Kathleen's perfected presentation.

She braced herself for the flawlessly executed extravagance, the carefully planned details, and idly wondered what theme her mother had gone with this year. They rounded another bend, nearing the last turn in the road, and Grace leaned forward in her seat as her childhood home came into view, frowning at the sight of the large Victorian. The candles that usually sat delicately on the center of each sill were missing. The garland that Kathleen obsessed over was absent. The twinkling lights that were always draped with near neurotic precision hadn't been hung. There wasn't even a wreath on the door!

Grace's heart lurched. "Slow down," she said to Luke, her voice catching in her pounding chest. Her eyes swept back and forth across the white Victorian farmhouse, trying to make sense of what she was seeing. Jane had implied it was the usual craziness, that she knew how it was. And she did! Christmas was a big deal in their house. Too big. But... "What's going on?"

She turned to Luke, searching his face for some sort of explanation, but he only shrugged. "What do you mean?"

"Where are the lights?" Her voice was shrill. She looked frantically toward the house, the bare stretch of yard. The naked wraparound porch. Why, it was the saddest house on the street. "The garland! All of it!"

Luke looked bewildered. "I...I don't know." He pulled to the side of the road and turned off the radio. They sat in silence, staring at the dark and uninviting house. Grace waited, hoping that at any moment, someone would flick a switch and the house would spring to life. Maybe they were waiting for her to arrive. Maybe Sophie wanted to surprise her. They waited, and with each second that ticked by, Grace knew the lights were not going to come on.

"My mother, as you know, is the Christmas Queen of Briar Creek." She started to laugh to ease her growing anxiety, gesturing with her arm to the irony of the situation. "This is downright depressing! What the heck has gotten into her? This isn't like her. Something must have—"

She stopped herself. Luke's gaze pierced her, his blue eyes filling with sympathy.

"Don't look at me like that," she muttered. "I don't need you feeling sorry for me."

Luke opened his mouth to say something but she opened the car door before he could continue. "You can drop me here," she said.

"But it's slick, and your bags—" He stopped when he saw her expression. In a huff, he put the car into park. "Fine."

Grace climbed out of the car, her feet slipping on the unpaved road. The cold wind stung her face, but the air felt fresh and clear. She breathed in large gulps, desperate to rejuvenate herself from the suffocating heat and the overwhelming awareness of his proximity.

Luke came around the front of the vehicle, extending her bags, and she took them from his grip, struggling to meet his stare.

"Thank you for the ride," she said tightly. The heat of his gaze made her momentarily forget they were standing outside in the middle of a snowstorm. She lowered her eyes to the ground, tracing a loop in the fresh powder with the tip of her black leather boot.

"Let me bring your bags to the door. I won't come in." His breath escaped in white clouds, and he thrust his hands deep inside his pockets, showing no signs of moving.

Grace adjusted her handbag and quickly slung a duffel bag over her shoulder. She stacked the smaller duffel bag on top of the roller case and grabbed the handle of the last bag with her free hand. She struggled for balance then righted herself, lifting her chin when Luke started to protest.

"This is ridiculous," he said.

"I'm fine." The weight of the duffel bag made her shoulder throb, and she could already feel her palms burn from the friction of the handle. "I've managed just fine on my own all these years, after all."

Something passed through Luke's eyes, and for a moment she dared to hope it was remorse. She held her breath, waiting for him to say something, anything that would make her feel less alone in her disappointment, but his jaw pulsed, and his mouth thinned to a grim line. "Have a good night, Grace. And Merry Christmas."

Grace stepped back, rattled by his dismissive edge, his gruff tone. What had he expected? For her to come back into town and throw her arms around him the first chance she had? They were over, long over, and that was his doing. He'd made his choice and she'd been forced to live with it. For years she had tried to banish his image, to focus on her work, her new life, even her new relationship. It was easier to stay away, to not dwell on the past, and now, not an hour past driving across the town border, she was right back where she started. Stung by the man who had the ability to hurt her the most.

Christmas was still a week away. Did he not intend to see her before then? Not want to? Was he letting her go this easily? Again?

What a fool she had been to think he would care, or have regrets. He probably hadn't thought of her at all in the past five years. To him, she was just a girl he used to know, his little Honeybee, a fond memory of his child-hood. He was a married man—well, a widowed man.

She blinked back tears; if they fell, she'd blame them on the wind. What was wrong with her, getting upset about Luke, now after all this time? There had been only one woman on his mind for the past five years, and it wasn't her.

Barely able to look at him, she managed something of a goodbye and began walking away, only slowing her pace when she feared she might slip on the icy road. The last thing she needed was for Luke to come to her rescue again.

The old Victorian farmhouse she had known and loved

so well came closer, like some twisted version of its former self. From somewhere beyond the darkness of the front room she thought she saw the flickering of a Christmas tree. Well, that was something.

She straightened her spine, hefting her bags to get a better grip. Luke was watching her from his car—she knew it. She could feel his eyes on her back. His headlights were guiding her way, and she fought the urge to turn back and look at him.

What must he be thinking of her? She glared into the snow. Nothing, she reminded herself. He was being a gentleman, like he always was. He was just lending a helping hand.

There was absolutely nothing more to it than that.

CHAPTER 4

Jane poked her head around the arched doorway that separated the kitchen from the den at the back of the farmhouse. Sophie was curled up in the armchair, flipping through the pages of a well-worn book and describing the pictures in an excited tone to her little rag doll. She looked so small in the armchair, so innocent, that Jane felt her heartstrings tug, and she had to look away. Hot tears prickled the back of her eyes, and she blinked before they could spill, darting her gaze to Anna, who was watching her impassively from the center island.

"Just checking on Sophie." Jane sighed through a forced smile and wiped her hands on her apron before picking up a wooden spoon. She distractedly stirred the tomato sauce that was simmering on the stovetop.

Anna murmured something terse and resumed chopping vegetables for the salad. Honestly! Jane had had about enough of Anna these days, and she knew it was only about to get worse once Grace showed up.

If she showed up.

"I hope Grace is okay," she said, turning to the window. The snow was falling harder now. She didn't even want to think about the condition of the roads.

"She just got her car stuck in some ditch," Anna huffed. "And she said she would call if there was a problem."

"I know," Jane said. Though she didn't feel the least bit reassured, she decided to keep the rest of her concern to herself. She certainly wasn't going to get any empathy from Anna on this one. Jane busied herself by adding another generous dusting of dried herbs to the bubbling sauce. Keeping her hands occupied had been the best tactic to keep her mind from wandering down paths she wanted to avoid of late.

"Don't overspice it," came Anna's warning.

Jane hesitated. With her back to her sister, she closed her eyes and counted to five, willing herself not to say something that would pick a fight or that she would later come to regret. Given that Anna was the certified chef in the family, one might assume she would be cooking tonight, but somehow that task, like so much else these days, had fallen to Jane. It was Christmas, the first Christmas without their father. Someone had to hold the family together, and it seemed like that person would be her.

With forced calm and a silent plea for patience, Jane set the container of herbs back on the counter and turned to Anna, smiling pleasantly. "Dinner should be ready soon," she said. "I'm sure Grace will be hungry after her drive."

Anna rolled her eyes. "I don't understand why you're making such a big deal about her coming home. She's the one who chose to stay away until now."

Jane inhaled sharply and released a slow breath. *One,*

two, three. "I understand where you're coming from, Anna. I guess I can't help but feel excited, though." She shrugged. "Maybe if she sees how much she missed us, she'll be inclined to visit more often."

Anna scoffed. "Don't bet on it." She began ripping the romaine with clenched fists, careless in her task but successful in making her feelings known.

Jane gritted her teeth, her nostrils flaring in reproach. Yes, they were grieving, each in her own way, but the tension was reaching a breaking point, and Jane was beginning to lose the battle with her own will. This Christmas was hard on her too, but she didn't have the luxury of falling apart the way her family could. She had Sophie to think about, and no matter how deeply her heart was aching, she was not going to allow her child's Christmas to be spoiled.

Jane shook her head and turned back to her sauce, gripping the side of the counter for support. The clock above the range ticked by another minute. *Please, Grace, get here soon.*

More than forty-five minutes had passed since she'd hung up with Grace, and she had been unable to get through since. She turned to the window, feeling slightly more relaxed to see that the snowfall was turning to light flurries. The roads might be slick, but Grace knew her way around town. It was ingrained in them the way home was. It didn't matter how long you were gone; once you were back, it was as if you had never left.

Not that she would know. But that's what people said.

"Do me a favor and don't be too hard on her," Jane suddenly burst out, flashing Anna an angry glance over her shoulder. "Sophie is thrilled to have Grace with us for the holiday, and I don't want any more tension for her. She's a child, and she deserves to have a happy Christmas without being bogged down by issues she could never understand."

"Whoa! What's got you so worked up?"

"Nothing," Jane muttered, feeling her eyebrows draw to a point. "Just...be nice."

Anna fixed her blue eyes on Jane, her mouth thinning. She went back to ripping the lettuce, tossing it carelessly into a large bowl.

Jane released a dramatic sigh. Between her mother refusing to decorate for the holiday and Anna acting like a petulant child, Jane had been counting the hours until Grace's arrival. Her oldest sister may not have been around much in recent years, but at least she wouldn't add to the negativity.

"So why isn't Adam here?"

"What?" Jane jumped at the sound of her husband's name—her lying, cheating husband. She stirred the sauce more quickly, her heart pounding. Finally, she gave the same excuse Adam had given her: "I told you. He has to work late."

Silence fell on the kitchen. Jane watched the bubbles form and pop in the sauce as she waited for her nerves to steady.

It was becoming increasingly difficult to hide the truth from her family. She was running out of excuses for Adam's continued absence, and the more lies she told, the less she was convinced her mother and sister were buying them. She knew she should tell them, and under normal circumstances she would have and they would have responded appropriately, with hugs and comfort, hot tea and a tissue for her tears. But it had been a long time since she'd been able to rely on either her mother or Anna. They were depending on her these days to keep the family from completely crumbling. They had no idea how unfit she was for the position.

Many times she had thought of telling them, especially when Anna was being especially brusque or difficult, but all it took was one glance at her mother's pale and drawn face to make her clamp her mouth shut. Jane knew it wouldn't help her to dump her grief on someone who had more than her share already. This Christmas was going to be hard enough for Kathleen to get through without the added worry of her daughter's and granddaughter's welfare and happiness. If there was one gift Jane could give her mother this year, it was to minimize the pain in any way possible.

It was the same approach she was taking with Sophie, she reminded herself with newfound resolve. She deserved to have one last Christmas before her family was ripped apart.

Jane turned off the burner and set the wooden spoon on a ceramic holder. "I think I'll go wait in the living room for Grace," she said breathlessly, untying her apron. She didn't wait for Anna to answer as she strode out of the kitchen and into the dark room at the front of the house, where she slumped onto the window seat, relaxing her shoulders. The only chance she had to be herself anymore was when she was alone, but she was hoping Grace would change that.

Grace loved their family, Jane was certain of this, but time and physical distance lent her a certain level of detachment. Jane knew that Grace was just as devastated by the death of their father as they all were—deep down, they had sensed she was his favorite, after all. But Grace wasn't here every day living with the ups and downs of her family's emotions. She was able to go back to her life after the funeral, whereas Jane and Anna had been forced to deal with the fallout. Anna resented Grace for this, and God knew she didn't keep the sentiment hidden, but Jane saw it differently. Jane saw Grace as her perfect ally: someone who loved her but wasn't very close to her anymore. She could tell her sister about Adam's treacherous behavior without hurting her further. Oh, Grace would feel bad for her, of course, but she wouldn't let it bring her down.

Yes, she was exactly what Jane needed right now. And thankfully, she would be here any minute. Just the thought of it made Jane's heart swell with something close to hope.

In the distance she heard her mother mutter something to Anna about Sophie getting hungry. Anna's sharp retort was laced with resentment when she said, "We're still waiting on Princess Grace, Mom. It's her world isn't it? Jane practically has the red carpet rolled out!"

Jane frowned and turned back to the window, leaning her cheek against the icy cold pane as she looked down the street to the cheerfully decorated homes. She knew all of the families, of course, and she could picture them inside, gathered around a tall, beautifully decorated tree, sipping hot cocoas, or laughing over a big meal. She wished for a moment she could duck out of the house, run down the street, and invite herself in. They'd welcome her, after all. But no, instead she had to be stuck in *this* house.

Well, she supposed she should be grateful that after a

long, firm discussion with her mother, they had managed a sad, skinny Christmas tree so Sophie wouldn't sense something was amiss.

Anna's voice from the kitchen cut through her thoughts. She was speaking to their mother again. "No, Jane said he has to work." There was a pointed pause. "She implied he wasn't coming."

Jane's temperature rose and she held her breath, craning to hear her mother's response.

"Adam's such a hard worker," Kathleen murmured, and Jane rolled her eyes, turning back to the vast bay window.

Adam worked hard, all right. Hard at chasing women, or at least one woman in particular. Jane's face burned with shame when she thought of the humiliation he had brought on her—the horror she had felt in her discovery, while he went about his dirty business as if she were none the wiser. She pressed her hand against the cold glass of the window, not caring if she left her fingerprints behind. She swiped a tear from her cheek before it had a chance to fall and sniffed hard, releasing a ragged breath. The last thing she needed was to be caught crying. It would only make everything worse than it was. And it was pretty bad already.

She swept her gaze gloomily across the street, searching up the road for an oncoming car, and it was then that she saw her. Her breath caught in her chest, igniting a spark of joy she no longer knew existed. Grace had come home. She was really here. Tears stung her eyes and she didn't even think to swipe them away.

Growing up, Grace had meant everything to her—she was the oldest, the most sophisticated, and the sister that

Jane most greatly admired. She had long ago given up thinking that Grace would ever return to Briar Creek for good, and eventually she had learned to go about her daily and often monthly routines without missing her. Seeing her now, knowing she had made the effort to come here, that she had come because Jane asked her to, filled Jane's heart with an ache so deep, she thought she would burst into tears right then and there.

She dashed to the door and flung it open, not even caring that the cold wind flew through the hallway. She hugged her sweater around her body as Grace turned onto the snow-covered stone path leading up to the porch, but her bright smile faded when she saw the shadow in Grace's normally bright green eyes.

"Jane." Grace's expression lifted into a smile that didn't quite reach her eyes. "The house—it's so dark." Fear laced her tone as she took the porch steps. "Jane, what's going on?"

Jane only shook her head, swallowing the lump that had formed in her throat. Everything would be better now. It certainly couldn't get any worse.

"Oh my, you're really here!" She pulled Grace into her arms for a hug before the reunion could be shared with her mother and Anna, whom she could already hear coming down the hall behind her.

Against the cries of rare delight from her mother and less enthusiastic greetings from Anna, Jane pressed her mouth against her sister's damp hair, whispering urgently, "I tried to warn you."

CHAPTER 5

Grace set her fork on the edge of the plate and glanced around the table, frowning at the sight of her mother, who sat at the head. Kathleen was hunched, listlessly dragging her fork over the fine, ivory porcelain china edged with a hand-painted holly design.

Grace looked away, back to her own half-eaten meal, and darted her eyes over to Anna, who was making an entire production out of her dismissive body language. Her head was down, eyes fixed to her plate, from which she took quick, robotic bites. Anna was obviously upset, and something told Grace it went well beyond their father's absence. She'd barely said more than three words since Grace had arrived, and all had been spoken in clipped, curt tones.

Feeling Jane's stare, Grace shifted to meet her youngest sister's gaze, her heart pulling tight at the apologetic grin Jane offered. With a small smile, Grace lowered her eyes and poked at her meal, stifling a heavy sigh. So it wasn't going to be a warm and fuzzy Christmas. She hadn't had one of those in years; in theory, she had no room for disappointment.

"So, Sophie," she said with false cheer, as she turned her attention on the little girl beside Jane, who was shifting restlessly in the stiff, open-backed Queen Anne chair. "What grade are you in now?"

Sophie let out a giggle and clamped her hand over her mouth. "I don't have a grade, silly! I'm too little!"

Jane tilted her head. "She's only four," she explained. "She goes to preschool three mornings a week."

Grace squinted, quickly doing the math. Sophie looked so much bigger than the last time she had seen her, and that had only been nine months ago. Her brown hair was thin and silky then; now it was thick and past her shoulders. Jane had fastened a sweet little white barrette on one side. Sitting close, Grace was struck by how much the mother and daughter resembled each other. Just looking at her little niece, she could almost picture Jane, so small, sitting at this very table. She smiled at the image, but she couldn't deny the part of her that ached with longing.

Derek had claimed she was feeling emotional, sentimental, when she returned from her father's funeral and told him she wanted to have a child. Not then, but someday. He'd stared at her, unblinking, and then placed two heavy hands on her shoulders, his gentle tone telling her it was the grief talking. They'd never discussed children, or any concrete plans for their supposed future together really, and Grace had suspected this would be Derek's response. But hearing it confirmed... He'd left her no choice.

Grace smiled at her niece, thinking of how it would

feel to have her own little girl like Sophie one day. She glanced at Jane, feeling happy for her despite her own dull sadness.

Jane had gotten it right. She'd followed the path of least resistance. The path Grace herself could have taken. And didn't.

Grace inhaled sharply. "She's so grown up. She's like . . . a real kid!" She pursed her lips at the derisive snort that came from Anna's end of the table.

"Nice to see that you're awake over there," Grace observed, and immediately regretted her words when she heard the sharpness of her tone.

Anna's turquoise blue eyes narrowed ever so briefly. "Nice that you finally deigned to honor us with your presence after all these years," she said. "I'm sure Dad would have appreciated it when he was still alive."

"Anna!" Jane cried out, but Anna simply shrugged, slid another pointed glance at Grace, and returned to her food.

Grace sat back in her chair, waiting for her pulse to steady. Her chest heaved with each breath, and she didn't dare meet her mother's eyes. A deadly hush had fallen over the room, one that seemed capable of lingering long beyond the dinner. One that threatened to ruin the evening and hover in the background until she finally went back to New York.

Anna had spoken the words that everyone had been thinking, including Grace. She had hoped she would be met with happiness and warmth, that her time away from this town, this house, them, would be understood. She also wanted to do something positive for her family by coming home for Christmas, something that went beyond solidarity or a promise to Jane. Perhaps she had overestimated how much she meant to them.

She swallowed the ache that scratched at her throat and stared at her plate.

"Dinner is delicious," Jane announced, her words falling on silence. Lowering her voice, she urged, "Eat a few more vegetables, honey."

Grace glanced up to see Sophie making a face. "Oh, no thank you, sweetheart," she said. "I really don't like them."

Despite the weight in the room, Grace heard herself chuckle in surprise. "Did she just call you *sweetheart*?"

Jane nodded, grinning. "She doesn't understand how to use terms of endearment yet." She smiled proudly down at her daughter, sliding her hand down the length of Sophie's ash brown locks—the same color as her own. "It's even funnier when she does it with Adam," she said. A shadow briefly passed over her face, and she reached for her water glass.

Grace frowned. "Adam couldn't join us this evening?" She felt rude for not asking about him earlier, but the mood among the women didn't lend itself to thinking of much outside the confines of these four walls.

Well, with the exception of Luke.

Grace took a long sip of her wine as her pulse quickened. She could still see him standing in that biting cold, the wind blowing his hair over his forehead, his blue eyes piercing and sharp. She gritted her teeth against the hold he still had on her.

Jane glanced nervously around the table. "Oh, Adam had to work late. Client dinner or something."

She fiddled with her napkin and Grace nodded, seeing

nothing wrong in Adam working late, but wondering why Jane seemed to think otherwise. Derek worked late most nights at his investment banking firm, and she hadn't thought twice about it in all their time together. She suspected there was more going on than Jane was letting on. She made a mental note to ask her mother about it later.

Her mother. Grace sighed at the sight of her, now staring dreamily out the window. Her plate was untouched, her wineglass the same. There would be no asking her mother anything, it seemed. Kathleen was the one who needed holding up right now.

"The tree looks really pretty, Mom," Grace fibbed and was granted a thin smile in return.

"It's not as nice as the tree at *our* house!" Sophie announced.

Grace felt inexplicably relieved to turn her attention back to her niece. It seemed she was the only one in the house who wasn't hiding something, or stewing in silent emotion. "Oh no?"

Sophie shook her adamantly. "Nope. Grandma's tree is all droopy and there aren't enough ornaments! Santa's *not* going to be impressed," she added.

"I didn't see a point in climbing into the attic to fetch the boxes this year," Kathleen replied, and Grace glanced at Jane, whose eyes flashed in desperation.

"So, Grace," Jane said, clearing her throat. "You didn't tell us who gave you a ride home tonight. A real Christmas hero, I take it, swooping in to save the day." She forced a cheerful smile that didn't quite meet her eyes.

Something like that. Grace stared at her plate, feeling the hot blush stain her cheeks. "It was Luke," she muttered, not daring to meet her family's eyes. She was convinced that even her mother had perked up at this tidbit.

"Luke *Hastings*?" Jane drawled.

Grace straightened her shoulders and leaned back against her chair with a lift of her chin. She had broken her own rule by saying his name aloud. It felt oddly exhilarating. "None other." She managed a thin smile and shifted the broccoli spears from one side of her plate to the other.

A heavy silence covered the room like a warm winter blanket. "Is Luke your husband?" Sophie finally interjected, and the table erupted into laughter for the first time that evening, even if it was laced with wariness, a guarded and abrasive edge to mask the nervous undercurrent.

"No," Grace said simply. She tried to ignore the tightness in her chest at the suggestion. Luke had been a husband once. Just not hers.

Sophie wrinkled her nose. "Well then, where's your husband?"

Grace faltered, shifting her eyes to Jane for support and seeing only amusement roll through her expression. "I don't have a husband."

"You don't?" Sophie cried. "Aunt Anna doesn't have a husband. Now Grandma doesn't have one either."

Grace met the panic in Jane's hazel eyes. "Well, your mommy has a husband," she said, trying to steer the conversation into more positive territory, but again a shadow fell over Jane's face.

Sophie nodded proudly and beamed at her mother. "The best one there is. Isn't that right, honey?"

Jane gave a tight smile. "The best one there is," she said softly.

"Wait," Anna said, startling Grace enough to cause her to drop her fork. "What about Derek? Unless—"

Derek. Closing her eyes at the magnitude of her step backward, Grace thought of the man she had spent eighteen months of her life with and came up flat. The only face she could see was Luke's. That strong, chiseled jaw; the bold, roman nose with the slight bump on the profile from the time he broke it sledding. The deep blue eyes that twinkled in the sunlight and darkened to navy when he pulled her in for a kiss. The little scar on the right corner of his lip that disappeared when he smiled. Grace cleared her throat and looked directly at Anna. "We broke up."

"I didn't know that!" Jane interrupted. Her eyes creased with such concern that Grace felt her mouth curve into a half smile. Leave it to Jane to still care. Jane cared about everyone. It was probably why, as the youngest of the three sisters, she was the only one to have so much love in her life. A husband. A child.

Grace pressed her lips together.

She supposed she could have tried to hold on to Derek a little longer, just to get through the holidays, but she knew it was pointless. It would have only complicated things knowing the end was in sight, that she was holding on to something that wouldn't and couldn't last. They hadn't even set a wedding date, and, worse, that had never worried her. She and Derek were not meant to be.

On paper, she and Derek looked like the perfect match. With his tall, lean frame and classic facial features, he fit the role he played as well as he filled a designer suit. He could light up a room with his smile, cause middle-aged women to blush with a glint of his eye. The thing that made him so irresistible—at least to Grace—was the cool, confident way he approached his life and the warmth and generosity he extended to those around him. What he didn't spend from his Wall Street earnings on his lush, lavish lifestyle, he gave to charity. He served on seven boards, and hosted an annual fundraiser for the children's hospital. He was kind to the elderly. He was good to his mother. He was good to her. He was...perfect. Almost.

He just wasn't Luke. And he couldn't offer any of the hundreds of wonderful things Luke could have.

Once.

With Anna and Jane gone, Kathleen sighed and set the last dish in the sink. "Well, I think I'll turn in for the night," she said, reaching over to flick off the kitchen light as if that was that. The room fell dark, the light from the moon traced shadows over her face.

It was only seven thirty, but Grace didn't argue. It had been a long, tense dinner, and if her mother wanted to be by herself, Grace wasn't going to stop her. If anything, she welcomed the chance to be alone. She'd had about enough family time for one night, and she needed time to process everything. She hadn't dragged herself to Briar Creek without a hearty helping of trepidation, and in one evening all of her worst fears had come true. And then some.

She'd thought that at the very least she'd be comforted with an ornately decorated home, a cozy holiday film playing in the background, a row of matching stockings hanging above a crackling fire, and the usual wild-eyed look her mother reserved for this time of year. Just the thing that would force her out of her funk and bring out her Christmas spirit. Instead, she was left with only a heavier heart. Oh, and a fresh image of Luke to boot.

If she were still writing, she might find some escape. But she wasn't writing much these days, and she hadn't for months. With the current state of her career, she wasn't sure she would ever write again.

Grace wrapped her hand around the old banister and retraced the familiar steps to the top landing. Her room was the second on the left, and the master bedroom door at the far end of the hall was already closed. A light filtered through the crack under the six-panel cherry door, and Grace hesitated before turning the glass knob to her room. She chuckled when the knob on the inside fell to her feet with a loud thud against the polished floorboards. Bending to pick up the heavy glass ball, she jiggled it back into place, shaking her head. In all this time, it had never been fixed. She was pleased to find it wasn't. At least one thing in this old house was unchanged.

Crossing the room, Grace plunked one of her bags on top of the desk near the window. She turned, taking it all in.

The bedspread still covered the twin bed in a pink and white floral print. Matching curtains donned the windows, framing the window seat where she would sit and write for hours, scribbling by hand in soft leather-bound journals.

She pulled opened the closet door and, sure enough, hanging on the back of the door was Luke's varsity jacket. The one she never could bring herself to give back.

Setting her jaw, Grace shut the closet more forcefully than she had intended, and wandered over to her bed. She climbed up onto it, amused at how high it was. It felt foreign and much too firm. She tapped the pillow. Lumpy. She laughed when she realized her toes hung off the edge, and she wiggled them, trying to remember if it had always been this way. It must have. She flicked on her bedside lamp, frowning at the pink frilly shade, recalling when she and her mother picked that out together, thinking it was the height of sophistication, and hopped off the bed.

Her bookshelf was still stacked with her favorite classics, and she grazed her finger over the spines, smiling at the familiar titles, and the memories they evoked. She'd alphabetized them all by author, and it took no time at all to find the complete Nancy Drew collection, arranged by publication date. She retrieved the first in the series, rubbing her hand over the pristine cover, and opened it to a random page, idly reading a paragraph before returning it to its proper spot.

Her sisters had always thought she was crazy, that her books meant too much to her, that she was strange about them, refusing to lend them out to anyone, getting panicky if someone dog-eared a page or even *thought* about using one as a coaster. Even now, she shuddered at the possibility.

Her dad had understood. He understood a lot of things. Whenever Anna made fun of her, or her mother would frown with confusion, her father would quietly meet Grace's eye across the room and wink. That was all it took.

Grace swallowed the lump in her throat and turned away from the bookcase. Tomorrow she'd go over to the shop. She always felt better at Main Street Books, no matter how rough the day had been.

She knew it was because of the store that she'd become

a writer—before her father took over the store, she loved the crowded atmosphere, the musty smell of paper. There was no greater thrill than the discovery of a great new book, and no bigger comfort than being able to curl up with it in one of the old English armchairs dotted throughout the store, hidden by shelves of books that reached the ceiling, escaping the world for just a little bit.

Hot tears prickled the back of her eyes, and her throat felt raw and scratchy. Heaving a sigh, Grace busied herself by unpacking, carefully arranging her clothes in the chest of drawers that was now empty, and hiding the Christmas presents in the cedar chest at the foot of the bed, in case Sophie came looking for them. She took a hot shower, wrapping herself in one of the big fluffy white towels her mother always stocked in the linen cabinet, deciding that when she got back to New York, she would invest in some herself. When she found her own apartment, that was. She couldn't live on her friend Angie's sofa forever, and she couldn't exactly go back to the sleek, stunning apartment she had shared with Derek, even if it did have a king-sized bed that would accommodate the entire length of her, toes and all.

Enough worry for one night, she decided. When her wet hair was combed and her face was moisturized, she turned down the bed and hesitated.

Had they kept it? After all these years? Or had they known to hide it, to put it somewhere she would never have to see it again?

If the varsity jacket was any indication, then it was still here. The room was untouched, more or less, and a small part of Grace resented her mother for that. Why couldn't she have been like half the other parents Grace knew of and turned the space into a sewing room or something?

Knowing the urge would keep her awake long into the night until she finally gave in and faced her fear, Grace climbed down onto her hands and knees, reaching her arm deep under the curtain of the dust ruffle, her hand sweeping the floor until there—*there it was*. Her breath caught in her chest as she tugged the box toward herself and set it on her lap.

She could feel her heart thumping as she slowly lifted the lid, immediately wishing she hadn't when she saw the corsage Luke had given her for their senior prom— its pale pink petals were dry and withered, brown and crisp at the edges. But it was still beautiful. She lifted it gingerly out of the box and set it on the floor beside her. She pulled out a few other items, pausing to hold them in her hands, remembering the importance they once held, before setting them next to the corsage, her heart growing heavy.

Underneath a few old yearbooks she found the item she had been waiting for. A thick, leather-bound photo album. Ten years of history wrapped neatly into one little book. The proof that once upon a time he had been hers, she had been his, and she had meant something to him, possibly more than she had even known. Or maybe less than she had thought.

She paused, recalling his gruff dismissal of her tonight. Had she really been hoping for more? If so, she was an even bigger fool than she thought.

Grace closed her eyes, remembering the last time they had spoken, the day her world had slipped out from under her and everything she had counted on, hoped for, and believed in just vanished. A knot wedged in her throat and she opened her eyes, willing herself to the present moment, frantically placing the items back in the order she had found them, the delicate corsage on top.

She climbed into bed, flicked off the lamp, and snuggled under the soft flannel sheets and the heavy down comforter. Nearly five years had passed since that day, and if today was any evidence, a lot had changed since then. She'd grown, moved on, and established a whole new life for herself. She'd reached her greatest career dreams, and seen them crumble down around her. She'd dated men, maybe even cared about a few. Hell, she'd been *engaged*. She'd had an adult relationship with Derek—a relationship built on real life and not childish pipe dreams or ideals.

Despite it all, lying here on her too-hard mattress in her prissy little-girl bedroom, Grace felt like no time had passed at all. She was the same girl who had fled Briar Creek in tears, desperate and lost, and wondering where on earth she was expected to go from here. She thought she'd found her way. Yet now she was right back where she started.

CHAPTER 6

Luke caught Mark's eye as he pushed through the glass door of the diner, and even from a counter-length's distance, he could see the flicker of anticipation register in his cousin's gaze. Not bothering with pleasantries, Luke plunked himself onto a swivel stool and turned over his coffee mug.

"How long have you known?" he demanded.

Mark held his stare, nonplussed. He filled Luke's mug within a half inch of the brim. "So you saw her, then?"

"Did you think I wouldn't?" Luke clenched his jaw and distractedly poured some milk into the coffee. He took a sip, not even tasting it.

"I take it things didn't go so well," Mark said.

"You could say that." Luke pushed his mug to the side and spread his elbows on the Formica surface, folding his hands. He lifted his chin. "Did Molly and Kara know about it?" he asked, referring to his younger sisters. Molly was on break from grad school for the holidays, and surely she and Kara would find this bit of information newsworthy.

Mark set the coffee pot back on its burner. "Everyone knew, Luke."

Luke hissed out a breath. "Unbelievable." He looked around the room, and sure enough there was Jackson Jones, Briar Creek's mayor, watching him with interest from across the room. Near the window sat Nate McAllister and his brother Rhys. All good guys, guys he had known all his life, people Luke might even classify as friends. But not today. Today no one in this town was his friend. For a fleeting moment he understood why Grace ran from small-town life. Living here, half the locals knew your business before you did. He turned back to Mark and said, "So you all conspired to keep this from me. As if I wouldn't find out."

Mark lowered his voice. "We all know this time of year is rough for you. We were only trying to help."

Luke shook his head and stared out the window at the front of the room. The snow had continued through the night, leaving downtown Briar Creek a veritable winter wonderland. Frost collected on the bottoms of the diner windows, which had been decorated with a hand-painted snowman and snowflake design. On the sidewalk, throngs of people bustled along the sidewalks, wrapped in colorful scarves, clutching shopping bags bursting with shiny, wrapped packages. At the post office across the street, a line was already forming out the garland-draped door.

Yep, it was beginning to feel a lot like Christmas, all right. And he didn't like it one bit.

"Doesn't this music drive you crazy after a while?" Luke asked Mark, gesturing to the speaker tucked into the corner of the ceiling. Mark shrugged and slid a steaming plate of hash to Arnie Schultz, who ate at least two meals here a day. The fact that Luke knew this wasn't lost on him—he really needed to get out more. He just…couldn't.

"Sure I can't get you anything?" Mark asked.

Luke frowned. Since winter break started last week, he had been in here each morning, unable to stand the emptiness of his house. Weekends were especially tough, and Luke made a point early on to keep himself busy. He had dinner with his mother or Mark once or twice a week, breakfast at the diner with the newspaper on Saturdays. And Sundays. School breaks were lonely times— especially summer, when it seemed everyone around him was grabbing their sweetheart by the arm, heading off to the lake or a picnic in the park. Still, nothing compared to Christmas break.

Last year, his first Christmas since Helen died, had been unbearable. He had been determined to have a better handle on it this year. And then Grace Madison had to come back to town.

Luke rubbed a hand over his face and turned back to Mark. "I'll take a Western omelet," he said, and let Mark refill his coffee. Growing up in the same small community, the two were more like brothers than cousins. They were born the same year, and both knew how it felt to lose a father at an early age, even if under different circumstances. Luke was one of the few people who knew how much it hurt Mark when his father up and left town without so much as a glance back at his wife or two young sons. His own father had tried to step in and make up for his brother's wayward act, and when he died shortly thereafter, Mark took the news almost as hard as Luke and his sisters. Luke thought they had an unspoken pact, a loyalty. But this…He gritted his teeth.

"So you mean to tell me that I've been in here every morning this week, and you chose not to mention this?"

A twinkle sparked Mark's brown eyes. "Yep."

"It's not funny," Luke reprimanded, but Mark's mouth twitched. "You knew I was bound to find out. Were you waiting for me to come in one morning and tell you?"

"Yep." Mark tipped his head, fighting a smile. "Come on, Luke. Do you really blame me? We all knew how you'd react to hearing that Grace was back. I didn't want to have to be the one to tell you."

"And how was I expected to react?" he demanded.

Mark shrugged, eyed him up and down. "Pretty much like this. Agitated. Restless. Conflicted. We all know how you feel about Grace."

"Felt," Luke corrected. "How I *felt* about Grace," he said, and Mark lifted an eyebrow, saying nothing. Luke's chest tightened and he rubbed his jaw, scratching at the morning stubble, thinking of Helen, of her long, blond hair and her sweet smile.

"Sorry," Mark said as an afterthought, and Luke grimaced, giving a slight nod.

"It's okay," he said.

"No, no it's not. It was insensitive." Mark heaved a sigh. "I feel like a jerk."

Luke offered a small smile, holding up a hand. "Let it go."

Mark glanced around the room and tipped his head toward a booth at the far end of the room. "Want to sit? I've been here since six and I could use a break." He turned to the kitchen. "Hey, Vince! Order me up another Western. Rye toast."

Mark grabbed a carafe of coffee and a mug for himself

and the two men settled into the booth. "So, tell me. What happened?"

Luke relayed the events of the night before, replaying them as he had more than a dozen times throughout the night. He stuck to the facts, telling himself it was easier that way, refusing to hint even to himself that he'd actually felt something when he saw Grace again. And he had felt a lot of things—anger, hurt, frustration, guilt. But he'd felt other things, too. Things he didn't want to feel. Things he shouldn't feel. Things he should have stopped feeling a long time ago.

By the time he'd gotten to the point in the story where he'd dropped Grace off three houses away from the Madison residence, dragging three bags behind her and refusing his help, their food was up. Mark stood to collect it, promptly returning, a sly grin forming at the corners of his mouth. "Can't say I'm surprised," he said. "That girl always did have a fiery temper."

"She's a determined woman," Luke agreed. He didn't elaborate that he still liked that about her, aggravating as it was. It had never failed to escape him that the one trait he admired most in her was the one that had ultimately divided them.

Mark salted his hash browns and passed the shaker to Luke. "Do you remember that time in college when Grace saw that magazine picture of a couch she wanted? I was visiting that weekend, and it was all she could talk about."

Luke nodded, smiling at the memory. "White slip-covered," he mused, recalling the way she had breathed the words.

Mark chuckled and tore off a piece of toast. "She had

that tattered navy couch, and she went out and bought I don't even know how many yards of fabric—"

"She bought a drop cloth," Luke said as the memory became clearer. "She couldn't afford fabric."

"She couldn't afford a sewing machine either," Mark said.

"Nope." Luke grinned, remembering the set to her fine jaw, the fierceness in her eyes. "She sewed an entire fitted slipcover by hand."

Mark shook his head in wonder. "How long did that take her?"

It would have taken most people weeks, and that would have been people who knew how to sew. "Two days," he said, his mouth twitching. She had stayed up all night, kneeling on the floor, cutting and pinning, and running the needle through the thick, difficult material. By the time she had finished, her fingers were bruised and calloused, but the pride in her face was what he remembered the most.

"It was a beautiful couch," Mark commented.

Luke nodded. "It was," he murmured.

He hadn't thought about that couch in a long time, and he wondered what had happened to it. She probably sold it, he decided. It was a busy time. A murky time. Grace was finishing her graduate program—he'd already completed his the previous spring—and decisions for the future were quickly being made. If he had known then how fleeting their time would be together, he might have paid closer attention.

"Remember that birthday cake she made you that one year?" Mark said, still traveling down memory lane. He shook his head, smiling ruefully. "That thing must have been eight layers thick. Never seen anything like it, not even in culinary school." He shrugged. "Guess that's why she became some famous writer, huh? She never was the type to quit. She always sees things through to the end."

Not me, Luke thought grimly. *Not us.*

There was a time when he thought he and Grace would grow old together, that they would carry on the rest of their lives as they always had. He'd thought Grace felt the same way, that she wanted the same things. He thought a life together would be enough for her.

He'd been wrong.

"So are you going to see her again?" Mark asked, and Luke startled, sloshing his coffee.

"No," he said firmly, but then sat back, squinting into his plate. Seeing Grace last night had been an accident, a chance meeting. Seeing her by choice meant something different altogether. It would be admitting to himself that something was still there, and he didn't want anything to be there. He just wanted her to go away. And stay away.

"Well, good luck trying," Mark said. He cut into his omelet with the side of his fork, saying nothing more.

Luke narrowed his eyes in suspicion. "What's that supposed to mean?"

"It's a small town, Luke. She's bound to be around."

"Well, she's not sticking around for long," Luke announced, frowning at his plate of untouched food. "You know this town was never good enough for her."

Mark looked at him. "You're still planning on coming to my party tonight, right? Don't even think about trying to get out of it."

"I'm still coming," Luke said. He knew Mark was

right, that he needed to get out more, try to move on. But not with Grace. Definitely not with Grace.

"Good." Mark nodded. "I wasn't sure you would still come."

"Why?" Luke began and then stopped. "Wait. Don't tell me she's—"

Mark leaned back in his seat. "I have no idea if Grace will be there. She has friends here. It's possible."

Luke gritted his teeth. "Let's just hope she doesn't show up. She'll know I'm going, of course. You're my family, after all."

"Well, I'm not sure how you're going to manage to avoid her unless you lock yourself up in that depressing house of yours."

Luke blinked. This was news to him. "You think my house is depressing?"

Mark pushed away his plate and set his palms flat on the table. "Luke, it's Christmas, and yours is the only house I know without a tree."

Luke's mind wandered to the Madisons' house, and then, inevitably, to Grace. "So?" Luke scowled. "Lots of houses don't have trees."

Mark's brow creased with concern. "You have not changed a thing in that house since Helen died. And I know you didn't even like the way she decorated it."

Luke felt his blood begin to course through his veins. He shifted his weight against the back of the bench, not liking where this conversation was going. "It's my home. It suits me fine," he said, but one glance at Mark told him his cousin wasn't buying it. Mark had seen the lavender hand soaps in the bathroom. The throw pillows on the bed. The faux floral arrangement that anchored the dining room table. The dishtowels that depicted little birds and butterflies.

"I'm just saying . . . it's not the kind of place you could bring a woman to. Not as a bachelor."

"Who said I wanted to bring a woman over?" Luke asked. The mere thought of it caused his temper to stir. "That was Helen's home as much as mine."

"And the storefront?" Mark lifted an eyebrow.

"What about it?" His mind flew to the image of the empty storefront next door to the bookshop, the way it had looked so vacant and lifeless the night before.

"You paid that lease through the end of the year without trying to break it or sublet it. And you renewed the lease last year. You planning to do the same come January?"

Lifting his fork, Luke ate half the omelet quickly, not tasting any of it. He didn't expect Mark to understand why he continued to throw good money at a piece of empty real estate, at a storefront that had never even opened, that only served as a reminder of Helen's vacancy in this world.

It was more than a reminder.

"It's all I have left of her," he said bluntly.

"Helen is gone, Luke," Mark said quietly, his expression pained.

Luke refused to agree with that statement. He knew she was never coming back, he had accepted it a long time ago despite what those around him believed. His wife was dead. Gone.

She had died five days after Christmas, nearly two years ago, from a brain aneurysm. He had come home that day, his mind reeling with the knowledge of what he must do, the certainty of what he must tell her, and he had found her lying there, her cheeks pale.

He had lived the past twenty-three and a half months knowing she was gone, that there was nothing he could have done to have prevented it. It wasn't denial that kept him clinging to her, or a lack of acceptance that made that house his own silent prison. It was plain and simple guilt.

He hadn't been fair to Helen as her husband. And so help him, he would honor her as his widower. It was the least he could do.

CHAPTER 7

By the time Jane's car rounded the bend, Grace was already jogging in place, ready to get a start on the day. It had been a long, sleepless night, and the morning hadn't brought much more relief. She hadn't expected this Christmas to be the same as those she so fondly remembered, but she hadn't expected this, either. Why hadn't Jane mentioned how bad things had gotten? She intended to find out the answer to that. Today.

Her cashmere-gloved hand gripped her handbag at the shoulder as she bolted out into the crisp mid-morning air. The sun was shining bright, reflecting off the blanket of white snow that covered everything from tree branches to roofs, and the world around her glistened. Her feet crunched on the frozen snow as she awkwardly leapt over snowdrifts that had collected overnight. She'd offered to shovel earlier that morning, but her mother had been against it, insisting with alarming intensity that she would see to it herself. Grace had persisted until she finally realized it would be a way for Kathleen to keep busy and occupy her thoughts, and so she let the idea drop.

Now, seeing how much had accumulated overnight, she wished she had gone ahead and done it before her mother could protest. Still, when her mother set her mind to something, she wouldn't be swayed. It was a trait Grace had picked up from her, along with the green eyes and wavy, chestnut hair. Tenacity, her father always called it, with a twinkle in his eye. It was the type of energy that could wear people down, but not Ray Madison. He'd loved that intensity in his wife, and fostered it in his daughters. It was one of the things Grace admired most about her dad—she could share her wildest dream, muse about the craziest idea, and he would only smile and tell her to go for it. He never held her back. But in the end, maybe that had been the one time he let her down. He'd always told her to go after her dreams, and somewhere along the way she'd learned that if someone loved you, they supported you along the way. And Luke . . . hadn't.

"You didn't shovel the driveway?" Jane asked as Grace climbed into the passenger seat.

Grace bit back a sigh of frustration and tossed up her hands. "She wants to do it herself!" Her voice was shrill, and she became suddenly aware of Sophie sitting in the backseat of the car. She turned to face her, her heart crumbling at the sight of the pink-cheeked little girl bundled up in an ear-flapped hat topped with an oversized red pom-pom.

"Hey, kiddo, I like your hat," she said.

"Thanks! I like your hair," Sophie said, and Grace touched her uninteresting locks, feeling oddly warmed by the compliment.

An hour ago, she had been thinking about Derek again, or forcing herself to, at least. After Kathleen had gone to take a shower, Grace had quietly cleared the kitchen table, wiped it down with a damp cloth, and then stood at the sink, running water until it steamed and soap bubbles threatened to spill onto the floor, clutching the counter with two hands, wondering what the hell she was doing here and how the heck she could leave now.

And where would she even go? Most of her stuff was in storage. Angie was having family over for the holiday, so Grace had cleared out her few belongings, bringing them all with her to Briar Creek. She'd been living out of suitcases for months, and while Angie was a good sport, she sensed she was coming very close to overstaying her welcome in the small one-bedroom apartment.

She had a few thousand dollars left to her name—she winced to think of how quickly she had blown through her money, how reckless she had been, how sure she had been that there would always be more.

It would be enough to find an apartment, certainly nothing compared to the lifestyle she was used to with Derek, but she needed to figure out where the next paycheck would come from first.

And right now, she hadn't a clue.

"I'm sorry to hear about you and Derek," Jane said now, and Grace swiveled back around in her seat. "I don't remember. Had you guys set a date?"

Grace pursed her lips. "No." She didn't mention that this had been just as much her doing as his. They both knew they were forcing something that wasn't there.

Silence stretched. Grace slid a glance at her sister, who stared at her sadly as they sat at a red light.

"Don't look at me like that," she pleaded. "Seriously, I'm over it. It's fine. The timing is bad, that's all."

Jane nodded thoughtfully and focused on the road as the light turned green. "Did you guys have a big fight? I mean, did something happen that made you realize you couldn't go through with it?"

"How are you so sure that I broke up with him?" Grace asked through an amused smile, but Jane blanched.

Her sister's hand flew to her mouth, and her hazel eyes were wide. "I'm sorry, Grace. I wasn't thinking."

Grace laughed softly. "Don't worry. I broke up with him." The story of her life, wasn't it? Too bad it wasn't a story worthy of another best-selling novel. Or even a novel her publisher was willing to buy.

Her stomach stirred with unease. She couldn't think about that now. She had other things to worry about at the moment.

"Well, I'm glad you ended it when you did, then," Jane said. "It's a lot easier to get out now, because once you're married…"

Grace frowned, staring at her sister's profile. "Is everything okay?" she asked as she pulled off her gloves.

Jane smiled tightly but kept her eyes fixed on the road. "Of course. Why would you ask?"

The vagueness of her tone proved what Grace had suspected. Everything was not okay. Grace pinched her lips, considering her youngest sister's behavior last night at dinner, Adam's strange absence, the general way she avoided discussing him. Something was up, and she intended to get to the bottom of it.

With Sophie in earshot, she decided not to press the topic. They were coming up on town, and in the light of day, it looked even more offensive in its lavish décor.

Storefronts were edged with twinkling lights and donned with wreaths and holly, lampposts were wrapped in pine garland, secured with cheerful red bows, and portly Santas were parked at various street corners, waving bells, collecting for charity. Children climbed the snowbanks that rolled between the sidewalks and roads, squealing with joy.

"You sure you don't want to come shopping with me?" Jane asked, as they turned onto Main Street.

Grace shook her head and stared out onto the town square. The town's tree stood tall in the center, decorated with oversized bulbs. Skaters glided over the ice of a frozen pond. The gazebo was ornately wrapped with red ribbon, so each post looked like a giant candy cane.

Grace tutted under her breath. She supposed she should feel happy she was being spared this sort of festive cheer back at home, but for some reason, it only made her feel more distressed that her mother was choosing to sit this Christmas out. Kathleen *was* Christmas. It was her thing. Her holiday. Her passion. If she couldn't muster up the energy for the holidays, what hope was there for her, or any of them, for that matter?

At the corner just ahead was Hastings, the local diner owned by Luke's cousin, Mark. She had seen Mark briefly at her father's funeral, standing near the back of the room, his unruly brown hair flopping over his forehead, his eyes set deep, like Luke's. He had nodded to her from across the room, and she had given him a small smile in response. It was all she could do under the circumstances, and speaking to him would have only brought more pain to the surface, more than she could handle in one day. She'd missed his easygoing manner and friendly banter, but the sight of him had shaken her, causing her to sweep her eyes over the rest of the room with a pounding of her heart.

When she realized that Luke was not with him—not there at all—she had felt both relieved and hurt. His absence was conscious, of course. Deliberate. And for the life of her she couldn't decide on the thought process that had led him to stay away. After how close Luke and her father had been, did he really not care to be there? Or did he just not want to see her?

She had told Luke he had been right to stay away, even if her heart said different.

Hastings was alive and buzzing from what she could see, proving that some things stood the test of time. The windows had been decorated in a winter scene, making it difficult to see through to the inside. She'd like to go in and say hello to Mark—he was an old friend, after all. She'd spent many summer afternoons in the back of his old convertible—the one he'd restored himself—with Luke's arm around her as Mark drove them all out to the lake, laughing and singing to whatever tune was playing on the radio, the sun warming their skin, the wind whipping her hair. She smiled now at the memory, but her heart started to ache with sadness.

"Just drop me off at the bookstore," she told Jane. She frowned, realizing something. "Who's running the store now? Did Mom hire someone to help?"

Beside her, Jane was thin-lipped, her eyes focused on the road. Her brow was knit, and alarm quickened Grace's pulse. "Jane?" she demanded, as fear sent a wave of ice over her stomach. "What is it?"

With a sigh, Jane slumped her shoulders. "The store isn't how you remember it, Grace."

"What are you talking about? I was there last night!"

Jane's eyes widened. "You didn't go inside, did you?"

"No. I couldn't find a key." Grace narrowed her gaze. "What are you trying to tell me?" She stared at her sister, her breath turning ragged with concern. That shop was all she had left in Briar Creek. Her last truly happy memory. If something happened to it...

"You have to understand that a lot has changed, Grace. Since Dad died..." Jane trailed off, a heavy silence finishing her thought. "Well, you'll see."

"Jane," Grace said impatiently, "I was there last night. There's nothing to see." She motioned to the brick storefront with the wide, white-trimmed windows and cheerful red center door, relief sinking in as Jane pulled the car to a stop. "God, by the way you're talking, you would think it was closed or something!"

"It *is* closed, Grace."

"What?" She darted her eyes to the shop, now directly in front of them. The CLOSED sign was turned in the glass window of the door. Beyond the bay windows that housed a selection of children's books, the room was dark and unwelcoming. "I can't believe it," she gasped, her jaw slackening at the sight. "I don't understand."

She turned to Jane, searching her face in confusion, looking for some answer that would shed light on the chain of events that had led to this. Main Street Books was her father's pride and joy. He'd left his English-teaching job to buy it—it had been his lifelong dream, and she was the one standing by his side when he opened it.

She bit her lip, willing herself not to burst into tears right then and there.

Jane let out a long breath. She glanced to the backseat to check on Sophie. "I don't really know what to say, Grace," she said, shaking her head sadly. "Mom hasn't been up to running it, and she couldn't afford to bring someone in to do the job for her. She's turned down countless jobs. She can't even handle her own workload," she said, referring to Kathleen's work as an interior design consultant. She used to say that there wasn't a house in all of Briar Creek she hadn't been invited to improve.

Sensing her lack of conviction, Jane continued, "It's not only about paying someone to man the counter. There's the bookkeeping, the upkeep, the inventory, the bills...the *rent*."

Grace frowned, realizing her sister had a point. She glanced blearily out the window, grimacing at the state of the quaint shop. She remembered it looking charming and literary in an authentic type of way. Now it just looked dusty and sad.

"When did it close?" she asked quietly.

"Pretty much right when he died," Jane admitted. "Mom implied it wasn't doing well long before that... Let's just say he was lucky to sell a book a week."

"He didn't do it for the money," Grace said.

"I know."

Grace closed her eyes. "So what now, then?" she asked.

"The lease is good through the end of the year," Jane said. "After that..." She didn't finish the statement, and Grace was grateful for that.

"And Mom?" she asked. Jane tipped her head in confusion. "Mom's okay with it shutting down?"

"Oh, you know Mom. She never loved this place like Dad did. She loved it because he did, and I know she feels sad about it closing, but it's a reality, and I think she's accepted it." Jane paused, lowering her eyes. "I should have told you sooner, Grace. I just…I didn't know how. None of us did."

"Yes, you should have told me," she said, setting her jaw. Surprise flickered in Jane's bright eyes, quickly shadowed by disappointment. "You should have at least told me before driving me over here."

"I'm sorry," Jane said, deflating against the back of her seat. She looked weary and drawn, Grace noticed with a ripple of shame. "You're right. I guess I was hoping that Anna or Mom would." She slid her a rueful glance. "They're not good for much these days."

Grace managed a small smile. "No," she agreed. "They certainly aren't."

She leaned back against her own headrest, staring impassively at the bookstore, trying to summon a clearer image of what it had looked like when her father was still alive. Had the paint always been peeling? Had the windows always needed a wash?

"I still have the keys," Jane said, and Grace perked up. "I thought you'd want to go in." *While you still can*, came the unspoken words, and Grace felt her throat lock up. So much had changed. So much was gone.

"I'd like that," she said, accepting the small metal keychain with the engraved image of an open book. It was the one her father always carried in his pocket. When Grace was younger, she would examine it until her eyes strained, trying to decipher which book it was—she never had figured it out. She rubbed her fingers over the key. "Thank you."

"You sure you don't want to come shopping with us,

instead? It could be fun." Jane's eyes were pleading, her mouth curved with forced encouragement.

"Not today," Grace sighed. "It's not easy being back. When I was back for Dad's—" She cleared her throat. "When I came here in the spring, I felt like everyone was staring at me."

Jane shrugged. "Everyone here is your friend, Grace. Besides, you're sort of a famous person to everyone now."

Grace felt her lip curl. "Oh, please don't."

"The one about the girl who meets the artist in Spain was my favorite, although—"

"Jane, can we please talk about something else?" Grace rubbed her forehead, suddenly feeling weary.

"What? Why shouldn't I take some pride in my oldest sister's success?" Jane asked.

"Because I'm not much of a success anymore, that's why," Grace muttered.

Jane clucked her tongue. "Oh, silliness. So you had a few bad reviews."

"Scathing," Grace corrected her. She locked her sister's eyes. "Scathing reviews, Jane."

Jane sloughed it off. "So? You'll write another one. Win 'em over again."

"It doesn't work that way," Grace said.

Jane frowned. "Don't be so defeatist. It isn't like you."

Grace sighed and splayed her hands over her jeans, studying her chipped manicure. No, she supposed it wasn't like her at all. Usually when Grace wanted something, she went for it. Nothing to stop her or stand in her way. So wasn't it ironic that when it came to the two things in life that mattered most outside her family—her career and Luke—she had been beaten down entirely?

"Maybe I'm afraid. Rejection stings, you know," she said, trying to sound casual. The truth was she was afraid—afraid of the final blow, the confirmation that something that mattered so much had slipped through her fingers.

Oh, she'd thought of giving it one last go, but she had a track record with that type of performance. She knew how it felt when your last chance was taken from you. When hope finally disappeared. Luke had taught her that lesson. The hard way, of course.

"I can imagine," Jane said, an edge creeping into her tone. After a pause, she abruptly flashed a smile. "Come on, come with us. We'll grab a hot chocolate and get your nails fixed. Don't bring yourself down further. You worry me when you get like this."

Grace gave a half smile, appreciating her sister's worry even if she didn't need it. Or want it. She knew what Jane was referring to—Luke. It always came back to Luke.

She glanced back at the shop, and then turned to Jane, patting her hand. "I think this is where I need to be."

Jane nodded, and squeezed her hand. "I'm glad you came back, Grace," she said, her voice cracking slightly. She blinked quickly, her eyes remained fixed on her lap. "It means more than you know."

Grace swallowed the lump in her throat. "I'm glad I came back, too," she said, and her pulse skipped a beat at the words.

"It'll mean a lot to have you at Sophie's pageant tomorrow, too. Why don't you come over beforehand and help with the cookies for the bake sale?"

"I'm going to be an angel!" Sophie cried proudly from the backseat, and Grace brightened at the joy in her niece's smile, her sadness inexplicably and wholeheart-edly replaced with complete and utter happiness.

Her chest pulled, leaving her breathless for one star-tling moment, as she gazed into the little girl's face. Had she really almost given this all up? The possibility of pure, simple, happiness? For a long time she had con-vinced herself that she was happy in New York, in her elegant apartment with sweeping skyline views, planning to marry a man whose understanding of her barely dipped below the surface. She had thought she was fulfilled, that it could be enough—that she would make it enough. She had been wrong.

But then, she had been wrong about a lot of things.

CHAPTER 8

Grace waited until Jane was out of sight before turning to face the crimson-painted door. She heaved a breath for courage and slid the key into the slot. It stuck as she tried to turn the lock, but after a little wiggling, it turned a quarter turn to the right with a slight clicking sound. Slowly, Grace turned the knob and pushed the door open, aware of the heaviness of her heart as she took one careful step after another, her eyes sweeping the room. A jingle of bells welcomed her across the threshold, but the store was otherwise silent and lifeless.

She soaked it all in, fearfully at first, looking for signs of change or disruption, and then, with some relief, she allowed each memory to come quietly flooding back.

The old chenille armchair with its fading red fabric was still wedged between the last two shelves, which were still packed tight with a rainbow of book covers. The strong bookcases in warm wood tones grazed the ceiling, and she ran a finger over one of the handwritten signs her father had affixed to each shelf, listing the category.

Grace glanced at the hard-covered spines of some first editions, tucked securely behind a glass case, remembering how she had shelved some of the titles herself, and then frowned to realize they had never sold. Venturing farther into the room, she smiled at the sight of the finely polished, rich cherrywood counter.

She pressed her lips together, willing herself not to cry, when she pictured her father standing proudly behind it, just as he had been the last time she came through that door. She could see him sliding her a warm smile, telling her to come into the back room with a conspiratorial wink, and she'd quicken her pace, following eagerly, waiting to see what new books had arrived since her last visit.

Next Grace walked into the room that housed storage and a small desk, sighing at its empty yet chaotic state. Boxes of unopened books were stacked in the far corner. The coffee machine that her father kept percolating throughout the day looked like nothing more than a useless toy. The file cabinets were full of neatly organized papers. Anywhere else, the sensitive papers would have been taken away for safekeeping, but here in Briar Creek, there was so little crime it never occurred to anyone to secure them.

Nothing exciting ever happened in Briar Creek.

That's what she had always thought, wasn't it? In a way, she supposed it was true. People were born and raised here; they went about their lives surrounded by the same faces and places they had seen every day. There was no sense of wonder, no possibility. But was that really so bad? She wasn't so sure anymore.

Flicking off the lights, Grace closed the door behind her and ventured back into the storefront, winding her way through the maze of ceiling-high shelves, pausing here and there to study the titles. When she came full circle, she wandered over to the chair nearest the window and plopped herself into it, her heart feeling like a brick.

The morning sun had been replaced with thick clouds, and the sky had turned gray. It had started snowing again, and she watched as large, thick snowflakes danced their way through the air, her mind far away. She couldn't remember the last time she had sat and watched the snow. In New York there were too many distractions, too much to get done. She was too busy to notice something so simple. Instead, she let it fade into the background, assuming it would always be there. She took it for granted. She was good at that.

A hot tear laced its way down Grace's cheek and she brushed it away, but another quickly trailed in its path. The knot in her throat ached, and she swallowed hard as the tears fell as freely as the snow on the other side of the glass.

What would her father think of her now? If he were still here, standing behind that counter, what would he say to her in this moment? She squeezed her eyes closed, and tried to summon his voice, his words of wisdom, knowing he would have the right thing to say. The words that would make it all better.

She could still remember the pride bursting in his voice when she'd sold her first novel and the unabashed joy when she hit the best-seller list quickly after. But now...Now what would he have said? Would he have looked at her sadly, told her she couldn't win them all, told her to keep going?

One thing was certain. He wouldn't have told her to call it quits. And that's exactly what she wanted to do.

She opened her eyes, inhaling sharply when she saw Luke standing outside the window, his face creased with concern. Jolting from the slumped position in her chair, she smiled reflexively, and then cursed herself for doing so. This man had broken her heart—shattered it, really. He didn't deserve a smile. He didn't deserve anything.

Luke held up a hand, his mouth curved into a lop-sided grin, and her pulse skipped a beat. In that one brief moment, she could see the boy she had fallen in love with, the boy who could make her stomach flip-flop with a slow smile. Then just as quickly, he transformed back to the man he now was. The man who had married someone else. The man who had planned an entire future without her in it.

She stood as he entered the store, frantically wiping at any lingering evidence of her tears. His presence seemed larger than usual in the cramped, crowded room, and she felt backed into the corner, forced to confront the one person she had hoped to avoid.

In the light of day, she allowed herself a proper look at the man who had once been her entire world, from the tousled, espresso-brown locks that spilled over his forehead to the sparkling blue eyes that still sent a shiver down her spine. She'd forgotten how tall he was—at least six feet—but she didn't forget the contours of his body, the way her fingers felt against the smooth plane of his chest. She wished she could forget. But then, life could be cruel. Sometimes memories were too sharp. Some things were best left in the past.

His mouth tugged into a smile. "Hi, Honeybee," he said, and then, noticing the disapproval in her face, he held up his hands. "Sorry."

She crossed her arms over her chest. "It's okay," she said, even though it wasn't. A nickname implied an intimacy they no longer shared. It was a spoken memory, a reminder of their history—one she hadn't forgotten, try as she might.

"I can leave if you want." He held her stare as if in a dare, challenging her to tell him to go. And oh, how she wanted to do just that. But a larger part of her couldn't bring herself to tear her gaze from those piercing eyes.

Grace glanced around the shop, suddenly not wanting to be alone here with its haunting memories and the emotions they brought to the surface. Everything in it, right down to the old, dusty books, felt like they belonged in a different time. "No, it's okay. It's strange being here by myself, honestly." Unsettling. Wrong. This was her father's space. It came alive when he was here. And now...

"I saw you in the window," he continued. His voice was low and gentle and achingly familiar, and it took everything in her not to collapse into the warm safety of his arms, to hear his thick, rich voice tell her it would all be okay. Then she remembered that he couldn't offer her that comfort anymore, and the distance between their bodies proved it. "Are you all right?"

Grace shrugged and jutted out her chin, willing herself to stay strong. His deep blue eyes penetrated hers, making her feel raw and exposed, and she glanced away, hugging her arms around her chest as she moved to the back of the room and studied the thermostat. It was freezing in here. She was too distracted to notice before, but now, she wasn't sure how she could tolerate it much longer.

The radiator hissed as it warmed up, and Grace

remained hovered over it, waiting. Luke was behind her now, a silent force in the empty store. "Did you know it was closing?" she asked, glancing at him.

"I knew it hadn't been opened since—" He stopped himself, running a hand through his wavy hair. "I didn't feel it was my place to say anything last night. I was hoping it wasn't a permanent decision."

"Well, looks like it is," she said bitterly, and then stopped herself. This wasn't his fault. Many things were his fault, but not this. She wasn't sure anyone was really to blame for Main Street Books going under, and that was what made her feel most helpless, she realized. "My sisters are busy with other things, and my mom, well...she isn't up for the challenge, I guess you could say."

His brow knitted. "How is she?"

She hated the concern in his voice, in the slant of his eyes. Yet, more than that, she hated how good it felt to be here talking with him. The one person who could understand.

Grace blew out a breath. It was so cold in the room she could almost see it plume in front of her. "She's hanging in there, I suppose." She slid him another glance. "But if someone's looking to enter the Holiday House contest, I'd say this is the year to do it."

Luke tossed his head back, his rich, booming laughter echoing off the walls. Grace smiled against her will, her heart aching in her chest. She had missed that sound—the thick, deep rumble that left you craving more. She waited for him to stop, defusing the sound with her own willful chuckle.

"I thought she stopped competing years ago," he said, and Grace slid him a smile.

He remembered. He remembered things about her life. Things that Derek never knew or never cared to ask. She tried to imagine telling Derek—sleek, flashy, glamorous Derek—about her family's Christmas traditions and found herself laughing even louder than Luke just had.

"Sorry," she said, noticing Luke's confused expression. Composing herself, she turned back to the radiator, placing her palms on the metal coils, absorbing their faint heat. "I was only . . . never mind."

An awkward silence stretched across the room, and Grace began racking her brain desperately for something to say. Something to make him stay and talk, to get him to leave—she didn't know anymore.

"How's Mark?" she blurted, fixing her eyes on him. She could tell by the sparkle that passed through his blue irises that he had been watching her the entire time, and she couldn't fight the flush of pleasure that spread up her face at the idea of it.

"He's good," he said. "He probably wants to see you while you're in town."

"I'd like that," she said. She glanced away. The room was much too quiet. She wished there was a radio or something. Even Christmas carols would do.

She stared at her hands, thinking of what to say, an excuse to leave. She couldn't stay here much longer—what was the point? She could sit in that armchair all day, clinging to the past, of a time that was lost, or she could quietly say goodbye, close the door behind her, and go. A long time ago, she'd made the decision to leave the past in the past, to put distance between things that were once hers and were no longer. This bookstore was no different than her relationship with Luke in many ways: it represented a happier time in her life. A time she could never get back. A time better forgotten.

Still, the thought of letting go of it was . . . unbearable.

She drew a breath and turned to face him. She'd tell him she had to meet Jane, that she was only stopping in to get something. He was probably as desperate to make an exit as she was. He'd only come in because he'd seen her crying, after all. She didn't need his pity. She didn't need anything from him.

"I—" she began but he cut her off before she could finish her thought.

"I read your book," he said and she froze. From four feet away she could see his eyes flash with intensity, the way they always did when he had something on his mind. "I read all your books."

Oh. Grace felt a hot blush creep slowly up her face. "All of them, eh?" she forced a smile, but her heart began a slow and steady drum.

"All of them," he repeated, his rich voice so smooth, so concrete, that she felt herself waver.

There was a time when she would have been flattered, maybe even found hope where none existed. She was amazed at how few people in her personal circle took the time to read her work—Derek never had. But Luke had cared enough to read her book. Books. *All of them.* She winced when she considered what he thought of the last one—the flop.

"Probably wishing you could buy back the time you spent on that last one," she managed with a brittle smile.

He frowned. "Hardly. I loved it. I love everything you—" He stopped. "I love everything you write. I always did."

She nodded thoughtfully. That much was true. Back in high school and then into college, he had been her biggest fan aside from her father. He read everything she wrote, encouraging her to keep at it, even when she herself didn't see much point. "It's only a matter of time," he would say. "It just takes the right story."

She could still remember the day she got the call—someone wanted to buy her book. She'd made it. The dream she had worked so hard for had come true. Her heart soared and then raced, and then her mind immediately flitted to Luke. If there was one person she longed to share the celebration with, it was him.

By then, it was too late. Luke was gone. Out of her life. She called her father instead. It was the happiest day of her life, but she couldn't stop thinking of the one person who was missing from it. Even then, when her dreams were realized, she was still thinking about Luke and the part of her dream that had never come true.

Her heart was beating quickly, and she felt flushed and agitated. There were too many memories in this room—too much potential for nostalgia. Luke's presence wasn't helping either, especially when he was looking as handsome as ever. She allowed her gaze to drift over the length of him, from the long legs to the strong, wide shoulders. Her eyes lingered on his square jaw, that full mouth.

"I should probably get going," she said suddenly, surprising herself.

Luke looked momentarily startled, but he said nothing, nodding instead. For a moment her stomach fluttered with hope that he was disappointed, that he would have preferred to have stayed and talked, but she pushed the thought away quickly. Even if he wanted that, and she was certain he did not, it wasn't what she wanted.

What she wanted was to be far away from Luke, from this town, to be back in New York, where he couldn't touch her or look at her like that. She shifted the weight on her feet, lowering her eyes to the floor.

Yes, that's exactly what she wanted.

"I'm sorry about the store," he said evenly. "I know how much it meant to you."

Grace swallowed the knot that had wedged in her throat. "Sometimes I wonder if I ever would have become a writer if it hadn't been for this place," she mused. She looked around the room, misty-eyed. Her voice hitched when she said, "I love it here."

"And there's nothing that can be done? To save it?"

Grace gave a defeated shrug. "Doesn't look that way." Even if she could scrounge up the money to get it running again, it didn't seem that anyone in her family was willing to oversee it, and Jane had a point that getting a manager wasn't enough. They needed a real owner. Someone who would love this place as much as her dad did.

As she did.

She turned to the vast stretch of the polished wood counter, her father's image so clear in her mind that it caused her breath to catch. And suddenly she knew. She knew exactly what her father would have said to her. *Well, how bad do you want it?* That's what he would have said.

More than anything else, she decided firmly.

CHAPTER 9

Luke plunged his hands deep into his pockets, rolling back on his heels as he watched Grace struggling with the old brass lock. He knew better than to offer his help—it would only spark a fire in her eyes, a defiant lift of her chin—and so he said nothing, and waited. He didn't know what he would say when she finally turned to him, but he was suddenly filled with the strange and all-consuming realization that he wasn't ready to let her go. Not yet. Even though he knew he should. He really, really should.

This time of the year was hard enough without her turning up to make it worse.

"There!" Grace smirked in satisfaction and stuffed the key ring into her pocket. In the crisp, winter light, her eyes blazed an arresting shade of green. The sun peeking out behind dense clouds glimmered off her hair, highlighting the bronze hues. After all this time, her beauty still had a hold over him.

"Which way are you going?" he hedged. She was wary around him, guarded, and he felt like he was clinging to a slippery fish, trying to get a grip on something that was determined to slide through his fingers, back into the great wide world. Free.

Her expression fell as she swept her eyes up the snow-covered street, over the garland-draped storefronts that blasted seasonal tunes through speakers and the thoughtfully placed wreaths that hung from every red-ribbon-wrapped streetlamp. Someone had even set felt Santa hats atop each fire hydrant. Luke curled his lip. There was no escaping it. Christmas was upon them, with all its garish reminders.

"I don't know. I might try to find Jane. Or maybe I'll head over to the café and get a coffee while I wait for her to finish her shopping. I'm depending on her for a ride today."

"Any update on the car?"

Grace rubbed her nose, which was turning pink from the cold, biting wind. With her rosy cheeks and pale skin, her eyes looked bright and vivid. She shivered into her coat. "I called this morning. I managed to bash a head-light, and they had to call for the part. It should be ready by Saturday."

"Good. Wouldn't want you getting stuck in town any longer than you had to be here." He set his jaw.

"It would take more than a smashed up rental car to keep me caged up in this town." She gave a small laugh, but the best he could manage was a tight smile. Her words stung, bringing him right back to a time and place he had tried to forget.

Boring town. That's what she'd called Briar Creek. Boring town, boring life.

He had sat in silence, realization taking a firm hold

like a hard rock that had settled into his belly, and he knew that everything he had ever assumed or planned for would never be. This town could never give her what she needed, and neither could he. She would never be fulfilled here. She'd resent him. Blame him. Hate him.

A part of him had hoped she would come back to town with her tail between her legs, admitting that Briar Creek was where she belonged, that she'd been foolish to think the big city could offer something more meaningful. But when she finally did return...

He stiffened his back. It was too late.

His heart panged as his thoughts flew to Helen, and he heaved a breath that escaped in a burst of white cloud. "Well, if you're headed to the Fireside Café," he said, referring to Anna's café a few blocks down Main Street, "I'll walk with you. I'm parked over in that direction, anyway," he added, to be sure she didn't get the wrong idea.

The truth was that he didn't know what the hell he was doing, or why he had come into the bookstore at all. He had walked down Main Street for another look at the storefront next to Ray's shop, for another reminder of Helen, and once again it was Grace who snagged his attention.

Grace averted her gaze, chewing on the inside of her lip. He should have known better than to suggest it, especially if last night proved anything. She didn't do well with feeling coerced into things—if anything, it made her do the opposite. She was a woman of her own mind, stubborn enough to drive him crazy like no one else could, and she liked to think through things at her own pace, come around to an idea when she was ready. It was just too bad that he had discovered this trait in hindsight. It was an observation that only distance and perhaps a little maturity could reveal.

She hesitated, her eyes shifting from his, but then her shoulders relaxed. "Okay," she sighed, jamming her hands into her pockets.

Luke tried to shrug off the sting of her reluctance. Did she really hate him this much?

They wandered in silence, skimming past the ornately decorated window displays without commenting, even for some of the particularly nice ones, like the one inspired by *The Nutcracker*, with toy soldiers that marched to a beat of a drum and a Christmas tree that grew before your very eyes.

They didn't have far to walk, five blocks at most, and Luke found himself wishing for once that Briar Creek was a little bigger. Anna had opened the Fireside Café just months before he and Grace had broken up and she had moved to New York. There was a grand opening party, and Grace wore a black dress with thin straps that kept slipping down her bare arms. He could still remember the silkiness of her skin as he slid the straps back in place throughout the evening, the pride that came in knowing she was his. After the party, they went home to his house and made long, slow love until they fell asleep in each other's arms, waking up intertwined to the light slicing through the trees in the thick forest surrounding his house, reaching for each other under the warm covers.

"Remember that night of your sister's opening?" he asked, his voice lilting at the end with hope that she remembered it the way he did.

A smile stretched across her face and she nodded, sliding him a glance as they reached the corner and paused at the intersection. "That was a nice night. One of the last fond memories I have of this place," she murmured, breaking his stare. Her cheeks flushed a darker shade of pink that he knew had nothing to do with the freezing temperature.

"Ah, well." He clenched his teeth, kicking himself for bringing it up at all. Why do that to himself? To her? It would only serve as a fresh reminder of what happened a few months later—an ironic contrast to the perfection of that day. "You did well for yourself in the end. You were probably right to leave this old town, really."

She lifted a brow, pursing her pretty lips. He did his best to keep his expression impassive, even though his chest felt like it was being wrung through a vise. This stilted chit-chat did nothing but pain him, remind him of the consequences of their actions.

Somehow in the past five years he had gone from knowing the details of her daily routine to having no clue how she spent her time. Or with whom.

He drew a sharp breath, pushing the thought away. He'd imagined what her life would be like, how she spent her days, her weekends. Her nights. He could never be certain of the details, and somehow, over time, she had become another person to him—a woman who lived in another city, spent time with people he had never met, went places he had never visited. Now he realized there was some truth to his musings. Who was she now? This Grace, the one standing beside him, the one whose life had gone on for five years without him?

With a twist of the gut he realized exactly who she was. She was the one who got away. Maybe everyone had one of those.

"You're right," she said lightly, but he thought he detected an undertone of regret. "I'm not really sure what I would have accomplished if I had stayed here. My life would have been a lot different, that's for sure." She left the essence of her thoughts unspoken. Her opinion noncommittal. Different, not better. Not worse. Just...different.

She held his stare, challenging him to say something, looking to scratch up old wounds, and he forced himself to stay put, to not waver under the heat of her intensity. She was looking for a reaction, and damn it, he wasn't going to give her one.

She knew exactly what her life would have been if she had never insisted on leaving. They would have gotten married, had a few kids, alternated Sunday dinners with their families. They would have lived in the house he had instead shared with Helen.

He stepped off the curb, quickening his pace. Just being here with Grace made him feel uneasy, agitated. The wind was picking up, but he stared right into it. It was better than facing Grace. Just being here reminded him of too many things he would rather forget.

"Not like my life is anything fabulous these days," Grace continued, and Luke studied her. He'd imagined sleek New York restaurants, a chic, modern apartment, and Grace, happier than ever, Briar Creek long forgotten. Along with everyone in it. He expected that Grace had gotten the life she had wanted. The one she wanted more than him.

"I find that hard to believe."

"Come on now," she said, catching his furrowed brow. "You can't say you don't know that my last book was a bust. You read it. It—"

"It was wonderful," he finished, unable to stop himself. He had devoured each of her books, ordering them online and keeping them in his desk at work so that no one in town got the wrong idea. He would lie awake at night and tell himself it was nothing, that lots of people remained friends with old girlfriends, that the past was the past and Grace was only someone he used to know. Still, he knew deep down it was more than that. Grace was gone, he had lost her forever, but when he sat down and read her books, for a brief period of time at least, it was like he was alone with her again.

"Honestly, Grace. It was a great book. I loved it."

She snorted. Only Grace could turn that sound into something pretty, elegant. "Well, I don't believe you. And besides, it doesn't matter if you liked it or not. No one else did."

"It used to matter to you if I liked your work," he pointed out.

She shifted her gaze. "Yes. It did." She seemed to hesitate. "But then, a lot of things used to matter to me, Luke."

"For example?"

"You used to matter."

Her words were a punch to the gut. "And I don't anymore?" She shrugged, infuriating him. As quickly as that, all pleasantries were over. "Very nice, Grace."

Her eyes flashed on him, green and vivid. "What do you expect, Luke? You were the one who gave up on me. You showed me how little I mattered. Was I supposed to hold on while you went on with your life?"

"You broke up with me, Grace," he reminded her, but he clung to her last words. She really had let go, moved on.

She had been doing just as he imagined with her life. She never stopped to think about him. Maybe it was wrong of him to have hoped she had.

"And what choice did you give me?" she demanded. They had stopped walking now, and she stood in front of him, lifting herself to full height, so close to him that he could see the freckles that dusted her nose.

"You had plenty of choices," he growled.

Her gaze narrowed. "And so did you."

He held her stare, his heart thundering in his chest, and then shrugged. Shrugged off the pain, the hurt, the frustration that had lingered for years and was now bubbling at the surface.

He had plenty of choices, she was right about that. And leave it to Grace to home in on the one thing that had nagged him all these years. Had he made the right one?

All this time it had been easier to blame Grace, to hold her solely accountable for the demise of their relationship. Perhaps it wasn't that black and white; perhaps he had given up, let her slip away.

But no. *No.* He wasn't going to let her turn this on him. Inhaling sharply, he huffed out a breath. "Grace, you were the one who decided to leave this town. And me. You have no one to blame but yourself for your choices."

"True enough," she said. "Yet, seeing how quickly you moved on, it's a good thing I didn't give up everything for you."

Luke narrowed his eyes; his stomach burned. She couldn't go there. He wouldn't stand for it. "Don't bring Helen into this."

"Why shouldn't I? She played a part in all of this, too." Luke's eyes flashed wide with warning, and Grace had the sense to stop herself, her pupils darkening with what he knew to be shame.

Luke glared at her, wanting nothing more than to turn and walk away right then and there. Forever, this time. His chest was pounding, and his ragged breath escaped in white clouds of frost.

"Well," Grace huffed, resuming her pace as she took quick strides down Main Street. The sidewalks were slick despite the salt that covered the patches of ice, and busy shoppers weaved past them, flashing them curious glances. "We were young then. Foolish. In the throes of passion, as they say!" She paused, becoming more somber. "You know how it is with first loves—you think you'll never find another, that it will last forever. And you proved to me that it wouldn't. *Twice*."

He frowned. "Twice?"

"First when you laughed at my dreams—"

Oh, now this was unfair! "I didn't laugh at your dreams."

But she wasn't listening. "Then when you got engaged to Helen."

Luke gave her a level stare. There was nothing he could say.

"And then!" She stopped, her eyes laced with pain so deep he felt his pulse skip. "And then when I came back for you," she whispered angrily, "and you had a chance to set it right between us again. And you *didn't*." The anguish in her face shocked him, made him ache in a way he had only experienced a few times in his life. His chest burned with regret, with shame, and guilt.

Always guilt.

"Guess that's three times," she said on a brittle laugh, turning her profile to him once more.

He lowered his head, contemplating her words. Was that all she had taken from the experience? It was so one-sided. So goddamned unreasonable of her! "What did you expect me to do, Grace? I made a promise to Helen, and I couldn't go back on it."

"So you married her out of obligation?"

"No," he said flatly. "I married her because she wanted the same things as me. A boring little life in this boring little town."

She scowled. "Stop."

"What?" he pressed. "Isn't that what you said? That Briar Creek is boring, that you could never live your life here? That if I loved you, I wouldn't force you to stay?"

She paused. "Maybe, but—"

"No buts. You said that. And I took you at your word." He stared at her stonily. "I loved you, Grace, and I didn't want to force you to stay here."

"So you let me go?" Her voice pitched, pulling at his heart, and he nodded his reply.

"Yes," he lied. He had watched her walk away, out of his life, but he had never let her go. No matter how much he wished he could.

She turned away, and this time he felt like she was slipping away for good, like they had exchanged the last words that needed to be said. And somehow, in that moment, he wanted to grab her by the shoulders and pull her toward him, and do what he should have done five years ago. He wanted to feel the familiar curves of her body against his chest, smell her sweet, coconut-scented hair, and feel complete again. No one knew him like Grace. She didn't take explaining; she didn't require a recounting of his memories. She had been there. She had lived them. She was part of him.

"I wish I had never come back," she mused, but her tone was angry, accusatory. "It's all different! It's all changed!" She tossed her hands into the air, shaking her head. A tear slipped down her cheek, and he forced his hands to remain put, resisting the urge to wipe it away, to comfort her.

He glanced at her sidelong, giving her a slow grin, jabbing her ribs gently with his elbow, hoping to cheer her up. "Aw, now, it's not that different. Still the boring little town with the same boring people we've known since we were kids and will know until we…" He stopped short of the word. This Christmas was hard enough for both of them.

"It's not boring," Grace sniffed.

"What?" Luke cajoled but she'd surprised him. Something within him stirred. If he hadn't known better, he might have called it hope.

He pushed it away, firmly. He thought of that morning, that day Helen had died. The thought running through his head. And he suddenly wished Grace hadn't come back, either.

She was just passing through, eager to leave. Only in town long enough to mess with his head. And his heart.

"It's not boring," she repeated. "I was…young then. Foolish."

A question burned within him, eroding his stomach, twisting it raw. It had haunted him every night leading up to his wedding day, hovered in the recesses of his mind when he stood at the altar and pledged his vows, lingered throughout every day of his marriage right up until that morning. The morning he decided to find out once and for all.

Now Grace was here, the conversation was broached, and he could ask her, finally have his answer. He opened his mouth, and stopped himself. What would it matter, what could it change? He had married another woman, and now he mourned her death. Grace had left him, then come back for him, and he had turned her away. Nothing she could say now could change the chain of events, and any revelation might only add to his distress, confirm that all of it was unnecessary, that it could have all been so different. So very different.

"Things worked out the way they were meant to," he muttered, trying to sound more convincing than he felt.

She shrugged, and stared despondently down the street. He followed her gaze, trying to see what she saw. In the town square a group of children were having a snowball fight, and he recognized the boys from the school. Shoppers wrapped in woolly scarves, carrying paper bags stuffed with wrapped packages, trekked across the shoveled paths. The Christmas tree stood proud in the center of it all, beckoning a sense of cheer he couldn't bring himself to feel.

"Maybe," was all she said, and they lapsed into silence.

Luke leaned against the brick building that housed the Fireside Café. Through the window edged in twinkling lights he could see that, as usual, the place was filled. Groups of friends clutched steaming mugs of tea and leaned over tables chatting excitedly. A few customers had claimed armchairs near the blazing fireplace, engrossed in books or magazines. Near the window, Luke spotted a couple on a date. The woman was pretty, laughing at something the man was saying, and Luke had to tear his eyes away as disappointment swelled within him. He wondered if he would ever have a moment like that again.

"I should get going," he said.

Grace nodded almost imperceptibly, her eyes boring through his, and his heart skipped a beat as he waited for her to say what was on her mind.

"Okay," she finally said.

He stuffed his hands in his pockets, took a step backward. "I'll see you, Grace."

"Yeah, sure," she said, watching him retreat, and suddenly he wasn't so sure they would see each other, and the thought terrified him. This couldn't be how it ended; this couldn't be their last conversation.

"I'll see you before you leave, Grace," he said, his voice cutting loud and clear through the crisp, still air. "Even if it's just to wish you a Merry Christmas."

She raised a brow but her lips twisted with pleasure. "I thought you weren't feeling up for Christmas this year."

He grinned. "What can I say? We Scrooges need to stick together."

Her mouth curved into a delicious, slow smile, and his pulse quickened. "I'll see you around, Luke," she said, and just like that, she was gone.

Walking back to his car, Luke was aware of the bounce in his step, of the race of his heart. He fumbled in his pocket for his keys, smiling to himself, until he thought of going home to the house that reminded him of Helen, and then he felt the smile drain from his face.

Helen had been sweet and kind and easy to love. She would never have asked for more than he could give her, never demanded that he sacrifice more than he felt possible. She had wanted the same things as him; she hadn't pushed him away or asked for the impossible. He had been safe with Helen. He had been comfortable. With Helen, he could have the life that they both wanted, the one he had told Grace he needed. The one he realized might not be enough.

It wasn't that he hadn't loved Helen. It was that he had loved Grace, too. And it was a lot easier to live with that guilt when he didn't have to confront it face-to-face.

CHAPTER 10

Anna's gaze lingered cool and steady as Grace weaved her way through the crowded tables to the gleaming wood bakery counter at the back of the café. "Talking with Luke, I see," she said archly.

Grace released a breath, still feeling rattled from the morning's events. "Why didn't you tell me about the bookstore?" she asked, refusing to get into a conversation about Luke.

Two days in a row. Chances were high she'd see him again around town tomorrow, unless she opted to sit inside the house all day, and after last night and this morning, she had no intention of that. She wasn't sure she could bear the sight of him again or the way her body responded to the curve of those lips and the shadow in his eyes, but the thought of not seeing him again made her heart hurt more than she cared to admit.

Anna heaved a dramatic sigh and straightened a tray of blueberry scones. "I was waiting for this."

"Why didn't you tell me?" Grace repeated, her voice rising at Anna's nonchalance.

Ann tipped her head, fixing her stare. "Do you really want to get into this now?"

Grace felt her brow pinch. "Yes!" she cried, loudly enough for the barista behind the industrial-sized espresso machine to glance her way. She lowered her voice and leaned over the counter. "Yes, I do want to get into this now. I want to know why my family decided to close down our father's bookstore months ago without consulting me on the matter."

Anna released another sigh and shifted her eyes around the room. She turned to one of the other girls behind the counter, who was plating a tray of thick, fragrant chocolate chip cookies the size of a small planet, and said lowly, "I'll be back in five minutes."

Five minutes. Grace felt her temper flare. Here she was, asking to discuss the fate of their family's bookshop—her father's passion, his life's work—and all Anna could spare her was *five minutes*.

"I skipped breakfast. Can I get you anything while I'm at it?" Anna asked, almost as an afterthought, and Grace shook her head. She'd barely eaten dinner last night or breakfast this morning and her stomach felt raw and empty, but she had no appetite. How could she enjoy a meal when everything her father had worked for was turning to dust? The thought of sitting here, eating a scone, pretending like nothing was amiss...impossible.

She glanced at Anna, who was carrying an admittedly delicious-looking crumble-top muffin and hot tea to a table in the corner, where they wouldn't be overheard.

"I can't believe you haven't told me about this," Grace blurted as she hung her coat on the back of a chair. She slid into her seat, staring expectantly at her middle sister, who calmly broke her muffin in half and took a bite.

Growing up, Anna had always been the most difficult of the three sisters. They said middle children were easygoing by nature, but such was not the case with the Madison girls. No, Anna was as headstrong and determined as Grace, and with only a two-year age difference, competition tended to brew strong and steady. Perhaps it was from watching the two older sisters go at it that Jane remained so laid-back and quiet, Grace had often reflected. There were times, she knew, where Anna could make her downright angry, like now. Mostly, though, Grace knew she had her sister to thank for a lot of the success she had in life, and that Anna could probably say the same if she stopped and thought about it.

This café was living proof of what a little incentive could do. Anna had worked all through high school and culinary school, saving every penny, refusing to part with so much as a few dollars for a Saturday night movie. By the time she had graduated, she was able to fund the start-up of the Fireside Café, which had thrived ever since.

Anna tucked a strand of blond hair behind her ear. "I should have told you. I'm sorry."

Well, that was something. And more than she had expected after Anna's behavior the night before. Grace relaxed her shoulders, feeling her defensive edge melt into the back of her seat. "I'm just so shocked," she said. "Jane said that Mom is at peace with the store closing. Is that true?"

Anna shrugged and briefly met Grace's inquisitive eyes. "I'm not really sure what choice she has."

"Well, has she talked to the bank? Maybe she could get a loan or a mortgage on the house—"

Anna was shaking her head. "No, Grace. It's too much

for her on top of her own work, and it's too much of a risk. Do you know how much money that place was bringing in for the past few years?" Without waiting for Grace to answer, she said, "Less than the rent, that's how much. It's in the red. It's a liability, and right now Mom needs all the security she can get."

"I'm worried about Mom."

"If you're so worried," Anna said, "then don't show her how upset you are about the bookstore. Disappointment is one thing, but don't attack her. It's not her fault. It's no one's fault."

Grace studied the pattern of the wood on the tabletop. Christmas music played softly in the background, barely audible over the lively buzz in the room. All around her, people were chatting, occasionally bursting into laughter, enjoying the holiday cheer. As much as she hated to admit it, Anna had a point. A good one. Still, something in her couldn't accept it. It meant too much. "It's just—" Her voice hitched. "It's the last piece of Dad we have."

For the first time since she had arrived, Grace noted that her sister looked genuinely saddened. Her blue eyes were flat; her pretty lips were turned down. "I know," she said softly. "Don't think this wasn't hard for me, too. For all of us." She drew a sharp breath and met Grace's eye. "We've struggled with this, and I think that's why none of us wanted to tell you. It would have made it worse for us than it already was."

"Because you knew I would be upset?"

"Because we knew how you would react. We knew you would do . . . this." She waved her hand in the air, gesturing at Grace across the table in exasperation.

Grace glared at her sister. "And how should I react?

Like you? Should I shrug it off and say, 'Oh well, too bad'?"

"No. But it's frankly unfair for you to get into a snit when you haven't even been around for the past five years," she said, her expression hardening. "You think you have a right to start questioning us for our reasoning, but the truth is that you weren't part of the decision process because you haven't been a part of this family in a very long time."

"That's not fair."

Anna lifted a perfectly plucked brow. "Isn't it?"

Grace pouted, fumbling with a napkin on the table. This entire trip was a disaster, one blow after another. She thought that by coming back she'd be helping her family, but so far it seemed like they were continuing on without her, making decisions without consulting her, treating her like a random cousin instead of something more.

She nestled back in her chair, looking around the crowded room, festively decorated for the season. A tree was tucked in one corner, blinking with colored lights, and the bakery counter was draped with glittering tinsel. From the ceiling, oversized, metallic ornaments in jewel tones hung by wire; stockings hung merrily from the crackling fireplace, whose hearth was the inspiration behind the establishment. She could recall how impressed she was the night it opened, and she was still shaken by the fact that Luke remembered that night at all. She thought of it often—too often perhaps. It was one of the last nights she could remember feeling like he was hers, and she clung to it on those lonely days, remembering the way his face looked on the pillow the next morning, so close to hers. She could close her eyes and see that grin, that sleepy, happy grin.

Her heart clenched. "Business is booming here, I see," she commented, desperate for a distraction.

"It's been amazing," Anna brightened. "Sometimes I still have to pinch myself."

Grace smiled, her chest swelling with sudden pride for her younger sister. Despite their rocky relationship, she still loved the girl. "I missed you, Anna," she said quietly. "I know you probably don't believe that, but it's the truth."

Anna's eyes widened ever so slightly in surprise before she offered a sad smile. "I kept wondering if you were ever going to come back."

"Well, you know why I had to leave," Grace replied, shifting in her seat. The chair suddenly felt too stiff, the room too hot. She wished she'd had the foresight to at least ask for a cup of coffee. Weeks of bad sleep were catching up with her.

"Yes, I know why, but I can't say that I understand why you had to stay away. I mean, not even a visit?" Anna fixed her blue gaze and Grace held her eyes, struggling with her mounting emotions. "All because of Luke?"

Grace's temper stirred. "I don't expect you to understand. You've never had a long-term relationship, so you can't even begin to imagine the pain that comes when it ends."

Anna's eyes flashed. "Don't give me that, Grace. We're not talking about me."

"Why don't we?" Grace said, and then pressed her lips together, exhaling deeply through her nose. This isn't what she had come here to do. Arguing with her sister was nothing new, but for a few days, she was hoping they could take some comfort in each other—support each other, not push each other around.

"Okay, fine. I have never had a long-term relationship. I wasn't as lucky as you were."

"What? Oh, please, Anna. You're a beautiful girl, the prettiest of us all. Do you know why you don't have a boyfriend? Because you're too picky, that's why. And because... because you're too involved in this place!" She waved her arm around the café, rolling her eyes.

"Fair enough," Anna said. "I take full responsibility for my decisions and my priorities. I'm happy running this place. I neither have the time nor the desire for a boyfriend, much less a husband."

Grace frowned, unconvinced. Anna was staring listlessly out the window now, and her profile made her look younger somehow, the somber expression made her seem vulnerable, which was not a look she often wore. "It only leads to heartache, anyway."

Anna turned to her. "I'm sorry to hear about you and Derek."

Grace dragged her thoughts away from Luke. "Oh. Oh, right. Thanks."

"You don't seem too broken up about it," Anna observed.

Grace shrugged. "It wasn't right. I knew it all along, but I guess I was forcing something that wasn't there."

Anna nodded, saying nothing for a moment. "Do you want to talk about Luke?"

"What's there to talk about?" Grace said with as much composure as she could muster. Her heartbeat took speed and she gripped the napkin in her hand until it formed a tight ball. "That's ancient history."

Anna eyed her watchfully. "If you say so." With one last sip of tea, she set her mug on top of her empty plate.

"I should get back to the kitchen," she said. "I have to go over the menu for tomorrow. Did you know we're now open for dinner? Just on weekends, but I'm hoping to expand that soon."

Grace didn't know that, and shame bit at her. "I'll let you go then."

Begrudgingly, she slid back her chair. This conversation had been fruitless, though honestly, what had she been expecting? For Anna to tell her it was all a mistake and Main Street Books was going to stay open? Jane had already explained the situation; maybe Grace needed Anna to confirm it, even if it wasn't what she wanted to hear.

"You going to the pageant tomorrow?" she asked.

"Yep," Anna said, and then her expression transformed with sudden interest. "And you know who else will be there, of course."

Grace's pulse skipped a beat. She wasn't sure how many more surprises she could handle right now. "Adam?"

Anna wrinkled her nose. "Of course Adam!" She laughed, shaking her head, staring at Grace as if she were half crazy. Maybe she was. "But you know who else . . ."

No, she didn't. And this game was not funny. "Who?"

"Luke." Anna stared at her, wide blue eyes disguised with innocence.

Luke. Of course he would be there. It was a school pageant. The school where he worked. The school that housed the preschool.

Grace closed her eyes and put her hand to her forehead, feeling shaky and sick. She really should have eaten something this morning. "Of course," she said weakly. "I didn't even think of that."

"Are you mad I told you?"

"No," Grace said. She drew a breath, her mind running wild with the thought of seeing him again, and she couldn't fight the quiver of excitement that zipped through her core. She shrugged into her coat, buttoning it slowly, thoughtfully. Would he be sitting in the audience or backstage? Would he be expecting her there? Would he be pleased? He didn't keep in touch with her family anymore, but Briar Creek was small, so surely he knew that Sophie would be participating...

"Well, if you feel like getting out tonight, there's a party at Mark's house. An annual Christmas bash."

"I thought you didn't like Mark," she said.

Anna let her eyes roam. "It's a fun party. Everyone will be there." Everyone including Luke, they both knew. "You should come. We can go together."

Grace felt her cheeks flush, and she nodded. She'd been a fool to think she could come back to Briar Creek without seeing Luke. And yet her sister was extending an olive branch, so she was going to accept it. "Okay."

"Good." Anna gathered her plate and mug and pushed in her chair.

Grace hesitated, not ready to admit defeat just yet. "I guess there's really nothing to be done about the bookstore then?"

"Not unless you have the cash for another year-long lease."

Grace huffed. Of course she didn't have that kind of money, not if she was going to find a new place in New York. She hoped to be out of Angie's apartment by the end of the year, and that would require every penny she had. Her first novel might have done well, but that was years ago. She and Derek lived an expensive lifestyle, and she'd been foolish enough to think that everything she produced would be met with the same result. How wrong she had been, she thought bitterly.

"You seem to be doing very well for yourself," Grace pointed out.

"Uh-uh. No." Anna stepped behind the counter. She folded her arms across her chest. "One business is enough for me, thank you very much. Besides, my passion is food, not books."

Grace decided to press the topic while she had the opportunity. "It would be a loan, to get us through."

Anna gave her a withering smile. "Even if I had that kind of money—and I don't—you still have to find someone to run the store." She tipped her head. "What, are you up for the job?"

"No," Grace shot back. "I...oh, never mind!" She tossed her hands up in exasperation, not bothering to say goodbye as she stomped out of the café and into the cold, crisp air. She took a big gulp of a winter breeze, waiting for the heat in her cheeks to fade, for her head to clear. No matter how hard she tried to fight it, Anna had sprinkled a little water on the idea that had planted itself in her head, and Grace knew full well what happened when one took root.

CHAPTER 11

The party was in full swing by the time Grace and Anna arrived, casually late and only after Grace had run out of excuses to stall. She hung her coat on the rack with the others and waited for Anna to do the same, her eyes scanning the festively decorated room for any sign of Luke.

Mark had moved since the last time she'd been to one of his Christmas parties, and this new house was small but sleek, with an open floor plan and modern furnishings balanced by the rustic beamed ceiling. The living room was filled with people she remembered from school, acquaintances she had lost touch with over time. There was Brett, Mark's brother, passing out appetizers. She smiled at the sight of him, so very much like Mark with his wavy dark hair and rich brown eyes. That was one thing New York didn't have on this town—the Hastings men were certainly a force to be reckoned with.

"I'm going to chat with Kara," Anna said. "Want to join me?"

"Kara?" Grace replied in alarm. She felt herself blanch at the mention of Luke's sister. "No, of course not. Why, is she here?"

But of course she was here. And Luke would be, too.

She could feel her heart begin to pound, but she didn't dare to look around for him. She would engross herself in conversations with old friends and make an early departure. Simple as that.

Something told her that was easier said than done.

Across the room, near the tree that was wrapped in colored lights and draped with tinsel, she spotted one of her closest friends from high school. Perfect.

"Ivy!" She waved desperately, smiling as her friend Ivy Birch squealed and ran over to her, giving her a hug.

"Oh my God, you're really here!" Ivy exclaimed, eyes dancing. "For how long? When did you get in? Oh my, so many questions, but first, take this. I'll be right back!" She thrust a drink in Grace's hand and dashed off to the makeshift bar table Mark had constructed in a corner of the living room. Grace took the opportunity to sweep her eyes over the crowd once more, this time noticing Mark, sloppy-grinned and laughing near the sofa, his arm draped around a woman Grace didn't recognize.

"Some things never change," she said to Anna, who was watching the scene with a disapproving frown.

"I'll be in the other room." Anna said brusquely, and then walked away.

"So, tell me, tell me," Ivy said, returning with a fresh drink in hand. Grace smiled in relief and leaned in, eager to hear what Ivy would ask her, wondering how she would frame her answer. What have you been up to? How's the writing going? Questions she was bound to hear and had hoped to avoid. Instead, all Ivy said was, "Have you seen Luke yet?"

Luke. Of course. It always came back to Luke.

She opened her mouth to say something, but it was too late. Mark had spotted her, and he was coming her way, holding up his hand in greeting. "Mark!" She smiled, feeling genuinely happy to see her old friend, and let him reach in for a hug. As she pressed her arms around his neck, her breath snagged when she spotted Luke over his cousin's shoulder.

Quickly, she untangled herself from Mark. "Nice party."

He shrugged, giving her a bashful grin. "You haven't missed much. Same party, different year."

"Well, traditions are nice," she managed, feeling the heat of Luke's gaze from behind the wall of Mark's body. What the hell was he doing? Was he not even going to say hello?

"Did you come alone?" Mark inquired, and Grace shook her head.

"I came with Anna," she explained, and Mark's smile faded. "She's around here somewhere."

"Hmm." Mark tipped back his beer and looked around the room with overt disinterest. Mark and Anna were chilly to each other, despite having attended the same culinary school, and it seemed five years hadn't changed matters.

She took the opportunity to pretend to look for Anna to instead steal a glance at Luke, who was now engrossed in a conversation with a petite blond woman, the very same woman that Mark had been chatting with a moment before. Her stomach tightened. So there it was, then. She had begun to wonder if Luke was having a hard time moving on from Helen, but clearly that wasn't the case at all.

"I should probably go find her," she said to Mark, hoping her tone didn't betray her hurt. "Catch up later?"

"I'd like that," Mark said, turning away from her.

Grace tugged at Ivy's arm and led her quickly to the expansive kitchen, lined with stainless steel appliances and gadgets. Safe inside, she drained the remains of her drink and set the glass down on the black granite counter with a bang. Anna and Kara were talking in the corner, laughing softly, but luckily Luke's sister's back was to her. "So what's new with you? How's the flower shop? Holidays must be a busy time of year," she said, forcing a casual tone as she refilled her glass from an open bottle of wine on the counter. She didn't bother to inspect if it was red or white—so long as it was alcohol, it would do.

"Uh-uh," Ivy said, shaking her head. "Me first. Did you see Luke?"

Grace emitted an exasperated sigh. "Well, he was standing right there. I'm sure you saw him, too."

"So, that's the first you've seen of him?" Ivy looked astonished.

"No." Grace paused. She really didn't feel like reliving the past two days, even with Ivy. She'd kept in touch with Ivy over the years, and Ivy had visited her in New York a few times, but like her sisters, she thought Ivy knew better than to push the topic of Luke. Being back in town seemed to have changed the rules, though. And being under the same roof at the moment probably left the subject unavoidable. "I've seen him."

"And?" Ivy pressed.

"And nothing," Grace finished. "There's nothing to talk about. Luke and I are ancient history. I've moved on."

"Oh, have you?" came the gruff response behind her.

The air locked in her chest as Grace whipped around to find Luke, standing tall above her, a glimmer of mirth flashing in his eyes.

"Oh. Hello," she managed, feeling the flush of heat creep up her neck. She took a sip of the cool white wine and then swept her fingers under the rim of her scoop-neck cashmere sweater, wishing she could peel it off before it clung completely to her sweating body.

The corner of Luke's mouth twitched and he leaned over her to grab a beer, so close that she had to lower her eyes, so close that she could smell the musk of his skin, feel the heat of his nearness.

She flung open her eyes, returning her glass to her lips with a shaking hand, eyeing him over the rim as he casually threw back his drink.

Why was he standing here? Tormenting her like this? Hadn't this morning been enough for one day?

"So you've moved on, eh?" His eyes locked with hers until her body went rigid, every ounce of her being working overtime to fight off the overwhelming sense of longing that was encroaching on her like a bad disease without a cure. To think he had once been hers, all hers, that handsome face, that smile, those lips.

She looked down at her glass. "That's right," she said. She shifted the weight on her feet, glanced up from the hood of her lashes. Damn it! He was still staring at her, still boring down on her, penetrating her with his eyes and that infuriating hint of a smile. "You're not the only one who found love. I moved on, too."

"Well, I'm relieved to hear that," he said, and she narrowed her gaze.

"Happy to be off the hook?"

"Happy to know you found happiness," he said.

"Well, I did," she fibbed.

"Well, good." His voice was gruff and he cleared his throat. He took another sip of his beer. "And all this time I was worried about you."

She scoffed. "Worried about me! Please."

His expression softened into something more sincere. "I was, Grace. I know you don't believe me."

"That's right, I don't," she snapped, turning away, looking for backup, but both Ivy and Anna had disappeared. In fact, the entire kitchen had mysteriously cleared out. "You really never loved me, did you?" she said bitterly, furiously wiping at a tear before it had time to fall. "You know what, forget it. I shouldn't have come to this party. I shouldn't be back here at all."

"Grace, wait." He grabbed her arm, forcing her to turn to him, to see the pain in his eyes. Of course he had loved her—she knew it then like she knew it now. She was being childish and silly, pushing him away because that's what she did. She pushed and pushed until he was gone, and there was no getting him back. "You know how much I loved you," he said softly, and then, with more force, "You know how you much you meant to me."

"I know," she admitted, letting her arm fall from his grip. They stood there in silence, neither one moving, waiting for something, though she wasn't sure what.

In the distance she could make out the sound of the stereo. She gritted her teeth, holding back a sigh. God help her, it was *their* song. They were playing *their* song.

She looked up at Luke, hooking her gaze on his stare, wondering if he had heard it, if he even remembered it. The shadow that came and went over his face gave her the answer.

"I think this about seals it," she said over an unhappy laugh. "Hands down, this is the worst Christmas ever."

Luke's mouth tugged into a lazy smile. "We used to love this song."

We used to love a lot of things. She looked away and took another sip of her wine before setting it on the counter. She wrapped her arms around herself, fingering the soft material of her sweater, wishing his arms were holding her tight instead. It was hard enough listening to this song, reliving those memories, but standing here alone with him brought it all much too close to the surface.

"I got you, babe." His voice was husky, deep like a growl, and she pressed her lips together to ward off a smile. "Babe," he said, in beat with the song.

She turned to him. He was grinning now, his blue eyes glittering. Confusion swept over her as she stared at him. He threw his head back, grinning, as he belted the song painfully off tune. Oh, how she had missed that grin. "They say we're young and we don't know— Come on, sing with me!" he chided.

"No," she said firmly.

He crooned the next line, forcing a chuckle to sputter from her lips at how badly he sang, then reached out to poke her shoulder with his finger, cajoling her into joining him. He wasn't going to let up. And she wasn't sure she wanted him to.

She smiled wanly and shakily tucked a strand of hair behind her ear. "Stop. We don't need this."

"Come on, maybe it will put it to rest. Maybe if we sing this song now it will give it a new meaning."

She raised an eyebrow, unconvinced. Still, she thought, as she brought her glass to her lips once more, he did have a point. Enough things were off-limits in her life as it was—all too painful in the emotions they stirred up—but if she could handle coming back to Briar Creek, then certainly she should be able to handle diffusing the power of one silly song.

He set his beer down and backed up, wiggling his fingers by invitation. His smile was contagious, his eyes so blue, brought out by the hue of his shirt, and her heart squeezed so tight she thought it might break.

Oh, to hell with it.

She yelled out the next line, wincing as her voice echoed off the empty walls, and he laughed, but as he took a step closer, his expression hardened, and she stiffened.

"Then put your little hand in mine," he sang softly, reaching down to take her hand, pulling her closer to him.

She stared at him, feeling the heat of his skin next to hers, his eyes so close she could see the flickers of color around his black pupils, count every eyelash if she wanted to. His lips hovered inches from her own, his fingers laced with hers, this time not letting her go. She reached her hand up and placed it on his chest, out of habit perhaps, or out of an urge too deep to restrain.

His free hand slid around her waist, sweeping her into the sway of the rhythm in one effortless movement, moving with her so naturally it was as if they had never spent a day apart. She closed her eyes and pressed her face against his shoulder, feeling the strength of him in her arms, the warmth of his body through his button-down shirt.

She knew the next verse and listened with a pounding heart as the muffled words came through the walls, over the raucous laughter and chatter in the next room. *I won't let go. I won't let go*, she chanted to herself. But that was exactly what she had done once, and now, being here in his arms like this, feeling his broad chest pressed against hers, his hand resting casually over the base of her spine, she wasn't sure how she would be able to let go again.

She'd stayed away all this time because she was afraid of this moment, afraid to feel something she shouldn't. To want something she could never have.

"Grace." His voice was husky and low, and she tilted her head up, her heart thundering in her chest, the world around her stopping as everything in that moment became about Luke, about the familiarity of his face so close to hers. His gaze was fixed on her mouth, and she parted her lips, sucking in a breath.

He stiffened. "We should probably get back to the party," he said, refusing to meet her eye as his arms dropped. He raked a hand through his dark hair and reached for his beer, quickly bringing it to his mouth.

Disappointment flooded her, but she refused to let him see it. She swallowed hard, feeling so vulnerable and stripped down that she might as well have been standing in the kitchen naked. "Yeah, probably." Seeing the pain in his eyes, she gave him a sad smile. "You go first. If we walk out there together we'll never hear the end of it," she added, forcing a small smile.

She waited until Luke left the kitchen, without another word or glance back, and then leaned back against the counter, releasing a shaky breath. It had meant nothing, nothing but an impulse to fall back into the routine that had once been so natural to them, and once Luke had realized what he was doing, he corrected himself.

She told herself to remember it was better this way. No good could come of slipping into their own ways. They were over, long over, and besides, she'd moved on. Or so he thought.

"Grace?" Ivy stood in the doorway, frowning. "You okay?"

Grace gave a wan smile. "Sure, of course."

"Mark's getting the karaoke machine out." She rolled her eyes.

"He always was the life of the party," Grace observed.

Ivy tipped her head. "You sure you're okay? We could leave if you want, go somewhere and talk. I'm sorry I brought up Luke. I shouldn't have—I don't know what I was thinking."

"No, it's fine, really," Grace lied. "I was just feeling nostalgic, being back here." She realized there was more truth in her statement than she had planned. Somehow, being at this party, being alone in the kitchen with Luke, so close to him it only made sense to lean in and kiss him, made her feel like no time had passed at all, that somehow the five years had never happened.

"Thinking about your dad?"

Grace paused as something occurred to her. "Did you know about Main Street Books?"

Ivy nodded, her face creased with guilt. "It's been a tough year for you, Grace."

"Here's the thing, Ivy. I've been thinking there might be a way to keep the store open."

"Really? That would be great!"

Grace licked her lips. "Keep this between you and me,

Ivy, but I really feel like there's still a chance for the place. Tell me: what do you know about that empty storefront next door?"

A strange expression took over Ivy's features. "I don't really know," she said after a pause. "Why?"

Grace hesitated, considering the idea that was taking shape, and then pushed it away with a shake of her head. "Nothing, forget it. It was a silly idea," she said. And that's exactly what it was. A stupid, silly idea. Saving that shop meant staying in town, and there was no way she could do that. Hell, she couldn't even handle staying at this party.

"If you don't mind, I think I would like to take you up on your offer," she said, thinking of how awkward it would be to see Luke's sisters, or to watch Luke talk with other people as if she weren't even in the room, as if he hadn't almost kissed her. Because he almost had—he most certainly almost had. "Mind if we head out?"

Ivy grinned. "Not at all."

Grace followed her friend through the hall, looking out of the corner of her eye for any sign of Luke as she shrugged on her coat, but as she stepped out the front door and into the cold, winter night, she realized as she saw the taillights of a black SUV growing smaller in the distance that he was already one step ahead of her.

CHAPTER 12

In the more than ten minutes since she had picked up Grace from their mother's house at noon sharp, not a word had yet been spoken. Exasperated, Jane turned up the volume on the car radio as a particularly happy jingle was starting. *Good*, she thought, feeling a bit better already. They could use a bit of cheer this afternoon.

"Do you mind?" Without waiting for an answer, Grace leaned over and switched off the car radio. Jane counted to three, waiting for it, and sure enough, Sophie's protest wailed from the back seat.

"Hey! Turn back on the music!" the small voice cried.

Jane pressed her lips together. *Stay calm.* "Auntie Grace doesn't want the music on right now, sweetheart." *She'd rather pout instead*, she finished to herself. She knew that Grace would be disappointed about the bookstore, but honestly! It was the pragmatic thing to do; surely Grace would see that too if she could stop and look at the facts.

"Oh!" Sophie grumbled in disappointment and then

kicked the back of the driver's seat, causing Jane to almost slam on the brakes in reaction.

"Santa's watching, Sophie!" she warned, even though she herself felt like doing nothing short of the same. Only to the back of someone else's chair.

She glanced at her sister. So much for thinking Grace would be there for her. Since she'd been back in town, her sister had been nothing but silent and brooding. Like everyone else in her family, Jane mused. It seemed she was the only one capable of pulling herself together for the season, putting on a game face, and forcing some Christmas cheer. She, of all people. If she stopped to think about it, she laughed.

Until she cried.

"I don't like Auntie Grace anymore! She's mean!" Sophie continued and Jane dropped her jaw, feigning horror, but secretly holding in a burst of laughter that was bubbling much too close to the surface.

Jane slid her eyes to Grace, who was staring out the window, seemingly oblivious to her niece's insults. It was typical of her sister. Grace was always able to find escape in her own mind and imagination. It was a trait Jane wished she too possessed, especially now.

"Let's be nice, Sophie. Apologize to your aunt." She made a show of pausing, rolling her eyes to Grace in mock exasperation, when what she really thought was, *That's my girl.*

Her heart warmed. Some days—in fact most days—it felt like the world was against her. Like she had no one on her side. And then Sophie would say something that would turn her mood around, lift her spirits.

She had Sophie, she reminded herself firmly each day. And that was all she needed.

"Don't you like Christmas music, Aunt Grace?" Sophie asked, and Jane took interest in this.

Grace pulled her attention back to them, frowning. "No, honey," she sighed after a moment. "I really don't like Christmas music. Not this year, at least."

Sophie fell silent, absorbing this unexpected response, her little forehead crinkled as she tried to understand. Perhaps Jane had sheltered her too much, she mused, glancing in the rear view mirror. Maybe Sophie was tougher than she had thought. Maybe she would handle the breakdown of their family better than Jane feared...

Well, not if she could help it.

"We're almost home now, and we can listen to music while we make our cookies!" Jane said brightly, as she turned down their street. She took in the houses, mostly boasting young, growing families, and felt a familiar pang in her chest.

She could still remember when she and Adam had purchased their home, just before Sophie was born. She remembered the sense of wonder that filled each room, the possibility of the four bedrooms on the second floor, the thought of filling this house with children, laughter.

What had happened to those dreams? She had thought Adam shared them, wanted the life they had planned for each other. The one that had meant more to her than her dreams of dancing, pursuing her ballet. She'd chucked it all, giving up her scholarship at the dance academy to marry Adam when he graduated from college, knowing that a life with him was enough for her. And it had been. She loved their life together, the role of wife and mother.

She had stayed the course, followed their predetermined path. She had done nothing wrong; it was he who had strayed—her lying, cheating, unfaithful husband. So why then did she lie awake at night wondering what she could have done differently, what she had missed? She had failed her family, herself, her child. She had been unable to keep her family together, and now Sophie would grow up in a broken home.

Jane blinked rapidly. She couldn't cry now, not with Grace here, and especially not in front of Sophie. She would protect her child some way or another. And maybe, just maybe, she could even give her the best Christmas gift of all this year: the security of knowing that her parents would stay together, that all would continue as it was intended to all along.

"I love your house," Grace said as Jane pulled into the driveway. It was shoveled; Adam had done that much at least. It was a small contribution to their family, and Jane was ashamed to realize how much it had meant to her. Somehow it signified more than she knew it should.

"Thanks," Jane said, tracing her gaze over the Dutch colonial. It was a beautiful house, a house she had thought she would live in forever, but now . . . Now it was only another source of uncertainty, another piece in the puzzle that had become her marriage and everything connected to it. She'd always assumed that if Adam filed for divorce that he would let her keep the house, but now, looking up at the house with its crisp white siding, black shutters, and hunter green door, she wasn't so sure if she could even live there without him. It would be a constant reminder of the hope she had once felt and the dream she had lost.

Foolishness! She was going down a dark road, imagining worst case scenarios. To hear herself think, why it was as if she was already planning for a divorce—and she wasn't. She most certainly was not.

Aware that Grace was staring at her, Jane jolted herself back to her surroundings. "Sorry," she muttered, turning off the ignition. She popped the locks and scrambled out of her seat before Grace could pry into her thoughts, and opened the back door, releasing Sophie from her car seat.

"I can't believe she still has to sit in one of those," Grace observed. She was hovering on the opposite side of the car, hands in her pocket, and as Jane caught her eye, something in her softened. She'd missed Grace. A lot. It was easy to forget that Grace had suffered her own disappointments recently, too.

It's not all about you, Jane. Although sometimes it felt that way, especially with no one to confide in. Oh, she had friends, but it wasn't the same as a sister, and deep down she knew her sisters were always her closest friends, even when they didn't always get along or went for years without face-to-face contact. Grace always made a point of keeping in touch via email or phone. Jane always felt a knot in her heart on the days her inbox sat empty.

"She's only four," Jane said, "but I know what you mean. I don't remember sitting in one of these at her age."

Grace shrugged. "Times change. I remember sitting on the armrest in the front seat. Right in between Mom and Dad. I liked being high up so I could see out the windshield."

Jane snorted and then burst out laughing, imagining her own daughter doing such a thing—ludicrous! It felt good to laugh. She hadn't done enough of it lately. "I wish I could remember that!"

"I miss those days," Grace said, her voice so low that it was nearly lost in a chilling burst of wind.

Jane shuddered and rubbed her arms over her ivory down parka. "Come on inside. It's freezing out here," she said, coming around the car to place an arm around her oldest sister's waist, her earlier hostility already fading.

Grace was her sister. She knew her and loved her like few in this world could, and she needed to remember that, focus on it. It was becoming so much easier to stop trusting in people, to assume they would let you down in the end, the way her husband had. The one person who had vowed to love her forever.

Once inside, Jane set the kettle to boil for tea and placed Sophie's red snow boots near the radiator to dry. She took Sophie by the hand and brought her into the family room—the *family* room!—where she scrolled through the channels until she found a Christmas show long enough to keep Sophie distracted while she prepped the ingredients for the cookies. The tree sparkled in the corner, standing tall enough to skim the ceiling, proudly boasting all the ornaments she and Adam had collected over the years. It had pained her to hang each one. Normally, they did it together, but this year Adam had told her to go ahead and set it up without him. Busy at "the office" ... of course.

She'd kept her mind occupied that night stringing popcorn, until the garland could have wrapped the tree fifteen times over. It was all she could do to keep her thoughts from trailing to what her husband was doing. Or who he was with.

Jane walked over to the hearth and straightened the knit stockings. Three in a row. She had thought someday there would be a fourth, maybe even a fifth—now she would be lucky to hold on to the three. The thought of only two stockings hanging from the mantel by next Christmas sliced at her heart. She turned away, brushing a tear quickly and inhaling a shaky sigh.

"Grace?" When her sister didn't answer, she wandered into the kitchen, finding it empty and the teakettle whistling. Turning off the gas, she set the kettle on the back burner, tipping her head as she saw Grace in the hallway. "Grace?" she repeated, stepping closer, and then halting in her path when she saw her sister staring at the framed photo that hung near the base of the stairs.

Their wedding photo.

"There you are," she breathed, becoming aware of the pounding of her heart.

"You look so young in this," Grace mused, barely giving her a glance.

"Well, I *was* young," Jane said as she stepped closer, aware of the defensive edge creeping into her tone. It pained her to look at that photo, to reflect on the excitement of the day, to recall the overwhelming sense of anticipation she had felt. What a stupid, stupid girl, she thought now.

"Nineteen, right?"

Jane nodded. "Adam was only twenty-two," she said, frowning at the image of his handsome, younger face. They were so innocent. He had proposed when she was just eighteen and she had said yes, thinking at that time that all she wanted was to be a wife and a mother. Now she was filled with regret, thinking of what her life might have been if she'd been more practical, more self-protective. Less foolish.

But then, she wouldn't have had Sophie.

"Guess you guys were meant to be," Grace said, but something in her tone made Jane pause. It was less of an observation than a question.

When Jane only responded with a mild shrug, Grace continued, her eyes turning wistful. "First love," she said, her voice drifting low, barely audible.

Jane narrowed her gaze. "I often wonder how many first loves even make it for the long haul. When you're young and naïve, you don't realize what the world has in store for you, you know? You think that nothing else matters so long as you're with him, that your love won't fade, that it will get you through anything." She scowled.

Grace turned to her, frowning. "Is everything okay?"

Jane's pulse skipped. She could feel her body heat rise. She'd broken a promise to herself, letting her emotions get the better of her. "Of course. Why wouldn't it be?" Her voice hitched, but she maintained an even expression.

Grace clearly wasn't buying it. "Because if it isn't, you can tell me, you know," she said. "I'm your sister. That's what I'm here for."

Jane gave a nervous chuckle, cutting the air with her hand to show how silly the conversation was, but her chest felt like it was being wrung through a vise. She could tell her, right now. She could finally open the floodgates, cry on someone's shoulder. But she couldn't. She had kept it inside for so long that she was no longer certain what would happen when she released it—somehow saying it aloud made it real. A fact. Not just a silly notion in her head.

Her husband was having an affair.

Grace could never understand, not any more than Anna. Neither of her sisters had been married, or had a child. Anna had never even been in love as far as she knew, and Grace—well, Grace was clearly incapable of commitment. When things didn't suit her exactly as she wanted, she fled. She didn't know the first thing about compromise. Sacrifice. What it took to keep a family together.

She knew what her sisters would say. What they would tell her to do. And she couldn't. She wouldn't. She... didn't want it to come to that. The *D* word.

Even if deep down she knew it probably should.

"Everything's fine," Jane said, trying to look perplexed. Switching gears, she said, "Besides, it's really me who should be asking you if everything is okay. You were really quiet in the car on the way over here."

Grace turned her attention from the photograph, her shoulders deflating on a sigh. "I saw Luke last night."

Aha. Jane gave her an encouraging smile and tipped her head in the direction of the kitchen. "Let's have something warm to drink and chat."

Grace smiled. "I don't know what I'd do without you, Jane. Mom's in her own world and Anna..."

"Anna is just being Anna?" Jane arched a brow and opened a cabinet, searching for her peppermint tea leaves.

"I guess so," Grace said slowly, "but I feel like something else is going on with her. She's always been focused and busy, but now she seems...detached. I don't even think she's very happy to see me." Grace chuckled softly but Jane could detect the undertone of pain.

"Don't worry about Anna," she said gently, sliding into a bar stool at the kitchen island. "She'll come around. She's dealing with the loss in her own way. I think it's harder on everyone at Christmas."

"Tell me about it," Grace muttered. She listlessly stirred some sugar into her tea.

Grateful for an excuse not to think about her crumbling marriage, Jane asked, "What's going on with you and Luke?"

Grace's eyes flew open as she met her gaze. "Luke? There's nothing going on with Luke and me. I...saw him. Again," she added.

Jane pinched her lips, hiding a smile. For someone who insisted there was nothing going on, it sure seemed like there was a lot not being said. "You know he'll be at the pageant tonight, too. I hope you're okay with that."

She watched as her sister tried to put on a show of surprise, perhaps even disappointment. "Oh, yeah...Anna told me." She shrugged. "That's fine, I guess."

Jane nodded, hiding her upturned mouth behind the rim of her cup. "He's great with the kids," she continued. "He was voted Teacher of the Year three years in a row. You know he's the principal now, right?"

Grace took a great interest in picking up her mug, taking a sip. "Oh," was all she said.

"This is his second year, but I get the feeling he misses being in the classroom."

Grace's eyebrows drew to a point. "You talk with him?"

Jane shook her head. "Idle gossip."

There was a lot of gossip about Luke these days. He was considered a real catch in a town like this, with his good looks and thoughtful personality. With the money Luke inherited from his father's investment stakes in three local ski resorts, he could have had any career in the world, and here he was, a teacher-turned-principal at the same elementary school he had attended. Lots of the single women in town found this swoon-worthy, but Jane knew Luke's career path, and specifically the location, had only served to infuriate Grace.

Grace had always wanted something more for herself. Something glamorous. And she'd found it.

Jane stared into her steaming tea. Where would life have brought her if she had opted for something more glamorous herself, she wondered. Would she have ever made it as a dancer? Or would she have failed and ended up right where she began?

She guessed she'd never know.

Grace inhaled audibly and Jane gauged her sister's mood, wondering how far she could push her. It seemed that Grace was determined to feign nonchalance, but Jane knew better. Luke was not easily forgotten.

When she was younger, Luke was like the cool big brother she'd never had—it had been a loss to her when he was no longer a part of their lives. No one in the family would admit it, making a silent allegiance not to speculate or question, but they'd all secretly wished that Grace would smooth things over, bring Luke back into their lives again. Instead, they had quietly drifted away, watching from a distance as he moved on with his life.

"His father would have been proud," Jane said, thinking of Mr. Hastings, who had died in a car accident when she was only a bit older than Sophie. She could barely remember him, but Rosemary Hastings (or *Madame* Hastings, as she liked to go by during class time) always spoke of him fondly after her ballet class was over. Jane was often the last to leave the studio, desperate for five more minutes at the barre, and so she alone would accompany

Madame Hastings out of the building, out into the cool evening air, often accepting a ride home if it was too dark or rainy to ride her bike. She knew from the stories Luke's mother told, from the faraway gleam in her eye, that his father had been a good man. Just like her own.

"Dad would have been proud, too," she added, knowing how close he and Luke had been.

A wave of exasperation crossed Grace's face. "What are you getting at, Jane?"

Jane frowned. "Nothing," she said, backtracking. She had gone too far. Pushed a sensitive subject. She should have known Grace would react this way. After all, up until yesterday Luke's name was still off-limits. He was not to be discussed in Grace's presence. Ever. Her reaction now was proof of what happened if they broke that promise. "I'm sorry. You brought him up, so I figured it was okay to talk about him."

Grace relaxed her stance. "No, I'm sorry. It's my problem, not yours." She trailed off, shaking her head. "I don't want to talk about him."

"Fair enough."

Grace eyed her. "I mean, do you know . . . has he dated anyone since . . ." She stopped herself, and straightened her back. "Forget it. I don't know why I asked."

Jane hesitated. "He keeps to himself," she said, matter-of-factly, and Grace pursed her lips, seeming satisfied with the response.

Jane set her empty tea mug on the counter and stood, pushing back her chair and crossing to the pantry to retrieve the ingredients for the cookies. She'd been promising Sophie all day that they'd decorate sugar cut-out cookies, and she wasn't about to go back on her word.

Right now, all she could offer her daughter were the small, simple things. The rest was out of her control.

The phone at the far end of the room rang, reverberating off the hushed kitchen walls, and Jane gasped, wondering if... She darted her gaze to her sister, who was peering at her, confusion folding her soft features. "Are you going to get that?" she asked.

"What?" Jane said. She stared at the phone. Her pulse kicked with each trill. "Sure, of course."

She lifted her chin and crossed the room with a stride more confident than she felt, answering on what she knew to be the last ring. "Hello?" she said briskly, folding her free arm tight across her waist as she leaned back against the wall.

It was Adam. "Hey."

"Oh, hello," she said brightly. *Fake it 'til you make it.* That was her motto these days, even if it did make her feel like a silly, stupid fool. She gritted her teeth bitterly, drifting her eyes away from Grace's curious stare. "How's work going?"

"What?" Adam grumbled. There was a ruffling of papers. He sounded distracted. Uninterested. And she was beginning to feel desperate. "I was calling about tonight. I have to work late, so don't wait up for me."

Her heart sank. She could feel the blood rushing in her veins. She willed her voice to remain steady, calm. "Okay. Sophie has her pageant tonight." Her voice was shrill, even to her own ears.

She wished Grace would stop watching her.

"That's tonight?" Adam repeated. "Oh, crap."

Jane bit down on her lip. She motioned to Grace to check on Sophie, hoping that her daughter's ears wouldn't perk up at the thought of her father on the phone, that she wouldn't overhear something she shouldn't. She waited with a pounding heart until Grace exited the kitchen, and then crossed the room quickly, shutting herself inside the pantry.

"Yes, that's tonight, Adam," she hissed. "I reminded you last night."

"No, you didn't," he accused, and Jane felt her blood pressure soar.

"Yes," she said flatly. "I did."

"I must not have heard," he replied.

Jane narrowed her eyes. *More like you must not have been listening*, she thought bitterly. It was happening more and more, no matter how hard she tried to fight it. He'd walk through the door at whatever hour he deigned to come home, mutter a greeting, and walk past her, leaving her standing in shock, mouth open expectantly, feeling like she didn't even exist. She tried to brush it off, wear him down, volunteer information about her day, tell him something funny that Sophie had said that morning, and sometimes she got a little smile, a hint of an acknowledgment, but more often than not, he said nothing, not even meeting her eye.

She pressed her hand over her face. Her husband did not see her anymore. What was she even holding on to?

Don't say anything you'll regret, she reminded herself. "Well, it starts at six," she said.

"Six!"

What else did he have to do at six, she wondered. Dinner two towns over at a hotel restaurant with his mistress? She'd seen the receipts, the credit card statements. When they arrived in the mail, she pored over them, her hands trembling as her eyes scanned the list. It was her only way of knowing it was still going on. Her only way of feeling remotely in control of her reality.

It amazed her that he still let her pay the bills. That he thought she was so blind, so trusting, so stupid, that she would buy his lies about these client meetings. "Client meeting tonight?" she inquired, bracing herself.

"I guess I can see if I can change it," he muttered.

Jane clenched her hand tighter around the receiver. "Well, I'm sure it will mean a lot to Sophie to have you there."

"Of course," he said, his tone softening, and for one, daring second, Jane felt her spirits rise. She held her breath, wondering if he had a change of heart, if the thought of sitting side by side, watching their daughter perform in the preschool chorus warmed him to her, made him remember the woman he had fallen in love with, the woman who had given him the child he loved so dearly. "I would never want to disappoint Sophie."

And me? Jane knew it was silly, immature, but she couldn't help it. How could he care so much for their child and so little for her? She hadn't cheated. She hadn't lied. She had done exactly what she had promised to do. And it wasn't enough.

She blinked back the hot tears that blurred her vision. "So, I'll see you tonight, then."

"Don't bother waiting for me," he informed her. "I'll come straight to the school from the office." His words translated into the usual: he would arrive on his terms, his schedule. He would do what was convenient for him.

A flash of anger burst through her core, quickly drying her self-pitying tears. How could she care about a man like this? A man who never stopped to show her consideration, who didn't ever think about her plans, her feelings? Why would she even want a life with this man? A man who cheated on her, lied to her, and looked straight through her?

She knew the reason why: Sophie.

She wanted to give her child a family. Adam may have stopped trying, so now she would have to fight for both of them. For all three of them.

She hung up the phone and set it on a shelf next to a box of oatmeal, letting out a long, shaky breath. She pressed her palms against her eyes, enjoying the brief indulgence of hiding in the self-inflicted darkness, escaping her harsh reality for a second more. *Get a grip, get a grip.*

Right. She counted to three and then released her hands, squared her shoulders, and pushed open the pantry door.

Grace and Sophie were standing in the kitchen, staring at her with bewildered expressions. With all the happiness she could muster, Jane plastered a toothy grin on her face. "So!" she exclaimed, rubbing her hands together with excitement. "Who's ready to make some cookies?"

CHAPTER
13

Grace discreetly scanned the dimly lit auditorium of the Briar Creek Grade School, her heart drumming in her chest. She scoffed at her own nonsense and turned her attention back to her mother, who had accompanied her this evening. From across the mass of people, Grace caught the flicker of a familiar face, the wave of a hand. "There's Anna," she said, quickening her step.

She wanted to get to her seat and stay there. She'd already noticed more than a few people she recognized— they'd be curious to know how long she was in town, what she had been up to, if she knew about Luke being single again...She smiled politely at the people she recognized as she shuffled into her row and collapsed into one of the empty chairs Anna had covered with her scarf, coat, and handbag.

See, this is what Luke had never understood. In Briar Creek everyone knew everybody else. They knew your business. They married people they had seen in diapers. It was the same recycled life over and over again. He didn't mind that; instead, he took comfort in it. But she . . . Well, she didn't know what she wanted anymore.

There was a time when she thought that big-city life was a necessity, that her soul would shrivel up and die without the exhilaration. Yet all it took was ten minutes of Luke's presence to leave her wavering.

"Is Jane sitting with us?" she asked as she shrugged out of her coat. She purposefully omitted mentioning Adam, waiting instead to see if Anna might shed some light.

"I haven't seen her yet," Anna said, giving a cursory glance to the back of the room.

Grace craned her neck to look for them and then, catching the heated stare of Mrs. Hastings, she whipped around. She felt herself blanch as her pulse began to race.

"Is everything okay?" Anna asked, bemused.

"What?" Grace frowned. Her chest heaved with each breath; her neck felt sweaty, slick. She unraveled her scarf—Luke's scarf—and tucked it into her lap guiltily. She'd only brought it so she could return it to him, but the night was colder than she'd expected and so she'd innocently tied it on. There was no denying that Rosemary Hastings recognized its origin. "Everything is fine. Just fine." She opened the program and pretended to become immediately engrossed.

Mrs. Hastings. *Luke's mother.* What must she think of her! Rationally, she knew that Mrs. Hastings would harbor no hard feelings—after all, Luke had moved on with his life after their breakup, married, settled down. People broke up all the time; surely she understood that. Five years had passed; she wouldn't still be caught up with Luke's broken heart over the woman he hadn't married. That would be ridiculous, preposterous!

And honestly, Grace convinced herself, it was Luke who had decided they were truly finished for good.

She kept her head low, feeling the flush of heat creep its way up her neck. It was absurd, she knew. She was nearly thirty years old now; she was an adult. She had moved on, as had Luke. There was no reason why she shouldn't be able to walk over to Mrs. Hastings and greet her with a warm smile, catch up on things at the ballet studio, and ask about her daughters, Luke's sisters.

Oh my God, are they here, too?

Grace pressed her palm against her stomach in an effort to settle it. This was craziness. She had successfully avoided Kara and Molly at Mark's party. If they were searching for a confrontation, she would have faced it last night. Besides, she and Luke were a thing of the past. Of course Luke's family would be happy to see her, as she was them... sort of.

No matter how many ways she looked at it, she couldn't fight the resounding feeling that she had let them down. All of them. Luke's family. Hers. Luke and Grace, Grace and Luke. They were... a thing. A fixture. A given. No one expected them to break up, to live separate lives. They were supposed to carry on as they always had: together, right here in Briar Creek.

And then Grace had to go and mess everything up.

"Don't look now," she whispered to Anna, "but Mrs. Hastings is sitting three rows behind us."

"I know," said Anna mildly. "I saw her when I walked in." She paused, and Grace set her jaw. She turned the page in her program. "Wait. Don't—don't tell me you're afraid."

Grace shot her a sideways glance. "I'm not *afraid*!"

she hissed. Oh, but she was. She was very afraid. Afraid of being met with a cool reception. Afraid of the confirmation of the damage she had done. Afraid of knowing she had upset people she cared about. Ruined things far deeper than she had intended.

Beside her, Anna chuckled. Her honey blond hair danced around her shoulders, brushing Grace's coat. "You're really still hung up on this, aren't you?"

Grace frowned. "Hung up on what?"

"Luke!"

Grace gritted her teeth. "Shhh!" she said forcefully, her heart squeezing in alarm. She lowered her tone, her frown deepening. "Someone will hear you."

Anna shrugged. "So?"

Bristling, Grace settled back into her chair, pulling her gray peacoat tightly around her shoulders for shelter. Oh, if she could just disappear into it. Pull it over her head. Maybe she could climb on all fours out the row and up the aisle once the lights went out... "I'm not hung up on it," she said, pursing her lips. Honestly!

Anna turned to face the stage. "Could have fooled me," she said, and Grace's temper stirred. She should have known that Anna wouldn't understand. Anna was unflappable; she was always the cool girl at school, always so calm, so assured. Life came easily to Anna, and she took it in stride. Grace had always admired that about her middle sister, but her father had always told her to embrace her emotions, even if they felt erratic at times, overwhelming. It was what made her dig deep, what made her pour her soul into her words, her thoughts. To everyone around her.

Especially Luke.

Well, she'd done a darn good job of tempering those

intense emotions in the past five years. And Derek was living proof. With him she had been safe, sheltered from the fear of raw, searing pain. With him she had been able to be breezy and aloof—she could let things roll off her shoulders with a grin or a shrug. She could have had an easy life with him, but not a fulfilled one. She had thought she could live without passion, and she could—she preferred it that way. But she couldn't live without the one thing he refused to give her. She knew that now.

She drew a sharp breath and chewed on her lower lip to steady herself. The lights were dimming, and the buzz of conversation slowly faded until an expectant hush fell over the room.

A commotion at the end of the row stirred her attention from the stage. She glanced over to see Jane awkwardly climbing over people and finally sliding into one of the two coat-covered seats near their mother. Grace narrowed her gaze. Adam was nowhere in sight.

Leaning over, Jane smiled at her sisters, fluttered her fingers in the air, mouthed "hi," and then settled back into her seat. She looked harried, rumpled even. And her eyes shone bright. Too bright. Grace gave a small smile in return, her mouth quickly forming a thin line of unease as she turned her focus back to the front of the room.

Something was definitely not right. Between the time of year, Adam's long hours, and Jane's distracted edge, Grace was beginning to have the sneaking suspicion that Adam might be having problems at work. Not that Jane would ever admit to it—she wouldn't want to worry them.

Grace smiled sadly. Leave it to Jane to always worry so much about everyone else. It wasn't at all surprising to her that her baby sister was the only one of them to have a child of her own. It was a natural fit for her. *Even if she would have made a wonderful dancer*, she couldn't help but think.

Anna tapped her knee as the red velvet curtains parted. "Speak of the devil," Anna said, jutting her chin toward the stage. Grace followed her gaze, and watched with bated breath as Luke strode out onto the stage, all thoughts about Jane and Adam replaced with something far more personal. And dangerous.

He gripped the mike, tapping it twice and then breaking into an easy grin that caused her stomach to flip-flop. He spoke to the crowd in assured, measured tones, his voice smooth and rich, just like she remembered it. She could barely follow what he was saying, whom he was thanking, any of it—no, her attention was centered completely on the handsome face, the twinkle in his eye she could make out even from this distance, the casual, confident presence he exuded. All eyes were on him, but sitting here, seven rows from the stage, Grace felt like she was alone in the room with him. She stared at him boldly, raking her eyes over his length, indulging in the broad shoulders, the muscular forearms where he'd rolled back his shirtsleeves.

The crowd chuckled at something he said—something she'd missed—and she snapped back to attention. Her stomach stirred with uneasiness. It didn't feel right to be sitting here, watching Luke in this new role that he played so well. Principal. She couldn't say she was surprised, but a part of her felt stung. It reminded her of how deep his roots were in this town. How firmly planted he was. How stubborn he had been about giving it up. So she was expected to give up her dreams, so he could stay here in Briar Creek? What choice had he left her with?

She glanced to her right, her lip curling at the sight of a woman of about her own age watching Luke's every move with rapt attention. No wonder he had been awarded Teacher of the Year so many times and then selected as school principal—the crowd loved him, especially the women. He thrived in his role, in this life he had insisted on, wanted, lived without her. And even though Grace had been the one to leave, she suddenly felt very left behind.

Luke's life had gone on without her in more ways than one. And to think of how much she had struggled to let go—the lengths she had gone to! Her heart panged, and she lowered her eyes, folding her hands in her lap, twisting at the smooth wool fringe of Luke's scarf. She would give it back to him as soon as she had a chance tonight. No use hanging on to any part of a man who had so easily moved on with his life and found so much happiness without her.

She listened with growing disappointment as he finished his introduction, and then applauded with the rest of the auditorium as the third grade class took the stage and performed an energetic version of "Rudolph, the Red-Nosed Reindeer," followed by a rather pretty rendition of "Deck the Halls" from the first grade class. By the time the fourth grade band was setting up, prepping instruments, Grace began to feel the strain of Mrs. Hastings sitting behind her, and as the flutes led off, she rubbed her neck, making a casual show of twisting ever so slightly in her chair, turning straight into the penetrating gaze of Luke's mother, who was flanked by her daughters. How had she missed that before?

Heart pounding, Grace swung around once more. The woman hated her; it was clear as day. Even in the dark room, she could see the narrowed eyes, the thin, disapproving line of her crimson-painted lips. It was sad, really, and a loss. She had always enjoyed her time with Luke's mother, who seemed so independent and free-spirited. Grace had been in awe of her, if slightly intimidated, but she'd be lying if she said she hadn't admired her. Rosemary spoke her mind and she had a steely determination when it came to following her passion for ballet. Surely, she would understand why Grace felt the need to pursue her own dreams, but maybe not when it came to breaking the heart of Rosemary's only son.

Grace shifted in her chair as a group of cherub-cheeked children took the stage in a scraggly single-file line among the *aw*s of the crowd. Sophie stood at the end of the row, looking simply perfect in the costume she had shown Grace earlier at her house.

Her heart began to ache as she thought back on the afternoon at Jane's, spent baking cookies, fussing over Sophie's pink and white room, hearing about her ballet classes, and chatting excitedly about the pageant. She swallowed the knot in her throat. Was that the life she could have had if she'd stayed in Briar Creek? She imagined how it would have been—a cozy little house, with a child or two, and Luke...

Enough. She had made her decision, she had pursued her dream, and she had seen it through. The only reason why she was thinking this way was because of recent events; it was silly to forget everything else the past few years had brought her. She would be doing herself a disservice to dismiss everything else she had achieved. Life wasn't defined by one event, and one breakup, one hiccup in an otherwise solid career, wasn't the end of the world.

Besides, she knew herself, and she never would have been okay with following in Jane's path. It only looked rosy because it was the path she hadn't chosen.

Anna elbowed her, gesturing to their niece, and Grace smiled, sitting straighter in her chair.

"She looks nervous," Grace whispered.

Anna nodded and leaned in to Grace's ear. "She gets stage fright. At her dance recital last spring, she peed all over the stage, poor thing."

Grace's hand flew to her mouth before she could laugh. "Oh, the poor little thing." And to think she had been so excited about tonight's pageant.

"She'll be okay tonight," Anna assured her. "Luke's been getting them so excited for it; there won't be room for nerves."

Grace felt her smile fade. She swept her eyes over the width of the stage as the children shuffled into three groups of angels, each wearing a tinsel-wrapped hoop attached to a headband and a set of bent-wire wings hooked over their tiny shoulders. A young woman, obviously the teacher, dressed in a black skirt and red sweater stood off to the side, beaming at the children and giving sidelong glances to the audience. Immediately, Grace recognized her as the woman from the party the night before. The one who was chatting up first Mark and then Luke. With her bouncy blond ringlets and sparkling blue eyes, Grace could imagine that the children simply adored her. She couldn't help it—she wondered if Luke did, too. They probably worked together, saw each other every day. Surely Luke would move on with his life eventually. He was still young. Still handsome. The catch of a small town like this, no doubt.

Her stomach began to hurt.

She gritted her teeth, trying desperately to focus on Sophie, who stared with wide eyes at her bouncy teacher, giving a nervous smile. When the music started, the small, high voices filled the room, faintly at first, and then with more confidence as Miss Ringlets encouraged them along. By the middle of the song, Sophie was positively beaming with pride, her small face filled with a wide, excited smile that revealed all her tiny baby teeth, her eyes shiny and full of hope.

Tears prickled the back of Grace's eyes and she clenched a fist, the ache in her throat growing stronger. For a while she had thought that if Derek could agree to one child—just one—that she would be fulfilled. Or almost fulfilled. Sure, their relationship might not have been everything she could have imagined, but their lives were simple, easy, and secure, without the complications that come from that heartbreaking kind of love she knew all too well. She and Derek were partners; they lived separate lives and came to each other at the end of the day. They were companions; they shared the same goals. Until they didn't.

She could live with affection instead of love. She could live with understanding instead of passion. She thought she could at least. But she couldn't live without a child.

Luke would have been a great father, she considered grimly. Of course.

Grace blinked rapidly as the children finished their song, and as the crowd burst into applause, she joined them, clapping until her hands hurt nearly as much as her heart. As the children waved and followed their perky teacher off stage, Grace's gaze lingered on her sweet little niece as she disappeared into the wings. Smiling sadly, she was leaning over to say something to Anna when her eyes snapped to a familiar figure.

Standing in the shadows, near the edge of the plush red curtain, Luke was staring at her from under his hooded brows, his gaze penetrating even from a distance. Grace's chest rose and fell with each breath until she tore her eyes from his, her heart pounding.

Had he been watching her this entire time? Fighting for composure, Grace fixed her gaze on the program in her hands, on the crudely drawn image of a snowman with a carrot nose that some girl from the kindergarten class had created. Everything in her wanted to look up, to see if he was still watching her, to try to discern that look in his eyes—was it anger? Sadness? Or maybe...

She could look up and know, for certain, connect with him in some small way, but as strong as the urge may have been, she forced her gaze to remain low and steady. Glancing up to realize that it was anger or disappointment in his eyes would be hard enough, but realizing that he had turned away would be considerably more heartbreaking.

CHAPTER
14

No matter how hard he tried to ignore Grace's presence, his eyes were pulled to her image, the vision having some intoxicating effect he couldn't quite shake.

He supposed he should have known that Grace would be here to see Sophie, but he hadn't expected to be confronted with her the second he walked onstage tonight. The sight of her had startled him, and he had nearly forgotten everything he had planned to say. Improvisation had never been his strong suit, but what choice did he have but to wing it?

Damn it if Grace still didn't have some power on him—the ability to make him lose sight of everything— and anyone—that mattered, that he had worked for. He was reckless when it came to Grace—last night at Mark's party had been proof of that.

Luckily from the pats on the back he was receiving, he assumed he had pulled it off. And the kids had, too. The night had been a success; everyone was in the Christmas spirit. Everyone besides him.

Luke stood at the back of the cafeteria and sipped his eggnog. The room had been decorated over the last few days to depict a winter wonderland—hundreds of paper snowflakes hung from the rafters, twinkling lights framed the doorways and windows, and the tables were covered with shimmery white cloths. Music blared from the speakers—holiday music, of course, Luke noted with a grimace.

He took another sip of the overly sweet drink, wondering how long he would have to stay. From his vantage point near the door, he could make an easy exit, but as the head of the pageant, and principal of the school, someone would be bound to come looking for him at some point or another. Best to stay.

"Loved the pageant!" crooned a voice in his ear. He turned to see Miss Johnson, or *Nicole*, he supposed, standing at his side. She was new this year, in charge of the pre-K class, and with the personality to match her perky blond ringlets, she was perfect for the job.

But not for him. He'd hired her himself, but it was obvious she took the job offer as an invitation to something far more personal. More than one of his colleagues had given him a suggestive wink when Nicole strode into the faculty lounge earlier this fall, and he could only assume that the new teacher had received the same reaction. It wasn't often that Briar Creek boasted a newcomer; most of the folks in town had been born and raised in the community. So when the pretty, petite blonde with big, bright eyes and an eager smile had arrived, everyone had thought, *Perfect*.

Everyone but Luke, that was.

Luke gave Nicole a tight smile, determined to maintain

a professional distance. The fact that he was her boss was a convenient excuse. "Thanks. No disasters, luckily."

Except Grace Madison sitting front and center.

"Is this an annual thing for you?" Nicole asked, leaning back against the wall. She was showing no signs of leaving as she curved her pretty little mouth into a smile.

Luke shifted the weight on his feet and glanced around the room, wondering if Grace had stuck around, or if she'd already gone home with her mother. He stopped himself—what did it matter if Grace was here or not?

"Only my second year," he said, forcing his gaze back to Nicole. She was being friendly, he knew, but there was something in her eyes that made him uneasy. Regardless of what people might have told her, he wasn't ready to jump back into the dating pool—with anyone. Not even—

"Grace!"

His pulse skipped a beat at the sound of her name, his attention immediately zapped to life. He stiffened, trying to look outwardly casual, even though inside his heart was thumping. He followed the voice to his left, where Grace's sister Jane was standing with little Sophie.

"She's such a sweetheart," Nicole murmured, having followed his gaze.

Realizing she was referring to Sophie, he nodded in agreement. "She is."

He didn't see much of Jane anywhere other than around town, but he couldn't help but favor the little girl while rehearsing the pageant this year. She was a sweet thing, a little shy at first, but delightfully charming once she warmed up. The kind of child he imagined himself having one day.

His stomach stirred. That door had closed.

Sophie twirled around, showing off her angel wings with a grin that made him smile. He remembered what had happened at last year's dance recital, which he faithfully attended each year in support of his mother's studio, and he was pleased that the little extra coaching he'd given Sophie had resulted in a positive experience for her.

"You know her family, don't you?" Nicole pressed.

Luke drained his glass, nodding noncommittally. "Oh, I know almost everyone in town," he said through a polite smile. With a lift of his empty glass, he said, "Well, I think I might go make the rounds. See you after the holiday break."

The disappointment that flattened her usually bright eyes didn't go unnoticed. "Merry Christmas," Nicole said with a sad smile.

Luke quickened his pace, striding to the back of the room with a pounding heart, trying not to notice Grace picking up Sophie, making a grand show of congratulating her. He needed to get to the far end of the room, away from the Madisons. It was all suddenly too much.

"Luke?" He halted, darted his eyes to the left, and then hooked his gaze on his mother. He sighed in relief. "Where are you dashing off to?" she inquired.

He held his mother's eyes, unwavering in their hold on him. He couldn't lie to her if he tried, and he didn't really want to. He and his mother had always been close. As the only son, he'd always held a special place with her, especially after his father's life was cut so short. He'd stopped being her little boy a long time ago, instead taking on the role of helping out and doing his best to take care of his mother and two younger sisters. His father had left his wife and three children with financial security for life, but

Luke knew how much his mother depended on him. And he her, if he was honest.

Now, at thirty, he had to admit that he was still the child, and she was still the parent, no matter how much he prided himself on being the surrogate head of the family.

"Grace Madison is here, if you must know," he said, giving his mother a grim smile, trying his best to show that he didn't care, that it didn't affect him. The soft look that fell over her eyes told him she knew otherwise.

"I saw her," she said, reaching out to pat his arm. "I made a point of it."

"Mother," he warned.

"What?" she cried. "Can you blame me? I heard that girl was coming back to town and I wanted to take a good look."

He glanced at her sidelong, frowning. "Didn't you see her at the funeral?"

"Oh, well, that was different," she tutted. "I didn't want to make a point of staring at such a somber event."

"Now you can?"

She shrugged. "What can I say? The gloves are off!" Her lips curved into a mischievous smile. "Settle down, Luke. You know how much I always loved Grace."

Luke paused. "I know."

Rosemary shifted her eyes in the direction where he knew Grace and her family to be and then ushered him over to the edge of the room. From a three-tiered silver tray she plucked a sugar cookie shaped like a candy cane. She nibbled it, smiling at what she experienced, and then helped herself to another. "They put cream cheese in the dough," she said with a wink. She took a third. "Nice touch."

Despite his mood, Luke chuckled. "And to think you maintain a dancer's figure," he mused.

His mother raised her eyebrows in mock indignation. "For your information, I don't only teach eight classes a day. I also *demonstrate*. It's tough work for a lady of my age."

Luke smiled, shaking his head. He could banter with her all night about her poor eating habits, but he had other things on his mind. "So did she say anything to you?" he asked. His voice sounded strained, and he cleared his throat. He couldn't look his mother in the eye as he waited for her reply.

"No," she said lightly. "She was sitting a few rows in front of me. Poor thing looked downright terrified when she saw me, though. I could see the whites all around her eyes!"

Luke's gaze returned to his mother, who was feasting on another cookie. "Well, you can be a very intimidating woman, you know."

"Nonsense. Only in my studio. Besides, Grace knows I've always had a fondness for her. There was a time when I thought she would become my daughter in-law, after all."

She paused, alarm sweeping her face, as her eyes flashed on his. "I'm sorry, Luke. I—I don't know what I was saying. It's the cookies...the sugar. It's messing with my head."

"It's fine," he said gruffly

She shook her head, frowning. "No, it's not. This is a difficult time for you. For all of us. We loved Helen."

Luke nodded. "I know."

They lapsed into silence, standing side by side, staring

at the clusters of parents and children, listening to the happy din over the jingle of the music. It all felt like a slap in the face, like some callous reminder of what everyone else had and he didn't. What he had lost. It was hard enough losing Helen, reliving that experience every year at this time, but it was also becoming increasingly difficult to think of everything that went with her—children, family, generations, shared experiences.

Although, maybe all of those things were gone before she died. And maybe that was why he was having such a hard time living with himself.

"I should go say hello to her," Rosemary offered, and Luke forced his attention back to the present. Back to Grace. *It always came back to Grace.*

"Have you spoken to Kathleen Madison recently?" he asked. The two women had always been friendly, even after their children had gone their separate ways. It was through his mother that Luke gleaned most of his insight into the Madisons' lives these days, but Rosemary also knew to keep a distance. She only discussed Grace's family when he asked. He tried not to, even when he wanted to.

His mother shook her head, her brow furrowing in concern. "No, I haven't. I've tried calling a few times but she hasn't seemed up for socializing. Betty next door told me that Kathleen wasn't going to judge the Holiday House contest this year." She gave a sad sigh. "It won't be the same without her."

"Their house isn't even decorated," he added.

His mother's eyes widened. A natural reaction, Luke determined, given that Kathleen was famous for her Christmas decorations, but she surprised him by saying, "When did you go by their house?"

Crap. Luke rubbed the stubble on his chin and thrust his hands in his pockets. "I drove Grace home the other night. She needed a ride." He looked around the room, uncomfortably aware of his mother's watchful stare. There was a heavy pause.

"I see," she said pointedly.

He loosened his shoulders. "It wasn't like that," he insisted. The twitch in her lips sent a flicker of impatience through him. "She needed a ride, Mom. That's all. Her car broke down."

He didn't appreciate the way his mother cocked an eyebrow suggestively. "If you say so," she said.

"Mother," he muttered. He reached for a cookie and ate it quickly. "It's not like that with us. I moved on; Grace has moved on. Besides, she isn't even in town for long."

"And if she were?"

If, if, if. There were always so many ifs when it came to Grace. He looked his mother square in the eye. "It wouldn't make a lick of difference."

"Well," said Rosemary, "I should go see Jane. I have something I've been meaning to discuss with her, and now is the perfect opportunity."

Luke nodded, relieved to be set free of the conversation, and walked over to the drinks table to refill his cup.

"Hey there." The voice in his ear made him jump, almost spilling his eggnog, and he turned around, his eyes locking on Grace's alarmed gaze.

"Sorry," she said. "Didn't mean to scare you."

"It's fine." It wasn't like him to be so jumpy, but knowing Grace was nearby had unnerved him, left him feeling shifty and agitated. Her mere presence brought back every kiss they'd ever shared, every laugh and every smile, even every tear. He didn't want to go there or think about the past. He'd made his decision, he'd lived with it. It was too easy to slip back into what they once had, and he couldn't do that. Not now. Not ever.

His eyes shifted to the door. He'd hoped to dodge her, slip out of the party without any further exchange, but now she had cornered him.

"I wanted to give this to you," she said, holding out his scarf.

He took it from her and draped it over his arm, trying his best to ignore the wave of disappointment that their final connection to one another had just been severed. "Thanks. You could have kept it, though."

"It's okay," she replied. "Between all of us girls, my mother has a supply."

Luke set his paper cup on a nearby table, darting his vision from the curious gaze of Mrs. Carson, the head of the parents' association, behind the punch bowl. Catching his eye, she glanced meaningfully at Grace, her eyes widening ever so slightly.

He set his jaw and turned away. Just what he needed. Since Helen died, he had been promoted to Briar Creek's most eligible bachelor in the eyes of the women's auxiliary board, the PTA, and every other fundraising committee around town. Mark had been tickled to have finally slipped in ranking, having suffered through years of nosy inquiries into his love life by the women around town. Luke supposed it was incentive enough to move on with his life once and for all—anything was worth escaping this unwanted attention. Anything but getting involved with Grace again, that was.

Wouldn't they love that, he thought, narrowing his eyes.

"Don't turn around now, but I think we're giving some of the locals something to talk about," he warned, and Grace laughed softly, that lovely, melodious sound that forced him to smile. No one had a laugh like Grace.

But then, Grace was one of a kind.

"If I didn't want to induce a cardiac arrest, I might be inclined to grab you by the lapels and kiss you right here and now," she quipped. "It would serve them right, old gossips."

Luke rubbed the back of his neck and thrust his hands in his pockets. "Did you enjoy the show?" he asked, hoping to steer the conversation back to more neutral territory.

"Oh, I loved it." Grace smiled warmly, but a strange shadow came over her eyes. "Sophie was just darling," she said, her voice fading.

Luke glanced across the room to where Sophie stood with the rest of the Madisons. Adam was there too—Jane's husband. A friendly enough guy, but not one he knew well.

"She's a sweetheart," he observed. "My mom enjoys teaching her ballet."

At the mention of his mother, Grace's cheeks flushed. "I saw your mother earlier. I—I didn't get a chance to say hello," she finished.

So she was feeling a little nervous then, wasn't she? *Well, good*, Luke couldn't help but feeling. It shouldn't be so easy for her, to come back to town after all this time, after the chaos she had left in her exit. He'd stuck around, lived out the repercussions of their breakup, the hounding questions from anyone and everyone who was disappointed in their outcome. Did she honestly think she could come back here without facing some consequence? That she could stride into town and mess everything up, and stroll right back out again?

"Well, she's over there talking to Jane," he offered. "Why don't you go over and say hello?"

Alarm flashed through Grace's emerald gaze and she glanced away quickly. "Oh, I will. Later," she said.

"I'm sure she'd like that. She was always fond of you." He grinned, noting the relief that spread over her delicate features.

"She always meant a lot to me," Grace said, smiling sadly. She lifted her chin, shrugging off the sentimental turn in the conversation. He was too grateful to be stung by the gesture. She'd built a wall up around herself, but so help him, he wouldn't let her tear down his. Not now. Not after everything.

"I have to admit, I was sort of surprised to see you up there tonight."

Luke shrugged. "Comes with the territory."

"Congratulations on the promotion, by the way."

Luke stared at her, and after a pause gave a simple nod. It was always a sore spot with him, the way she'd been less than supportive in him choosing to take a teaching position in Briar Creek, in the very school they had both attended as children. It was unglamorous to her, predictable. He wasn't challenging himself, she'd told him. He was settling.

She couldn't understand that it was what he wanted to do, or why. Ray Madison had been like the father he never had through his adolescence, and it was because of his stories that Luke chose to follow in his path, just as

Grace had followed hers. It wasn't lost on him that Grace wouldn't have her father any other way, but somehow she expected different from Luke.

Maybe it was because Ray had never stood in the way of her dreams the way she felt he had.

Grace pursed her pretty lips. She'd painted them a dark shade of red—a festive color, he noticed with a twinge of irony. He wondered what that was all about. He tried not to consider that it would have anything to do with seeing him tonight. After all, she'd just admitted that she hadn't expected to see him.

"I meant that it was surprising to see you lead the show," she said. Leaning in closer, she lowered her voice to a conspiratorial whisper: "I mean, last I checked, you weren't exactly gung-ho about Christmas."

Luke listened to the sweet voice in his ear, felt the tingle of her breath on his skin. From this close proximity, he could smell the sweet scent of her shampoo, feel the heat of her body close to his. It was so familiar, so right—Luke stopped himself.

It was so wrong.

He pulled back, straightening his spine. "Do you think I had 'em fooled?"

She grinned and his groin stirred. *Damn it.* "Completely," she said.

He matched her smile, relaxing into the moment, and then stopped himself. It was too natural to fall under her charm, to get caught up in the depth of their connection. He couldn't have that.

"I guess we're the only two Scrooges in this room," he said, glancing around at all the smiling families, the laughing children. He grinned, hoping to replace the ache in her

heart with a joke, but one look into her eyes cut him straight
to the gut. This could have been them—if she had stayed,
they could have been among these happy, smiling families,
instead of two lonely people, standing on the edges, left out.

Helen. His breath stalled on her image. This is exactly
why it was not good for him to be standing here, spending
any more time with Grace. If he and Grace had made it,
then he and Helen would never have married, never even
met, never would have shared anything. Shame churned
his stomach raw, and he swallowed the acidic taste that
filled his mouth. He reached back to the table for his eggnog, ignoring Mrs. Carson's piercing gaze.

"Helen died right after Christmas," he said suddenly.
He needed to say it, needed to speak her name out loud in
front of the one person who had the power to make him
forget her altogether.

Beside him, Grace had paled, her eyes were dark and
hollowed, and when they met his, she averted her gaze.
"I'm sorry," she said on a breath. "I didn't know that part."

"Why would you?" He suddenly turned angry. He
didn't need her here, didn't want her here. He just wanted
to be alone. He didn't want to be reminded of what a terri-
ble husband he had been, especially now, when he should
be honoring the wife he had betrayed.

"I guess you have a valid reason for hating Christmas
then," she said grimly, and Luke felt himself waver at the
kindness in her tone. It was the first time he felt he could
let down his defenses—the first time he felt she wouldn't
try to take Helen's memory from him, replace it with
something lustful, passionate, and wrong. So wrong.

He forced a grin. "What's your excuse?" His heart
skipped a beat when he thought of Ray. Of course.

Grace only huffed out a breath. She glanced around the room, and even in profile he could see the strain on her face. "Oh, I don't know. I guess you could say that life hasn't been working out for me lately."

"You mean with your father," he said. He ran a hand through his hair, fixing his eyes on her. "Grace, I'm sorry."

"Don't be. It's not just that." She halted, frowning. "Well, of course it is. But...it's other things too. I guess—I guess you could say that life hasn't turned out the way I had hoped it would." Her voice cracked on her last words and she forced a brave grin, attempting to mask the pain with laughter—a trick he understood all too well. Her eyes shone bright, betraying her.

He expected to be relieved, almost vindicated to hear her confession—to know that she had regretted her path, the one that had led her away from him. But hearing her words, watching her fight for composure and hold her head high, he felt overcome with sadness. Not for the pain she was going through, but for time lost, and hopes unfulfilled.

She had been so insistent about leaving, about going out into the world. She needed experiences, stimulation. Excitement. Everything she could never find here, she'd said. And she'd gone, left him. It had all meant more to her than he did.

Or so he had thought.

He could still remember the way he felt when he saw her walk up his driveway that warm spring day, six months since he had last seen her. He had come home from work, knowing Helen would be arriving any minute, and there she was. Grace.

"Hi, Honeybee," he'd said, as naturally as if he'd seen

her that morning and kissed her goodbye after breakfast instead of Helen. It was always that way with Grace; they could always leave off as if no time had passed.

He'd stood, unable to move or step forward, the air locked in his chest, his mind racing. He was frozen with conflicting thoughts, paralyzed with desire he fought to deny as she strode toward him. He remembered the way the sun caught her hair, the way her eyes shifted. She was nervous. And that was when he knew what she had come to say and dread pooled in his gut.

"I've missed you," she said, and he'd stood, holding her stare, gripping his keys, his breathing labored and heavy. He couldn't say it back, no matter how true it was. It was too late.

He shook his head, anger coursing through his veins. How easy for her to come here, looking like this, standing so close, after all this time. As if he'd been waiting for this day, hoping she would come to her senses. Come back to him.

"I've met someone, Grace," he said, and she lifted her chin.

"I know."

He exhaled. He stared at her, watching as she chewed on her lip and smoothed her hands over the skirt of her dress, giving him that questioning look that made his heart ache like it never could for anyone but her. A thousand questions ran through his mind, but he didn't have time for them all, and he wasn't sure he wanted to know the answers. It would only make this more difficult than it had to be.

"Look, it's not a good time. Helen will be here soon."

She arched a brow, pinching her lips in displeasure. "Helen? Is that her name?"

"How long are you in town for, Grace?" Luke looked down the street, bracing himself for the sight of Helen's car rounding the bend. As much as he dreaded her finding him like this, he was almost wishing she would appear, save him from these unwanted emotions. With Helen he was safe. Their life was simple and easy. By this time tomorrow he'd forget Grace all over again, he'd go back to his routine, the established life he had with Helen. And he'd be content.

Grace followed his gaze and then turned to him, frowning. "As long as you want me to be."

Luke hesitated. No, she wasn't going to put this on him. She had come here to set him up—to make him take the fall. She'd regret her decision in time, come to resent him. She'd leave him sooner or later; if not now, then someday. They didn't want the same things anymore. Maybe once they had, but they were young then—children! Ten years was a long time to know someone, and he *knew* Grace. He knew what she was capable of, and he knew what she wanted. If she wasn't true to herself, she would never be happy living here in Briar Creek. And he wasn't going to be the one to drag her down or hold her back.

"You should go, Grace," he said. "I've moved on," he forced himself to add.

She took a step closer, never breaking his stare as she closed the distance between their bodies. He gripped the keys harder, feeling them embed in his palm. He'd forgotten how beautiful she was, how perfect she was to him. All these months away from her, he'd pushed her from his mind, eventually replacing the image with Helen's. Sweet, loving Helen.

"Do you expect me to believe that what you have with

her is the same as what we have?" Grace said. She was standing so close he could see the flecks of gold in her eyes, the indentation on the bottom lip.

"Of course it's not the same."

Her lips curved in satisfaction and she leaned forward. "I didn't think so," she murmured as she slid her arm up his shoulder, pulling him close as her lips grazed his.

He groaned into her mouth—a silent plea to stop—but soon he was kissing her, forcefully, angrily even, pressing her body close against his chest, feeling the contours of her breasts against his racing heart. She smelled like coconut, like that favorite shampoo of hers, and he drank in her scent, his tongue parting her lips, exploring her mouth, tasting her warmth.

She felt so good, so right, and that was the problem. There was nothing like kissing Grace. They just fell into place; they knew every step of the dance, every way to satisfy the other's needs. So he stood there, in the middle of the afternoon, in broad daylight, in front of the house he had expected to be their home, and he kissed her for the last time, savoring every last sweet touch, until he finally tore his lips from hers.

His eyes flashed on hers. His pulse was thundering. He swallowed hard, wondering if he had it in him. "I'm engaged, Grace."

She was close enough for him to feel her stiffen. "Do you love her?" she whispered.

He sucked in a breath. What did it matter? What mattered was that he and Grace were over. Through. Helen could give him things that Grace never could. And Grace... "I can't give you the life you want, Grace."

Her mouth spread into a grim line. "That's not what

I asked." She glared at him, and he swore to himself in that moment that he couldn't go through with it. Her lips turned downward, her voice softer, pleading almost. "Do you love her?"

She stood, waiting, her eyes filling with tears, her lower lip quivering. He looked to his left. In the distance he could see Helen's car approaching.

Shifting his gaze back to Grace, he stared deep into her eyes, committing them to memory, knowing it would be the last time he saw her this close.

"It's too late," he said firmly.

He expected her to sob, to protest, to fight. She didn't. She only nodded her head sadly, gave him one last long look, and walked away.

Grace always fought for what she wanted, he told himself. She didn't give up, didn't back down. That was what he needed to believe to be sure he had made the right choice.

But he hadn't taken one thing into account—she only gave up when the fight was over. When hope was truly lost. And maybe, just maybe, on that warm spring day, when she'd come back, looking for a second chance, he'd taken that hope from her. He imagined she was happy with the outcome, that her life had become everything she had intended, and that she never could have been satisfied with the life he could have given her.

Yet now, standing here in the cafeteria of the school they had both attended as children, so close to him that he could smell that coconut shampoo, she was telling him that life hadn't turned out the way she hoped it would.

I guess that makes two of us, he thought.

CHAPTER
15

Grace watched in frustration as the alarm clock on her nightstand hit midnight, and sighed in defeat. No matter how much she wanted to escape into the blissful unconsciousness of sleep, her mind was too busy replaying conversations with Luke to relax into slumber. Like it or not, she was awake, and if she had to be, it was probably better to start distracting herself from thoughts that only brought her confusion and sadness.

Tossing the frilly pink comforter off her warm and toasty body, she slipped her toes out from under the thick blankets and tucked them into the slippers at the side of her bed. She'd learned at a young age that socks and slippers were needed in this big, drafty house—the hardwood floors could be particularly cold at this hour. Shrugging a wool cardigan over her flannel pajama top, Grace walked quietly to the door, turning the handle ever so slowly, and then peered out into the hall.

Her mother's door at the far end was closed, and the house was dark. The light of a full moon guided her path as she crept down the stairs, careful to avoid the steps that were especially creaky—it was a trick she and Anna had mastered as teenagers, when they would sneak downstairs for a late night movie. Or worse.

She grinned to herself, thinking back on the few times she had snuck out to meet Luke, recalling the thrill of rebellion rushing the blood through her veins as she ran through the dark street to his car, waiting at the top of the bend. The feel of his warm lips on hers as he pulled her near, closing the distance between their bodies eagerly.

She paused at the landing, thinking she had heard something, craning her ear. It was only the wind rustling through the branches—the birch trees had been known to snap when the storms got the best of them. She'd check in the morning, see what she could collect for kindling.

Rounding the corner to the kitchen, she flicked on the light and screamed in alarm. Kathleen sat immobile, completely unaffected by her daughter's reaction.

"You scared me!" Grace shouted at her mother, who was sitting at the kitchen table, her expression blank. Grace put a hand to heart, feeling it race against her palm. "What the heck are you doing down here?" she exclaimed, trying to steady her breath.

"Same thing as you, I suppose," Kathleen said. "Couldn't sleep."

"So you were sitting here in the dark? How about turning on a light?" Grace frowned, not enjoying her fright at all, and crossed to the stove. She lifted the warm kettle, gauging the remaining water by the weight, and then turned on the gas.

"I like sitting in the dark," Kathleen said. "It's peaceful."

Grace placed a hand on the counter and stared at her mother, feeling unsettled. She didn't like the idea of her mother sitting at the kitchen table, late at night, without bothering to turn a light on. Was it a regular thing, a habit?

"I'm worried about you, Mom."

There. She had said it.

Kathleen heaved a weary breath. "There's always something to worry about, Grace. I could even say that I'm worried about you."

Grace folded her arms and leaned back against the kitchen island. "Me? Why?"

Kathleen tipped her head, holding her gaze, and Grace felt caught. She suddenly wished she had never come downstairs at all. She wasn't up for an honest conversation. She preferred to think about something other than her messy life for a little while. She was here to help her mother, to support her—not the other way around.

"You didn't tell me that you had called off your engagement," her mother began.

Grace drew a breath. "It's fine, Mom," she said, holding up a hand. "Really. It's...fine." And it was. The sad thing was that it really was fine. Disappointing, yes, but not because she had lost Derek. More because she was back to square one. Starting over. Twenty-nine and alone. She had finally figured out what she wanted out of her life, only when it might be too late.

"I saw you talking with Luke Hastings tonight," Kathleen said quietly. "How did that go?"

The teakettle began to whistle, and Grace turned her back to her mother, grateful for the opportunity to hide her face. Her mother had always said Grace's expressions spoke a thousand words, and she didn't feel like giving any insight into her emotions right now, especially when she didn't even understand them herself.

"It was fine," she said as she poured the boiling water into her favorite mug with the chipped handle. She dipped a teabag into the steaming liquid and cupped the mug with both hands, pivoting to face her mother, hoping that she could maintain a cool, unfazed façade. "I saw him yesterday, too. He was at Mark's party, and earlier he came into the shop."

Her mother's eyes darkened as Grace pulled out a chair and joined her at the table. "You went into the bookstore?"

Grace nodded. "Jane had a key." She paused to take a tentative sip of her tea. Still too hot to drink, she swirled the teabag around in the water with a spoon, wondering how to broach the subject without being completely insensitive. "I have to admit that I was a little … surprised to find it closed."

She stole a glance across the table, noting the dismay in her mother's drooping lips. "There wasn't any other choice, honey. It wasn't an easy decision for any of us, but what else were we supposed to do?"

"I'm not blaming anyone," Grace said. At least, she wasn't anymore. "I just wish something could be done to save it."

"You and me both, but unless you have a brilliant idea, I'm at a loss. Your sisters and I have talked about this at length. We don't see another option."

Grace felt her temper stir. "Why didn't any of you tell me about this? I'm part of this family, too. And you know how much that store means to me. Way more than it ever meant to Anna or Jane."

Kathleen sunk her head into her hands and rubbed her

face. When she pulled her fingers from her eyes, Grace was discomfited by how old she looked, how worn out. This hadn't been easy for her; she would be wise to remember that, to have patience.

"Perhaps we should have told you," she admitted. "Maybe it wasn't right, but we've gotten used to making decisions without you, Grace. You haven't been home since..." She trailed off and looked into the distance for a long moment, then turned her attention back to Grace. "What would you have done if we had told you?"

Grace didn't appreciate the insinuation, but she decided to let it go. To defend herself would be exhausting for everyone, only serving to make her feel more guilty, to make them relive old wounds. She hadn't come back to town in years, and when she finally did, her father was gone. She knew it. They knew it. They were all thinking it, but none of them were saying it. Part of her wished they would; it might lance the pain that had haunted her for months.

She took a long drink of her tea and lifted her palms in defeat. "I wish there was something I could have done."

"We all feel that way. But now it's time to move on, accept it for what it is."

Grace nodded, suddenly feeling tired enough to collapse into bed, her earlier restless energy replaced with the depressing weight of hopelessness. She finished what was left of her tea in silence, her heart feeling heavier with each sip.

"Guess I'm tired after all," she admitted. "You coming up?"

"I think I'll stay down here a little longer," Kathleen said.

Grace hesitated. "I could keep you company if you'd like," she said, but Kathleen shook her head, shooing her off with a flutter of the wrist.

"I'm fine, honey. You go to bed, get your rest."

It didn't sit well, leaving her mother in the kitchen, alone. The image of her sitting here in the dark all that time bothered Grace. How long had she been down here? How long would it have continued had she not found her? Grace set her empty mug on the top rack of the dishwasher.

"Feel like going into town tomorrow?" she hedged, forcing a smile. "It might be fun," she lied. "We could do a little Christmas shopping, maybe grab lunch at the café?"

Kathleen made a little face and shook her head. "Another time, Grace," she said, and the relief that Grace had expected to feel was replaced with a tightening of her heart. The last thing she wanted to do was celebrate the holiday season, but somehow seeing her mother follow suit felt wrong, and sad.

"Come on, Mom," she sparred. "You love Christmas! We could get a peppermint hot chocolate, maybe come back and watch one of those made for TV movies—"

"Grace." Her mother's voice was firmer this time, insistent. "Not this year."

Grace decided to let it drop. "Good night, then, Mom."

Grace shuffled back up the stairs to her room. She toed off her slippers and clambered into bed, not bothering to remove her sweater. With the covers pulled up to her chin, she curled onto her side and stared out the window onto the snow-covered stretch of forest behind the house, which looked silver in the moonlight.

Hot tears pooled in her eyes and then laced their way down her nose, where they made their escape, soaking her pillowcase. She sniffed hard and wiped a few away, but they only reappeared, and she finally gave up.

She hadn't been this miserable since she'd first gone to New York. She'd expected glamour and excitement but that had soon worn off, and instead she was working as a receptionist at a newspaper instead of as something more interesting, living in a studio apartment that was so small she could touch the front door with her outstretched leg while she lay on the twin mattress that served as both a bed and couch.

Loneliness was nothing new to her—but at least she usually had her other true love, her life's passion to fall back on, to keep her company. And it had eventually made at least several parts of her life a little easier.

Now even her writing had failed her—she couldn't remember the last time she had turned on her laptop. It sat on the bottom of one of her bags, patient and waiting, but she knew it wouldn't be put to use on this trip. The only thing it was useful for these days was email, and even then it only served to deliver more bad news. Bad reviews. Disappointed correspondence from her editor. Even her agent wasn't returning her calls these days! They'd all encouraged her to take some time away, collect her thoughts. Well, then what?

She was childless. Unmarried. Alone. And broke. Oh...and homeless. Yes, there was that problem to figure out, too.

She couldn't depend on royalties from her first two books forever. Sure, she was getting by. She wasn't going to starve—*yet*. Still, she needed something more. A purpose. Something to make her feel whole again. Something to make her happy.

Main Street Books.

Her breath hitched mid-sob and her chest began to thump with excitement. She could do it, couldn't she? Yes... maybe she could!

She quickly brushed the remaining tears from her face and sniffed loudly, her mind reeling with possibilities, her fingers itching to scurry from this bed and get busy. Oh, if only daylight would come sooner!

She might have ruined all her other opportunities for happiness, but there was still one thing she could save. Main Street Books had two weeks left on the lease. And one thing was for certain: she never walked away from anything—or anyone—without a fight.

CHAPTER 16

From his familiar perch at Hastings, Luke stared at his menu, his mind on anything but the words.

"In all these years, I have never seen you so indecisive," Mark commented.

"Nothing seems to suit me this morning."

"You could always try the Fireside Café," Mark bantered, knowing full well that Luke wouldn't step foot in that establishment any more than he would. Mark and Anna had a restless dynamic, but Anna unnerved Luke with her cool gaze and no-nonsense attitude, and she stirred up way too many memories of Grace.

"Yeah, right." Luke took a swig of his coffee and glanced at the blackboard, perusing the Saturday specials. "I'll have the gingerbread pancakes today."

"Side of bacon?"

"Why not?" He hunched over the counter and stared into his coffee. He was exhausted, having slept for barely more than an hour the night before and about the same the previous two nights, and his right eye was starting to twitch. It had been doing that a lot lately, and he had given up any hope of it going away soon, or at least not until the New Year, when everything finally settled down.

Yeah, he'd feel a lot better come January, when he was back at work, Grace was gone, and life would return to normal.

He rubbed a hand over his face. If only he didn't have to decide on that lease before then.

"Seen any more of Grace?" Mark asked. He leaned back against the counter and tossed a dishcloth over his shoulder.

"Why are you asking me this?" Luke took another sip of his coffee. "You know I don't want to talk about her."

"Ah, but see, I think you do," Mark said. "I think you haven't stopped thinking about her since she came back to town. And I think you've thought about her a long time before that, too." He paused. "Besides, you two looked pretty cozy at the party Thursday night."

Luke narrowed his gaze. "Why don't you focus on your own love life instead of mine?"

"My own love life?" Mark scoffed. "You know I don't believe in that nonsense."

Luke shook his head, turning to look around the room. If only he could be more like Mark. The guy had never committed to any woman, never given his heart away. He was happy as a clam, running this dive, doing what he wanted to do, not busy thinking about things that weighed you down. He was free of all the heartaches, all the ups and downs.

It sounded nice, when you stopped to think about it.

"Come on now, you really plan to stay single forever?" Luke asked.

Mark stared at him. "And you don't?"

"Point taken." Luke couldn't help but grin ruefully.

Mark helped himself to a mug of coffee, drinking it black, as he had always done. "Come on, Luke. We're different, you and me. I like my independence, I like doing my thing. But you—" He shook his head. He wasn't buying it any more than Luke was. "You don't like being alone, Luke. And, if I may be frank, it doesn't suit you."

Luke guffawed, almost spitting his coffee back into his mug. "What the hell is that supposed to mean?"

Mark's eyes roamed over him. "It means look at you. Sitting here every morning you aren't at work, going home to that empty house. You say you don't like the way it's decorated now, but the truth is that you like a woman's touch."

"That's not it." Luke shook his head.

"No?" Disbelief danced through Mark's brown eyes. "Then why do you still have those floral pillows on your bed?"

"Paisley," Luke muttered into his coffee mug. He drained the remains, grimacing at the dregs at the bottom.

Mark leaned almost imperceptibly forward, his eyes sparked with mirth. "What was that?"

"Paisley," Luke said firmly. "They're not floral. They're... paisley."

Mark laughed heartily, attracting the attention of a few other lone men at the counter. A good ol' boys club of Briar Creek widowers, Luke thought to himself. He stared stonily at Mark, not finding any of this remotely funny.

Why should he expect Mark to understand? Mark had never been married, much less in love. "You can't understand," he snapped. "You've never lost someone you loved."

As soon as he said the words, he regretted them. The shadows that darkened Mark's face sent a wash of shame over his gut. Of course Mark knew how it felt to lose someone you loved. His father had walked out on their family when Mark was ten years old. He'd never heard from him since.

"I'm sorry," Luke said. "That wasn't fair."

With a shrug, Mark stepped forward and refilled his mug. "If you're not ready to move on from Helen, that's your business. I want you to be happy, that's all."

Happy. Luke couldn't exactly remember the last time he had been happy. There had been a time when he felt content, but happiness ... well, that was reserved for a life free of regrets or indecision. Or guilt.

"So you didn't answer my question," Mark said.

"About seeing Grace again?" Luke's eyes flew open. "Let it go, man!"

"Sorry, cousin, but I can't." Mark lifted his hands helplessly.

"And why is that?"

Mark slid his eyes in the direction of the door. "Because she just walked in."

Luke stiffened. Without turning his head, he followed Mark's gaze to the front of the crowded room, his pulse quickening as Grace spared him a tight smile.

Bet she's regretting stopping in here this morning, he mused. But then, she knew Mark was his cousin. This was a family joint; he thought she could respect that. Much the same way that he avoided the Fireside Café.

His brow knitted as he stared at his hands splayed on the Formica counter. What was this, a mob town? A he-had-his-turf, she-had-hers type of understanding? How juvenile could it get? He was thinking like a kid, not like a thirty-year-old man.

Maybe that's who he was with Grace—the boy he was back when he knew her. She had a way of bringing out the kid in him, and not always in a good way.

He took a long, slow sip of coffee, hoping to look occupied as Mark came around the counter and gave Grace a proper greeting.

"Grace!" Luke could hear the grin in his cousin's voice. He kept his eyes trained on the kitchen window, waiting for the pancakes he wished he hadn't ordered. Now he'd be forced to stick around, when what he really should do was leave. "To what do I owe the honor?" Mark continued.

Grace slid into the empty stool next to Luke, and he turned to her. "Hello."

"I hope it's okay that I'm here," she said.

Luke's brow knit, but Mark bellowed, "Of course, it's okay. Coffee?" he asked, as he finished filling a mug.

"Thanks."

Luke slid her the creamer and then, after a pause, reached down the length of the counter for those multicolored sweetener packets she liked.

"You remembered how I like my coffee," she noted, and he thought he could detect a flicker of wonder in her tone.

"Honeybee, I remember the first time you ever tried coffee," he said, chuckling. The bitter brew had clearly come as a surprise, but determined even at age fourteen, she hid her grimace and drank the entire cup.

She laughed, tossing her head back until her chestnut hair cascaded over the back of her coat. Sobering, she stirred not one but two blue packets into her small mug, shaking her head. "I was hoping you wouldn't remember that," she said ruefully.

Luke was aware of Mark's eyes on him as he set the pancakes in front of him. Refusing to meet his stare, Luke doused his stack with syrup and took a bite. He nudged his head in the direction of Grace's mug. "Doesn't look like much has changed," he said.

"I do still like it sweet," she admitted.

"Guess the girl I knew is still there," he mused. "New York didn't change you too much."

"I'm still here," she said quietly, avoiding his gaze. "I'm still the same girl you knew."

Luke pulled in a breath, slowly blowing it out. He didn't want to hear this—he didn't want to believe that the Grace he knew and loved and had spent every day of ten years talking to and laughing with was sitting right next to him. It hurt too much to think that she was still there, and that she had been all this time.

"Can I get you something to eat?" Mark cut in.

Grace looked at his plate, twisting her mouth. "Those pancakes do look good."

"Another stack, coming up," Mark announced. "On the house."

"Aw, thanks," she said.

"No thanks needed. I was disappointed we didn't have more of a chance to talk at the party."

"Oh, I—had to leave. My mom…needed me." Grace took a nonchalant sip of her coffee, her eyes revealing nothing.

"Yeah, a lot of people had to leave early that night." Mark slid Luke a glance. "We've missed you around here, Grace."

There was a long pause. Finally, Grace said, "Well, it has been a long time."

"Next time don't stay away so long." Mark grinned and Luke reflexively narrowed his eyes.

It was so easy for him, Luke thought. He could love Grace as a friend, for who she was, not what she was to him. He wasn't invested, not the way Luke was.

"Well, there's a chance I might be sticking around a little longer than I expected," Grace said, and Luke almost choked on his coffee. He swallowed the large gulp, covering his mouth with his hand.

What the hell did she say? He suddenly wished his mug contained something a little harder than coffee.

"Really?" Mark said and Luke glanced up, locking on to his cousin's wide eyes.

Don't even think about smirking, he silently warned.

"I'm sure you know that my dad's bookshop is closed," Grace said. She drew her shoulders up, beaming proudly. "Well, I have an idea that might save it."

Luke's gut knotted. "What's that?"

Even before she opened her mouth, he knew. He knew the way Grace thought, the way her brain churned, and he just knew with Grace, she was going to be focusing on something bigger and better. *Expansion.*

"Well, I noticed that there's an empty storefront next door," she said, and Luke's pulse stilled. He refused to look at Mark, whose stare he could feel burning a hole through him.

"Uh-huh," he grunted. He shoveled another forkful of pancakes into his mouth.

"Now I don't want to give too much away," she grinned, and he could see the light in her eyes—the light that took hold when she got one of those ideas of hers. When she got inspired. "I mean, it might not work or anything..."

"You're thinking of growing the store?" Mark offered.

"Something like that," she replied, with a knowing wink.

Luke knew this was the perfect time to mention that he was the current lessee of that space she had her eye on, but he couldn't bring himself to say it. Handing over this bit of information was like handing over Helen, giving her up. It would give way to endless questions he didn't want to answer and, frankly, wasn't ready to yet. He didn't want to have to explain or justify anything to Grace, or anyone else for that matter. He wanted to do what he needed to do, even if it was contrary to what everyone else expected from him.

"So you're going to reopen the store?" His eye was starting to twitch again.

She bristled. "Well, I guess so, temporarily at least. I mean, technically it's still ours until the end of the year. And after that, well... we'll see!"

He didn't like the way she was talking, this vague sense of time. Staying a little longer than expected was one thing, but moving back permanently was another. And infinitely worse. "Don't you have to get back to New York?" he asked.

She shrugged. "It's not like I have a job waiting for me."

Mark glanced at him and then back to Grace. "Yeah, how are things going in New York, Grace? You uh... seeing anyone?"

Luke fixed his gaze on his cousin. Hard. Mark refused to meet his eye. *Typical*, Luke thought to himself.

Silence stretched and Luke became faintly aware that he was nervous. The anticipation of hearing more about Grace's current life had reached its peak. Everything he had never known, never wanted to know deep down, was about to be revealed. He wasn't sure he was ready to hear it.

"Nope," she said briskly. She tucked a strand of hair behind her ear and played with the back of her earring—something she did when she was nervous. A pink glow heated her cheeks and she looked down, smiling sadly. "I dated someone for a while, but that's over now."

Luke felt his jaw tense. So she *had* moved on. His saliva suddenly tasted metallic. Grace—his Grace—had been noticed by another. This man, this stranger to him, had spent time with her, kissed her, held her . . . He stopped himself. He'd told himself he wanted her to be happy, and he did. Just not with someone else. It might not have been fair of him, but he couldn't help it.

"I figured a pretty girl like you would have been snatched up, married by now," Mark said with a grin. "Career got you too busy?"

"No," she said hurriedly. She looked down at the table. "We were engaged, actually. But . . . that's over now."

Luke glanced at Mark as his stomach dropped into his gut. Engaged.

"Sorry to hear it didn't work out," Mark said smoothly.

Grace shrugged. "I—I guess I haven't found what I'm looking for yet. Or . . ." She hesitated. "I guess that I haven't been lucky enough to find someone who wants the same things that I do."

"And what's that?" Luke heard himself ask, his tone a notch sharper than he had planned.

Grace squared her shoulders, lifted her chin. "It doesn't matter," she said, and he stared at her profile, looking for something, a hint into her soul perhaps, maybe a glance into her heart. But she had hardened again, putting up that wall.

He had lost her.

Her pancakes were up and they ate, chatting idly about people in town, both taking a twisted interest in condemning the tinsel and lights that Mark had shamelessly hung all over the diner.

When she'd finished the last of her food, she set down her fork and smiled. "I was hungry," she admitted.

He fought off a grin. "I noticed."

"Hey!" She swatted him with her napkin and then tossed it onto her plate. "I haven't eaten much since I've been back in town. I woke up feeling better this morning."

He smiled at her. "I'm glad to hear that."

"Well," she said, standing. "I should probably get to my car. It's supposed to be ready today."

"See you around, Grace," he said, watching her shrug back into her coat, button it all the way to the top.

She gave him a slow smile, the kind that made him want to stand and take her into his arms, pull her close and bring her mouth to his. "See you then," she said, and with one last wave to Mark, she turned on her heel.

He watched her retreat until the door closed behind her with a jingle, and then he stared at the space she had consumed, reveling from the encounter.

Mark's whistle pulled his attention back, and he swung around, facing the counter. "What?" he demanded.

Mark shook his head, his laughter a low and steady rumble. "I don't envy you."

"What's that supposed to mean?"

"I mean Grace Madison, your first love, strolls into town looking like that, and then announces she might intend to stay?"

"Please. I don't need to be reminded."

"What the hell are you going to do about that storefront, Luke?" Mark said, coming closer. "You can't hold on to it forever, you know."

"I know," Luke lied. He glowered into his empty mug and pushed it away. He ran his hands over his face, breathing deep.

"She's going to find out who's leasing the space," Mark reminded him and Luke closed his eyes, desperate to block out reality.

It was all crashing down on him at once. Now, when he should be mourning his wife's death, when he should be honoring her life, thinking of her and only her, the way he should have all along, he couldn't stop thinking about Grace. Like always.

And now with the storefront, he was once again forced to make a decision and choose between the two women he had loved, the two women who consumed his past and who continued to haunt him, making it impossible to move on with his life in any direction at all.

That lease expired at the end of the year. He had eleven days to make a decision. His fist tightened in his lap. It always came back to this, didn't it? Helen or Grace. Grace or Helen.

And somehow one always prevailed. It just wasn't necessarily the right one.

CHAPTER 17

Grace flicked on the windshield wipers and squinted into the distance as the morning's snowfall grew heavier. The tires crunched on the snow as she drove down the road, past the quaint homes decorated with red and green wreaths and garlands, some with silly-looking snowmen in the front yard.

Jane's garage door was closed, and a swell of disappointment took hold that she might not be home. Grace realized that she should have called first, but her excitement had gotten the better of her. She had the day all planned. She would talk to Jane, then Anna, and then she would go over to Main Street Books.

The door opened on the third tap, and Grace's expectant smile faded when she saw the flat, dead look in Jane's eyes. Her sister's naturally rosy complexion was peaked, and dark circles had formed under her eyes. Her hair was limp, and she was still in her bathrobe.

"Are you sick?"

Jane pulled the belt of her purple robe tighter and

glanced behind her like a furtive cat. "No," she blurted. Hesitating, she motioned into the hall with her head. "Come on in."

Grace's heart sunk; she couldn't help it. She'd come here full of good spirits, and now she was feeling that heavy weight in her chest again. The whole point of coming back to Briar Creek for Christmas was to try to help her family, to be there for them and support them—God knows they needed it. And here she was, finally feeling useful, finally able to think of a way to bring a little hope back into their lives, and she couldn't even share it with any of them.

"Sophie is coloring in the family room," Jane said quietly. "I'd rather not disturb her. She's usually not quiet for long, and I—I needed a few moments of peace. For myself." She closed her eyes and rubbed her temples, causing Grace to frown.

Okay, now something was definitely wrong. Grace stood in the entranceway, her feet planted on the rug, which was doing a good job of soaking up the snow from her boots. "I can leave if you want," she hedged, uncertain if she should even remove her coat.

"No. No, stay. Adam had to go into the office, and I could use the company, honestly." Jane held out her arms. "Hand me your coat."

Grace hesitated, regretting her decision to show up unannounced. "Really, I can come back later."

"No, no, it's okay," Jane said, but her smile was forced, her eyes still flat.

Frowning, Grace followed Jane into the kitchen, pausing as Jane leaned her head in to check on Sophie, pressed a finger to her lips, and flashed a look of warning to Grace. Grace slid across the floorboards on socked feet, happy to see that in this newer-construction house, nothing creaked like it did back at home.

They sat down at the kitchen table. Jane didn't offer coffee and Grace didn't ask for any. She'd had enough at the diner.

"So you're not sick," Grace established.

Jane looked momentarily confused. "What? No, I'm tired, that's all." She blinked rapidly, as if about to cry.

Grace leaned forward, whispering urgently, "Then what is going on? You're scaring me! Is it…Dad? Is it Christmas? That you miss him?" She knew that their mother was falling apart, but Jane had seemed so stoic, so unflappable. Had she been in denial, was it only all surfacing now, days before Christmas?

"It's not Dad," Jane said. "I mean, of course, it's hard. For all of us. But, it's not that. That's all there…in the background. A dull pain that never really goes away but you somehow have to learn to live with anyway, you know?"

Grace nodded. She knew. Too well. She'd been living with that type of pain for years. It was the kind of pain that came with losing someone you loved. The kind of ache that never truly went away, and had a tendency of creeping back up, resurfacing, reminding you, no matter how badly you tried to block it out and shield yourself from it.

"So what is it, then? Did something happen?"

Jane rubbed her hands over the surface of the table, stretching out her long, thin fingers. She slumped over, idly playing with the chip of an engagement stone that sat on her left hand. "It's Adam," she said eventually, so quietly that Grace had to strain to hear.

Grace narrowed her eyes in concentration. "Adam?" she repeated. "Is he okay?"

"No, he's fine. I'm the one who isn't fine."

Grace drew a sharp breath, feeling the frustration fill her chest. She sat back in her chair, staring levelly at her sister. "Jane, you've lost me. What the hell is going on?"

Jane hesitated, wavering over something. "It's nothing," she finally said.

Grace eyed her. "I don't believe you."

"Then don't." Jane shrugged as her frown deepened.

Grace softened her stance. Speaking more gently, she urged, "Jane, you're visibly upset, and you've told me you're not fine. You're not sick, so that means something else is going on. If you don't want to tell me, I understand. You should talk to someone. I can call Anna or Mom—"

"No!" The insistency in Jane's voice caused Grace to freeze and she stared at her youngest sister, refusing to back down.

Jane slumped back in her chair, pouting. "Adam and I had a fight last night. That's all."

"Well, married people must fight all the time," she offered, but Jane just glared at her.

She shook her head. "It's not like that, Grace. It's more serious than that."

Grace studied Jane across the table, noticing the weariness in her shoulders, the emptiness in her eyes. She knew that look. The look of the hopeless. The look she had seen in her own eyes one too many times. It was the look of knowing exactly what you wanted in life, and having no control as it was taken from you.

"Do you think you'll be able to work it out?" she asked quietly, hoping this was a safe question, one that would bring her one step closer to understanding Jane's situation without upsetting her sister further.

Jane swallowed. Her nose had turned bright red, and she pulled a balled-up tissue from the pocket of her robe and swabbed her eyes. "I'm not sure," she said through a sudden sob that came from somewhere deep within her.

Grace frowned. "How long has this been going on?"

Jane rolled her eyes, throwing up her hands. "Months. Since Dad died. Maybe longer. I'm..." She started to cry, and Grace felt her heart snap in half, watching her sister's shoulders shake up and down as she tried to muffle her sobs into the shawl of her robe. "I'm so exhausted!" she wailed, crying harder, and then sniffling hard, abruptly stopping.

"I can't let Sophie see me like this," she whispered, her eyes wild and urgent.

"No, no, of course not." Grace pinched her lips and pushed her chair back from the table, walking over to the entrance to the family room, where Sophie was sitting on a blanket on the floor, having a tea party with her dolls. Behind her the Christmas tree twinkled magically, and a fire was dying down in the hearth. Grace allowed her gaze to linger on the three matching stockings hung perfectly from the mantel, which was decked out with family photos of Christmases past.

Perfect. That's what she always thought of Jane's life. Even when this path hadn't been her ideal lifestyle, she had known it was perfect for Jane. Exactly what her sister wanted. Coming back here, Grace had seen how wonderful all this could be, this simple family life. So warm and cozy. So intrinsically fulfilling. So unlike her fast-paced life in New York.

Now the illusion was shattered.

She smiled at her little niece, who didn't even notice her in the doorway, and slipped away. Jane was at the stovetop when she came back into the kitchen. Her face was still red and blotchy, her cheeks still sunken, but she had stopped crying.

"She's playing with her toys," Grace reassured her.

Jane nodded. "If she notices anything is wrong, I'm going to tell her I have a cold."

A thought came to Grace and she tipped her head. "Why don't you let me take Sophie for tonight? It might be a nice break for you, one less thing to worry about."

Jane turned from her, her brow creasing. "I don't know..."

"It might cheer Mom up, to have her around," Grace pressed. "And it would be nice for me to have some alone time with her, spoil her a bit. I'll take her to the Winter Festival." She smiled, though Jane didn't return the gesture. "Only for a night, Jane. It would give you a chance to focus on yourself for a change and take care of the things you need to."

Jane looked pensive as she filled two mugs with hot water. "It might give me a chance to clear my head," she murmured.

"Then it's settled," Grace said before Jane could say anything more.

They walked back to the table with the mugs, falling into silence as they sipped their tea. It was taking everything Grace had to not ask Jane for more details about what was bothering her, but she knew that Jane would open up to her when she was ready. Besides, she thought to herself, there were some things best kept between the two people involved. Complications no outside party could understand.

"Thanks," Jane said through a watery smile. As she started to get up, she suddenly turned to Grace. "Why did you stop by? Was there something you needed?"

Grace smiled. "Just wanted to say hello," she lied.

Anna was in the café when Grace pushed through the front door an hour later, clutching Sophie's mittened hand. Seeing her sister behind the bakery counter, chatting easily with a woman Grace recognized from the pageant the night before, she knew it was now or never. She would have loved to have run the idea by Jane first, maybe take an ally with her into the meeting, but this was something she would have to do alone.

Squaring her shoulders, Grace strode across the room, plastering a big, bright smile on her face as she approached the display case filled with mouth-watering pastries and cakes.

"Grace," Anna said, looking slightly startled. "You're in a good mood today."

"I am," Grace concurred. A flutter of nerves zipped through her stomach and she drew a breath. "And that's what I wanted to talk to you about."

Anna frowned. "Me?"

"Got a few minutes?" Grace asked. She glanced around the café. It was busy, but not bustling. The woman had left the counter and was now sitting near the window, sipping a cappuccino. "I could wait for your break, if you prefer."

"No," Anna said hesitantly. "I could use a break, actually."

"Good." Her heart was doing jumping jacks as she turned to her niece. "Sophie, say hello to Aunt Anna."

"Can I have a hot chocolate with extra marshmallows?" Sophie asked, and the two women burst into laughter.

"Sure thing, sweetheart." Anna looked at Grace. "Give me a minute. I'll meet you over at the table near the fireplace."

Grace walked over to the set of armchairs that nestled around a coffee table in front of the roaring fire and set up the coloring book and crayons Sophie had brought. It was cozy and warm and wonderfully inviting, and a thrill of anticipation zipped down her spine as she watched the flames dance in the hearth and inhaled the rich aroma of fresh coffee. This was exactly what she had in mind for Main Street Books! Only the customers wouldn't be reading magazines or surfing the net. They'd be reading books bought in the very same store. It would be a win-win situation for the café portion as well as the bookstore.

Now to make sure that Anna saw her vision, too.

"I went ahead and made you a peppermint latte," Anna said, coming up from behind her and placing a frothy mug on the table. A dusting of cocoa covered the foam, and an old-fashioned candy cane was tucked into one side.

Grace smiled. As much as she hated all things Christmas these days, she couldn't help feel a little tingle of something as the waft of sweet peppermint filled her senses.

"Thanks," she said, taking a sip.

"Here you go, Sophie." Anna handed their niece a

snowman-shaped mug and settled herself into the opposite chair, curling her feet up under her as she sat. "I hate
to cut right to it, but you have me a little curious. Last
time I saw you, you were broken up over Dad's store, now
you're positively glowing." She paused, her eyes growing
wide. "Did you get back together with your fiancé?"

"What?" Grace exclaimed, almost sloshing her latte
in shock. She swallowed hard and set the mug back on
the table, where her trembling hands wouldn't do further
damage. "No," she said firmly. Never. "Derek and I are
over, and I meant it when I said I was fine with that, actually." He was a good man, but he wasn't the man for her.
She'd accepted that. No one was to blame.

She pressed her lips together. Why was it so easy to
see it that way with Derek, but never with Luke?

"If you say so." Anna didn't look convinced. Leaning
back against the red velvet throw pillow, she clutched her
mug in both hands and said, "So what is it then? What has
you all bright-eyed and grinning? If it isn't Derek then—"
Her eyes darkened. "Oh my God, did you and Luke...do
something?"

"What?" Grace felt the blood drain from her face,
and she was happy she'd had the foresight to set her mug
down. "God, no! Why would you think such a thing?"

Despite her protests, curiosity built within her, filling her
chest with a sense of something awfully close to hope. After
everything she and Luke had been through, Anna wouldn't
toss something like that out there lightly. Unless...

"Did...someone say something to you?" she asked,
holding her breath.

Anna gave a knowing smirk. "I saw the way you two
were getting cozy near the punch last night, that's all."

Grace sighed and turned away, trying to banish the memory of her conversation with Luke from her mind. She had set out to hand him back his scarf and walk away, but he had pulled her in and kept her there. She never was good at walking away from that man.

In the fireplace, the flames crackled, casting a warm glow on the row of stockings hung from the mantel. They were the red felt kind that she remembered making in school, right down to the hand-painted glitter names on the white trim. She smiled at a distant memory, running home from school, asking her mother to hang her creation, and Kathleen's pinched brow, the flash of horror that no, no, it wouldn't match the others, it wouldn't go with the theme she had created for that year.

That was the year of the twelve days of Christmas. Grace's "official" stocking had featured two turtle doves. Her father had taken the cheap, rejected stocking and hung it in the bookshop, off the counter. "So everyone can see how beautiful it is," he had said with a smile.

Grace blinked away the threat of tears and turned back to Anna. *Here it goes.*

"I actually had an idea I wanted to run by you specifically," she began. "It's about Main Street Books."

Anna frowned. "I was hoping we were past this." After a silence she said, "What kind of idea, Grace?"

The leery tone made Grace second guess herself, but not enough to let it drop. "I noticed that there was an empty storefront next door," she said casually.

"Oh. Yeah, it's been empty for years." Anna shrugged. Then, with newfound trepidation in her voice she asked, "Why? What do you have in mind for it?"

"Now, hear me out." Grace said quickly, licking her

lips. Her pulse was gaining speed as her mind raced to find the best way to propose the plan. "A lot of people who frequent bookshops like to linger, sit around, read..." *Have a cup of coffee*, she thought. "Main Street Books never really had that opportunity. What if we could create that experience? Give the customers a destination point?"

Anna locked her gaze from across the table. "Grace, you're speaking as if the shop is still open."

Grace was prepared for this. "Ah, but see, the lease doesn't end until the thirty-first. Technically, it's still open, even though no one is there to run it."

"And you're going to run it? Until the end of the month? For like... another week and a half?"

Grace held up a palm. "Well, there's more," she said.

Anna groaned. "Get on with it!" Despite her outward impatience, Grace detected a hint of interest. She wanted to hear the rest, even if she didn't want to admit it.

"I haven't thought through all the details yet. I didn't want to get ahead of myself." Grace ignored the flash of mirth that sparked Anna's bright blue eyes. "I figured that while I'm here, in town, I might... spruce the place up a bit."

Anna nodded slowly. "Spruce it up a bit?" She drew a breath and released it slowly. "Go on."

"Now don't freak out," Grace began. Her heart was positively pounding now. This was it. She was going to lay it all on the line. If Anna guffawed, cackled at her expense, it would be over. Hope lost. If she could only hear her out, think about it, she might see that it could work. "I was thinking that a way to revive the shop would be to expand into the next storefront with an... an adjoining café," she blurted out the rest, staring at the foam of her latte, bracing herself.

"A café," Anna repeated after a beat.

"That's right. It would make the bookstore more of a destination point."

"And am I correct in assuming that I would have something to do with this café?"

Grace looked up at her pleadingly. "Well, it's clear that this place is a hit. You yourself said how successful it is. You have no competition in town other than Hastings, really. Why not expand?"

Anna rubbed her finger over her bottom lip and stared at her. The silence stretched for what felt like minutes, until she finally said, "Where would we get the money to pay for the lease? The entire reason we had to close Main Street Books is because we couldn't afford it, remember?"

Grace swallowed the excitement that was building in her chest, refusing to show any outward emotion for fear of scaring Anna off. So far, this conversation was going considerably better than she had planned. She had expected Anna to snort in laughter, to shake her head and tell her to stop dreaming. If she didn't know better, she might say that Anna was actually considering this. Now they just had to figure out a way to make it happen.

"I have a bit of money saved," Grace said. "It would help with the first few months of the lease, but the rest would be a risk. I can't lie. I'm assuming there would be some initial construction costs."

Anna peered at her, seeming to mull this over. "And who would run the bookstore?"

"Well, I thought you or someone from here could

oversee the café and that I might be in charge of the books."

Anna's jaw slacked. "You?" She stared at her, unblinking, and Grace gave her a weak smile in return. "You're moving back to Briar Creek?"

Grace broke her stare and looked around the room, taking a sip of her sweet peppermint drink. It tasted like Christmas in a cup. She rather liked it.

"Well, that's all dependent."

"On?"

Grace widened her eyes. "On this, of course!"

Anna closed her eyes and began to laugh, and Grace felt her heart sink. She had thought Anna was actually considering this, that it might truly happen, and in that moment, it had felt so real—all of it. Even the prospect of moving back. She could see herself standing behind Dad's counter, ringing up the till, recommending books. Stacking new inventory with a little smile on her face...

She almost felt...happy. It felt like what she was meant to do.

"I'm sorry, Grace," Anna said, composing herself. "I shouldn't be laughing. I'm so stunned, you see. You leave town for five years, refusing to come back, and now you're saying you want to stay?"

Grace nodded. She lifted her chin, pursing her lips. That's right. That's exactly what she was saying. It might sound ludicrous, but there was nothing wrong with it. What was so wrong about wanting to come home?

"What about your writing?"

Grace lowered her eyes. There was that question again. "I can write from anywhere." Technically she could, if she chose to. That was another issue she didn't want to think about right now.

Right now, Anna was showing signs of support, and Grace wouldn't let anything tear her thoughts from this possibility.

"Tell you what," Anna said, standing. "Find out what the rent is on that empty storefront and then we'll talk some more."

Grace's pulse kicked. She opened her mouth to speak, but her breath wedged in her throat. "Oh my—are you—you mean—"

Anna grinned. "I might live to regret this, but your idea might work. If we can figure out a way to pay for it all, that is."

Grace nodded her head furiously, her heart swelling with excitement. "I'll let you get back to work then."

"See you, Grace." Anna stopped halfway to the counter and turned, smiling wide. It was the happiest Grace had seen her since she'd been back in town, and the sight of it tugged at her heartstrings. Anna was far too beautiful a girl to ever be caught frowning.

"Just for the record, I'd really like it if you stayed."

"Me too!" Sophie said, coming over to take her hand.

Grace looked down at Sophie and felt something within her break. Holding the little hand in hers, thinking of the joy that Sophie brought to her sister—the comfort, even in times like this—Grace knew more than ever that this was where she belonged. She might have run from it before, thinking it was boring, simple, uninspiring, but now she knew that Briar Creek, and everyone in it, was what she needed to fill that hole in her heart that had been there ever since the day she had left.

Grace grinned at her sister. "Talk to you later, Anna."

She gathered up Sophie's things and helped her put on her coat. She put on her own coat, turned on her heel, and pushed through the door, Sophie's small hand in hers, feeling the blood pump through her veins. Out on the sidewalk, she almost jogged all the way to Main Street Books, with Sophie giggling at the thrill of it, not even minding the chill whipping through her hair or the goofy smile plastered on her face that drew curious frowns from passersby. Let them talk, let them *all* talk! She was finally getting somewhere. After months of agonizing over her fate, pacing Manhattan in search of a sense of purpose, she had finally found one—in the one place she had least expected to find it.

She felt flushed, hot with excitement, and the cold air felt invigorating as it slapped at her warm cheeks. Her coat was unbuttoned, flying behind her, as she quickened her pace, at last rounding the corner to the shop. After making a quick note of the management company's number on the plaque outside the storefront next door, she let herself into Main Street Books with the key she had never given back to Jane.

It was colder in here today, and it felt dustier, too. Still, hard work was never something she had been afraid of— without it, she wasn't sure what she would do.

She tossed her coat on a chair, and, after selecting a stack of picture books for Sophie, she set to work, starting with pulling the financial documents from the file cabinets so she could go over them later. Then she began clearing out the overflowing shelves. She went on instinct, placing anything that she didn't think would ever sell in a big box for donation. Next, she took stock of the new inventory in the back room—the boxes her father had never even opened. It didn't feel right, doing this without him, but somehow, standing there, hunched over the new titles, she couldn't help but feel him looking down on her.

She hoped he was at least.

CHAPTER 18

Gray clouds rolled in over the mountains as thick white flakes of snow fell slow and steady, collecting on the bare treetops stretching as far as the eye could see. Luke turned from the window and crouched to stoke the fire, adding another log to the flames. He rolled back on his heels and stood, sweeping his gaze over the expanse of the room, suddenly feeling the house was too large for him.

The soaring wall of glass ran perpendicular to the oversized stone hearth, and Luke lost himself in the view once more, wondering if he could really give it all up. He'd thought of it, more than once, but no matter what had happened here or the memories it held, he couldn't let it go.

Then again, letting go had never been his strong suit.

He'd had the house built six years ago, and even now, regardless of the jokes that Mark might crack, he knew it suited his needs. Tucked into the forest, on a long, winding street off Mountain Road, the red-cedar log cabin was hardly a cabin at all. He'd taken a good percentage of his inheritance and had it built, knowing it would be the house he would live in for life. Not a detail went unnoticed, and the modern-rustic details had been created exactly according to his vision, from the hand-hewn beamed ceilings to the multileveled decks looking out over the mountain chains.

He loved this house, but its sheer size sometimes reminded him of how empty it was. How empty his life was.

He tore his gaze from the window once again. Now what?

It had been a long morning, and no matter how hard he tried to fill it with useful tasks, he couldn't tear his mind away from Grace, or the conversation he'd had with her that morning.

Grace Madison. Back in Briar Creek. He had never thought it possible. He thought she could never live here, that doing so would be a sacrifice, not a choice of her own free will. And yet, her announcement was delivered with a smile.

His gut knotted. Every doubt had been absolved; every nagging question that lingered in the recesses of his mind over the years had been answered. But not in the way he had hoped.

All this time he had wondered what would have happened if he had made a different choice all those years ago. He wondered if he had done the right thing in letting her go, sticking with the woman who loved him and their life, who saw it as enough, rather than as a compromise.

Grace had made it clear when she left for New York how badly she needed to get out of this little town. He'd been planning to propose when they finished their master's programs—he had been waiting for the house to be ready first. *Their* house, he thought grimly.

The plans had all been in place, hadn't they? And then she had to go and mess it all up—tell him she could never be inspired in this town, that there was nothing new for her, that if he loved her, he wouldn't keep her here.

What choice had she given him? He let her go.

What she was really asking was for him to go with her. And he couldn't. He just couldn't. She thought he hadn't loved her enough; he thought she hadn't loved him enough. At the end of the day, they wanted different things. It was as simple as that.

Yet now...now his worst fears were confirmed. He'd let her go that fateful spring day when she'd come back for him, convincing himself that if she stayed she would come to resent him. He was sure of it. Almost. It was the little part of him that wasn't sure that could never rest.

And now he knew for sure. She was moving back to Briar Creek. And she seemed downright happy about it. Luke exhaled deeply and shook his head clear of the mounting fog. He crossed the room to switch on a light and grab a soda when he realized the only thing inside his fridge was an expired carton of eggs and a long list of condiments. A trip to the store was the last thing he needed right now, what with all those tacky decorations and the holiday music and the in-your-face cheer. He didn't feel cheerful right now.

Even if Grace might be moving back to town.

It would be a challenge to keep his feelings under control, but he'd had years of experience. He was used to being tormented by her image, and in some ways it might be easier when she was close by. She would no longer be a mystery. She would be a tangible, accessible, beautiful woman—*Stop right there, Luke.*

He walked down the hall to the closed door at the very end and brought his fingers to the handle, closing his eyes. With a thumping heart, he turned the knob, hearing the click of the latch, and he pushed the door inward an inch. Was he really doing this? This was Helen's haven, her studio, filled with her things.

A knock at the door startled him, and he quickly pulled the door closed tight behind him. Rubbing his sweaty palms on his jeans, he retraced his path down the hall, noticing his mother through one of the windows that framed the solid door.

"Hey there," he said, ushering her inside.

She pecked him on the cheek, and he reflexively swabbed his face with his fingers. His mother loved her lipstick almost as much as she loved the ballet.

"One of my students made me this," she said, thrusting into his hands what appeared to be a chocolate cheesecake garnished with crushed candy canes. "As *if* I could eat such a thing and still wear tights!"

Luke fought off a smile. He seemed to recall that only the night before his mother couldn't get enough sugar cookies into her hands, but he decided not to point this out. Cookies were one thing; an entire cheesecake, he presumed, was another.

"Why don't you save it and we'll eat it on Christmas. I'm sure Mark and Brett will make short work of this."

"Well, I could," his mother said hesitantly. "I didn't know if we were still doing a family dinner this year."

Luke furrowed his brow. "Why wouldn't we?"

"Well, we all know how you feel about Christmas."

She made a furtive show of shifting her eyes over his house. "I mean, you still don't even have a tree! So, forgive me for not wanting to assume you'd be coming over to celebrate the holiday."

Luke lifted his shoulders in exasperation. "Mother, I am still coming over for Christmas dinner. I may not have much holiday spirit these days, but I always come over for the family meal. I came last year, didn't I?" He forced a grin, hoping to lessen the strain. "You know I can't resist your twice-baked potatoes."

Rosemary beamed. "Then it's settled."

"How about a cup of tea?" he asked, deciding he could use the company.

"Don't mind if I do," his mother said, already sliding off her coat. "This house is much too large for one person. It's not healthy for you to stay here alone all the time."

Luke ignored the insinuation. "It's my home, even if it is...big."

"Big!" Rosemary scoffed. "The scale of these rooms is positively dramatic!"

Luke bit back a sigh. His mother had a point. It had become much too easy for him to hole up in this enormous house, all by himself, for days on end. Tonight was a perfect example of how destructive this kind of behavior could be. He was going down a dangerous path, thinking about things he shouldn't, and it only served to make him feel worse.

"It's the style of the house," he said. "Besides, your house isn't exactly small," he said, with a lift of the eyebrow.

"Your father left us comfortable, but my situation is entirely different," she said, regarding him closely.

"How's that?"

"I raised three children in that house! I needed the space!"

Luke felt his temper flare. He didn't need to be reminded of his single status. "How's rehearsal for *The Nutcracker* coming along?" he asked abruptly, as he took her cashmere scarf and coat and hung them both on the rack near the door.

Rosemary made a grand production of rolling her eyes. "Don't get me started. Besides," she added, walking toward the kitchen. "I'm not here to discuss my boring old life. I'm here to talk about you."

Luke drew a hand over his weary face. He stood in the hall, watching his mother retreat, and summoned up the energy to reply. "Great," he muttered to himself.

He wandered to the back of the house and sat down at the kitchen counter, while Rosemary helped herself to a box of tea in the cabinet above the sink. A stack of unopened Christmas cards was strewn next to the empty fruit bowl, and he quickly shoved them in a drawer before his mother could remark.

After she set the water to boil on the stove, and took it upon herself to wet a rag and wash down the already clean granite counter, ignoring his protests, Rosemary finally whirled around and met his eye. "I'm worried about you, Luke. It's going on two years now since Helen passed—"

"Mom," Luke groaned. He raked his hand through his hair in agitation.

"Now hear me out. I'm your mother, and sometimes you need to listen to what I have to say, whether you take my advice or not."

"Fine," Luke grumbled. "Let me have it."

"I'm not here to let you have it, Luke. I'm here to tell you that I understand."

Well, this wasn't what he had been expecting. Luke leaned forward. "Go on."

"I lost my spouse, too," she said quietly. "I know how it feels in a way that others cannot. And that's why I want to tell you that it's okay to move on. I sometimes wish someone had told me that."

Luke stiffened. "Mom."

Rosemary shook her head softly. "It's fine, Luke. I have a full life. Three children, a thriving business. But when you children were young... Well, there were many lonely nights." The teakettle began to whistle and she turned to pull it from the range, taking her time in filling two mugs until the steam curled toward the post and beam ceiling.

Sliding a mug to Luke, she looked him square in the eye. "I don't want you to be lonely. I want you to know it's okay to move on, to find love again. Maybe not now, but someday. Enough time has passed, but only you know when you are ready. And in case you didn't know it was okay, just in case you were feeling... guilty, well, I wanted to tell you what I wish someone had told me."

She lowered her eyes, looking sad and young all at once, and Luke's heart ached, thinking of his young, widowed mother, sitting alone in the house each night when he and his sisters had gone to bed. He didn't want that for her, as she didn't want it for him.

"Well, that's the thing, Mom. I *do* feel guilty." There. He had said it. Out loud. The relief he felt in that moment was like his chest finally being filled with air for the first time since Helen died.

Rosemary squinted. "Guilty for wanting to move on with your life?"

Luke shrugged. "That. But for other things too." He considered his words, wondering where to even begin. Something still haunted him, and he turned his face to his mother, ready to face the truth. "Did I seem happy to you on my wedding day?"

Surprise sharpened Rosemary's features. "Of course. Why would you ask such a thing?"

Luke frowned, shaking his head. "I don't know. I guess I never really knew if I was completely happy. If I felt the way I should feel."

Rosemary gave him a withering smile. "Marriage is wonderful, Luke, but it isn't without its challenges. Of course you were happy with Helen."

See, that was the thing. He was happy with her, or at least, he thought he was, until the doubts started creeping in, and something within him shifted. He could never seem to find his way back after that, no matter how desperately he tried. She was slipping away, he had lost her, and he couldn't make himself feel what he had once felt. If what he had felt was ever even real. Or enough.

"I don't know if that's exactly true." He couldn't meet his mother's eyes, but the heat of her gaze burned a hole straight through the empty part of his heart. "I don't know if I ever loved Helen the way I should have. The way she deserved to be loved."

"Luke." Rosemary's voice hitched on the word and she reached out and placed a hand on his arm. "These are normal feelings. You lost someone who meant the world to you, and now you're beating yourself up wondering what you could have done differently." She tutted. "You did the best you could, Luke. You loved her, and she loved you. I was there, trust me."

Luke took a sip of the tea, hoping to chase away the ache in his throat.

"If you didn't love her, you wouldn't be feeling the way you do," his mother added.

He lifted his eyebrow. She had a point.

Rosemary sighed. "This is about Grace, isn't it?"

Luke's eyes shot up to his mother's. He opened his mouth to protest and stopped. There was no sense in trying to deny it. "That obvious, huh?" He grinned sheepishly.

Rosemary's lips curved into a sly smile. "Just a hunch. I saw the way you two were canoodling over at the eggnog bowl last night," she added and a spark danced through her blue eyes.

"We weren't *canoodling*," he corrected. "We were talking. But, yes, this is about Grace." *Wasn't it always?* "I always felt like something was wrong. That I should have felt the same way for Helen as I did for Grace. And I didn't." There. It was out.

He waited for his mother to sneer, to shake her head in shame, but all she did was shrug and say, "So? How can you be expected to feel the same for two completely different people?"

He had never thought of it that way. Relief flooded him like a warm bath after a rough, dirty day, until he remembered how far his feelings had gone, and the familiar uneasiness returned.

"You and Grace knew each other for a long time, Luke. Since you were kids. You practically grew up together." She shook her head. "You can't expect Helen to have filled that same space."

Luke rubbed his hand over his chin in thought. "No. You're right."

But had he? Had he expected the impossible from her? Had he set his wife up to fail? It tore a hole through his gut to think he might have—that he might have waited and waited for something more, rather than enjoying what they had. That in the end he might have let her down in the worst way possible, all because his love for her was different. Not better. Not worse. Just different. "Thanks, Mom."

Rosemary paused. "Do what you will, but learn from me. Don't end up alone, Luke. You have a whole life waiting for you."

"But—"

Rosemary interrupted, "You know, I used to think I could never love another person like I loved your father, and the truth is, I couldn't. But that's not a reason to never love again, Luke, and it's not a reason to close off your heart to the possibilities. Each love is different. You aren't replacing that space in your heart. You're just filling another part of it."

Helen had filled a part of his heart, that much was true. She had shown him what constant, patient, quiet love could feel like. And he still wanted that, even if at one point he thought it wasn't enough.

"Oh my!" Rosemary announced suddenly, glancing at her watch. "I should run. Rehearsal for my sugarplum fairies, and based on yesterday's practice, this should be a long, tear-filled afternoon."

Luke chuckled, standing to walk his mother back to the door. "Don't be too hard on the girls, Mom."

"Who said anything about that?" she cried. "When I said tear-filled, I was talking about myself. If my two pink sugarplums don't nail their pirouettes, we'll be the laugh-ingstock of town come December twenty-third!"

Luke helped his mother slip into her coat and handed her the soft, red scarf. "Thanks for stopping by. And don't forget the cake."

Rosemary eyed the decadent dessert that was propped on a chair in the front hall and pursed her lips. "If I must, but you're taking home the leftovers on Christmas."

"Deal." Luke leaned in and gave his mother a peck on the cheek and opened the door. Raising his hand in a wave, he watched her scurry to her car, tucking his hands in his pockets as the wind whipped through his lambs' wool sweater.

He waited until his mother's car had disappeared out of sight and then picked up the phone. Without pausing to think, he dialed the Madisons' number. After all this time, he still knew it by heart.

He closed his eyes and waited as the first ring went through. It was time to confront his past, once and for all.

CHAPTER 19

The Winter Festival was yet another annual tradition in Briar Creek, one Grace had also missed for the last five years. But like Mark's party, little had changed in her absence, and she was grateful for it. There had been too much change recently. It was nice to know there were still some things she could rely on these days.

Most of the locals had gathered in the town square, which was alive with sparkling lights and decorations. Fragrant smells of roasted nuts and sweet chocolate rose over the crowd, and the fresh snowfall left the branches glittering. A band played Christmas music under the shelter of the gazebo, which was decked out in garland and red velvet ribbon. Colorful scarves fluttered in the wind as excited children bounded past, eager to take part in the festivities.

Grace held Sophie's hand tight, making sure the little girl didn't run off into the growing crowd, and steered them in the direction of the snowman-building contest.

"Oh, it doesn't start for another ten minutes," she said, looking around the festival for something to keep them busy in the meantime. Across the way, past the ice sculpting and snowshoe race track, she saw a stand for hot chocolate. She shrugged to herself. What Jane didn't know wouldn't hurt her, and it was Christmas after all. Why shouldn't her niece get two treats in one day?

"Why don't we get a hot chocolate before the contest starts?" she suggested. Leading a smiling Sophie toward the stand, she halted in the crunching snow when she saw the distinct form of Luke only a few yards away.

"What is it?" Sophie asked impatiently, while Grace hesitated. There was no way they would make it past him unnoticed.

Suddenly, she had an idea. "Your mommy ever show you how to make a snowball?"

"Of course, silly!" Sophie giggled, and then, following Grace's lead, bent down to scoop up two handfuls of snow.

"Well, watch this," Grace said, as she packed a snowball the size of a grapefruit. With her unsuspecting target in sight, she wound up about as well as a girl who had once been laughed off the softball team could. With as much force as she could manage with all her layers keeping her stiff, she launched her snowball at Luke just as a loud bell signaled the start of the speed skating race on the pond behind her, and he whirled around in time to collide with her effort at full force.

"Oh!"

Grace stared in horror at Luke, who stood unmoving, his face covered in snow. Beside her she heard Sophie mutter something about that "not being very nice," but she barely registered the words as she took in the sight before her, wondering whether she should flee the scene of the crime or deal with her punishment.

"It was supposed to hit your back—" she called out weakly, as Luke swiped at his face.

"You mean the back of my head?" He shook the snow off his glove and glanced over at her, the beginnings of a rueful smile forming on his lips.

She relaxed. "You know sports were never my strong area."

He cocked an eyebrow. "Neither was running, from what I recall."

And before she could sprint away, he reached down, scooped up a lump of snow and flung it at her, the impact silencing her mid-scream, landing right at the side of her head, knocking her hat askew.

"Jesus, that *hurt*!" she yelled, bending over and taking a hand to her head.

"Oh, God. Grace—I'm sorry—"

Before he could get the rest of his thought out, she stood up and flung another snowball at him, laughing devilishly, while Sophie squealed in glee. A mischievous grin flashed over Luke's features, and soon they were picking up snow as fast as they could, not even bothering to pack it or form it before hurling it at the other, until they were both covered from head to toe.

Luke finally held up his hands in surrender. "You win." He chuckled, shaking the snow from his hair, and Grace did the same, but all the while her eyes were on him, on the way his sleek wet hair clung to his forehead, and the way his strong hand casually pushed it back. The way his eyes looked bluer in the cool winter light, and the way his mouth was still pulled into a grin.

Her heart panged. How could she have ever walked away from him?

"You're all wet," she said, instantly stiffening at her words. "I mean—"

Luke let out an easy laugh. "It's okay. I'll dry." He looked down at Sophie. "What are you ladies up to?"

"We're about to enter the snowman-building contest," Grace said. She checked her watch. The hot chocolate would have to wait now.

"I build a heck of a snowman."

Grace hesitated, held his stare. "You could join us," she offered, her heart beginning to pound as she questioned her invitation. What the hell was she doing? She was only tempting herself, only opening the wounds, only allowing herself room for more pain.

Luke grinned. "Why not?"

Grace felt her eyes widen, but she forced a casual tone when she said, "Great." Just *great*.

He fell into step beside her as they retraced their path to the center of the festival, where children and adults alike were preparing for the event. "I was hoping to run into you, actually," he suddenly said.

Her heart skipped a beat. "Oh, yeah?"

"I called your house, and your mom mentioned you were here. She gave me your cell number, but I thought I'd look for you first."

Grace shifted her attention over to the festival, but she barely took any of it in. He had called her house? He was looking for her? Why?

She glanced at him sidelong. "Well, good thing you found me, then," she managed, and then quickly looked away, focusing instead on finding the patch of snow designated for their entry.

All around them were parents and their children—

families—and as the bell went off and Luke quickly got to work on a giant snowball for the base of the snowman, guiding an enthusiastic Sophie through the process in patient tones, Grace knew that this could have been them in a different life. If she had never left, if she had stayed behind and followed the path they had started, this is how it would have been. Luke, and her, and a child they loved, doing simple things like building a snowman together.

Tears prickled the back of her eyes and she swallowed the growing knot in her throat.

"Grace?"

She spun to look at him, at the concern that crinkled Luke's eyes. "Everything okay?"

"What? Oh, oh yes." She blinked rapidly and gave a watery smile. "Just the wind. It makes my eyes tear."

He held her gaze for a second longer and then smiled. "Then get to work, lady. I know how much you hate to lose."

She laughed, the moment quickly fading, and set to work building the snowman, which Sophie had decided should be a princess snowman, and for which Luke was able to find a tiara from the props table. When they were finished, they stepped back and admired their handiwork.

"Not too shabby," Grace said, tipping her head. In fact, it was not the most glamorous snowman she had ever seen, nor was it the best in the contest. It was, she decided to herself, one of the most lopsided, disproportional snowmen she had possibly ever seen in her life. She opened her mouth to suggest they quickly redo the head and face but the glow in Sophie's eyes as she stared at the messy creation stopped her.

Her priorities had been out of whack for too long already.

"Not too shabby at all," Luke repeated. He leaned into her ear, his breath so close it rustled her hair. "Oh, please. You know you're standing there thinking of how much better you could have done it yourself."

Grace pinched her lips. "No, it's better this way. It was a family effort."

He lifted his eyebrow. "A family effort?"

She bristled. "I meant with me and Sophie. I mean—oh, you know what I meant!" She tossed up her hands and stormed off to get one last prop from the picked-over selection, feeling Luke's gaze on her back.

He was still watching her when she came back, and his grin turned positively wolfish when they were awarded a basic participation ribbon.

"Stop it," she hissed, swatting his arm.

"I can't help it," he retorted gleefully. "It's the first time I've ever seen you lose. I need to see how you'll take it. Should I call an ambulance?"

"Stop," she said, but she was smiling too. "I've changed. I don't get hung up on things like this anymore."

He frowned, crossing his arms over his chest, clearly not believing a word of it. "Really?"

"Yes, really," she said, growing impatient.

He narrowed his gaze, studying her. Finally, he said, "I don't believe it."

"Well, you don't have to."

"I know you, Grace."

I know you, Grace. She closed her eyes, wishing she could hide behind them forever.

"You don't know me anymore," she said briskly. "I've been gone a long time. Maybe I've changed."

He leaned forward. "Maybe?" His eyes were gleaming, and she immediately knew she had misspoke.

"Okay, fine you win!"

"Aha!" He wagged a playful finger at her. "You're a determined woman, Grace. I always loved that about you. When you want something, you don't let anything stand in your way."

She grew silent. He was right. When she wanted something, she didn't back down easily. And right now what she wanted was to save her father's bookstore. And heal her broken heart.

"I should get Sophie that hot chocolate I promised her," she said, fighting off a shiver as a cool wind ripped through the festival. "It's getting too cold out here anyway. We should probably go home soon. I'm watching Sophie for the night to give Jane a break."

Luke nodded and thrust his hands into his pockets, looking pensive. "What are you doing later, after she goes to bed?"

"I don't know." She paused. "Why?"

"Want to meet me at the pub?" He motioned to the bar across the way, his tone becoming serious.

Meet Luke at the pub? Her stomach was doing jumping jacks as she stared at him, trying to soak more out of him, but finding her heart only twisting at his handsome face. "Um, sure, I guess. Eight o'clock sound good?"

He nodded. "I'll see you then," he said.

She stepped away. "Okay, see you then," she said. She held up a hand, a hint of a wave, and then led Sophie over to the stand for her hot chocolate. And as she handed over the wad of dollar bills and dared to glance back, the jolt she experienced when she realized he was still looking at her caused her to nearly spill the damn drink all over herself.

Luke wanted to meet her at the pub. He had sought her out, looked for her at the festival.

But why?

Time to find out. Drawing a sharp breath, Grace unlatched her seat belt and pushed open the door. The wind closed it for her with a heavy slam, and she shoved her hands deep into her pockets, bracing herself against the biting cold. Hoping her nerves wouldn't get the better of her, she walked quickly across the parking lot to the wooden door of the pub, the music loud enough to be heard through the solid oak. She'd worn heels, which was a vain choice, and her feet slipped across the ice. She cursed to herself, then lifted her chin. It wasn't often one had the chance to sit face-to-face with the one who got away. Heels, her best jeans, and a low-cut sleeveless blouse were in order. Even if it was about ten degrees below zero.

Inside, the room was dark, and strings of multicolored lights were hung from the bar, which stretched the length of the far wall. She swept her eyes around the establishment, trying not to look too obvious or desperate in her search, when her eyes locked with his. Her breath hitched at the sight.

Luke sat at the bar, his square jaw set, his blue eyes hooded by two lethal brows. His gaze was unwavering in its intensity; the hold he had over her rendered her powerless. A spasm of lust zipped through her stomach and she drew in a breath, willing herself not to give in to attraction, because that's all it was by now. Plain and simple attraction. Sure, she had loved him once, but that was over. Ancient history. She couldn't expect to suddenly find the man repulsive, though. Especially when he looked like he did tonight.

She edged closer, her lips curving into a slow smile, and his expression matched hers. As she neared his body, she could smell the musk of his aftershave, that hint of sandalwood she would recognize anywhere.

Luke was leaning on an elbow resting on the bar. His shoulders were wide and sculpted, and she could make out the curves of his biceps through his navy merino sweater. Her fingers itched to reach out and trace their way down the contours of his body, to feel his hard chest under his sweater.

She lowered her gaze, but her stomach only flipped as her eyes came to rest on his thick, muscled thighs. She could still remember how hard and strong they felt under her palms when he lay himself on top of her. She closed her eyes and her breath snagged in her throat.

"Been waiting long?" she asked, hovering near him as his eyes roamed over her face, his lips giving the first hint of a smile, his eyes shadowing something infinitely deeper.

He shrugged. "Nah." He lifted his chin in the direction of a booth. "Want to sit at a table?"

She nodded as he stood. "Sure."

She slid into the dimly lit booth, noticing how high the seatbacks were, how enclosed she felt with only a candle to light the table and Luke so close, staring at her like he hadn't known her for most of his life, like he was seeing her for the first time.

She shrugged her coat off her shoulders and leaned

back against it, tucking a strand of hair behind her ear as she studied the drinks menu. The heat of Luke's gaze was burning a hole right through her heart, and she couldn't bear to meet his eyes, not when she didn't know what he was thinking. Not when she didn't know what to say.

It seemed that Christmas had hit the bar, too. Spiked eggnog, something called a Santa's Little Helper, even an oddly intriguing concoction named Naughty and Nice. She scanned the wine list. "I think I'll have the Cabernet."

"And here I thought you'd go for the Mistletoe Martini." Luke grinned.

The waiter appeared at their table and Grace hesitated. "I'll have the, um...Special Snowflake," she said quickly before she could change her mind. She glanced guiltily at Luke, whose eyes gleamed with interest. "Don't even start. I know what you're going to say."

Luke ordered a beer and then leaned across the table. "And what would that be?"

"Oh, that the name suits me. That I think I'm better than this town."

Luke frowned. "I never thought that. I was just surprised to see you participating in all the Christmas cheer. First the festival and now the holiday libations. What's next, those little battery-operated earrings shaped like tree lights?"

Her lips twisted into a smile. "Very funny. It was a moment of weakness. You know how much I like eggnog."

"I know how much you like Christmas," Luke bantered. "You are the Christmas Queen's daughter after all."

Thinking of her mother, Grace felt her spirits deflate. It didn't seem like anyone she was close to was looking forward to Christmas this year. Well, other than Sophie. She grinned at the thought of her little niece, but her expression fell when she caught Luke's gaze across the table. She straightened her back against the wooden bench. No use thinking about what might have been.

"I was surprised you suggested this," she admitted, sliding the drink menu to the end of the table.

"Long overdue," he said.

Grace frowned and pulled her napkin into her lap, so she could take her nervous energy out on the soft, pliable paper. "First chance you've had, maybe. I have been gone a while."

"Second chance, perhaps," he said. He huffed out a breath and ran a hand through his hair, pushing a deep brown lock from his forehead. "I've never really forgotten that day—that day you came back."

The air closed in Grace's chest. She held his eyes, not daring to speak. Finally, she managed, "Really?"

All this time it had seemed so easy for him. She had shown up at his house, stood in his driveway and asked for another chance. She had kissed him, knowing he had a girlfriend, hoping the sensation of her lips on his would remind him of what they shared.

The look in his eyes when he told her to go, that she was too late, was seared into her memory, and her heart burned with shame. She had overestimated him and the love he had for her. She had thought they meant something, but then she realized in that one brief moment that maybe they never had. Maybe what they shared was a silly kind of love, a love between two kids who had never known anyone else. She was holding on to something Luke had let go of, and she had made a fool of herself trying to win back the heart of a man who no longer belonged to her. He had moved on so quickly. It was easy for him to let her go.

At least, that's what she had thought.

"I try not to think of that day," she said tightly, gritting her teeth, holding back the emotion that threatened to creep into her voice. She couldn't let him see how badly he had hurt her, how betrayed she had felt, how shattered.

No one knew she had come back that day. She didn't stop to see her parents, her sisters, no one. When Luke pushed her away, told her to leave, she promised herself then and there that she would never return to Briar Creek. She couldn't bear to stay in this town another second longer than she had to—every street she passed, every shop, every bend in the road—everything reminded her of him.

She had driven back to New York immediately, not stopping for anything but gas, and her tears had nearly blinded her all the way to her lonely apartment. She had cried for days, unable to get out of bed, to eat, or even to write. Bit by bit she had pulled herself together, her only resolve that she banish any thought of him, that she only think of the future, not the past, and that she never, ever let herself get so close to another person again. If you didn't get close, you couldn't get hurt.

It had worked, so far. She had dated, found companionship, and even almost gotten married. But she hadn't found love. She didn't need love. She didn't want it.

"I can't stop thinking about it," Luke said.

She stared at him, looking for a hint of a smile, a flicker of something in his eyes that would lighten the mood, but all she saw was the set of his jaw, the thin line of his mouth, the shadow in his eyes.

The waiter appeared with their order and quickly left.

Grace took a sip of her drink, feeling her spirits lift with the sweet taste. Luke left his mug of beer untouched, sitting between them on the table. He looked hunched, haunted, like a man with a burden he couldn't shed. This wasn't the Luke she knew—but then, who was the person she thought she knew so well?

"Why do you think about it?" she sighed. She peered at him, feeling her face crumble at the memory. "What does it matter now?"

Luke shook his head, glancing away. "It shouldn't matter. I know that. But it does. I...I've thought about it over the years, playing back the things you said, the look on your face." He huffed out a breath, looking down at his tented fingers. "I wondered if I made a mistake."

Grace almost didn't dare speak. Everything she had hoped and wished for was finally being spoken, but the joy of the moment had come years too late.

"Then you shouldn't have gotten married," she said firmly.

Anguish pulled at Luke's rugged features, and Grace fought back a flicker of guilt. Did he think he could say these things to her, play with her heart, make her doubt every decision she had made for the past five years without some kind of price?

No, she wasn't going to let him off that easy. If he had any doubts, he should have voiced them then. Or kept his mouth shut now. She didn't like living a life based on woulda-coulda-shouldas. It only led to remorse and regret, and the longing to change things that could never be changed.

Her heart wrenched when she thought of the time that had passed, the pain she had suffered. She had stayed away from this town, kept her family at arm's length, and now he was telling her that he had always wondered if he had made a mistake? Well, it was too late to go back and change it.

"Maybe I shouldn't have," he surprised her by saying.

She eyed him across the table. "I thought you said you loved Helen. You loved her so much you rejected me, sent me away."

"I couldn't trust you anymore, Grace," he hissed, leaning closer across the table until Grace could see the blue in his eyes flash. "Don't you see? You left me first. You were determined to move out of this town, claiming you needed something more. You wanted a life I couldn't give you."

"I came back, Luke," she insisted, meeting him halfway across the table, glaring into his eyes.

"And what did you expect me to do?" he asked, pulling back. He stared at her, his breath heavy. "Believe that you suddenly had a change of heart?"

She stared at him for a long, silent moment, finally nodding her head. "Yes." It was so simple; none of it had to turn out the way it had.

Luke shook his head. "You say that now, but I know you, Grace. You would have been miserable if you had stayed."

She inhaled sharply, holding his stare. She had no way of knowing if he was right or not. She'd like to think she could have stayed, that she had meant it when she told him she had made a mistake and that he was worth sacrificing everything else. Still, there was no way of knowing if she would have lived to regret her decision, if she would have felt trapped in this town, stifled. Bored.

Now it was different. She had lived the city life for five years, gotten that thrill of excitement out of her system. She had made a success of herself. And a failure. She had seen where it all left her in the end.

"Maybe you're right," she said softly. She shook her head, shrugging. "I don't know. All I know is that I missed you, and it killed me to see how quickly you had moved on. Six months was all it took for you to get over me."

"You have no idea how much you crushed me when you left, Grace. I thought it was going to be you and me. For life."

Grace looked down at her Special Snowflake, feeling like the name was taunting her, reminding her of a choice she had lived to regret. *Boring town.* She'd yearned for more, and look where it had gotten her. It really could have been them. She really could have had it all. She didn't know at the time what she had then. Everything that mattered.

"Then why Helen?"

Luke tossed his hands in the air. "With Helen, I knew I was with someone who wanted the same things I did. Someone who was going to be satisfied with the life we shared. I didn't have to worry about not being good enough."

"You were good enough," Grace said. "You...*are* good enough."

He stared at her, his eyes roaming her face, searching for something she couldn't quite determine. The truth maybe. It killed her to think he didn't trust her anymore. That she had broken the bond that they had shared for so long.

"Why didn't you ever ask me to marry you?" she

asked. It was a question she had mulled over for a long time. They had always talked about a future, of course, and they were young enough at the time that marriage didn't seem urgent. At least not to her. "We were together for so long and then, within months of meeting Helen, you proposed to her."

His mouth thinned. "Do you want to know why I asked Helen to marry me so quickly? Because I learned from you that when you find someone who you can care about, you don't let her go."

"You let me go," she retorted.

"Yes," he said. "I did. And I also decided to come back to you."

A gasp lodged in her throat. "What?"

Luke rubbed a hand over his face. He looked suddenly ashen, drawn. As if he had aged ten years since they had sat down. His beer remained untouched and he pushed it to the side, heaving a deep breath.

"I wasn't a good husband to Helen, and it's something I've had to live with since her death." He stopped and stared at the table, and Grace could see the labored rise and fall of his chest. "I thought I loved her, and I did, I did love Helen." He paused. "But maybe I didn't love her enough."

Grace narrowed her eyes. "Go on."

"There was a part of me that always wondered what life would have been like if I had taken the other path." He looked up at her. "If I had gone back to you that day you came to my house."

Grace tipped her head. "That's a destructive way of thinking." She should know.

"Yes. It is." He took a sip of his beer and set it back

on the table. "I think it's part of the reason I'm having so much trouble letting go. I—I betrayed Helen."

Grace squinted at him. "Betrayed her? How?"

"Helen and I had a life, and for a while, I was content. I had my job, the house, my family close by—"

"Everything you wanted," she pointed out. "Everything you would have lost if you had moved to New York with me."

"Everything I thought I would have lost," he said. "Then, after a while, I started to realize that I *had* lost something. I lost you, Grace."

Grace could feel the blood coursing through her veins, and she stared at him, barely able to believe what she was hearing and certainly not daring herself to speak.

"Things with Helen weren't going well that last year of our marriage. I was busy with my job and she was busy working on a new business idea. She was very artistic. She liked making clothes. Designing them. That type of thing."

Grace frowned and something deep within her felt sorry for Helen. She hated this woman by default, the woman who had won Luke, the woman who slept in his bed and could call him her own. She didn't even know Helen, and now she felt like a real person, with real interests. She might have even liked her, been friends, had the circumstances been different.

"Something wasn't there anymore with us," he continued. "It was like we were on two different paths, friends more than…" He stopped himself. "I blamed myself for it. I wondered if I really loved her, if I had ever loved her. I wondered if she was the one for me, if I had married in haste or…" He lowered his gaze. "Married the wrong person."

He huffed out a breath and locked her eyes, and Grace waited for him to continue, her heart thundering. "I decided to see for myself, erase the doubts. I tracked you down, to see if I had made a mistake in believing that you wouldn't have really stuck around."

Grace's mind whirled, racing with possibilities she couldn't even count. When had this been? What phase in her life had she been in at that point? Was she already with Derek? What would she have said if he had knocked on her door, if she had opened it and seen him standing there? Luke. Her Luke.

"You never came," she said.

He shook his head. "I didn't want to come without having some kind of discussion with Helen. It felt too underhanded, too...sly. Instead, I was going to confront her and ask for a separation."

Grace furrowed her brow in confusion. "But you never did."

"I couldn't," he said.

"Why not?"

A heavy silence settled over the table and the sound of Christmas music filled the gap, like a mocking reminder of their less than cheerful conversation, and all the joy they should be feeling but couldn't. Luke stared at the table, his jaw set, his brow furrowed. Finally, he looked up, his eyes locking with hers. "Because the morning I knew I had to do it, I took a long walk, to clear my head, to sort out everything I would say to her. And when I came home—" He kept his gaze fixed squarely on Grace, and she could see his chest rising with each heavy breath.

"I couldn't tell her," he said. "Because when I walked into the room to tell her, she was gone."

Luke waited for Grace to say something. To tell him what a monster he was, what a horrible husband he had been to his wife. Her silence was much worse.

"So now you know." He reached for his beer and took a long, hearty sip. He had kept these feelings bottled up for years, telling no one, perpetuating a lie and feeling increasingly disgusted with himself. Now the truth was out, though it didn't bring any relief. Not that he had expected it to. "I betrayed Helen when she needed me the most. She died never knowing the truth."

Grace frowned. "I think she died believing she had your love. And she did."

He stared at her. He hadn't expected that.

"I was unfaithful to her, Grace. Emotionally." Didn't she get it? Didn't she see it? Grace knew him better than anyone. His feelings for her were part of this big, sticky mess. If anyone could set him straight on this matter, it was her. She alone could tell him he had been foolish, he had wasted his heart and been cruel. How could she find any excuse for what he had done?

"*Unfaithful* is a pretty extreme word in this instance."

"I had feelings for someone else," he insisted, and she inhaled sharply, breaking his stare.

When she looked at him again, she spoke cautiously. "You and I have a shared history. A long one. That can be a powerful thing. It doesn't just go away."

He shook his head. "I hadn't made peace with my past. For some reason I was compelled to find closure."

"She didn't know that," Grace countered. "She might have known you were having problems, but she didn't know about any feelings you might have had for me." She shifted her eyes on the last word. "You said yourself that you were going to tell her. You didn't have the chance. Isn't it better that way?"

No, no it wasn't better that way. The last thoughts he had of his wife were of leaving her. He had walked through the front door, calling her name, telling himself he would finally come clean with himself, with her. He would clear the air of the past, confront his demons, and then he would know for sure if he could move on with Helen or not.

"The last conversation I planned to have with her was to tell her I wanted to leave her," he explained. "What kind of man does that make me?"

"I don't know. Human? I think you're being too hard on yourself, Luke."

"She died never knowing I had strayed, never knowing what my real intentions were." His gut tightened with self-hatred. "She died living a lie, and I was the one who created it. How cruel is that?"

"Relationships are complicated, Luke. You and I both know that." Grace gave him a small smile, but her eyes were sad, pleading. "I feel partly responsible for the way you've let this haunt you."

"You? Why?"

She shook her head, gazing blearily into the distance. "If I had never come back that day, never kissed you or questioned you about marrying her, you never would have had a reason to doubt your feelings for her."

He swallowed hard. "I guess not."

She pulled her bottom lip over her top, studying the table. "I'm sorry for that, then."

"Don't be," he said quickly. "You didn't know. You came back and I—I pushed you away. Then I wondered... A part of me always wondered, Grace. I was never going to find peace with this situation or my decision, and so I was left to imagine alternate outcomes. What life would have been like if I had asked you to stay that day. What life could have been like if I had gone to New York with you in the first place."

She frowned at this. "That's sort of how I felt once I got there," she said with a lift of her eyebrow, and Luke felt his stomach roll over.

"I always figured you never looked back," he said.

She snorted. "*Tried* to never look back is more like it. Especially after..." Her voice trailed off, but he knew. After that day. The day she had come back for him.

"I thought of you a lot, Grace," he said softly. "Too much, I guess. It's why I read all your books. It was my only connection to you."

A shadow fell over her face. "I don't like to talk about my books anymore."

"Why not?"

Her eyebrows drew together. Her mouth was a thin,

grim line. "I went after my dream. I sacrificed everything for it. And it all came crashing down."

"Oh, now," he said, reaching out to take her hand. She flinched as his fingers grazed her smooth skin, but she didn't pull away. He patted it twice, fighting the urge to take it in his, lace his fingers through hers the way he used to. "So the last one didn't do as well as the others. It happens. Don't be so hard on yourself."

"You should talk."

He grinned. "Touché."

After a pause she said, "There is something I don't understand, though."

He swallowed the remains of his beer. "What's that?"

"Helen died two years ago. You were planning on coming to see me that day. Why didn't you come after?"

Rubbing a hand over the stubble on his chin, he looked at the far wall, where a woman inserted a coin into an old-fashioned jukebox and then began swinging her hips to a corny Christmas tune. A man, presumably her boyfriend, jostled his way to her side, and they fell into soft laughter as they moved to the beat of the music, the woman crooning along to the words. An oldie but goodie. Helen had liked that song, he thought, closing his eyes briefly.

Dragging his eyes back to Grace, he found her expression primed, curious. He drew a breath, letting it out with force. He had been waiting for this. It was the question anyone would have asked. The question he himself had denied. "I wasn't emotionally faithful to Helen while she was alive," he said. "It didn't seem right to betray her after her death."

It was easier to blame Grace, to think of her as the temptress, the woman who had a permanent place in his heart that should have only belonged to Helen. If he could banish Grace and any thought of her from his life, he wouldn't have to be reminded of how much he had failed Helen in the end.

"So you were going to let it go then?" she asked. "Just pretend you and I never meant anything to each other?"

Luke shrugged. "Guess so."

Grace nodded softly. "I assume that me showing up in town this week hasn't helped matters."

Luke spared a wry grin. "Not really. If anything, it's brought everything to the surface. This time of year is always tough for me," he added, clearing his throat.

Grace sighed and reached down for her coat, pulling it around her shoulders as she slid one arm into the sleeve, followed by the other. She stared at him, the anger he had so recently seen replaced with sadness. Affection, if he didn't know better. The look of an old friend who you could still count on, no matter how many years had passed.

"So you're really sticking around then?" he asked, his pulse stalling on the question. As much as it pained him to see her, he couldn't bear the thought of her leaving again, moving on with life, going on without him.

"I don't know for sure yet," she said. "I've realized that I'm needed here. And it feels good to be needed."

"You always did like to have a purpose."

"Well, I don't have much purpose in New York these days," she said with a brittle smile.

Luke slid his empty beer glass around the table, swirling the condensation that formed in its path. He didn't know what to say, and he didn't trust himself to speak. He wanted to tell her to never go back, but the man in him that had always been there knew that when it came to Grace, he never wanted to be the person who would stand in the way of her dreams.

So she'd had a bump in the road. He knew Grace, and he knew that if she went back to New York, eventually she'd land on her feet again.

"I can keep my distance if that will make it easier," she said, looking at him.

It was what he wanted, what he needed, but somehow, hearing her offer it, his heart seized. She was right there, within his reach, and he couldn't let her slip for a third time.

"No," he said, shaking his head. "It's fine. This is your town as much as it is mine."

He gave a grim smile as she dipped her chin once in understanding and then slid out of the booth. She hesitated at the table, her green eyes bright as they latched onto his. Her brown hair fell around her shoulders in loose waves, and she brushed a strand from her collar, heaving a breath.

"Just so you know, I would have said yes."

His breath caught. He was so jarred from the silent pleasure of absorbing her beauty that it took him a split second to connect her words with the meaning.

"If you had shown up at my door and asked if I meant it when I said I would move back here for you," she said, "I would have said yes. I meant it. I still . . ." She shook her head. "Never mind. It doesn't matter now. What's done is done. Let's leave it at that."

She turned on her heel and walked toward the door, the sound of her determined stride fading as each step created more distance between their bodies.

Luke felt the weight of her words. The answer he had been afraid to hear. She would have said yes. Then. And now?

She pushed through the door and he waited, hoping she would turn around, look at him, even come back to the table. But she didn't turn around or even glance over her shoulder, and the door swung shut behind her, with only a cold gust of air filling the space she had left in her departure.

Let her go, he told himself. *It's what you do best.*

He'd had his chance. With her. With love. Hell, even with marriage. And look at him now. He wouldn't be going through all of that again only to wind up in exactly the same place. Only worse.

His mind flew to Helen, of how close he had come to leaving her that fateful day. Instead, he had poured himself into being the best husband he could be, only now, when it was too late. Helen was gone. She had loved him, died thinking he had loved her, and he had.

He replayed the day, imagining the alternative. Helen was in her studio when her aneurysm occurred. She was sewing, making a skirt out of soft pink cotton. If he had walked into that room and found her still sitting there, the machine still humming as she worked the foot pedal, would he have had the heart to tell her anything other than hello?

It was easy now, in retrospect, to focus on his state of mind at the moment, to remember the thoughts that had consumed his time. He and Helen were fading into a routine, their honeymoon phase was over, and all he could wonder was whether or not he could have something different—make that something better—with someone else. With Grace. It was so easy to focus on the drama of that relationship, of the excitement and the uncertainty it yielded.

He had loved Grace. Loved her for the sparkle in her eyes, for the sense of adventure in her spirit. For that restless need to fulfill herself in every possible way. And he had loved Helen. Loved the way she would sit at the sewing machine, making beautiful things, singing out of tune when she didn't think he was listening. He loved them both, just differently. His downfall had been trying to compare his feelings.

Luke stood, suddenly knowing what he had to do. Slapping a twenty-dollar bill on the table, he pushed through the pub and out the front door, ignoring the blast of frozen air, his footsteps halting only once he reached the sidewalk and saw Grace standing in the parking lot, her back to him.

The air was still, the wind having died down with the temperature drop, and the only sound that could be heard was the crunch of the snow under his boots.

Luke watched as Grace stood in front of her rental car, keys in hand, but not moving. His breath was ragged, and he stood perfectly still, unable to move or take a step closer to her, fearful that if he did he might scare her away forever.

Suddenly she turned, her eyes locking with his across the stretch of the parking lot. Her mouth was a thin, flat line. The sparkle in her eyes was gone. Even now, she looked so beautiful, he could stand here staring at her all night.

"Grace," he said, his voice husky. "Wait."

He took a step, and then another, closing the distance

between their bodies with increased speed until his arms reached out and grabbed hers, pulling the length of her close against the hard wall of his chest until he couldn't tell where his body ended and hers began. His mouth found hers, hungry in its need to be filled with her taste. She moaned into his mouth, wrapping her arms around his shoulders as she pressed into him. His tongue parted her lips, exploring her greedily, and she responded, lacing her tongue with his, silently begging him for more.

Their bodies fused, and he tightened his hold on her, his groin warming at the sensation of her curves under the bulk of her coat. He closed his eyes, remembering the way she felt under his hands, the smooth flare of her hips under the cup of his palm, the excitement that tingled through him when his fingers traced lower.

Parting her legs with his knee, he pulled her closer, grunting as his tongue searched hers, his mouth guiding his way, all rational thoughts having escaped. He pressed his leg higher, feeling that warm space between her thighs, his belly coiling as she pressed against him.

He ran his fingers through her hair, letting each smooth strand lace its way through his fingertips. As his arousal mounted, he tore his swollen lips from hers, groaning as he buried his face in her warmth, his mouth exploring the crook of her neck, the delicate earlobe nestled in a mound of coconut-scented hair.

He pulled her close, and she curled her face into his neck, gripping him to her panting body until he couldn't breathe. He gulped the cold night air, raising a hand from her waist to stroke her hair, and cradle her head. The lights from the pub flickered green and red, and slowly, effortlessly, it began to snow. Large flakes traced their way through the night sky, shining brilliantly in the back-drop of the blinking strings of lights, slowly coming to rest on the top of Grace's head, where they melted into each rich, chestnut strand.

Luke smiled into her hair. After all this time, she had found a way back to him. He had dreamed of this moment so many times, of holding her in his arms, kissing her, just being with her again, and now she was finally here. And no matter how much he wanted to believe that this time she would stay, that nothing would come between them again, he didn't dare.

He had loved and lost so many people, including Grace, more than once. He couldn't make her stay with him any more than he could push her away—and God knows he had tried.

The only thing he could do was hold her tight, close his eyes, and live in this moment.

CHAPTER
21

Sunlight poured in through the gap in the drapes, stirring Jane from a deep slumber. She opened her eyes and glanced over her shoulder, already knowing that Adam was not there by the temperature of the bed, the way the sheets were still tucked neatly in place, the blanket intact.

His side of the bed remained turned up, with the sham on top of the pillow, the comforter pulled taut. When he first started sleeping on the couch, claiming he had fallen asleep watching television, Jane had taken a strange pleasure in having the room all to herself, liking the fact that she could sit in bed reading longer, or crack the spine on her book if she woke in the middle of the night. There was something indulgent about having a bed all to herself as a married person; it was a rare treat.

Unfortunately, it wasn't rare anymore. And the pleasure of it had long since been replaced with the heavy reminder of their circumstances.

Jane lay on her back and stared at the ceiling, listening for sounds of life. Adam often woke before her and could be heard making his breakfast of toast and coffee, usually stirring Sophie from her slumber. But this morning Sophie was with her mother and Grace, and that meant there would be no buffer, that when Jane went downstairs, she would be alone with Adam.

She wasn't sure she could bear it.

She lay in bed for several more minutes, contemplating staying there until he left for "work," as he often did on Sundays. And Saturdays. She was tempted, very tempted, but she also knew that would be the coward's way out. Her husband was having an affair, and she wasn't going to close her eyes to the cold, harsh truth for another day.

She changed quickly and ran a brush through her hair before slipping down the stairs. The house was unnaturally quiet without Sophie's childish energy, and a pang squeezed Jane's chest when she thought of the implications of divorce. There would be a handful of nights each week where Adam would have Sophie, when Jane would wake to an empty, still house. She couldn't stand the thought.

It wasn't fair.

Adam was sitting at the kitchen table, chewing on a wedge of toast, scrutinizing the newspaper. Pausing in the doorway, Jane took a deep breath.

"Hey there," she said, forcing her tone to remain light. She pulled a mug from the shelf and filled it with freshly brewed coffee.

"Hey," was the grunted response.

She paused, waiting for more, and when none came, she pressed, "Sleep well last night?"

She regretted her words as soon as they had slipped from her lips. They seemed a calculated reminder of the fact that they no longer shared a bed and, with the exceptions of a few nights here or there, hadn't in a long time.

Jane tried to do the math, wondering when it had all began. It had happened so naturally, so seamlessly, that she hadn't noticed until it was already set in motion. Irreversible. Much like the affair.

If Adam was fazed he didn't show it, instead shrugging noncommittally. "I guess."

She waited for him to ask how she had slept, where Sophie was, something, but he only flicked the paper with his wrist, shifting his eyes to another headline.

"I waited up for you last night," she said. She leaned against the counter and fixed a stony gaze on him. He didn't meet her eye.

"I had a crisis at the office. We have a big meeting on Tuesday." He flicked the paper again. "I thought I told you."

"No," she said, wandering over to the table and taking a seat opposite him. She took a sip of her coffee. It tasted burned and acidic, and she pushed it away.

After a pause she continued, "Sophie spent the night with my mother and Grace. I thought it would have been a good time to talk."

Adam heaved a sigh and set down the newspaper. He turned to look at her, his expression hard and unrelenting. His eyes were deliberately flat and emotionless. Bored. "What is there to discuss, Jane?"

She flung her eyes open wide. "You. Me. What are we going to do, Adam?" Her voice was shrill and she pressed her mouth shut, angry at herself.

He thinned his lips and went about slowly folding his paper. "I don't know," he said.

A wave of fury heated Jane's blood. "I can't live like

this much longer. It's not fair to me. It's not fair to our daughter."

"Well, what do you want me to say, Jane?" He stared at her, his eyes unflinching, and something within her shifted. *Who was this man?*

A month ago—heck, even a week ago—she would have wanted him to say he was sorry, that he would stop seeing his floozy and make a determined effort to make this marriage work. She would have forgiven him, taken him back, looked toward the future, even. Now, sitting here, staring into his cold, ice-blue eyes, she wasn't sure she could stomach that.

Adam had not only cheated on her; he had cheated on their family. He had betrayed her trust, broken her heart, and lied to her. And she had put up with it, hoping it would go away. Until today.

It stopped here.

"I want you to tell me you are not having an affair, that this is all a figment of my imagination."

His jaw tensed and a shadow crossed his eyes. She held his stare in challenge, waiting to see if he would break. If he would have the nerve to lie to her face, when he was sitting so close she could smell the musk of his soap from his morning shower.

"Why are you causing trouble? I was sitting here, having a nice relaxing breakfast..."

She rolled her eyes, unable to stop herself. "Are you going to stop seeing her?"

He flashed her an angry look. "What do you think?"

She gave him a withering smile. "I don't think you are going to stop seeing her. I don't think you are willing to even try."

Adam leaned back in his chair and folded his arms across his chest. "What do you want from me?" he asked.

"What do I *want* from you? What I *want* is for you to stand by the promises you made to me. What I *want* is for you to treat me the way you did when we first met." She could feel her face collapse, and she blinked back the tears that prickled her eyes. "What happened to us, Adam?" she asked softly.

He shook his head. "I don't know."

"We used to have fun," she said. "You used to love me. You used to think I was pretty."

"You are pretty," he said, but his tone seemed forced, obliging.

It didn't matter now, she told herself. He had vacated their marriage a long time ago, just as he had left their marriage bed. The only thing tying him to her was this house they both shared. And their child.

"I don't think you've left me any choice," she finally said.

He didn't look at her when he said, "No, I don't think I have." He inhaled deeply. "I'm sorry, Jane."

"Sorry?" She laughed bitterly. "For which part?"

He shrugged. "For all of it."

"Please," she hissed, pushing her chair back from the table. She couldn't sit here and live this sham of a life for another minute. She had done everything she could to hold this together, to put on a brave face, and pretend nothing was going on. She would continue to pretend all right, but not in front of Adam. "You destroyed our marriage. And our family. But you will not destroy Christmas. Not for me, and certainly not for Sophie."

She emptied her coffee into the sink and rinsed her

mug. Fury blinded her vision and hot tears fell into the sink. She brushed them away quickly, before Adam could see the effect he had on her.

"If you want to have Sophie for Christmas, that's fine," he said.

Panic swept over her, stopping her pulse. "What are you saying?"

He stood, his face lined with anguish, and stared at her. "I'm saying that I'm moving out." His voice was low and even. Determined, she decided, realizing with a sinking heart that he had known this all along but had been waiting for the right moment to tell her.

"Today?"

He nodded. "I think it's best."

The wife in her wanted to know where he was going, if he had somewhere to stay, if he would be okay, but she stopped herself just in time, clamping her mouth shut.

"Me too," she said, her tone clipped.

She knew where he was going all right, and the thought of it only cemented her resolve. It was time to move on, start living her life again, instead of treading water in a marriage that was sinking.

"What will—" He stopped, his mouth thinning. "What will we tell Sophie?"

"I don't think we should tell her anything until after Christmas," Jane said. "It's only a few days away, and she deserves to experience the magic of the holiday like every other child does. Our unhappiness shouldn't spoil it for her. You can stop by in the morning, when she opens her gifts."

He nodded wearily. "I wish it didn't have to be this way."

Jane gave a mirthless snort. "Please." She slammed her mug into the top tray of the dishwasher. "This was all your doing. You set this in motion."

"In case you haven't noticed, I haven't been happy in a long time, Jane," he shot back.

She met his gaze. "Are you happy now, Adam?"

He stared at her. After a pause he said, "Yes," and Jane's heart dropped into the pit of her stomach.

She gave him an icy smile. "Well, good for you. Then I guess it was all worth it."

She turned and walked down the hall, her heart thundering in her chest. She could hear the blood rushing in her ears, and her vision felt foggy. For a second she worried she might pass out, and she didn't even bother to put on her coat as she grabbed it off the hook in the mudroom. She slipped on her shoes, not caring that they didn't match her outfit, and walked out the back door of the house.

The snow on the back stairs hadn't been shoveled and ice filled her shoes, melting against her bare feet. The wind cut at her face, slicing through her thin cotton shirt, but she didn't care. It wasn't until she had marched around the side of the house, down the driveway, and past two neighboring houses that the heat in her blood cooled and she finally shrugged on her wool coat, stuffing her frozen hands deep into the pockets.

She walked in the direction opposite the route she knew he would take to leave, so she wouldn't have to see him again, face another curt exchange. She walked until the street ended, and then she walked the cul-de-sac, plastering a toothy smile when Mrs. Banks drove past and waved.

She wouldn't let him win, she told herself. If anything,

she would show him. She would land on her feet, she would find happiness, she would be better off. Someday.

She gritted her teeth, thinking of what she had given up for that man—every inch of herself she had poured into domestic life, into creating a home for them, a family. Nearly six years of her life! And he had thrown it all back in her face, showing her it wasn't good enough. It hadn't made him happy.

Jane swallowed a sob and clasped a hand to her mouth, pressing her teeth into her fingers, stifling the sound that came from somewhere deep inside her. It was the sound of grief and pain so raw she didn't know how to contain it. She knew that sound. She had heard it once before. When her father died.

She glanced around the street, hoping that no one had seen her, and then headed back to the house, her heart all at once quickening with relief and then sinking low when she saw that Adam's car was not there. He was gone. The life she knew was gone. That quickly. It was all over.

She couldn't go back in that house. Not when it was so empty and still. She needed to be with the few people left in this world who loved her, and who would never leave her. She needed to be with her daughter.

The roads to her mother's house were cleared, and Jane spent the short drive trying to compose herself in a fruitless effort to disguise her anguish. By the time she pulled into the familiar driveway, her eyes were dry, if not a little skirting and wild, and her face was clear of any sign of tears. It was the best she could hope for under the circumstances.

She climbed the steps to the wraparound front porch

and knocked on the door, smiling as she heard the faint trill of Sophie's voice. "Mommy's here!" The pounding of Sophie's heels approaching swelled her heart and threatened to pool her eyes with fresh tears.

"Hi, honey!" she exclaimed, bending down to embrace her child the moment the door was flung open. She pulled Sophie close, burying her face in her daughter's thick, silky hair, inhaling the smell of her sweetness. "Did you have fun?" she asked when she finally released her.

Sophie nodded energetically. "Oh, yes. Auntie Grace gave me *two* hot chocolates!" Her eyes danced with illicit excitement.

Jane laughed and took her hand, crossing into the warm hallway and closing the door behind her. Inside, it was as if nothing had changed—this morning had never happened. But one step closer into the house and she was instantly reminded of how much she had lost in the past year. Here it was, four days before Christmas, and aside from the half-heartedly decorated tree, you would never even know it.

"Hi, Mom," she said, smiling at Kathleen, who was standing at the kitchen counter, slicing an apple into wedges. She gave her a kiss on the cheek, noticing for the first time how papery her mother's skin felt.

She frowned, thinking of how much time had passed.

"Grandma is making me a snack!" Sophie explained.

Jane opened her eyes and smiled brightly. "Were you a good girl for Grandma?"

"Isn't she always," Kathleen said, giving Sophie an indulgent smile. It seemed her granddaughter was the only person who could brighten her mood these days. "Though I think that Grace got a bit more attention during this visit."

"Where is Grace, anyway?" Jane looked around the room.

"She went into town," Kathleen told her, carrying the plate of apples to the table, where Sophie was waiting. "Didn't say why, but I can't help wondering if it has something to do with Luke Hastings."

Jane frowned. "Luke? Why would you think that? You know how she feels about him."

Kathleen grinned mysteriously. "I'm just saying... You'll have to ask her."

Jane bit back a sigh and sat down at the table. She knew what Grace was doing in town this early in the day and it had absolutely nothing to do with Luke. Anna had called her yesterday to discuss Grace's plan for Main Street Books, but Jane certainly wasn't going to mention that tidbit to her mother. The woman had had enough disappointments for one year, and Jane knew all too well how it felt to know you couldn't handle another.

"She went out with him last night, you know," Kathleen added pointedly.

Jane felt her jaw slacken. "Grace went out with *Luke*? Mom...what?"

Kathleen's lips twisted. It was the closest to her old self that Jane had seen her in months, and it tore at her heart, making her realize how much she had missed her mother. How much she needed her.

She had tried so hard to keep the details of her crumbling home life to herself, to put on a happy face for her mother, to not add any stress to a grieving widow's life, but now she felt like she was unraveling, that the truth had to spill out or she would break. She wanted to burst into tears and pour her heart out, and she wanted her mother to take her into her arms and tell her it would all be all right.

She glanced at Sophie, who was happily munching an apple slice, and paused. She was a mother, too, now. Things were different.

"Where did they go?" she asked brusquely, getting back to the topic of Grace and Luke. Grace and Luke. Just the sound of it—it was preposterous! After everything they had gone through, certainly they weren't finding their way back to each other now. Things like that didn't happen . . . Did they?

Her heart fluttered but she pushed the thought back. Adam was cheating on her. He was moving in with his girlfriend. His lover. His tramp. The woman he wanted to be with instead of her. It wasn't the same. She and Adam were never going to find their way back to each other. She needed to learn how to accept that.

Or want that.

Her hand shook as she reached for an apple slice. She glanced up to see Kathleen staring at her, her eyes squinting with curiosity.

"So, tell me," Jane said hurriedly. "How did this even happen?"

Her mother shrugged. "Luke called here looking for her, and according to Sophie he spent some time with them at the festival. Not twenty minutes after Sophie's head hit that pillow, Grace was flying out this door to meet an unnamed friend. That's all I know."

Jane stared at her mother, aghast. Both women knew that Grace's heartbreak over Luke had kept her from Briar Creek for five years. She had missed out on holidays, birthdays, time they could never have back, all because she couldn't bear to face that man again. And now she was cavorting with him. The man whose named could not be spoken. The man who had married another, and who now held a torch for his deceased wife, two years after her passing.

It pained Jane to watch Luke's distress, even from a distance. Out of loyalty to Grace she had stepped back from his life, soon even fading away from Mrs. Hastings, who had been such an inspiration to her when she practiced ballet through her youth. She knew that Helen's death had been a shock, a horrible tragedy, really, and she knew that Luke had never recovered from it. Never moved on. Everyone knew.

"Did she say anything to you when she came home last night?" Jane asked.

"I was already asleep," her mother replied.

Jane nodded slowly, trying to make sense of this information. She looked at Sophie, who was finishing the last slice of apple, and back to Kathleen, who looked pale, troubled.

"Is everything okay, Jane?" her mother asked.

Jane sucked in a breath. "Of course." She forced a smile. "Why would you say such a thing?"

"You looked sad for a minute there," Kathleen observed.

Jane swallowed the knot in her throat. She wiped Sophie's mouth with a napkin and carried the plate to the sink. From the kitchen window, she could see children playing in the backyard of the house next door, making snow angels. Her heart felt heavy, like she couldn't fight through this for another day. It all seemed so unfair, so lost.

"Maybe I'll go into town and see if I can find Grace," she announced, and her mother nodded. "See if she gives me any details of her big date."

"Don't tell her I said anything," Kathleen warned.

"I won't," Jane said, as she began gathering Sophie's things. She was going into town to find Grace all right, but it wasn't to hear about her supposed date with Luke—Jane knew better than to take that at face value.

No, she had other things on her mind today. And if she didn't talk to someone about it soon, she might end up just as sour as the rest of her family by Christmas day.

CHAPTER
22

Grace pulled the last box of decorations out of the car and slammed the door shut with her hip. Walking carefully across the icy sidewalk to the front steps of Main Street Books, she placed the box on top of the others, panting at her efforts. It was really a task for two, but she couldn't tell her mother about her plans, and Jane and Anna were obviously busy with other things.

Grace frowned as she pulled out her key and unlocked the shop. She had been worried about Jane since she left her yesterday—when she wasn't worried about her own problems, that is.

She still couldn't quite believe how things had changed in such a short amount of time. Luke had kissed her. Kissed her properly. And damn if she didn't enjoy every second of it.

She'd replayed the taste of his lips on hers over and over again from the moment she had reluctantly pulled herself free of his embrace, and the sensation of his body close to hers was the first memory to greet her when she opened her eyes this morning.

Well, all the more reason to get busy. She had a purpose for the day, and it had started as soon as her bare feet hit the cold, hardwood floors. While her mother was still asleep, she'd ventured into the attic, where at least three dozen boxes were labeled "Christmas." Leave it to the former Christmas Queen to have an entire store's worth of decorations on hand. She'd never notice that a few measly boxes were missing. A few lights. A mini tree, a few small bulbs. It was just the thing Grace needed to spruce up the store and get it noticed again. A sale before the New Year would hopefully stir up interest for the expansion.

Her breath caught on the idea.

A shuffling on the sidewalk caught her attention, and as she slid one of the heavier boxes over the threshold, she paused, turning to look over her shoulder.

"Mrs. Hastings," she said, somewhat breathlessly. She stood, feeling the flush of guilt heat her cheeks, and wiped her dusty hands on her jeans before reaching out a hand.

Rosemary tutted it aside. "Come over here and give me a good hard squeeze, Grace. After five years, I'm long overdue."

Grace smiled as relief swept her and she skipped down the stoop and into Rosemary's open arms. When she released her, she thought she saw tears in the older woman's bright eyes, but Luke's mother simply sniffed and patted her cheek.

"It's been too long," she said. "Tell me you won't run off this time without at least saying goodbye."

Oh. That. Grace lowered her eyes, her stomach knotting. It had been immature, rash, to not say a proper goodbye to Rosemary. At the time, she couldn't face her, couldn't explain that she was choosing her dream over

Rosemary's son. Maybe it was because she didn't want to acknowledge the part of her that doubted her decision.

"I promise," she muttered with a limp smile, forcing her gaze back to Rosemary, whose eyes had now shifted to the shop.

"Are you—are you reopening the store?"

Grace nodded. "Not officially, you could say, but yes. I thought it needed one last try before the lease expires for good."

Rosemary stared at her. "You never could sit still and relax, could you?" she asked, a hint of affection creeping into her tone.

Grace slid her a shy smile. "Guess not."

"What does your mother think about all of this?"

"Oh, um. She doesn't know, actually." Grace shifted the weight on her feet, shivering in the cold winter morning. The sky was gray, and snow was predicted before noon. She stared at the boxes, at the hint of a wreath peeking out of the bottom container, and chewed her lip.

"I've tried to reach out to her," Rosemary said.

"It seems she's been keeping to herself a lot these days," Grace apologized.

Rosemary sighed. "Well, all in good time, I suppose. I'll keep trying."

"Thanks for that."

Rosemary patted her on the cheek once more. "Still as beautiful as ever. Tell me, will you be able to see *The Nutcracker* while you're in town? One performance only, thank goodness! Christmas Eve Eve."

Grace grinned. "So the twenty-third."

"You always were a smart one. I told Luke not to let you slip—" She stopped herself, her cheeks turning pink, and

Grace felt her pulse skip a beat. "I should go now, dear. We have a rehearsal today and high drama is expected. The girl playing Clara has turned into *quite* a diva, between you and me. You would think this was Broadway, not Briar Creek!" She pinched her lips, her gaze narrowing into the distance before turning back to Grace sharply. "Time to remind her who's running this show."

Grace chuckled. "It was good bumping into you."

"Oh, we didn't bump into each other," Rosemary said with a wink. "I saw you and made a point of coming this way."

Grace bit back a smile. "Well... thanks for that."

"Say hello to your mother for me. And to Jane," she added. "I keep wondering if she'll ever take me up on my offer. Maybe one day," she said wistfully.

Grace paused from lifting the second box. "What offer?"

Rosemary tightened her scarf around her slim neck. "To teach, of course! She always was the brightest star in my studio. When I think of how she gave up that dance scholarship to the academy..." She trailed off, shaking her head.

Grace gave a small smile, but her mind was already swarming with questions. What was going on with Jane? Ballet had always been her passion; Rosemary had not been flattering her when she called her the best in town. Wouldn't Jane have loved the opportunity to get back in the studio, teach children everything she had learned and mastered?

"Well, off I go!" Rosemary trilled. "I'll look for you in the audience Tuesday night!"

Grace waved until Rosemary turned away and then finished loading the boxes into the store. Just another topic to discuss with Jane, she decided. It seemed her youngest sister had become a downright mystery at this point.

Grunting as she picked up the heaviest box and carried it over to the counter, Grace couldn't help but feel pleased with the transformation of the shop. Yesterday, she and Sophie had cleared and dusted the overstocked shelves, reorganized the selections, and tagged all the books for clearance. With a little festive touch, she would be able to turn the sign on the door to OPEN in no time.

Even if the sign remained that way only until New Year's Eve.

Grace fought off the niggling sensation of doubt and squared her shoulders. No good came from thinking like that. After all, only a few days ago, she hadn't thought there was any chance at all that her father's store could survive. Now she was armed with Anna's support, and with a little luck they might be able to work out some kind of deal with the property manager for the space next door. Grace hadn't brought herself to do it yet, but she intended to call today.

Something was stopping her, and she recognized it as fear. Without that space, this store would be what it always was: a bookstore. Judging from the looks of things, that hadn't been enough to make it a success. To pull in a crowd, they needed that café space. She didn't know what she would do if she found out it was impossible. She wasn't quite ready for her last bit of hope to be crushed yet.

For now, she would focus on what she could control, and that was framing the windows with these strings of lights and hanging the wreath for all who passed by to see. She had to admit, it proved a nice distraction from thinking about Luke, too.

Luke. As his handsome image came clear in her mind, Grace sucked in a breath and squared her shoulders. Right. The wreath. She needed to hang this on the front door. Immediately.

Just keep busy.

Grace didn't stop working until the last strand of tinsel was removed from the box. She stepped back and admired her handiwork, grinning at the results. The store looked like a Christmas card, if she did say so herself.

The large display windows on either side of the door flickered with colored lights, illuminating the collection of Christmas books that she had artfully arranged. On the left window, she had even set up a little village of porcelain figures, right down to tiny skaters gliding on a pond. She knew these were among her mother's most prized decorations, but Kathleen must have had a collection larger than all the buildings and houses in Briar Creek—surely half a dozen could be spared.

Besides, it wasn't like they were being put to better use this year.

On each of the armchairs she loved so much, Grace had placed a plump red or green velvet pillow. She set a bowl of candy canes on the counter next to the miniature angel pine tree, complete with tiny bulbs and a garland tied with ribbons. If she didn't know better, she might think she was almost looking forward to Christmas.

She pushed the thought back. How callous of her. This was the first Christmas without her father. She should be following her mother's lead—this was not a year to celebrate.

A jingle from the front door caught her attention as she put the finishing touches in the children's books corner.

She wedged the last of the Christmas teddy bears onto an antique reading bench and stepped back.

"Hello?" she called, her heart beginning to thump. *Could it be Luke?* She held her breath, wondering if he would come looking for her yet. If he had changed his mind, if he wished he could take it all back.

Her pulse steadied when she saw Jane standing just inside the door, holding on to Sophie's mitten-covered hand, her expression awestruck. "My goodness, Grace!" she exclaimed, her hazel eyes wide.

Grace looked around, trying to picture the room through her sister's eyes. "Do you like it?" Trepidation laced her words. Maybe she had overstepped.

"Like it?" Jane repeated. She shook her head, leaning down to take a closer look at the window displays. When she turned to face Grace, her eyes were wet with tears. "I'm at a loss for words. It's...beautiful."

"Really?"

"It's beautiful, honey," Sophie said, showing all her teeth in a big grin, and Grace burst out laughing.

"Anna told me what you're planning. I'm so proud of you," Jane said, and Grace's heart swelled.

"I hope Dad would be proud."

"He is proud. Somewhere, somehow, he is." Jane smiled and then looked away.

Grace rolled back her shoulders, lifting her chin against her mounting emotions. "How did last night go?" she inquired as she unwrapped a candy cane for her niece.

Jane's expression faded. Her eyes darted to Sophie, who was happily enjoying her treat. After a pause, she said, "I heard *you* had an interesting night, actually."

Grace's eyes flashed. "Who told you?"

"Grandma," Sophie offered. "But we weren't supposed to tell."

"Oh, weren't you?" Grace shook her head. She should have known the news would travel. If you could call it that: news. It was more like a non-event really. Just two people who used to know each other, sharing a kiss...

"Grace?"

Grace jumped, noticing the interest pass through Jane's eyes. "Yes?" she asked, knowing she sounded as guilty as she felt.

"Something did happen last night!" Jane declared. She pinched her lips and wagged her finger. "I didn't believe it! I still can't."

Grace bristled. "What's so hard to believe?"

Jane blew out a breath. "All of it, I suppose. I mean, now, after all this time? After everything... You and Luke?"

"It's not me and Luke," Grace said haughtily. She straightened a stack of holiday cookbooks. She couldn't keep it up any longer. "Oh, God, Jane, I don't know what it is."

"Do you still have feelings for him?"

Grace didn't need to consider the question. "I don't think I ever stopped having feelings for him," she said, and Jane lifted an eyebrow.

"What about this fiancé you had? Derek?"

Grace plunked herself into the closest armchair and hugged a red throw pillow to her chest. "Oh, Derek. We never should have gotten engaged to begin with, honestly. We never wanted the same things."

Jane gently encouraged Sophie to amuse herself with a

book about one of Santa's reindeer and turned her attention back to Grace. "And you and Luke did?"

"I didn't know then what I wanted, Jane," Grace groaned. "And now I do."

"And what do you want?" Jane asked, unwrapping a candy cane for herself.

"What you have."

Jane released a bitter laugh. "What I have?"

Grace nodded. "Yes."

Jane lowered her voice, "Grace, you were over my house yesterday. I thought you understood—"

"I want a child, Jane. I want a family. I want it all."

Jane stared at her, her expression dark. Finally, she set the candy cane down on the counter with a small sigh. "Don't we all?"

Grace thought of Rosemary Hastings then, of the comment she had made about Jane. If Jane wanted more than she had, why was she turning away an opportunity to do something she loved? It didn't make sense, none of it did, but she decided not to ask. It was clear from Jane's mood that things with Adam hadn't gone well. What wasn't clear was how serious this was. Jane was sensitive, she always had been, and it was hard for Grace to determine if this was a bump in an otherwise seamless relationship or something a little more permanent.

"So you didn't tell me how last night went," she said as Jane's face paled.

"What do you plan to do about the shop?" her sister asked hurriedly. "I mean, you have it all decorated and cleaned up. Are you really planning on reopening it?"

"That's the plan. Then I'll see what our options are on the space next door."

"Mom has no idea, I was pleased to see that," Jane said. "She thought you were visiting Luke again."

Wouldn't that be nice, Grace thought. She stood and adjusted an ornament on the small tree. Just because she and Luke had kissed didn't mean it would happen again. Much as she wished it would. "I'm going to open it through the end of the year, see if I can raise a little money, rejuvenate the place. It would help with our plans for the expansion." It might lift her spirits, too.

Jane glanced around the room. "And if it all goes according to plan, you're really going to stay in Briar Creek and run the shop? Anna would help with the café?"

Grace felt her pulse quicken. She didn't want to give such a concrete answer, even though deep down she knew what she wanted. If things didn't go according to plan, did that mean she would go back to New York? Back to that empty life of meaningless relationships, fancy dinners with people who knew her only skin-deep, and maddening efforts to jumpstart a dying career?

"Yes," she declared firmly, surprising herself with the conviction of her tone. She had never sounded more sure of anything. "If I can save this shop, I'm going to run it. I'm going to move back to Briar Creek."

Jane tipped her head. "This is really what you want?" she asked, her tone questioning, wary.

Grace's cell phone on the counter vibrated and she reached for it, her pulse kicking when she saw the number she'd programmed into her phone before driving home last night. *Luke*.

She met Jane's gaze briefly, more certain than ever in her feelings. "This is exactly what I want."

Grace looked at her sister, at the smaller version sitting

cross-legged on the floor beside her, happily munching on a candy cane as she flipped pages in a picture book, at the perfect simplicity of their lives, the fulfillment, and felt her heart wrench. At the end of the day, what did she have? Herself. Derek, she supposed, at some point in time, but that was just as lonely. Luke and she didn't have many shared experiences these days, but they had history, and they knew each other. Inside and out. He got her. She didn't have to explain a thing.

God, listen to myself! This was exactly what she had hoped to avoid—her entire reason for staying away.

Four and a half years ago she'd come back, hoping Luke would give her a reason to return. And so help her, this time she wasn't going to leave town with a broken heart. This time, she hoped she could stay where she was meant to be all along.

CHAPTER 23

Luke set the phone down and closed his eyes. Grace was coming over tonight. She'd agreed to it. He glanced around the expansive living room, from the walls of windows looking over the mountains to the stone on the fireplace that soared to the vaulted ceilings.

Mark was right: he really hadn't changed anything in the past two years, and considering that Grace had been to this house dozens of times before, she would be sure to notice Helen's influence.

With a heavy heart, he grabbed a box out of the basement and did a round of the main rooms of the house, removing anything that was an obvious memento of his former life. There were no pictures from their marriage—he had taken those down right away, within days of Helen's passing.

He couldn't stand the sickening feeling every time he looked at them.

Instead, his house was filled with...well, girly things, as Mark would say. Frilly things. Things he saw in his sister's apartments, not Mark's. There were still throw pillows in a paisley print on the sofa and armchairs and throughout the master bedroom. Mark had called them floral, but whatever they were, they were not his style, and he set them into the box, along with bouquets of fake flowers, sweet-smelling candles, and hand soaps in various shades of purple. Lavender, Helen would have said.

When he had loaded two large boxes and sealed them shut, putting them away in a corner of the garage, he stood back and took a long look at his home. He had feared that taking away these items Helen had collected over their years together would make him feel like he had lost her all over again, make him feel empty and remind him that she was never coming back, but instead he felt a lightness in his chest that had been missing for so long, he barely recognized it.

Still, the rooms did look a little sparse, especially given their scale. Hands on hips, he surveyed the room. Cold, blank, and chilly. This wasn't a home he would want to visit, much less live in. Grimly, he considered his options. He hated Christmas. He really, really did. It was no longer a season of merriment and celebration—instead it was a painful reminder of what he no longer had.

Why, then, did he suddenly feel like that far corner of the living room could use a tree? A big, towering tree that skimmed the beams of the ceiling and glittered against the reflection of the arched window that encompassed the far wall.

He inhaled sharply as he glanced down at his watch. Grace would be here in a matter of hours. That gave him enough time if he hurried...

Without stopping to think about it further he grabbed his jacket and keys and darted out to the car.

● ● ●

The doorbell chimed at seven on the dot. Luke grinned to himself. When was Grace ever late? The answer to that was, of course, never. She didn't play games, and she lived her life with a focused intensity. He supposed that was one thing he could count on about her. She was a woman of integrity. He should have remembered that a long time ago, rather than letting his own self-preservation stand in the way.

"Hi there," she said, curving her lips into a shy smile.

He held the door open wide enough to let her pass. "Come on in," he said, even though he could have stared at her all night, just as she was, lit by the porch light, snow dusting her rich, chestnut locks, her cheeks rosy, her lips perfectly ripe.

"I hope you still like lasagna," he said, closing the door behind her and helping her out of her coat.

She threw him a glance. "You cooked? I figured we'd order a pizza or something."

"Believe it or not, I do cook. Though, admittedly, not often." He grinned. He knew how to cook all right, and he enjoyed it. But the truth was that it was depressing cooking for one, and whatever meals weren't consumed at Hastings or at his mother's or sisters' homes usually constituted something frozen and microwaveable.

"I'm impressed," she murmured.

"I was hoping you would be," he said, feeling more pleased than he wished to be. What was going on with him? He had known this girl since they were children, had dated her for a decade, had planned to marry her, have children with her! And now he was flirting with her as if this were their very first date.

Maybe it was, in a way. He wasn't quite sure how he felt about that. He wasn't used to feeling nervous around Grace. It made him feel vulnerable, and he didn't like feeling that way. Especially when he knew the pain she alone was capable of causing him.

"Wine?" he asked, as they entered the kitchen.

Grace nodded. "Thanks." She accepted a glass of Cabernet and took a small sip, glancing around the room.

Luke wondered what she thought of it all, if she noticed things that had changed since she'd last been here, if she was looking for signs of Helen, evidence of the life he had with another woman. He became aware of how strange it was to have her here, but so natural all at once.

Standing there in tight-fitting jeans that hugged her slim curves in all the right places and a black sweater so soft he had to fight the urge to reach out and graze her waist with his fingertips, she looked perfectly at home, at place. His stomach rolled when he thought of how right it felt to be with her here.

"The house looks nice," she said, pushing her hair back behind her shoulders.

"Thanks." He gestured to the living room. "Dinner won't be ready for a while. Want to have our wine in the living room?"

Grace nodded, following him through the kitchen and then halting as they rounded the hall. "I'm sorry. Is that—a Christmas tree?"

Was it ever. The Douglas fir stood next to the fireplace, a good twelve feet high, wrapped with twinkling white lights.

He turned to look at her, throwing her a grin. "I don't know how it got there."

Grace pursed her lips but he could see the glimmer in her bright green eyes. "I thought you wanted nothing to do with Christmas."

"I didn't bother with the ornaments," he pointed out, and then tossed up his hands. "What can I say? I had a change of heart."

She narrowed her eyes at him, her lips twisting. "Well, I have to admit that I, too, have lost the fight. Christmas has officially claimed me. I spent all morning decorating the store."

The store. His stomach knotted, and he could feel the smile fading from his face. He took a seat next to Grace on the soft leather couch and drank the smooth wine, letting it warm his throat. He had made great strides in the past day, and he felt like a new man for it. A better man, a free man. He was able to look back on his marriage to Helen with a smile, remember her laughter, and not be filled with shame and regret every time her face came to mind. He could live his life honoring her the right way, not holding on to some crippling need to live his life for her.

That's what he told himself, at least. And he believed it. But when it came to that store—Helen's dream—he couldn't bring himself to throw it away. Or give it away. Not yet.

"I ran into your mother today," Grace said, and Luke's pulse steadied with relief that they were off the subject of Main Street Books. She had hinted enough at her plans for him to be worried about her intentions for Helen's storefront next door.

"Was she nice to you?" he teased.

Grace slid him a rueful smile. "Of course. Though I admit I was a bit anxious about seeing her again."

"Why?"

Grace brushed at a nonexistent piece of lint on her pants. "Oh, you know … with everything."

Luke nodded and took a sip of his wine. It was still there, their past, like a cold, wet blanket. It would take some time before it thawed and warmed, but he wanted to see it through. He hoped she did, too.

"We have a lot of time to make up for," he said.

"Yes," she agreed with a sad chuckle.

When he glanced over at her, she was staring into the fireplace, the dancing flames painting a warm glow on her porcelain complexion. Her eyes looked flat and far away.

"Everything okay?" Doubt ate at him, leaving him with the twisting feeling of dread. Had she changed her mind about staying in town?

"I was just thinking of how things played out between us, the effects they had on everything else. I—I wish I had handled it differently. I wish that I had been able to come back here."

He swallowed the knot in his throat, refusing to feel any more guilt. She was a big girl, she had made her choice. Besides, she had been the one to leave him first. She had set all this in motion.

"If there is one thing I've learned in the past few days, it's that regret is the worst type of emotion." He met her eyes. "You can't change the past, Grace, and you have to tell yourself that everything that happened led us to this moment."

"This moment?" she repeated.

He held her gaze, managing a nod.

"You're right, I know." She gave a sad smile. "I miss

my father sometimes. I wish I could have seen him more often than his visits to New York. I wish...I'd never left."

Luke leaned over and tucked a strand of her hair back from her face, his fingertips tracing the smooth silk of her neck. Arousal burned deep inside him, and his pulse quickened. He reached over and took her wineglass from her hands, setting it on the coffee table. She stared into his eyes, expectation parting her mouth. He met her lips with his, their contact so light it was almost imperceptible, save the shiver that zipped down his spine at the sensation.

He grazed her mouth, slowly bringing her full lips to his. His hand came around her slim waist, his fingers warming at the softness of her sweater, itching to slide the material away and experience the even softer skin beneath.

She sighed into him and he parted her lips with his tongue, slowly lacing his tongue with hers and then pulling away to gaze into her eyes. The green of her irises shone in the firelight, the flames reflecting in the flecks of gold around her pupils. She lowered her eyes, smiling shyly, and her long, black lashes fluttered. He leaned in again as arousal burned deep and pressed her into his chest. He could feel every curve of her body as her ripe, firm breasts rose and fell with heavy breaths. He lowered his hand, caressing her waist, her hips, and then higher, to trace the contours of her breast and the swanlike arch of her neck. He kissed her lips, her neck, her ear, breathing deep into her skin, memorizing every taste of her skin, every touch.

The buzzing from the timer on the oven stirred his attention from her, and he groaned. He pulled away, throwing her a bashful grin. "We're being chaperoned."

Her lips were full and pink, and he brushed them with the back of his thumb, desperate to claim them with his mouth once more. Instead, he stood and crossed to the kitchen, his heart rate still elevated as she followed him into the room.

While the lasagna was cooling, he refilled their wineglasses and lifted his in a toast. Something he should have thought to do earlier, but desire had apparently gotten the better of him.

"To...moving forward," he said, clinking her glass with his.

She lowered her eyes, a smile playing at her lips before she brought the rim to her mouth. He watched as she tipped her head back, her glossy tendrils cascading over her shoulders, just like they had a hundred times before, so often he once took it for granted.

"I'm going to go freshen up before dinner," she said, taking a step backward. Her tone was laced with suggestion that knotted his groin. "Maybe you could find a little background music while I'm away."

He grinned and turned on the small radio he kept on the baker's rack near the table. He'd set two candles down in the center of the rustic pine plank, and he now drew a breath as he studied them.

Somehow it felt strange to light them, create an ambience for her, make this all...official. This was Grace after all, the girl he had seen without makeup countless times, the girl who wore sweatpants around him and with whom he had spent endless Friday nights on that very couch where he had just kissed her, sharing a pizza and watching a stupid movie. Now things felt formal. Although not in a bad way, he had to admit.

Five years had passed. He'd had a lot of experiences in that time, and he knew she had, too. In many ways, they were getting to know each other all over again.

He picked up the pack of matches sitting beside the candles and ran one over the rough black strip. By the time Grace reappeared in the alcove, the candles were lit and the bottle of wine was sitting in the middle of the table.

"I could get used to this," Grace murmured, coming around to pull out a chair.

"Then my plan's working," he said with a grin.

Grace tipped back another sip of her wine as he plated her a slice of steaming lasagna. Her expression had turned thoughtful, pensive—he knew that look.

"What is it?" he asked, his pulse skipping a beat.

"It's funny. That's all. I was so upset about the thought of having to see you when I came back to town—"

"Gee, thanks." But he knew what she meant. After all, he had felt the same way. "And now?"

"Now you've given me an extra reason to stay." A pink flush crept up her neck and landed on her cheeks. She took another sip of wine, and he bit back a smile.

"So you're really staying then?" he asked.

"I've got to do something with my life," she sighed, lifting her fork. "With my writing career going nowhere, I can't think of anything I'd rather do than run my dad's bookstore."

"Your writing career is not going nowhere," he said firmly.

She cocked an eyebrow and held his gaze. "Try telling my editor that." She forced a smile and he frowned.

"Maybe it's on hiatus. Maybe you're refueling your

creative energy. Maybe you need to try something different. Mix it up a bit."

She tipped her head. "Maybe. I...I have been feeling
a bit more relaxed, just being here. I don't feel the same
type of pressure to save my career, or turn it around."

"So, you're really going to focus on Main Street Books
then?" he asked, trying to remain calm as he thought of
Helen's empty storefront next door.

"It depends. I have a plan for it, but I first need to see
what evolves." After a pause, she said, "Only my sisters know the details, but I don't think I can keep it to
myself much longer. If I tell you, do you promise not to
tell anyone?"

"Of course."

She made a face. "Not your mother? Not Mark?"

Luke made a show of crossing his fingers over his
chest. "Cross my heart. Come on, Grace. You know you
can trust me."

It was the wrong thing to say. A heavy silence fell over
the room. Luke drew a deep breath and cut into his dinner.

After a beat, Grace said, "I mentioned that empty
storefront next to the shop."

Luke's heart felt like lead. "Yes?"

"I really shouldn't be telling you this. I don't want to
jinx it..." Her eyes were alive and dancing and Luke felt
the cold, icy wash of dread coat his stomach.

"Go on," he managed, his voice tight.

"Well, we have to first see about some details, but if we
could make it work, we would expand the bookshop and create an adjoining café." Perhaps noting his wide-eyed horror,
she elaborated, "It would be a second location for the Fireside Café. It wouldn't have the same name, of course, and it

would have a limited menu since we wouldn't be installing a kitchen, but it would be the same quality coffee and pastries." She grinned. "Secretly, I've been thinking that *The Annex* has a nice ring to it. Can't you see it, Luke? People could come in to browse, read, have a coffee. It wouldn't be a dusty old bookshop anymore, it would be a *destination*."

Oh, there she goes. The Grace he knew and loved so well. The Grace who latched onto a dream and followed it through. The Grace whose dreams he had tried to squander once. The Grace whose dreams he was about to crush all over again.

"Well, you could still turn the bookshop around without the café," he said mildly.

She frowned, disappointment shadowing her pretty face. "Oh. I don't know. Probably not. I mean, I really think it needs a little extra something."

"So what do you need to make all this happen?"

"Well, we first have to see if the space next door is even available, but I'm sure it is. Anna said it's been empty for years," she added, and he balled a fist in his lap. "Then it's really about negotiating a lease and financing the first year or two, especially with the initial renovation from the expansion. Anna's doing well, so I think she'd be willing to take the risk, and so would a bank, and I have a bit saved up that I'm happy to invest."

"And if the space next door isn't available?" He had to ask. He had to know.

She shrugged. "Well, then it would be up to me. Anna wouldn't be involved at that point and I'd be on my own. I'd have to choose between pouring everything I have— which isn't much—into saving the shop and seeing if it could turn a profit quickly, or . . ."

"Or going back to New York," he finished for her.

She nodded.

Luke set down his fork, his appetite lost. She was going to find out sooner or later, and it would be better coming from him. He dragged a hand through his hair and blew out a breath, staring at the table.

"Grace," he said. "I have something to tell you."

And you aren't going to like this one bit.

CHAPTER 24

Luke's face had turned ashen, and his blue eyes darkened to midnight. Grace felt her stomach knot with apprehension. She gripped her fork until her fingers cramped. He had something to tell her, and judging by his ominous tone and the shift in his gaze, it wasn't going to be good.

"If I didn't know better, I might think you were about to deliver some bad news," she said, forcing a nervous chuckle. She pressed her lips together when she saw the set to his jaw. "What is it you need to tell me, Luke? Is there some problem if I were to stay in Briar Creek?"

Luke took a sip of his wine. Stalling, buying time—whatever it was, it was becoming increasingly clear that whatever he had to tell her was hard for him. Panic quickened her pulse. Her chest heaved with each breath as she waited for him to finally deliver the blow.

"That empty storefront you want to lease," he said, and then paused.

She leaned forward. "Yes?"

He met her stare. "It's already leased."

Grace frowned and leaned back in her chair. A strange sense of relief washed over her. For a second there she had been worried he had something personal to tell her— a reason why they couldn't be together. This information, while disappointing, was something she could deal with, control. She might still be able to find a way to save her father's business, but if Luke changed his mind about her, she would really be left with nothing.

"That's strange. Anna said it's been empty for years." She picked up her fork and took another bite of food, contemplating the situation. "How do you know it's already leased?"

"It's been leased for two years," Luke replied.

"And empty?" Grace set down her fork. "That doesn't make any sense."

"Probably not," Luke muttered.

Grace pinched her lips and stared out the window at the falling snow. Well, if the person leasing it was letting it sit there empty, then they might be willing to let her sublease, or buy them out.

"Do you know who is leasing the space?"

Luke nodded. "Me."

Grace's eyes narrowed. "You?"

Luke lowered his gaze and Grace felt her heart drop into the pit of her stomach. What the hell was going on here?

"What for?" she asked.

"Helen had planned to open a shop there. A clothing store. She designed dresses, skirts, things like that."

Grace sighed, realizing that the subject of his deceased wife still stirred difficult feelings in him, even two years after her death. She stared at his face, lined with sadness, and looked down into her lap, feeling like a voyeur, watching him relive a memory she hadn't been a part of.

After a moment, she said, "So, she signed a long-term lease then?"

She chose her words delicately, not wanting to remind him of what he had lost, but selfishly needing some closure to the conversation. She hated to turn this dinner into a business transaction, and she didn't want to be callous and negotiate a sublease, but she needed that space in order to save Main Street Books.

To her surprise, Luke shook his head. "No. She signed an annual lease."

Confusion knit her brow. "Luke, I don't understand. Helen's been—" She stopped herself when she saw the force in his eyes.

"I've been renewing the lease," he said.

She gaped at him, the blood coursing through her veins. Helen had died two years ago. He had paid for the rent on that space all this time? She knew how much that kind of space went for—and it wasn't cheap. Not by Briar Creek standards, at least.

Luke slid back his chair and walked over to the sink, where he scrubbed at his plate. "I don't expect you to understand, Grace," he said, his back to her.

He was shutting down, pushing her away. Her heart began to twist, the familiar ache she had sworn she would never feel again threatened to break to the surface. Frantically, she searched for the right thing to say—something would make him face her again, come back to her. To the present. To the future. To *their* future.

"I understand what it's like to lose someone you love," she said slowly. She stared at the v-shaped span of his back, at the hard, chiseled curves of his shoulders that filled his camel sweater. "I know what it's like to want to hold on to something that you've lost."

She didn't know if she was speaking about him or her father, or both, but all she knew was that in this moment, she felt like she was on the verge of losing everything that had ever mattered to her. He knew how much her father's store had meant to her—it had triggered her love of books, inspired her to become a writer. Surely he wouldn't take that from her, not when it was all she had left of him.

Her breath caught in her chest when she realized this was exactly how Luke felt about the empty storefront next door. It was all he had left. Of Helen.

Grace closed her eyes, recognizing the magnitude of this moment, the hold the past still had on Luke. He wasn't ready to move on—not with her, not with anyone. He was still married to Helen in his heart, even if he thought their marriage and his feelings for her had ended long before she died.

"I should go," she said softly, pushing back her chair.

Luke had stopped scrubbing the plate but didn't move from his position. Instead he stood, hands gripping the counter edge on either side of him, head facing the window, his back firmly to her. The message couldn't have been clearer.

Say something to stop me, Luke, she silently begged as she inched her way toward the front hall. She paused in the doorway, to watch him, and wait. For a moment he opened his mouth, as if to say something, and her heart lurched with hope. *Give me the space*, she pleaded. *Show me you are ready to move forward.*

"I'm sorry, Grace," he said, and her chest heaved.

She stared at him for a long, silent moment. "Me too," she said bitterly, turning away.

Tears immediately sprang to her eyes, hot and blinding. She grabbed her coat, not bothering to put it on, and sprinted through the snow to her rental car. She turned the ignition with shaking hands, and then shifted her body to adjust the gears.

It was then that she saw him. Staring out the window at her, his face was lined, sad, his eyes hollow and dead. It was the face of a man who had lost everything. A man who had nothing left to live for.

Her hand froze on the gear stick. She could go in there, take him into her arms, and tell him how she felt, how she had cried a thousand tears for him.

Then she thought of what he had experienced during that time and her resolve strengthened. When she had lain in bed, crying into her pillow until the cotton sheet was soaked through, he had been sharing his life with another woman, building memories with her, laughing at her jokes, going out to dinner, climbing into bed beside her. Taking her hand. He hadn't come running for her when she needed him the most—and when he finally had . . . Well, it was too late, wasn't it?

Now he was a guilt-ridden man, crippled by the past, unable to move on.

And if his image taught her anything, it was that she couldn't live like that anymore. After five long years she was ready to move on, with or without him. He wouldn't hold her back any longer.

The bookstore was the only place she could be right now. Curled up in her favorite armchair, Grace stared out the window, looking past the cheerful decorations and onto the quiet street. Evenings were slow in downtown Briar Creek, and most storefronts closed by dinnertime. This was a town where families still ate together, gathered around big farm tables, sharing the events of their day.

Five years ago, she had shivered at the thought of spending her nights like this, but now she longed for it. She had almost lived the experience tonight, sitting with Luke at his kitchen table in front of the big bay window overlooking the snow-draped winter forest. Once again, their priorities weren't in line. Maybe they never would be.

And maybe that was all her fault. Maybe she was still paying the price for walking away all those years ago.

The street was lit by gas lamps, and from a shadow grew an image, appearing slowly in the frame of the large display window closest to her. Grace gasped as she stared at her mother's face, but if Kathleen had seen her, she made no show of it. Instead, her focus was centered on the porcelain village scene Grace had set up that morning.

Grace felt her stomach stir with unease. She didn't think her mother would be angry that she had snooped through the attic, but she couldn't be sure. If her mother was determined not to celebrate the holiday this year, there was a small chance she would find Grace's liberties insensitive. It was the last thing Grace wanted her to think.

Pulling herself up from the chair, Grace stood and hesitantly smiled at her mother.

Startled, Kathleen's eyes widened in surprise. Gingerly, she reached for the handle of the door and let herself inside.

"Hi, Mom," Grace said, her tone sounding guilty even to her own ears.

"Grace." Kathleen's voice was laced with astonishment. Her eyes swept the room, finally finding their way back to Grace. She blinked. "What is all this?"

Grace shifted the weight on her feet and shrugged. "I borrowed some of your decorations," she said, fingering the garland that swagged from the counter.

"I can see that!" Kathleen said, but her voice was filled with wonder, not hurt. "I meant the store. What is going on here? Why is it decorated?"

Grace swallowed, feeling her cheeks flush with heat. She couldn't stand here and lie to her mother's face, even if the truth might only set her up for more disappointment. Right now, she had to accept the fact that the expansion was not going to happen, and the reality was that the shop wouldn't survive as it now stood. She'd seen the account books. Her father had held on to the store because it meant the world to him. But in recent years, sales had plummeted. It needed more than a good dusting to survive another year. As much as Grace hated to admit it, she couldn't sink what was left of her savings into a lost cause.

"I was just sprucing the place up a bit." Grace shrugged. "I wasn't ready to let go of it yet."

Kathleen's face was pale, her eyes flashing and alert. She put a hand to her heart, shaking her head. "Your father would never let me in here to decorate," she said. "It's never looked better, Grace. The decorations. The windows. It looks so organized. So fresh! Did you do all this yourself?"

Grace nodded. "I've been working on it for the past two days."

"All this in two days!" Kathleen grinned ruefully. "And here I thought you'd snuck off to town to meet Luke."

"You weren't entirely wrong," Grace admitted. "I have been seeing a bit of him lately. I saw him again tonight, actually."

Kathleen arched an eyebrow. "How did that go?"

Grace tossed up her hands, her heart feeling heavy. "Luke and I have a lot of issues. Maybe we're just not meant to be."

Kathleen clucked her tongue. "Nonsense. You're a headstrong girl, Grace, and I've always admired that in you, even when I didn't tell you."

Grace blinked. Was this really how her mother felt? She . . . admired her?

"No, you never did tell me that, Mom."

"I should have told you more often, I know that now. Your father was so encouraging that I felt like I had no choice but to balance you out." She sighed. "He was always lifting you up, telling you to reach for the stars, and I suppose I was sitting there worried what would happen if you never grasped one."

"Is that why you never asked me much about my life in New York?" Grace asked, recalling the twinge of hurt she would feel whenever she called home in those early months, the emptiness she would feel when she hung up the phone. It stung her that her mother never asked about her apartment, her friends, her writing. When Grace offered, Kathleen would mutter something generic and change the topic. It didn't go unnoticed.

"I did," Kathleen insisted, frowning.

Grace shook her head, forcing a half smile to show it was ancient history, even though the hurt was still fresh. "Not really."

After a pause her mother said, "I'm sorry if you felt

that way, Grace. I knew that you had given this all up to go live in some one-room apartment above a convenience store or something. I was worried sick! I couldn't even think about it, so I guess I chose not to ask too many questions."

"It wasn't a convenience store," Grace corrected. "My first apartment was above a liquor store."

Alarm flashed in Kathleen's green eyes and she held a hand over her mouth, laughing. "See?" she cried. "This is what I'm talking about!"

Grace was laughing now too, thinking back on the experience. She really had come far, even if she had only made it full circle in the end. "It's a good thing you never visited that first apartment," she admitted. "You would have probably fainted."

"Oh, I know I would have!" Kathleen chuckled. "Still, we should have visited more. I never even met Derek..."

"It was my fault. I was busy. Preoccupied. If I had known then..." A hard lump wedged in her throat. No one could have predicted the heart attack that took her father. She knew it, but she still couldn't shake the guilt. The last time she had seen her father was nearly a year before his sudden death. "I wish I had come back sooner."

"He knew he was never far from your thoughts."

Grace walked over and wrapped her arms around her mother. The chill was still stuck to her coat, and when she breathed, she caught a whiff of fresh snow on the cool collar.

"You and I are more alike than we know, Mom," she said, pulling back.

"That's what your father used to say," Kathleen smiled, but there was a sadness in her eyes.

"I know," Grace said softly. "He used to tell me the same thing."

"I suppose that determination is a good quality. Only you would take on an endeavor like this old shop."

"Well, I love it. I'd do anything to keep it going."

Kathleen's eyes were sharp when she met her gaze. "What's that supposed to mean?"

Grace's pulse skipped a beat. "Just wishful thinking," she said.

"I haven't been in much of a Christmas spirit this year," Kathleen admitted.

"You have your reasons. Though I think everyone in town misses your gorgeous decorations."

Kathleen's lips twisted in pleasure. "I did waver a bit when I saw the judging panel for this year's contest."

"No one has a better eye than you," Grace agreed. "Is it too late to judge this year then?"

Kathleen nodded. "But..." she trailed off, tutting as she shook her head. "Silly."

"What?"

Kathleen wouldn't meet her eye. "It's not too late to enter. The judging is Christmas Eve, if you recall."

Oh, she recalled all right! She could remember how nearly every Christmas Eve of her youth was spent sitting in the living room, she and her sisters wearing identical holiday dresses, her mother perched on the edge of the armchair, barely breathing as she watched the judging panel drive slowly up to the house. When Grace was very little, she used to think her mother was waiting for Santa, but she soon realized that to her mother, the judging panel was Santa.

Later, Grace had claimed to be relieved when her

mother took on the role of judge, and the family was spared the palpable nervous energy Kathleen would exude until the phone inevitably rang in triumph, but deep down she missed the excitement. The thrill of waiting for the phone to ring, the camaraderie and the celebration.

"Are you thinking of entering?" she asked carefully.

"What? Oh, no. No...It's silly, really. Just..." Kathleen darted her eyes around the room, lingering on the teddy bear North Pole arrangement in the children's corner. "Well, there wouldn't be time, anyway. And really, what's the point in entering if you aren't going to win?"

Grace grinned. "Aha! I knew you still had it in you!"

"Grace!" Her mother looked panicked, stricken, as Grace grabbed her coat and bag.

"We have a lot of work to do, Mom."

"You mean you're going to help?" Kathleen's eyes danced with excitement, but she clasped her hands nervously, searching Grace's face.

"Of course." Grace made for the door, but Kathleen stopped her.

"Wait. Grace." Kathleen heaved a sigh, her expression collapsing. "Do you think...do you think your father would mind us doing this?"

Grace stared at her mother quizzically. "Mind?"

"It doesn't feel right to celebrate when he isn't here with us." Her voice broke on the end of her sentence and she drew a shaky breath. Her eyes were wet when she met Grace's once more. "So do you think...he would mind?"

Grace swallowed hard, willing herself not to cry. She reached out and took her mother's hand, giving it a tight squeeze. "I don't think anything would make him happier,

Mom," she said. "Now come on. This time Wednesday night, everyone is going to know that the Christmas Queen of Briar Creek is back in business."

"They'd better watch out!" Kathleen giggled.

"They don't stand a chance," Grace said through a grin. And as she and her mother stepped out in the quiet street, she felt a chill that had nothing to do with the wind whipping down the block.

CHAPTER
25

I can't get over that jerk," Anna hissed, after Grace finished telling her about the way things had ended with Luke the night before. She swiped her dust rag furiously over the last bookcase. "And here I actually thought you two might find a way back together."

Grace paused from the holiday selection display she was creating on the circular table near the center of the shop. Wouldn't that have been nice? She and Luke, together again . . . She sucked in a breath and squared her shoulders, focusing on arranging the books in neat stacks. There wasn't time to think about this nonsense right now. Luke had cost her too much already. She owed it to herself and her family to keep it together now.

"I think we're nearly ready," she announced, turning swiftly to glance over the room.

"It looks great," Anna said, following her gaze. From the festive window scenes to the twinkling lights that framed every doorway and window, to the welcoming bowls overflowing with candy canes and chocolates, it certainly was the best effort they could make under the circumstances.

"I'll put on some music," Grace suggested. The truth was that she was stalling, even if it was only for a minute. This was it—their last chance to save the store. Without the possibility of expanding, and with the lease expiring in a little more than a week, everything was now riding on this day, and the few more remaining.

"I'm a little nervous, Grace," Anna admitted, coming up behind her.

Grace looked up from the pile of CDs stacked behind her father's old desk. "Me too, but I'm glad you're here with me. It helps, not feeling like I'm the only one who wants to hold on to it."

Anna gave a small smile. "I gave you a hard time before, and I'm sorry about that. It's been hard, Grace."

Grace nodded. "I know." She set the disc in the stereo and pressed PLAY. Soon the soft sound of Christmas music filled the shop. "Now or never," she said to Anna, and the girls clasped each other's hands and ran over to the front door, each taking one side of the heavy sign they had garnished with tinsel and carefully dragging it down the front steps to the snow-covered street below.

Open! Main Street Books needed a second chance, and this was their way of giving it one. One last effort to see it through, to raise the funds to turn it around, to remind people of why it should be kept alive.

Now there was nothing else to do but wait. Wait for someone to come into the store and turn it all around for them.

Grace stared down the empty sidewalk. "You don't think this is a bad idea, do you?" She popped a peppermint in her mouth. Anxiety was leaving her queasy.

Anna rubbed her arms. "It might not work, I guess. I hope it does. And not because this store meant so much to Dad but because—" She paused. "Because I'd really like you to have a reason to stay."

Grace didn't want to think about that right now. She'd thought too much of staying, decided she might be able to build a life here, and then last night had sent her reeling in confusion all over again.

She shivered. "Come on. We'll catch colds standing out here without our coats."

Inside, the girls perched themselves behind the counter, staring silently at the door. After a good amount of time had passed, Grace fought back a sigh and announced, "I'll go make some fresh coffee."

She ducked into the back room and went through the task. If she didn't keep moving forward, she was in danger of sliding into the past. And she didn't want to think about the past anymore. Not any part of it.

When the pot was filled, she poured them each a mug and carried it into the storefront, halting in surprise when she heard Anna conversing with someone. A customer! Carefully, she set the mugs on the counter and wove her way through the stacks, feeling more hopeful already. If one person had already decided to stop in, surely more would follow. Books were a great gift for Christmas, after all, and maybe now that the shop had been closed for a few months, people would realize how much they had come to miss it.

Her face fell, however, when she noticed the person her sister was speaking to was only Ivy.

"Oh. Ivy." She tried to mask the disappointment in her tone. Of course her friend would be here to support her. The problem was they needed more than friends and family to help them now. "It's so nice of you to come in," she tried again, feeling the truth in her words. If only everyone who was supposed to have cared about her made the same effort.

She gritted her teeth as an image of Luke swam to the front of her mind.

"You mentioned you were hoping to try to save the store," Ivy said. "I didn't realize you were going to follow through."

Grace gave a modest shrug. After all, it was a modest effort. "Well, we're trying."

"It's wonderful!" Ivy gushed. "Honestly, I was just telling Anna how great the place looks!"

Grace couldn't help but smile. "Well, thanks. That means a lot. As does your support."

"So you're open then?"

"Not exactly." Grace hesitated. "We had hoped to expand, but that plan was thwarted."

Ivy turned in confusion to Anna, who explained, "We wanted to expand into the space next door, with a bookstore and café, but it seems that someone else has the lease on that store and isn't willing to relinquish it."

Ivy nodded slowly. "Luke," she said, her eyes flashing on Grace.

Grace straightened in surprise. "You knew?"

"I'm sorry, Grace," Ivy said softly. "I remember a few people mentioning that Helen had plans to open a boutique."

Silence fell over the room as the women took in the information. "Well, what's done is done. On to plan B."

"And a wonderful plan it is!" Ivy enthused. "In fact, I plan to buy all that I can carry. How much do I have here? Ten, eleven. I'll get a few more."

Grace laughed. "Ivy, it's fine. You've done enough." She didn't have the heart to tell her friend that it would take a lot more than ten or fifteen book sales to save the store. More like a few hundred. A few thousand.

This was really pointless.

While Anna guided Ivy to their children's book section, Grace walked over to the door and stared through the glass, out onto the sidewalk. Crowds of shoppers clutching shopping bags barely even looked through the windows or stopped to notice the sign. They'd given up on the bookstore. Maybe she should too. She didn't know why she had thought this could work. Her family had been right. Hell, the account books had been right. People had stopped shopping at Main Street Books a long time ago. It couldn't survive without a total transformation.

"No one's going to come in," Grace said, stepping back behind the counter. "People buy their books online now."

"Oh, don't say that!" Ivy said. She started placing stacks of books on the counter. Grace eyed them warily; it didn't feel right to take money from her friend, even if Ivy wanted to offer it. "After I pay for these, I'll go and tell everyone I know to come over."

"Even then, they wouldn't be back tomorrow. Or the day after. We need people shopping here every day. Every single day." She shook her head. "It's just not possible."

"They would have," Anna said. She started ringing up the items and placing them in paper bags. "If we could have turned this place into the type of establishment you described, with the café and the energy, they would have come. I know it. The moment you described it, I knew."

Grace looked at her sister. "Thanks, Anna."

"Well, every little bit helps," Ivy said, collecting her heaving shopping bags. "I'll go find a handsome gentlemen to carry these for me and let him know all about this fabulous sale you're having at the new and improved Main Street Books!"

Grace watched as Ivy struggled through the front door, barely managing an awkward wave goodbye. *New and improved* was a stretch. A little tinsel didn't go as far as she had hoped.

The sisters finished the entire pot of coffee and then started another. Grace knew Anna well enough to know they were both sharing the same thought. Each was wondering when they could admit defeat. When they could speak up and voice their opinion.

Grace decided it was her place to put an end to this.

"Oh, for God's sake," she heard Anna hiss. "It's Mark. Please don't tell me he's coming in here."

Graced perked up. She rather hoped he would. Mark was always up for a good time, and he had a knack for lifting her mood. The same couldn't be said for Anna, however. They hadn't gotten along since they were kids.

"Oh, come on, he's not so bad," she said, watching as his figure grew close.

"He's..." Anna trailed off. "I don't feel like dealing with him right now."

"Then let me," Grace said, plastering a genuine smile on her face as the bell above the door jingled and Mark poked his head around the door.

"Am I allowed to enter?" He grinned, and Grace felt her smile widen.

"Of course," she said. "So long as you're a genuine customer, that is."

"I seem to remember giving you pancakes on the house the other morning," he bantered, stomping the snow off his boots.

"Fair enough." She handed him a candy cane. "On the house."

"Thanks." His eyes shifted to Anna, his smile faltering slightly. "So," he said, giving Grace his full attention. "How's the sale going? Ivy came into the diner and told us all about it."

Grace frowned. Ivy had left the store nearly two hours ago. "No one else stopped by."

Mark looked momentarily panicked, realizing the impact of her words. "Oh. Oh, Grace. I'm sorry. I know how much this place means to you."

"And did you know?" Anna accused. "Did you know about Grace's plan to expand, about the way we had planned to save the shop?"

Grace fell silent. It was the most she'd heard Anna say to Mark in . . . years. Something had turned between them in culinary school. No one knew what happened, and neither Anna nor Mark was offering to tell.

Mark looked from one sister to the next, and then to the door. Despite her fury, Grace bit on her lip. He hadn't changed one bit. When he was faced with something serious, Mark fled. He ran from relationships, from houses, everything. But unlike her, he'd never run from Briar Creek. She'd give him that.

"And did you know," Anna pressed, "about Luke's attachment to the storefront next door?"

Mark's jaw flinched. "So he told you, then?" he asked

softly, and Grace nodded. He tossed up his hands, shaking his head. "For what it's worth, I've been telling him to let it go. I'm on your side here."

Grace shifted her gaze to Anna, who was staring stonily at Mark. "Do you think he'll change his mind?" Grace asked.

Mark shrugged. "I hope so, Grace. I wish I could tell you he would. But…" He stopped talking. There was nothing more to say.

"Well, you don't need to worry about buying anything," she said. "We'll be wrapping up here soon and the inventory will be donated to the Forest Ridge Hospital."

"It's really sad it's come to this," Mark said. He looked around the room, frowning. "You really did a nice job with the decorations."

"Well, it wasn't enough." As if it could have been. As if Christmas decorations alone could change the situation.

"At least let me buy a book."

"No," Grace said, her heart beginning to feel heavy. "Really, don't worry about it. Just give me a free cup of coffee next time I come into the diner."

Mark grinned. "Always." He edged back to the door. "There's still time, you know. Anything is possible."

"I'd rather not get my hopes up," Grace replied flatly.

"I get it." Mark paused. "Well, bye, Grace. Anna," he said, with a curt nod.

Grace turned around and leaned on the counter, hearing the door close. She stared at her sister, whose expression was the picture of displeasure. And disappointment.

"I feel a little sick," she admitted.

Anna nodded. "Me too. I mean, I run a business. I know how this works. I saw how the bookstore went downhill in the past few years. Somehow I still hoped something amazing would happen today."

After a pause Grace said, "I should probably get home and let you get back to the café."

"I suppose so," Anna said.

They walked around the room, collecting the candy dishes, and then worked together once more to haul the sign back into the storage room.

"Well, we tried," Grace said, as she flicked off the last of the lights and the room grew dim.

"Maybe Mark was right," Anna offered, but Grace knew she was only being kind. Anna never thought Mark was right about anything. "It's not over yet. Anything is possible."

Grace forced a smile. Maybe her sister needed to believe it, even if she didn't.

CHAPTER 26

Jane still couldn't believe it.

She had thought her mother's voice sounded strange when she called that morning and asked if Sophie could come over for a few hours to help with some stuff around the house, but sitting here now, in the driveway of her childhood home, she felt like she was a kid all over again. For a split second, all her troubles were gone, the pain of the past nine months had vanished. The magic of Christmas had appeared.

She hadn't thought it possible.

Still in shock, Jane climbed out of the car and quickly unfastened Sophie from her car seat. Hand in hand, they followed the cobblestone path to the front porch, which was wrapped in a fresh pine garland and holly berries. Matching wreaths hung from every window and door by a neat red velvet ribbon and from the corner of her eye, Jane spotted a ladder propped against the side of the old Victorian house.

Surely her mother hadn't climbed that herself! In this weather?

Jane narrowed her eyes. Grace. This must have been

Grace's doing—she'd seen what her sister had done to the store. She could only hope she hadn't pushed her mother too hard into this. If the woman needed to wallow, let her. Jane would love nothing more than to do the same.

The door opened before she could knock and Jane took a step back at the sight of her mother. Her shoulder-length hair was pulled up in a messy ponytail, dust was on her face and clothes, and she hadn't looked this happy since before Jane's father had died.

"Mom?"

"Well don't just stand there gaping," Kathleen ordered. "You're letting in the cold air!"

Jane pushed Sophie into the front hall and swept her eyes up the ornately decorated banister. The sound of Christmas music was coming from somewhere, and was that gingerbread she smelled?

Jane darted her gaze back to her mother. "Are you... *baking?*"

Kathleen nodded with excitement. "Gingerbread."

Jane stared at her mother, unable to blink. "For..."

"For the contest! Since I can't judge, I'm entering this year." Kathleen beamed.

Jane was bewildered. She looked around, noticing the stacks of boxes and decorations covering the entire surface of the dining room table. Turning back to her mother, she said, "But, you haven't entered that in years."

Kathleen shrugged. "So? No time like now to reclaim the throne."

Reclaim the throne? What the heck was going on here?

"Mom, are you feeling all right?" She glanced at Sophie, who had wandered off to play with a Santa figurine. One of many.

"Of course, I'm feeling all right!" Kathleen insisted, her face creasing with confusion.

Jane lowered her tone. "You're worrying me."

"Worrying you?" Kathleen laughed. "Jane, this is the best I've felt in a long time. Honestly."

Jane gave a tentative smile. She had to admit it had been a long time since she'd seen this side of her mother— her heart wrenched when she realized how much she'd missed her.

"What changed things?" she asked.

"I saw what Grace did to the store," Kathleen said, taking her coat.

"You did?" She wondered what else her mother knew about Grace's plans for the store, but she chewed her lip, not wanting to complicate matters.

"It's exquisite," Kathleen said. "It made me realize how much I've missed being surrounded by the spirit of Christmas. I was afraid it would make me miss your father more, but getting the house ready, seeing it come to life, brings back a lot of happy memories."

Jane smiled. "You don't know how good that is to hear, Mom."

Turning to Sophie, Kathleen said, "Want to help me build the gingerbread house, Sophie? You loved doing it last year, and this year we have some showing off to do!"

"Yeah!" Sophie cried, skipping into the hall, her pig-tails flying.

Jane frowned. "Oh, Mom. If you're entering the contest—"

Kathleen winked. "Sophie will be bringing *her* gingerbread house home with her tonight, isn't that right, sweetheart?" She grinned, triumphantly. "Whereas mine will become part of my gingerbread Christmas village window display. Can't you picture it, Jane?" she mused, wandering over to the bay window in the front of the house. "I'm going to set up a table right here, and instead of the porcelain village, I'll have gingerbread. That's my theme this year, you see. It was the jigsaw trim on the porch that inspired me. I don't know why I hadn't thought of it before, but as soon as the idea came to me, I knew I had to run with it!"

Jane pressed her lips together to keep her laughter from sputtering, but tears of joy sprang from her eyes instead. Her mother was back to her usual antics, already rambling about her plans, and Jane couldn't have asked for anything more in that moment.

Well, almost anything.

"Is Grace at the store, then?"

"She's upstairs, actually," came Kathleen's unexpected reply. "She came home about an hour ago."

Jane felt her brow furrow. "Oh, well. I might go say hello then."

"Yes, yes, but afterwards, if you aren't busy, I'd love your help with the decorations."

Jane stared at her mother for a long time, still in disbelief over the sudden transformation. "I can't think of a better way to spend the rest of my day," she said, and then sprinted up the stairs, careful not to disturb the garland that was so perfectly wrapped along the cherrywood banister.

The upstairs of the house showed pending signs of a Christmas makeover, too, Jane noted as she tapped on Grace's door. At least fifteen boxes had been popped open, their glittering contents on full display. "It's me," she said, trying the handle.

Grace was sitting on the floor, rifling through a box of ornaments, when Jane entered. She smiled when she looked up. "Hi."

"I thought you'd be at the store," Jane confessed.

"I was." Grace sighed. "I don't feel like talking about it." She shrugged and turned back to the ornaments, setting a few to her left and the rest to her right. It was then that Jane noticed the piles were being arranged by color. She didn't know whether to roll her eyes or laugh in delight.

"She put you to work then," Jane observed, crouching down to join her sister. She picked up a handful of small ornaments and began sorting them. "I can cover for you, if you want. If you need to get back to the shop."

"No. It was a stupid idea, really."

"Stupid idea?" Jane repeated, startled. "I thought it sounded brilliant, Grace! Even Mom was thrilled with the transformation. Think of what everyone else will say."

Grace shook her head and pulled out another handful of ornaments. "It doesn't matter. It isn't going to happen."

Jane felt her heart sink. She hadn't even realized until that moment how much she wanted Grace's endeavor to work. Not only for the shop, but also so that Grace wouldn't leave again.

"Do you want to tell me about it?" she asked.

"Not really," Grace replied.

They lapsed into silence, quietly sorting through the box of ornaments. Jane marveled that they had been so poorly stored to begin with, until she noticed the date on the box, and realized these hadn't been brought out in a while. Always one to keep things fresh, Kathleen scoffed at using the same Christmas decorations each year. Grace or Anna had probably stuffed all these into the box one year when Kathleen had asked for their help.

Jane eyed her eldest sister. Her mouth was a thin line, her brow narrowed in concentration on the task at hand. A curtain of silky chestnut brown hair fell in front of her face, and she didn't bother pushing it away as she scrutinized the objects in her hands.

"Well, I have something to talk about today," Jane finally said, breaking the silence. The moment the sentence was out, she wished she could take it back. Somehow the proclamation felt formal and prepared. Like it was another person speaking, another person's life. It still didn't feel real, but maybe it would when she finally said it out loud. "Adam and I are getting a divorce."

Grace snapped her attention to Jane. "*What*?"

Jane let out a breath she hadn't even realized she had been holding, and then promptly burst into tears. She covered her eyes with her hands, feeling the weight of her grief with each sob that racked her body.

The comfort of Grace's arms enveloping her only made her cry harder, and she wept into her sister's hair until she had no more tears left to cry. Depleted and weary, she pulled back, brushing at her swollen face with the back of her hand.

"Sorry," she blubbered, forcing a smile.

"You have nothing to be sorry about," Grace said gently. "I'm the one who should say sorry. I had no idea it was this bad."

Jane swallowed the last of her tears. "I didn't want to make things worse. Christmas was hard enough this year, and then with Sophie to think about, too...I tried to put on a brave face."

Grace gave her a sad smile. "You were always the strong one, Jane. Always thinking of others. So loyal."

Jane let out a bitter laugh. She sniffed, wiping her nose with the tissue Grace handed her. "Loyal to a fault."

Her blood stirred when she thought of Adam, who probably hadn't shed a single tear over the demise of their marriage, their family. He had simply faded away instead—found happiness and security with another woman, and then... poof! On he went with life. How perfectly easy for him. *Bastard.*

"What's that supposed to mean?" Grace asked.

"Adam's been having an affair." Just saying the words lifted ten pounds from her heavy heart. "He's a cheating sneak," she said, trying again. Her chest heaved and then lifted. She smiled. "He's a lying jerk."

She grinned. She hadn't felt this great in months.

Grace looked puzzled. Horrified, really. "What the hell are you smiling about, then?"

Jane shrugged, unable to temper her relief. "I have been holding this inside for months, trying to fight through and pretend my life wasn't crashing down around me. I have sat there and tried to cling to the good in that man for the sake of holding this family together, and now I don't have to. Adam is a lying, cheating bastard. And now that I have nothing left to fight for, I can finally admit it to myself. And it feels great!"

Grace stared at her. "I can't believe this."

Sobering, Jane admitted, "I can't believe it either, actually."

And she couldn't, not really. Adam had been absent from her life for so long that she had gotten used to not having that close bond with him anymore, of not sharing a bed, or even a meal, for that matter. Still, divorce entailed something bigger, and she wasn't sure she was ready for it yet.

"Are you going to be okay?" Grace asked slowly, and Jane knew what she meant.

"The truth is, I don't know," she said, feeling her chest seize up the way it always did when she thought about her future. "I gave up everything to marry Adam. I have no degree. I'm not qualified to do anything." She'd been a wife since she was nineteen, a mother since she was twenty-one. It was all she knew.

She sucked in a breath as her mind began to race. She couldn't panic—when she panicked, she became depressed, and she couldn't afford to feel that way. It wouldn't help her. Or her daughter.

"What about teaching ballet?" Grace suggested.

Jane felt her face color. "Oh, that," she said, trying to brush away the idea. Rosemary Hastings had been asking her to help out at the studio for years, and Jane had always found a reason to shut her down. It was tempting, but when Sophie was younger it wasn't really an option. And besides, there was Grace to consider.

"I saw her the other day and she mentioned something to me," Grace continued, searching her face. "She's asked you to work there before?"

Jane shrugged. She fumbled with the ornaments in her hand. "It didn't feel right," Jane said and then quickly added, "and I wasn't looking for a job then."

"Well, you are now!" Grace said. "And why wouldn't it feel right? You love ballet. You were the best dancer in town! And you were always Rosemary's pet."

Jane smiled. It was true. "It didn't feel right because

of Luke. Because it wasn't fair to you." There, she had said it.

Grace looked like she had been slapped across the face. "You are right, Jane," she said. "You are loyal to a fault."

"So you think I should call Rosemary?" Jane asked quietly.

"Yes," Grace said. "And if you don't, I will."

Jane felt her chest swell with relief. It wouldn't be a lot of money, but it was something. She chewed at her lip, imagining what it would be like to get back in the studio, to pass on everything she had learned. A little shiver zipped down her spine at the thought. She'd always regretted not having a career or something of her own, and she'd learned to temper that empty place in her heart when she thought of everything she was doing for her family instead. Now, she was being given an opportunity to live up to her accomplishments, follow her dreams.

Maybe it would all be okay, after all.

Something else was weighing on her mind now. "Are you going to move back to New York, then?"

Grace shrugged. "I don't know. I don't want to, but I don't really know what I want to do. Or where I really belong."

"You really don't think the bookstore can be saved?" Jane pressed. "I do."

Grace shook her head firmly. "It isn't going to work." She tossed a miniature green knit stocking into a pile. "Maybe it's a sign that I need to go back. That my life isn't here."

"Is this because of Luke or the store?"

"Both," Grace sighed. "Without the store, I don't really know what I could do here."

"What about your writing?" she asked, but Grace shook her head forcefully, and Jane knew better than to push the topic.

"It turns out," Grace suddenly said, her voice shrill with emotion, "that Luke has been leasing the empty storefront next to Main Street Books."

Jane stopped sorting the ornaments. "What? Why?"

Grace met her eyes. "For Helen."

Jane frowned, trying to make sense of this information. "But Helen..."

Grace hastily tossed the ornaments into their piles, accidentally tossing a green elf into the red pile. Without a word, Jane shifted it to its proper place. "Apparently Helen had leased that store for a boutique before she died."

"Wow." Jane tried to digest this information. She had not known Helen except in passing; she never could have known this. "He's having a hard time letting go," she surmised.

Grace nodded. "There's no room in his life for me. But then, maybe there never was."

Knowing she couldn't hold her opinion in much longer, Jane carefully said, "I think that's probably how he felt about you for a long time."

"Maybe I should have stayed with Derek," Grace mused. She gave a weak smile, but Jane didn't feel amused.

"You said that Derek couldn't give you the things you wanted. If that's true, then it wouldn't have lasted."

"I know." Grace shrugged. "As much as it hurts, being alone is better than being with the wrong person. At least then there's the hope of finding what you're looking for."

"Then maybe there's still hope for me," Jane said.

"Of course there is!" Grace shook her head. "You know, it's funny, because even now, with everything you've been through, I still think you've got a great life."

"Me?" Jane burst out laughing. "Oh, please, Grace. You don't need to try to cheer me up. I'm fully aware of how pathetic I am."

Grace frowned. "No, I mean it. You knew what you wanted early in life, Jane. I didn't."

"You always knew you wanted to be a writer. And look at you! A best-selling author!"

Grace stopped her. "I mean in my personal life. I was so focused on my career that I didn't think about everything else I wanted from my life, not really. And now... what's left?"

"Oh, Grace. I had no idea it was this bad."

"I know in my heart it was right to break up with Derek, but sometimes I wonder if I'll ever find a guy who makes me feel the way—"

"The way Luke does?"

Grace nodded. "Ridiculous, isn't it?"

"No," Jane said. "Lately I wonder if I'll ever find someone who made me feel the way Adam used to. Before he changed."

After a long silence, Grace said, "I still can't get over Adam. He loved you, Jane. I know he did. How could he do this to you?"

Jane shrugged. She had asked herself these questions a hundred times, and she still couldn't make any sense of it. "All this time, I've wondered what I could have done differently, and the truth is that yes, Adam strayed, but maybe a part of me let him do it. I'm not saying he's off the hook, but somewhere through all this, we both stopped trying. And now it's over."

"Oh, Jane. I'm so sorry."

"It is what it is," Jane said with a shrug to mask her pain. "I've tried to deny it. Now I have to find a way to move on with my life." She couldn't bring herself to think of the hardest part: sharing Sophie.

She closed her eyes, reminding herself that it would be better this way. She wouldn't be in knots all the time, she wouldn't be half present, only there in a physical sense with her mind wandering, worrying. She would have quality time with her daughter, and she would always be Sophie's mother.

That was one thing Adam could never take from her.

"Are you sure you're okay, Jane?"

Jane forced a half smile. "No. But I will be. I have to be."

"You gave up a lot to be with Adam," Grace said.

"Yes, but it didn't feel that way then. Only now. Now that it's over." She looked down at her hands. She was still wearing her wedding ring. She had tried taking it off that morning, but her finger felt bare. She'd kept rubbing her thumb over the spot where it used to be.

She drew a deep breath, releasing it slowly. One day at a time.

"So you really don't think you and Luke will find a way back to each other?" she asked, ready to turn the conversation back to Grace.

Grace pulled a disappointed face. "No. I don't think so."

"And you'd be okay with that?" When Grace didn't answer, she pressed, "The one thing I've learned in life is that you can get through a lot—painful, horrible things you never thought you could—but it's the regret that's hardest to move past."

Grace nodded softly. "Do you have regrets? About you and Adam?"

Jane considered the question. Finally, she said, "Yes and no. I did the best I could, even if I could have done things differently." She paused, thinking of Adam's lies, the way her heart had dropped to the pit of her stomach when she realized what he was up to that day when she'd stopped by his office unannounced and seen him with that woman, laughing as they strode down the street, his hand casually draped on the small of her back. She had started trembling so hard she had to sit in the car for forty-five minutes before she trusted herself to drive home. "I think my biggest regret is holding on to something that I had already lost."

"So what are you going to do now?"

"Move on." She shrugged. "How about you?"

Grace gave a coy smile. "I don't know. But you've given me a lot to think about."

"What are sisters for?" Jane grinned. She leaned in and gave Grace a hug. And for the first time in a long time, she felt hopeful again.

CHAPTER 27

It was evening by the time Jane and Sophie left. The house had undergone a transformation in a matter of hours, and Grace could hear the faint sounds of her mother humming Christmas carols as she finished wrapping lights around the tree branches in the front yard.

Behind them, the old Victorian farmhouse looked like a life-sized dollhouse, decked out for the holiday. The pitched roof was covered in a thick blanket of snow, the beaded spindles of the front porch were generously wrapped in fresh garland, and a candle lit each window. In the bay window, Grace could see the gingerbread village Kathleen had arranged in a winter scene.

The wind was sharp, but Kathleen didn't seem to mind. Her attention was rapt, and she barely heard Grace when she called out.

Grace sighed, trying again. Raising her voice, she shouted across the lawn, "I'm out of lights!"

With a disoriented frown, Kathleen turned, her expression lifting when she noticed Grace's progress. "Sure, honey. Go warm up. I'll be in soon."

Stomping the bulk of the snow off her boots before she went inside, Grace inhaled the deep, warm aroma of gingerbread and spice cake as she closed the door behind her. It had been a long day—a busy one—and while she was tired to the bone, she was grateful for it. It had been just like old times. Grace had been so busy she hadn't even stopped to really think about Luke. Or the bookshop. Or her mess of a life.

Until now.

She let out a weary breath as she set her coat and scarf on the back of a kitchen chair. Her fingers were red and chapped, and she ran them under the hot faucet until they tingled. A whole day had gone by without a word from Luke. When she thought of it, she felt incensed. After the way they left things off last night, she had hoped he might reach out to her, explain, or try to talk things through. Instead, nothing but silence.

She narrowed her eyes as she looked out the window, her mind filling with dark thoughts, until she recalled Jane's words to her that afternoon.

She had a lot of regrets about Luke. Was she only creating more?

Her cell phone buzzed from the depth of her pocket, and the air stalled in her lungs. Speak of the devil . . . could it be? Her heart was pounding as she considered what she would say to him, what her approach would be, until she saw the name on the display screen.

It was Derek.

It rang a third time and her mind whirled with possibilities. She hadn't spoken to him in a month, maybe more—she didn't even know what she would say to him. The thought of his voice and the routine of their life in

New York pulled her straight out of her childhood home, reminding her of the life she had, the one that was still waiting for her, there for the taking. If she wanted it.

She stared at the screen, at the name of the man she had spent so much time with but somehow never knew. And it was then that she knew what she needed to do.

She had built a life for herself, a successful one at that, but Briar Creek was her foundation. This was where she belonged.

Half an hour later, her car dragged to a stop on the slick mountain road. From a few hundred feet away, she could see the warm glow of Luke's windows through the snow-covered tree branches. She steadied her breath, gripping her fingers tighter around the wheel.

He might not want to see her. She might only make things worse. But she had to know. Just like she did the time she'd shown up on his driveway, unannounced, and told him she'd made a mistake.

She pulled into his driveway, and his front door opened before she was out of the car. Her stomach fluttered at the sight of him leaning against the doorjamb in a gray long-sleeve T-shirt and jeans, his muscular forearms folded against his chest. His hair was tousled, as if he had just woken up, and from the looks of it, there was a day's worth of stubble on his tight, square jaw.

She straightened her shoulders. This was it.

"Hey there," she said softly, barely managing a smile. Her pulse hammered as she waited for him to speak, to say something that would make her feel less vulnerable for showing up here like this.

"I didn't think you'd want to see me after last night."

She shrugged. "I didn't at first."

"What changed your mind then?"

"I didn't want to end things like the last time." This time, she needed to be sure.

He stared at her for a measured second and then his lips curved into a lopsided grin. "I'm sorry about last night," he said, and her stomach flipped.

Grace nodded, walking slowly up to the porch so she didn't have to answer. She passed through the open door with only a sidelong glance in his direction, her heart speeding up at the flash in his eyes. Damn it, would the image of this man ever stop having this effect on her?

Chagrined, she smiled to herself. She knew the answer to that question. It was the reason she was here.

"Wine?" he asked, tipping his head in the direction of the kitchen, and Grace felt her shoulders relax.

"I'd love some."

She followed him through the hall and watched in silence as he uncorked a bottle and filled two glasses.

"I didn't come here about the store," she began. She paused, accepting the outstretched glass and taking a sip of the warm, smooth wine. That wasn't true. Not entirely, at least. "I came here to . . . talk."

His eyes held hers with warm certainty. From his close distance she could smell the musk of his soap on his skin. She leaned into him ever so slightly, and then drew her back straight, averting her gaze.

With a grin, he gestured toward the living room, where the lights from the Christmas tree twinkled invitingly. "I have a lot to say, myself."

She led the way, feeling the heat of his stare, as his eyes lazily roamed over her blouse and jeans, wondering if he felt the same lust when he looked at her as she did for him. There was a time when they could feed off each other's touch more than food or water or even air. She closed her eyes, wondering if she would even feel that way again. No other man could light that fire in her.

"You go first," she said, sinking back into the couch.

Luke sat at the other end, a comfortable distance, she noted with disappointment. She braced herself for the inevitable. He wasn't ready to let go of the past—not any part of it.

Luke rubbed a hand over his jaw, making a faint scratching sound in the perfectly still room. "I don't really know where to begin," he sighed, and Grace pressed her nails into her palm. So here it was.

"It's okay, Luke," she said, giving him a level stare. "You don't owe me an explanation. You moved on with your life. I obviously complicated things for you by coming back."

"You did complicate things," he admitted. "But you also forced me out of this rut I've been living in."

She blinked. "Really?"

He nodded as a slow smile formed on his mouth. "You made me start thinking about everything I want out of life. Everything I can still maybe have. I thought it was too late, but maybe it's not."

Swallowing the lump in her throat, Grace opened her mouth to say something, but Luke leaned forward, silencing her with his mouth before she could form any words.

She parted her lips to his, releasing a breath as he slid his tongue along her lower lip and then slowly intertwined it with hers. She sighed into his mouth, quickly falling into the natural rhythm of their kiss, and something deep within her belly stirred as his mouth made its claim on hers.

His mouth never leaving hers, his tongue never hesitating, he leaned her back against the pillows, slowly guiding himself on top of her. She smiled through the kiss, enjoying the familiar weight of his body on hers. The way his shoulders felt so massive under her fingers, the way his hair smelled like soap and his skin smelled like sandalwood.

She ran her hands down the length of his back, warming under the heat of his body. His face was so close to hers, if she opened her eyes she could see every eyelash. Her heart ached with the memory of his touch, now so real, as if no time had passed.

His finger grazed the rim of her jeans and she quivered, nestling deeper into the cushion, under the wall of his chest above hers. He traced his finger under her sweater, circling her belly button and then higher, leaving a tingle in his path.

As his hand came up over the swell of her breasts he pushed the sweater higher, until it was over her head, leaving her feeling small under the bulk of his muscled form. She reached out her arms, pulling his sweater over his head, and then ran her fingers down the wall of his chest, over the hardened muscles of his taut stomach.

He lowered himself onto her, his mouth finding hers again, slowly this time, lighter. The tip of his tongue traced her lips and then circled her tongue before probing her mouth, and she welcomed him in, feeling the weight of his body on hers as his mouth pushed deeper.

His fingers traced their way up her stomach and she arched her back with need. The space between her thighs tingled with anticipation. Pulling the lace cup of her bra over her breast, he bent down and took his mouth to the tender flesh, teasing the bud between his teeth until she moaned. She combed her hands through his wavy locks, pressing his head into her breasts, her belly pulsing with each flick of his tongue as desire mounted.

Luke reached behind her and unhooked her bra, pushing it to the side. Her skin was cool beneath him, longing for the heat he could bring to her, and her breasts rose and fell as he stared into her eyes, brushing her hair away from her cheek with the back of his hand.

With sudden hunger, his mouth claimed hers, his tongue frantic in its exploration, its need to bring them closer, connect them on every level. He groaned into her and she parted her legs, imagining what it would be like to feel him inside her again.

Tearing his mouth from hers, he traced her neck with delicate kisses that caused her to shiver and writhe. Idly, he rubbed his thumb over her nipple until it peaked under his touch.

"I want you," he whispered, his voice low and husky, and she reached up and unhooked the button of his jeans, parting the zipper with a tug of her hands.

She was warm, ready for him. He slid her pants down her legs at an achingly slow speed, and her breath became labored as he ran his hand back up the length of her legs, angling to her inner thigh as he parted her knees. His fingers teased at the edge of her cotton panties and she sucked in a breath as they snuck under the elastic, stroking her until a fire was lit and she cried out.

With a small smile, he leaned into her, kissing her softly on the mouth as his hands slid the remains of her undergarments down her legs. As he centered himself over her, she traced her fingers down his back, tugging his boxers from his clenched and primed body, taking his firm butt in her hands as he guided himself inside her.

She gasped as the length of him filled her. She wrapped her legs around his waist, her hands clawing at his back, his neck, nestling through his silky hair. She lifted her hips to match his effort, the tension mounting with each stroke, and he wrapped his arms around her waist, pulling her so close she gasped for breath. His thrusts were smooth and deep, and he groaned into her ear, the heat of his breath causing her insides to pool, and she relaxed further into him, her mouth fumbling for his.

His mouth was frantic on hers, fast and hard in its urgency as his breath came in spurts. She lifted her hips, pulling her legs higher and then cried out as she broke. He tore his mouth from hers as he groaned on a thrust, and then collapsed onto her chest, panting.

His warmth still filled her as they lay there, spent, and a tingle of pleasure still coursed through her as he ran his fingertips lightly over her warm flesh.

"Just like old times," he said, and she could hear the smile in his voice.

She hesitated. "Yes, but maybe—"

"Maybe better?" he finished, and her lips twisted into a grin. "Maybe you should disappear for five years more often," he said.

No way in hell, she thought. She was right where she wanted to be, and this time, she wasn't going anywhere.

CHAPTER 28

Grace woke at the first hint of sunlight rising up over the mountains, filling the living room through the floor-to-ceiling windows. Foggy from sleep, she squinted at the unfamiliar surroundings for a split second before a delicious warmth spread over her body.

Smiling, she pulled the blanket higher. The weight of Luke's arm around her waist was heavy and secure, and she snuggled her back against the smooth plane of his chest, closing her eyes.

"Morning," he mumbled, nuzzling into the nape of her neck.

A shiver traced its way down her spine, and she pressed herself closer against him, feeling the heat of his bare skin against hers.

"Sleep well?" he asked, kissing her bare shoulder.

"Never better," she said, shifting herself on the plush rug so she faced him. He rolled over on his back and she settled against his chest. "Today is Christmas Eve Eve," she said, tracing her fingers over the ripples of his abdomen.

Luke snorted. "You sound like my mother," he said, combing his hair through his fingers.

She slid him a glance. "That's not something you should say to a woman you just slept with." She smiled, leaning in to kiss him. She had only intended a quick peck, but something about the touch of his tender flesh caused her belly to pool with warmth. She pulled back, and stared at the ceiling, smiling. She could stay here all day, exactly like this, but there was too much to do.

Besides, she and Luke would have many more moments like this.

"Oh, shoot," Luke groaned. "Tonight's *The Nutcracker*. My mother will be in rare form today."

"You think *your* mother will be in rare form?" Grace shot back. "My mother's decided to enter the Holiday House contest this year."

Luke's eyebrows drew to a point. "You're kidding me."

"I know!" Grace laughed. "I couldn't believe it myself, but when she came by the store and saw the way I had decorated it, I guess it brought that itch to the surface." She smiled, thinking of how much her mother had improved in the past few days, but when she looked over at Luke, her smile fell.

"What is it?" she asked, alarm causing her pulse to quicken.

After a pause, he shook his head. "Nothing," he said, pushing up into a sitting position. His bare chest rippled in all the right places, and Grace reached up and ran a hand languidly down his back.

He glanced back at her over his shoulder. "I should get dressed," he said, abruptly standing up.

Grace's pulse skipped a beat as she watched him retreat into the hall. She strained her ears, mentally following his path as he padded up the stairs to the bedroom, closing the door behind him.

She dressed quickly and combed her fingers through her hair to smooth it down. By the time she had folded the blankets and set them on the coffee table, she heard the click of the bedroom door, and shortly after Luke appeared, refusing to meet her eye.

"What's going on, Luke?" she asked, her heart began to race. "Was it last night? Was it too soon?"

"No. No, last night was…" He shoved his hands into his pockets. "It wasn't last night."

Exasperation filled her chest. "Then what, Luke? Something's wrong. I want to know what it is." She stared at him, her eyes pleading, but he looked away, determined to remain evasive. Distant.

She folded her arms across her chest, feeling alone and out of place. The fire in the hearth had burned out hours before, leaving the room cold and less welcoming than it had been the night before.

She shouldn't have come here. She expected too much from him, and now she was paying the price.

"I thought you were over our past," she said.

"I am."

She took a step toward him. "Then why the cold shoulder?"

Luke let his attention drift over the room. "A lot is happening at once, Grace."

Grace stared at him, her gaze narrowing, and then she sighed in disappointment. "You're clearly not ready for this, Luke. You say you don't want to keep living in this rut, but you like it there." Her eyes filled. "You don't want to move on, not really."

"That's not true."

"Yes, it is." She brushed at a tear before it could fall hating herself for coming back here, for letting herself get hurt again. "You don't want to move on because you can't let go of Helen."

Luke shook his head. "Stop."

"You think if you move on with your life—if you start living again—that you'll be forgetting her, hurting her somehow."

Luke dragged a hand down his face. He stared at the floor, his shoulders straining against his thin wool sweater. After a pause he shrugged, giving her a hooded stare. "Maybe," he said, his tone low and husky. "But it's how I feel."

"You blame me for it," she continued, realizing how clear it all was. "You can never move forward with me because I remind you of a part of yourself that you want to forget."

Luke's expression folded. He took a step forward, but she was already backing out of the room. "That's not true, Grace. I mean…" He stopped, running a hand through his hair, his eyes darting wildly.

"See?" she snapped. She shook her head and pushed past him. Her tears were hot and thick, blinding her path to the door, but she could have found her way with her eyes closed. She knew this house—every inch of it. Just the way she knew Luke.

She opened the closet door and grabbed her coat and bag.

"Stop!" Luke ordered, his tone firm enough to cause her to obey. "Grace. Please. Turn and look at me. Please."

She hesitated, sucking in a deep breath. With her back

to him, it was easy. She could leave, get in her car, drive away, and never look back. But she knew how that road ended. It ended back in New York, walking the lonely streets, thinking of him the way she had for the past five years, even when she'd tried so hard not to.

She closed her eyes. It would never be easy with Luke.

Slowly, she turned, almost wincing when she saw the pain in his eyes, wishing he didn't have this hold on her, that the sight of his face wouldn't make her heart wrench every time.

"What, Luke? What do you have to say?" She tossed up her hands. "What more is there?"

"I don't know," he said. "All I know is that I don't want you to walk out that door right now. I don't want you to walk out of my life."

"Then give me a reason to stay," she said, tightening her grip on her coat. "I told you once I would come back for you. I meant it then. And I mean it now."

"I want to believe that," he said.

Silence stretched and she didn't dare to breathe. She had taken a leap of faith once, and she had done it again by coming here last night. She needed something from him, something to show her they had a future. A chance.

"What about the storefront next to the bookstore?" she asked.

"What about it?"

Her temper stirred. "Helen is never going to open that store, Luke. You can keep renewing it and renewing it until you are ready to let go, but you are holding on to the past, and that store is tangible proof."

"And you mean to tell me that you aren't doing the same?" he snapped back.

Grace froze. "Excuse me?"

"You're clinging to the past just as much as I am, trying to save Main Street Books. You're holding on to your father, a part of your life and a whole set of memories that you want to keep with you."

"That's true. I am." She stared him down. "But I am still here, Luke. Right now. Standing here in front of you. I still have a chance, and you're the one who decides whether I can have it."

He let out a deep sigh, running both hands through his hair and gripping the roots. "Do you realize what you are asking of me, Grace?" he cried, his eyes flashing a piercing blue.

"I'm asking you to take what's in front of you before you lose it for good. Because if you let me walk away from you again, this time I won't be coming back." She paused, the magnitude of her words fueling her. "I know what I want now, more than I did back then. And it's you, Luke. I'm ready to move forward, but you have to be willing to do the same."

He broke her stare, shaking his head.

"Are you going to renew the lease on the store?" She had to know, he had to tell her. It was more than just a piece of space, more than just a roadblock to her hopes. It represented something larger—someone. He knew it, and she did, too.

She waited for an answer until she knew he wasn't going to give her the one she wanted to hear. "Why, Luke? Why?"

His eyes hardened. "It wouldn't be fair to Helen."

"If someone else wanted that space, would you give it up?"

He heaved a breath and crossed his arms over his chest. "I don't know."

She knew she should let it go, stop torturing herself, but she couldn't, not without hearing it from him first. He had to close the door so she could find the strength to walk away, permanently. "Probably?"

He shook his head softly, lowering his head. "It wouldn't be as difficult a choice."

The impact of his words hit her like a physical blow. "Then you and I are finally over." She stared at him, wishing it hadn't come to this, that he would say something, anything to take it all back, but it was hopeless. "For good."

She hadn't realized it until this moment, but somehow, all this time, she had still been clinging to him, whether it be out of hope, or out of denial, she had held on to Luke and their past the way he was now holding on to Helen. She had moved forward, but she was always alone, always missing the one thing she could never have. The part of her that was gone forever.

"Don't say that, Grace," he said, reaching out to grab her arm, but she recoiled on reflex, tearing free before his fingers could reach her. His eyes darkened with anguish and, finally, acceptance. "I do love you, you know," he said softly.

She shot him a look as her fingers turned the door handle. "I know," she said bitterly. "But we both know from experience that sometimes that isn't enough."

Turning away, she closed the door behind her. Standing on the snow-covered porch, she huffed out a breath. The day was young—so young that the streetlamps were still on in the distance, the dusk still fading into a gold swirl of clouds on the horizon.

She waited for the tears to come, for her heart to feel like it had been shattered, but instead she felt it harden with newfound resolve. After all this time, she finally had her closure. The hope was gone, but it didn't hurt as much as the burden of her regrets. She and Luke were simply not meant to be.

She'd fought for Luke. Twice now, and both times the message was clear. She could live with that—not that she had a choice in the matter.

Still, there was a part of her that sparked with need and a dream yet to come true. She may have lost Luke this morning, but there was still one thing left worth fighting for.

Grace spent the rest of the morning and afternoon in Main Street Books, continuing to clean out the back room and organize, doing everything she could to think about anything but Luke, before finally collapsing into her favorite chair. So many days had been spent in this place, so much hope had filled her then. She wanted to be a writer, to have her books line these shelves one day.

Frowning, she abruptly stood and crossed the room, weaving her way through the stacks until she came to the fiction section, then grazing her pointer finger over the spines until she found it. Madison. Grace Madison. A small smile came to her lips as she contemplated how much had changed since the last time she'd been here all those years ago. Her father had been so proud of her; she would have loved to have been with him in the back room when he popped the box on the shipment of her books—she could almost picture the gleam in his eye. Instead she'd been hundreds of miles away.

Her heart felt heavy as she wedged the book back into

its slot. Is this what she wanted for herself? To see every effort she had made come crumbling down around her? What had it all been for, then? The sacrifice, the effort. All for this?

No, she decided, plucking a pen from the desk. Definitely not.

With a notepad in hand, she settled herself into a chair, the words flowing faster than her fingers could record them. By the time the door jingled, clouds had covered the earlier sunlight, and she flicked on a lamp as she sprang from her chair. A customer? Could it be possible that things were turning around?

She set her notepad facedown on the counter, returned the pen to the cup, and turned to greet the newcomer with an ear-to-ear grin. Her pulse skipped when she saw the man in the doorway.

"Derek," she gasped.

"Your mom told me I could find you here," he said guardedly.

Her mother? Grace drew a deep breath. She supposed he'd stopped by the house. Oh, she didn't even want to know what Kathleen was thinking now... With his slick black overcoat and classically handsome features, her mother was sure to have given some sort of reaction.

"The address was listed," he explained. "I've never seen anything like it," he said with a grin. "It's like a giant gingerbread house."

She smiled, and something within her heart thawed. There was of course something about Derek that had drawn her to him in the first place. It just wasn't enough to keep her there.

"My mother would be pleased to hear that," she said.

"Well, pass it along for me." He grinned.

"I will."

Silence fell and Grace watched as Derek swept his gaze over the room. He looked tall and out of place in his polished shoes and cashmere scarf. She appraised him from a reserved distance—the black hair and piercing dark eyes, the strong Roman nose, and noble chin. A handsome man, there was no mistaking that. It felt surreal to think that only a matter of months ago, he was her fiancé. Standing here now, he felt like someone she barely knew, from a time and a place that was skin-deep, not ingrained in her soul.

And she knew then and there that no matter what happened with Luke or the store, she was not going back to New York.

"So..." she said, smiling nervously. She paused, waiting to see if he would take the pressure off the situation. "What brings you to Briar Creek?"

"You," he said simply. The smile had faded from his face, and he held her eyes until her stomach rolled over. There would always be something there—a connection of shared time together, of the possibility of a future—but she knew in her heart that she had made the right decision. No regrets.

"Me?" She tipped her head. "Oh, Derek."

He cleared his throat, gesturing to a bookshelf. "This is your father's store?" When she nodded, he said, "It's very...charming. I can see why you were always so fond of it."

Grace felt her stomach knot. She still couldn't bear the thought of clearing it out, shutting it all down on New Year's Eve. When she tried to imagine going through the process it felt surreal, impossible. She had a bad feeling she'd be in denial right up until the key was handed over to the management company. And it would take many years before she could walk down Main Street without a lump in her throat.

It wasn't any reason to run away. And neither was Luke.

"Well, it won't be around much longer, so you're lucky you got here before the door closed for good."

Derek frowned. "Grace—you love this place."

"I do. Unfortunately, not everyone else does." She gave a brave smile. "It had a good run. I'm thankful to have ever known it."

His frown deepened. "I'm sorry."

"Me too." She rubbed her arm, and sniffed. "I thought I could keep it going, actually, but I don't think that's very realistic."

Derek's brow knitted. "You were planning on staying here?"

She hesitated. "I *am* planning on staying here, actually."

She glanced at him from the shadow of her lashes. They both knew what it meant. Somehow things were less permanent if she was still in New York. They'd meet up, run into each other, and have the option to try again. It would only end the same way, though. They were friends, maybe even good friends, but not close friends. They could never think something more would last.

Derek held her eyes with his and pushed his lips off to the side. "Ah." He gave a lazy grin. "Well, don't I feel like a fool now."

She shook her head, taking a step closer to him. "Don't say that, Derek. You know I care about you. You also know why we could never work out."

"I know. I thought..." He inhaled deeply and shook his head, whistling out a breath. Locking her in a sidelong gaze he said, "This is really it, then? You're really staying here?"

"I am." She gave him a sad smile. "This is where I belong. New York was a learning experience for me. It made me realize what I want in life."

"I know." Derek lifted his eyes to the ceiling. After a pause he said, "I will miss you, you know."

"I'll miss you, too," she said softly.

Silence stretched and Grace looked around the room helplessly. She adjusted an ornament on the miniature tree, watched it catch the light and glimmer.

"It really is a shame this place is going out of business," Derek mused, catching her off guard.

"Well." She shrugged. She was exhausted, defeated. Deep down she'd had some ridiculous hope that the second she turned the sign on the door, throngs of people would be pushing their way in, but that wasn't the case at all. She'd been fighting since she got here—for Luke, for the shop. She was trying to revive the past.

She frowned at the thought. Wasn't that what she had accused Luke of doing?

"You'd think a place like this could prosper," Derek continued. He began wandering around, stopping periodically to pick up a book and glance at its cover. "It's so authentic. There aren't any other bookstores in town, are there?"

"No, just this one. I had some plans...Oh, it doesn't matter now," she huffed. "The shop is closing on New Year's Eve. There's really no way around it."

Derek looked up from the book he was holding. "No? A little freshening up and it could be good as new."

Grace shook her head adamantly. This was exactly

why she had fallen for Derek to begin with. He might not want children or family dinners or quiet evenings by the fire, but he did dream big, and she appreciated that quality. Too much, sometimes.

"Derek, no. Honestly, I've thought of everything. I had a plan and it fell through. The only other option now would be to totally renovate this entire store and even then... well, it would be a risk." People weren't stopping in, they didn't think to buy their books here, and without the revenue from the café to offset the costs, much less stir up foot traffic, it was a pipe dream. It was pointless.

"But if you had the money—"

Grace's heart dropped into her stomach. "No. Derek. I—I need to let go." The sooner she could do that, the sooner she could heal. Just being here now, giving up the fight, she found she could enjoy the time she had left, no matter how bittersweet.

"What are you going to do here, then?"

Grace tossed up her hands. She hadn't really figured that part out yet herself. "I don't know yet. All I know is that Briar Creek is where I need to be."

"This bookstore inspired you to become a writer, didn't it?" He tucked a book back into place on the cramped shelf and turned toward the door.

A wave of sadness washed over her. This was really goodbye for them. She hated goodbyes. There had been too many of them lately.

"It did," she said, pleased he had remembered.

He shook his head, taking one last look around. "A real shame to lose it then."

She nodded, unable to speak as tears prickled her eyes. *A real shame.*

"I have something for you before I go," he said.

She stared at him with interest. "What is it?"

He held out his hand and slipped something into hers. Her heart stilled. Her engagement ring.

"Why are you giving this back to me?" she asked, her breath hitching.

"It was my gift to you," he said. "It still is."

"Derek."

He held up a hand. "I know I'm not the man for you. I couldn't give you all those things you dreamed of—things money couldn't buy. I am who I am. I'm never going to be that person."

"I know," she said softly, and she suddenly realized what Luke meant when he said you could care for two people in wildly different ways. There were many parts of Derek she admired, even loved, but that didn't make him the right man for her.

"This is your ring, Grace. I gave it to you once, and you gave it back. Take it now and give yourself the life you dreamed of. Start with this place."

Tears blurred her vision as she stared at the ring in her palm. She hadn't seen it in months, since she'd slid it across the dinner table to him, and she admired how exquisite it was all over again. It was the most beautiful ring she had ever seen, but even when she had worn it, it had never felt right. It was too big, too flashy, and it represented a whole way of life that wasn't her.

"You're a good man," she said. She swallowed the lump in her throat and blinked, giving him a watery smile.

He reached over and wiped a tear from her cheek with the pad of his thumb. "Goodbye, Grace."

"Goodbye."

He reached over and gave her a hug, tight and short. With a nod of his head, he skipped down the steps, not bothering to pause as he took long strides across the snow-dusted sidewalk.

She wrapped her arms around herself, shivering as she watched Derek climb into a sleek Mercedes. It was the last time they'd see each other, she knew, and she smiled sadly, knowing that he'd move on soon enough, and that any girl would be lucky to have him. He was a good man, a decent man, but he wasn't the man for her.

Through the tinted windows she caught a glimpse of his wave and she smiled broader, her heart strings tugging as the car silently, smoothly, slid down the street. She watched it disappear at the corner, taking one last look at her past and the life she was leaving behind.

Turning to go back inside, the corner of her eye caught something across the street and she paused, blanching when she saw him standing so still, watching her from behind a large snowbank. Luke.

Heart thumping, she froze, considering lifting her hand in a wave and then wondering what she would even say. Before she could move, he thrust his hands into his pockets, turned on his heels, and walked away.

CHAPTER
29

Luke balled his hand into a fist. He quickened his pace to a near sprint, weaving in and out of blurred faces carrying shopping bags, chatting cheerfully all around him. His pulse was spinning, he could hear the blood rushing through his veins, and all he could see in front of him was Grace in the arms of another man.

Darting to get past a group of women who had slowed to check out the twinkling display in the toy store windows, Luke ground to a halt as he nearly collided with Mark.

"Whoa," his cousin chuckled, but his grin collapsed when he saw Luke's expression. "Everything okay?"

"No. No, everything's not okay," he growled.

Mark gestured toward Hastings. "Coffee on the house?"

Luke hesitated, and then shrugged his shoulders. He could use someone to talk to right now as much as he could use a distraction. The thought of going home to that empty house, now tainted with fresh memories of his night with Grace, was unappealing at best. It had taken years to get that woman out of his system, and now he had only cemented the image, the memory of her touch, the way her eyelids fell heavy as his lips met hers.

"Coffee sounds good," he said abruptly.

The men pushed through the crowded diner, finding an empty booth near the kitchen. Mark lifted his finger, catching the attention of one of the waiters behind the counter, and called for a pot of fresh brew. He turned over their mugs and settled back into his seat.

"You caught me at a good time. I was just going on break."

Luke grunted his response, and rested his head in his hand.

Mark blew out a low whistle. "Damn, Luke. You're looking even worse than usual."

Luke didn't bother to feed into his cousin's attempt at a joke. "Gee, thanks."

"Okay, what the hell is going on here?" Mark asked. "It's Grace, isn't it?"

Luke deepened his frown. For a self-confirmed bachelor, Mark knew a lot about women. "That obvious?"

"It was either that or your usual Christmas funk. With all the recent developments this past week, I took a gamble and went for the most obvious choice."

"You should take that strategy to the casinos," Luke bantered, starting to feel a little more like his old self.

"Nah. Why play the slots when your love life is so much more entertaining?"

"Happy to be at your service," Luke rolled his eyes and tipped back his mug. "But you're right. It is Grace."

"You giving up the storefront?" Mark asked, and

then, noticing Luke's expression, let out a sigh. "Does she know?"

Luke stared into his mug. "She knows all right."

"And she was none too happy about it?"

"Nope." Luke rubbed a hand over his forehead, recalling the hurt in her eyes. That store meant everything to her—to Ray. Luke's gut tightened at the memory of Grace's father. That store was the last piece of him around these parts. You couldn't think of Ray Madison without thinking of him standing behind the counter of that dusty old shop, glasses sliding down his nose, grin on his face as he flipped another page in some old classic.

"She's done a lot of work on the place," Mark continued.

Luke frowned. "How would you know?"

"I went in there yesterday. She and Anna were making a last-ditch effort to save the store, it seemed. Can't say they were very pleased to see me, though."

"Oh, come on. Grace has always liked you. Now Anna, on the other hand..." He forced a smile at the tension between the middle Madison sister and his cousin, even though his heart wasn't in it.

"You're seriously going to renew that lease? I saw what that place means to those girls. You can't do this, Luke." Mark gave him a level stare, obvious in his disapproval.

Luke felt his jaw set. "Let it drop."

Mark held up a palm. "Sorry. I hate to see you clinging to the past instead of living your life. Why not take the money you would spend renewing that lease every year and give it to charity instead?"

Luke frowned. He'd never thought of that before.

"Do you honestly think Helen would want you to hold on to that storefront for her?"

"It was her dream," Luke said, his voice firm, insistent.

"I know, but Luke…Helen's gone. She's never going to have that dream. Let someone else have it."

Luke shook his head. "It's not that simple," he insisted.

"Yes," Mark said. "Yes, it is."

Silence stretched and they sat huddled over coffee mugs, pretending to take interest in the bustle of the neighborhood joint, in the cheerful Christmas music reminding them that it was Christmas Eve Eve. It was hard to believe that only this morning Grace had been in his arms, drawing attention to that very fact.

"I should go," Luke finally said, leaning back against his seat to pull out his wallet.

"Dude, it's a buck thirty-nine. Please."

Luke arched a brow. "A buck thirty-nine for a cup of coffee? I remember when it was fifty cents."

"Get with the times, Luke," Mark said waving away his cash. "Open your eyes to the present."

Luke's lips thinned. "Thanks for the coffee."

"See you," Mark said, no longer smiling.

"Feel like coming over Saturday?" Luke asked. "The game's on."

Mark gave a half smile. "Sure."

"Think it's always going to be like this?" Luke grinned, trying to lighten the mood. "Two bachelors sitting around every weekend?"

"I used to think so," Mark said, "but the older I get, the more depressing that sounds."

Luke nodded slowly. "I know what you mean," he said. It did sound depressing. Depressing as hell. And wrong—just wrong.

He'd never pictured his life that way—not back when

he was with Grace, not when he was married to Helen, and not even now. He'd been given so many chances for happiness, to have the life he wanted, and he'd resisted every opportunity, doubted himself, and questioned it all.

Not anymore. He knew what he wanted. He'd always known. It wasn't about convincing himself anymore. It was all about taking the chance.

The house was so quiet he could hear the floorboards creak under his feet as he walked into the kitchen. He plunked down onto a counter stool, eyeing the evidence of the night before. The wineglasses, one still bearing the imprint of Grace's red lipstick on the rim, sat offensively on the counter, the dregs slightly pungent by now, reminding him of how quickly things could sour.

He dumped the remains down the sink and turned his attention to the stack of mail that had collected over the past few weeks. He could spot a Christmas card in the mail carrier's hands from here, and they now sat in front of him, a neat stack of red, white, and even green envelopes. It was the stamps, he'd learned early on. People who sent Christmas cards always made sure to include one of those holiday stamps with a depiction of a little snowman or a sprig of holly.

Well, he was glad they did. It saved him the displeasure of having to open their letter.

Now, shuffling through the envelopes and reading the return addresses, he felt a wave of shame take hold. Some of these people he hadn't spoken to in years, had blocked out of his life completely for no good reason other than because he couldn't deal with seeing anyone for a while there, and yet here they were, reaching out to him. Wishing him a Merry Christmas. Hoping the best for him.

What was so wrong with that?

Here goes nothing. He tore open the first envelope, smiling when he pulled out a family photo showing an old friend from college. He had a wife and two kids now. Luke felt his smile fade, and he put the card back in the envelope and to the side. Trying not to think of how badly that hurt, he opened another. And another.

He picked up a creamy white envelope, not bothering to glance at the return address, and stiffened when he saw the contents. It was a letter. A long letter. From Helen's mother.

The room went completely still as he scanned the handwritten note; the only sound he could make out was the pounding of his heart. When he came to the end, he started over at the beginning, slower this time, a raw ache forming in his throat as he read her words. The words from a grieving mother. From a woman he hadn't spoken to in two years. Out of guilt. Out of shame. Because he couldn't look her in the eye.

It didn't seem fair, somehow, for him to share his grief with her. Helen was her daughter, the person she had loved most in the world. And Luke...He couldn't say the same.

Gritting his teeth, he read the letter once more, focusing on the last paragraph again and again until the hopes Helen's mother expressed began to crack his hard shell and break through the surface, touching him in a place he had thought could never be healed.

Luke closed his eyes and turned the letter facedown on the table.

Down the dark hall, past the shadows of tree branches

that reflected off the cedar-planked walls, was the door that Luke kept firmly closed. Helen's studio. He hadn't been in there since the day he buried her. It felt too real, too raw, and too wrong, going through her stuff like that. It was Helen's space, filled with Helen's stuff. He knew Mark raised an eyebrow every time he came over, a silent judgment that it was time to move on.

Luke put his hand on the doorknob, gripping the cold metal in his palm. His heart was pounding, but something propelled him forward, and with one quick turn and thrust, the door swung open. The shade was pulled on the window above her desk, and Luke switched on a lamp, smiling sadly as the room came to life.

All of her things were here, in front of him. He stood above the desk, choosing not to sit, and picked up the framed photograph from their wedding day. It was a candid photo, caught when they thought no one was looking. Helen looked radiant, her smile so bright, it wrenched his chest. His brow pinched when he studied himself, and he pulled the frame closer, scrutinizing his expression.

He was smiling in that photo, gazing at Helen, who was looking at the camera, her eyes bright and cheerful, laughing at something... They looked so happy.

He frowned and set the photo exactly where it had been and then swept his eyes over the room. The back wall was lined with shelves filled with colorful fabrics. Helen's sewing machine was still perched on a table, as if waiting for her to come and put it to use. On a rack, dozens of beautiful dresses hung side by side. All handmade by Helen.

It had been her dream to open that shop. The lease had been signed, ready for occupancy on the first of January.

And she had died just before she could take the key and start designing her vision. She was going to paint the walls a pale blue, he remembered. She'd take all this stuff to the back room of the store, she promised, hinting that this room might make a good nursery one day.

Luke huffed out a breath. He'd held on to this room like he'd held on to that lease. And now he had a decision to make. He could keep that storefront for another year, preserve Helen's dream, or he could let it go. Let Grace have it.

The phone rang and he jumped, chuckling at himself as he steadied his pulse. He strode into the kitchen, where the phone sat on the counter, lifting his eyes to the ceiling when he saw who the caller was. She always had the best timing.

"Hello, Mother," he said with mock annoyance.

"Don't 'Hello, Mother' me!" Rosemary snapped. "I've got thirty prima donnas over here and I can't get the audio system to turn on."

Luke frowned. "Where are you?"

"Where am I?" Rosemary trilled. "I'm at the auditorium! Oh, for the love of Pete, don't even think about having so much as a sip of that cola with that costume on—take it off. Take. It. Off!" From somewhere in the distance, Luke could make out the sounds of a little girl's protests, a disappointed whine.

He covered the receiver so she couldn't hear his laughter, but Rosemary was sharp.

"Don't you laugh at me!" she cried, but before he could interject, she said, "Snowflakes do not laugh, they dance. And they don't dance in cola-stained costumes. This isn't the waltz of the dirty snowflakes!"

After a beat and a rustle of the phone, she breathed, "Sorry."

He pressed his lips together. "That's all right."

"So are you coming to the show?" she asked.

He pressed a palm to his forehead. Of course. *The Nutcracker.*

"It's Christmas Eve Eve," she huffed and Luke's pulse skipped a beat.

A memory of Grace lying in his arms, her skin so smooth under his fingertips, he was mesmerized, lulled, her hair falling loosely over her bare shoulders. He closed his eyes. He'd lost so many chances for happiness, was he really prepared to let another one go? For what? So he could feel like a man, feel like he had done the right thing, the honest thing?

Or just so he could be a fool?

"Something's—"

"Don't tell me something's come up!" Rosemary warned, her voice growing shrill. "The whole town comes to see this show and we don't have any music!"

Luke drew a breath. This is what he'd insisted on, what he claimed he wanted in life more than Grace at a certain time—to be right here, in Briar Creek, with a family who needed him to do things like fix audio systems or construct scenery. A simple life—a boring life—he knew it, Grace knew it, and every time he doubted his choice, he wondered if Grace had been right, if he could have had more. Now he knew, this quiet life, this boring life, was the life he wanted. And he had Helen to thank for that, for showing him that it really was where he was meant to be.

He'd thought that he hadn't needed to do any soul-searching the way Grace had, that he was certain of what he wanted as much then as he was now. Only he'd needed to live through it to know for certain. They both had.

He'd stayed the course, he'd love and lost, and, in the end, it all came back to Grace.

"Luke?" His mother's voice was panicked in his ear. "I really need you here."

"I'll be there in twenty minutes," he said to her obvious sigh of relief and set the phone back on the counter.

From the corner of his eye he caught the open door of Helen's studio. If he closed his eyes, he could almost picture her in there, behind the door, humming. Happy.

He smiled and ever so softly whispered, "Thank you," and as he turned down the hall, he could hear the sound of her soft voice, humming a tune over the *whirr* of her sewing machine.

He grabbed his coat and bolted out onto the porch. Christmas Eve Eve. The biggest day of the year for his mother and thus the entire Hastings family. He'd love nothing more than to run the whole way over to the Madisons' house, to beat down the door and claim the woman he loved, but just like five years ago, he had other people that needed him.

He'd waited this long for Grace. He would have to wait one more day, and hope it wasn't a day too late.

Grace leaned back in her chair and stared at the blinking cursor on her screen, doing a perfectly miserable job of fighting off a smile if she did say so herself. With a quick press of the button, the document went to print, and she darted into her father's old study, watching with a swell in her chest as the pages chugged out of the device, piling neatly.

She pulled the stack from the tray, a little stunned by how thick it was, and grinned. She hadn't thought it possible that she would write again, much less produce something she felt this good about, but inspiration had taken hold and well . . . she knew how that usually ended.

Her mother appeared in the open doorway, and leaned against the jamb. "Grace? What's that?"

Grace wavered. Her mother had never supported her writing, not outwardly at least, not the way her father had done. Things were different now, she reminded herself. This was a fresh start.

"It's a new book I'm working on, actually. I started

yesterday, and I haven't been able to stop." She didn't mention that she'd already passed the first chapter to her agent and had received a positive response. For now, she was happy to think that she was finally writing again.

"I saw the light under your door last night," Kathleen mused, stepping into the room. "I was wondering what you were up to." She held out a hand, "May I?"

On reflex, Grace pulled the manuscript against her chest. At her mother's crestfallen expression, she said, "It's not ready yet. But...I'm on to something here. I can feel it."

Kathleen grinned. "Maybe you'll let me read it when you're finished?"

Grace gave a slow smile. "That means a lot, Mom."

"There's one other thing you can do for me," Kathleen said, gesturing for her to follow.

Venturing into the hall, Grace looked around and sighed. The house looked like something out of a magazine. Kathleen had taken her theme to a new level, turning the Victorian home into a gingerbread house itself, right down to the metallic peppermint candy ornaments hanging invitingly from the front porch roof.

"Still more decorating, Mom? The judges will be here in only a few hours. Maybe we should leave well enough alone."

Kathleen's eyes burst open. "Oh, honey, I'm not lifting another finger on this house. Besides, you and I both know that no one in town can compete with this," she added, and Grace bit back a smile. "No, I've got some copies of your books and I was hoping...Maybe you could sign them for me?"

Stunned, Grace felt her cheeks flush. She hugged the

manuscript tighter to her, searching her mother's hopeful face.

"I read them all the day they came out, but... I didn't know how to properly discuss them. Your father was the literary buff. I let him call you about it."

Grace tipped her head, saying softly, "You didn't need to impress me with some serious discussion about the books, Mom."

Kathleen shrugged. "Oh, well. I just figured—"

"We both figured a lot of things," Grace said, giving her mother a sad smile. "All this time I thought maybe you didn't like them. Especially the last one..."

"Oh, that one was my favorite!" Kathleen gushed and after a shocked second, Grace burst out laughing. "What's so funny?"

"That's the one that flopped!"

Kathleen shook her head. "See? Shows what I know."

She led Grace into the bedroom, quickly retrieving three well-thumbed paperbacks from her nightstand drawer. "Your father had them on display on the shelves downstairs, but I like to keep my copies here."

Grace set her manuscript facedown on the bed and picked up the top book. Her first release. She opened the spine, frowning at how loose it was. "You've read this more than once?"

Kathleen nodded. "So will you do me the honor? I've only been waiting years for this."

Grace swallowed back the emotions that were building within her and took the pen, taking a moment to think of something special to write in each one.

"Don't read it right now," she said, handing the stack back to her mother.

Kathleen winked. "Thanks, honey."

Grace's eye lingered on the cover of the third book. Her *last* book, she should say. "It wasn't so bad," she said, giving a half smile. "You weren't the only person who told me they liked it, you know."

"Oh no?" Kathleen placed the books back in the drawer. "Who else? Your sisters?"

Grace pursed her lips, knowing not to take offense to her mother's unintentional insult. Of course her family would have to say they liked it—she stopped herself, realizing this wasn't true at all. Her mother had said she liked the books and that had meant more to her than any glowing review from a random stranger.

"Luke, actually," she said, tucking a strand of hair behind her ear. She avoided her mother's watchful eye and lifted her manuscript from the bed.

"Well, he was always your biggest fan," Kathleen pointed out.

"Yes," Grace murmured. "I suppose he was."

Was. Luke was a lot of things.

She waited for the hurt to pass. It was sharp but it would fade in time. She was counting on it.

The doorbell chimed and Kathleen sprang to the door. "Your sisters are here!" she cried and Grace gave a mild smile.

"I'll be right down," she said, walking to her room.

In her bedroom, she tucked the manuscript under her bed, on top of the box of memories of her past, secure in a place that was out of sight, but very close to her heart. She'd come back to it this evening maybe, or tomorrow. Right now, she needed to focus on the thing that mattered most— the thing she had let slip all those years ago. Her family.

From a distance she could hear the peals of Sophie's laughter, and she smiled sadly. She might not have everything she wanted for Christmas this year, but somehow next year was looking a lot more promising. Derek was gone, Luke was now a permanent part of her past, but through them both she had learned what she wanted. And when she set her mind to something, she made a point of seeing it happen.

With a newfound sense of hope, she dashed out into the hall and leaned over the ornately wrapped banister to see Anna, Jane, and Sophie huddled together, chatting happily, peeling off layers of winter clothing.

"Merry Christmas!" she called, as she bounded down the stairs.

"It's not Christmas yet!" Sophie cried, stricken. "Santa hasn't come!"

Grace chuckled and picked up her niece for a squeeze. "Don't worry, Santa is coming tonight, and I'm sure he'll bring you everything you wanted."

She glanced at Jane, who was smiling at her daughter. "I hope so," her sister said, giving her a nervous look.

"I know so," Grace said.

"You girls go get settled," Kathleen ordered, ushering them out of the hall. "I have a few last-minute things to do before the judging."

"I thought you said you were finished!" Grace said.

Kathleen threw her a look. "Don't you know me by now?"

Grace laughed and followed her sisters into the living room, where a roaring fire crackled invitingly. Six red velvet stockings hung from ceramic figurines. Sophie's hung right next to the one belonging to their father, who was still with them this Christmas, almost more than ever.

"We missed you at *The Nutcracker* last night," Jane said.

Grace sat on the couch, tucking her feet under her. Even though Sophie was too young to dance in the show, she had assumed Jane would mention her absence. "I was busy with some things. I'm sorry to have missed it."

"I thought maybe it was because of Luke."

Grace's heart skipped a beat. "Was he there?" she asked, hoping her tone was more casual than she felt.

"Of course," Jane said.

A heavy pause fell on the room. "Luke and I are over, so you can all stop thinking things."

"It's really sad," Jane said softly, running a hand over Sophie's hair. "He was like a brother to us growing up. A son to Dad."

Grace nodded. "I know. But I guess that store is the last bit of Helen he has left. And he isn't willing to part with it."

A heavy silence fell over the room and for a few minutes, Grace focused her attention on the golden flames dancing in the hearth. From somewhere, Kathleen had turned on Christmas music, and it filled the house at what her mother had always referred to as a "subtle" level. A trial run, Grace assumed, for the judges' tour.

"So that's the end of the road then?" Anna asked, her mouth a grim line. "We start clearing out the store at the end of the week?"

"I guess so," Jane said on a sigh.

"You know, the funny thing is that now more than before, I feel really sad about the thought of it closing,"

Anna said, and Jane nodded her head in agreement. "I mean, at first, it was all part of Dad passing away, like we lost every part of him at once, without time to process all of it. But this past week, thinking there was some hope to save the store..." She paused. "It felt like for a little while at least, a part of Dad was back."

"I know," Jane said.

Grace looked from one sister to the other and took a deep breath. "The store isn't closing."

Two sets of eyes fixed on hers. "Derek came to see me yesterday," she said. "He gave me back my engagement ring. It's worth enough to renew the lease. It will take a lot of work to get more customers in there, but we might be able to turn it around and make it successful."

"And you're willing to take the risk?" Anna asked. "Grace, even with the addition of the café, it was going to be a risk, but at least then there would be another source of revenue and foot traffic. That store never turned much of a profit."

"I know," Grace said. "Believe me, I know. I have to try. I can't let go yet."

Something in her heart softened with her own words. This was probably the way Luke felt. Whether she liked it or not, he had loved Helen, maybe not the way he loved her, but Helen had still been his wife, someone he had shared an enormous part of his life with. He had every reason to want to hold on to whatever fragment of her was left.

She smiled sadly, pulling a crimson chenille throw off the arm of the couch and wrapping it over her legs, knowing she would have to perfectly replace it before the judges came through. She forced a grin. "Guess this means you're stuck with me," she said and Jane whooped.

"Mom, get in here!" she called. "Grace has some news!"

The doorbell chimed and Kathleen's harried voice shouted back, "Oh my God, they're early, they're *early*! Places, everyone. *Places!*"

Giggling nervously, Grace fumbled with the blanket, her sisters grabbed Sophie, and they all hurried to their places. Kathleen had instructed them to stand in front of the towering Christmas tree that replaced the sad, stick-like thing that had stood here less than a week ago. Kathleen darted into the room and took them by the arms, placing the three sisters in back, Sophie neatly front and center. "This is it! This is *it!*" she trilled nervously, before smoothing her hands over her hips, squaring her shoulders and sailing to the front door.

A murmur of voices was heard from the hall, and Jane placed her hands on Sophie's shoulders to keep her from wandering off. "I have some news of my own," she whispered.

"What?" Grace whispered back, breaking into laughter when she caught Anna's wide eyes. They were perfectly ridiculous, huddled here, waiting for people to come and *ooh* and *aw* over their house, while their mother wrung her hands, beaming with pride she was careful not to show. It was just like the old days. The good old days.

"Rosemary hired me at the studio!" Jane whispered eagerly, and Grace had to smack her hand over her mouth to keep from cheering.

Anna clapped her hands together silently. "Well done, you!" she whispered, and then abruptly straightened her back, jutting her chin, as the sound of their mother's voice, crooning gaily, came closer.

Grace rolled her shoulders and plastered a pleasant

smile on her face as she waited for the judges to appear in the doorway, but her gasp could be heard above the Christmas music when Luke's handsome form appeared instead.

"Luke."

He slid her a lopsided grin. "Do you have a minute?"

She could feel Jane's fingers dig deep into her back, firmly pushing her away from their cozy huddle. Lurching to catch her step, Grace smiled nervously.

She glanced back at her sisters, who were grinning devilishly, and narrowed her gaze. Easy for them, all right.

"Let's go somewhere private," she whispered to Luke, grabbing a piece of his jacket and giving it a tug.

She waited until they were upstairs to speak. Closing her bedroom door behind her, she whirled around and demanded, "What the heck is going on?"

"I'm sorry, Grace," he began, but she held up a hand to stop him.

"Luke, please. Don't." She crossed the room and sat down on her bed, feeling exhausted and weary. "I understand. You don't need to explain."

"I do need to explain," he said, coming forward.

She shook her head. "It's okay, Luke. It doesn't have to end badly between us, not like the last time. I expected too much from you. I was wrong."

"You weren't wrong," he said. "You gave me a lot to think about." His blue eyes pierced hers and she winced, looking away quickly.

"You gave me a lot to think about, too," she said. Her heart fluttered when she thought of what she had accomplished. "After I left your place yesterday, I actually sat down and did some writing."

Luke's brow furrowed. "Really?"

She nodded and slid down off the bed, retrieving her pages from under the bed skirt. The lid of the memory box came loose, and a random picture slid onto the floorboards.

Luke bent down and picked it up. "Oh, wow," he murmured, staring at the photo with narrowed concentration. He sat down on the edge of the bed and she joined him, leaning over to see the photo.

She smiled sadly at the image. It was taken on one of those lazy summer days at the lake. She was wearing a light blue sundress, and the thin straps of her red bikini could be seen on her bronzed skin. She was sitting on a picnic blanket, next to Luke, her head resting on his shoulder.

Her heart panged at the memory. They were so young then; it was the summer after she graduated from high school. He had a madras plaid bathing suit that summer, and she smiled, happy that it was still as she remembered it. Luke looked young, like the image of the boy she had clung to all those lonely years in New York, and tanned, happy. His white T-shirt was pulled taught across his broad chest, and an arm was draped lazily over her shoulder.

Looking at the two people in this photo, it was like they were someone else, someone other than the two people sitting here now, side by side, in silence. They were so young then, so innocent. She'd be joining him at college in the fall. She remembered thinking they'd never have to be apart again. They had the whole world before them, their whole lives, and the only care in the world they had that afternoon was knowing they would have to wait until the next day to see each other again. They always had tomorrow, and they counted on that.

She stared at the picture, wondering who those people

were, trying to bring them to the surface of her mind. If they knew what lay in store, what would they have said? Would they have scoffed, turned their shoulder, given a casual laugh? They thought they had forever, that it would always be them, there couldn't ever be anyone else that would even come close.

They didn't know anything. All they knew was that they loved each other.

"Mark must have taken it," Grace said softly. She looked up at Luke's profile, at the pain in his eyes, the thin line of his mouth, and she felt something deep within herself break. For years she had hated him, hated him for turning her away, shunning her, breaking her heart.

"We've hurt each other a lot," she observed quietly, blinking rapidly.

He handed the picture back to her. "Yes. We have."

She hesitated, running her fingers over the front page of her manuscript. "I want you to have this," she said, placing it in his hands.

He frowned. "What is it?"

"Something I started working on yesterday. You gave me a lot to think about."

"I saw you," he blurted, meeting her gaze. "I saw you at the store. I came to see you."

She'd figured as much. "I told you I was engaged before. That was Derek. He came to give me something of mine. And to say goodbye."

His blue eyes flashed.

"It's hard to let go of the past," she said. "But if you don't, you never move forward. I learned that once already. The hard way." She slid him a sidelong glance. He was staring at the manuscript.

"I'm sorry about your dad's store. I know how much it meant to you." He rubbed the back of his neck. "You always said that store is what inspired you to become a writer, but something I never told you is that your dad was the one who inspired me to be a teacher."

Grace frowned. "Really?"

Luke nodded. "After my dad died, I struggled in school. Your dad talked so fondly of his days as a teacher." He shrugged. "Every day I walked into that classroom I thought of him."

Grace looked down at her hands. "I never knew that."

"I'm giving up the store. I'm going to start a charity with the money I've been putting toward the rent." He paused. "Grace...I want you to have the storefront. I want you to have your bookstore, the café, all of it."

She snapped her gaze to him. "Luke. Are you sure?"

He nodded once. "Certain."

She reached over and took his hand, feeling its strong grip, its familiar warmth. She never wanted to let it go, and maybe now she wouldn't have to. "I'd actually decided to keep it open even without the expansion. Now...Thank you, Luke."

"So you're staying in town then?"

She nodded. "This is where I'm needed. It's where I'm meant to be."

He inched toward her. "I've let too much time go by already. I can't let another chance pass me by."

Her breath caught. "What are you saying?"

"I'm saying that Helen will always be a part of me, like you always were. But I'm ready to move on. I need to move on. With you." He smiled. "I love you, Grace. A part of me always loved you."

Tears blurred her vision and she laughed, brushing them away. "That's the best Christmas gift anyone has ever given me."

He slid her a grin. "You're going to have to come up with something pretty special to top it, then."

She tapped the manuscript. "Take a look."

He frowned, holding her eyes sidelong, turning to the first page, and then the second. She held her breath, waiting for him to stop, to say something.

"This is about us," he said, his tone laced with wonder.

She nodded. "Yes."

He read another page, shaking his head with a smile. "It's wonderful," he said, and she blew out a breath she hadn't realized she'd been holding.

"Really?"

He turned to her, his eyes searching hers, his lips curling into a smile that made her heart fall to the deepest pit of her stomach. "How does it end?" he asked, his eyes crinkling at the sides.

She looked into his face, into the eyes of the man who knew her inside out and still loved her in spite of it. "I was sort of hoping you would tell me."

Luke's mouth slid into a lazy grin, and he leaned forward, grazing his lips with hers. "Honeybee, you and I will never reach the end. We'll keep going and going and going."

She smiled through the taste of his lips on hers, reaching up to wrap her arms around his shoulders. "I wouldn't have it any other way," she said.

When her Main Street restaurant is ravaged in a fire, Anna Madison is left at the mercy of Mark Hastings—the one man she's spent years pretending she doesn't need...

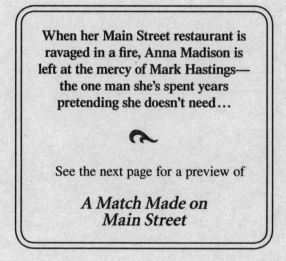

See the next page for a preview of

A Match Made on Main Street

CHAPTER 1

A strong friendship is *always* the best foundation for a lasting relationship."

Anna Madison stopped arranging the wild blueberry scones on a ceramic tray and frowned. *Not always*, she thought.

Up until now the chatter from the weekly book club had been nothing but a pleasant buzz, a lively and comfortable backdrop to an otherwise quiet morning in the shop, but now Anna strained her ears over the percolating coffee machine to hear the details of the conversation. Sliding the tray onto the polished wood counter, she narrowed her eyes at the group of women who were gathered around the antique farm table near the big bay window of Main Street Books—or The Annex, as the café extension was called—as they were every Saturday morning since the bookstore had reopened. From her distance behind the counter, she watched them sipping cappuccinos and enjoying fresh pastries, and wondered which of them would be foolish enough to make such a grand statement.

Her gaze fell on Rosemary Hastings, sitting at the head of the table, clutching this month's book club selection, *Sense and Sensibility,* with determined hands. Rosemary's ruby-stained lips were pinched with certainty, her back straight and proud, revealing years of professional dance training, her graying hair pulled back in her famous bun.

"I always told my children to start with a friendship first. If you build on that, true love will follow," she continued sagely. The rest of the group nodded their consent or politely sipped their coffee and tea, knowing better than to voice an opinion to the contrary. "Men and women are rarely only friends," she went on. "A friendship is just the beginning. In time it *always* blossoms into something more meaningful."

Oh, now this was too much! "Yeah right," Anna muttered. She shook her head and turned her attention to a basket of ginger-fig muffins, a popular item this morning, she noted with satisfaction as she mentally counted out just seven of the twelve she had brought over fresh from her primary restaurant, Fireside Café, down the road.

"Do you disagree, Anna?"

Well, now she'd done it. Anna glanced up to see Rosemary peering at her sharply from across the room, her head tipped in expectation. She sighed, feeling her shoulders sag slightly as ten pairs of eyes waited for her reply. She knew she should leave it—no good would come from starting an argument with Rosemary—and get on with her ever growing to-do list. In the month since Main Street Books had reopened, Anna was busier than she could have imagined. The expansion of the bookstore's café was a hit, just as her older sister, Grace, had predicted, and business at Fireside Café hadn't slowed either. She supposed she should be thrilled that everything was off to a good start—God knew she relied on both establishments to be a success so she could pay off the loan she'd taken out to help reinvent their late father's struggling store—but a business didn't run itself.

"What's that, Rosemary?" Anna's younger sister, Jane, came around the corner, clutching a stack of books to her chest. She glanced at the cover of the one on top and then slipped it into its proper slot in the cookbooks section, which bordered the café portion of the store.

"Your sister here was disagreeing with my statement that men and women cannot just be friends."

"Sure they can!" Jane smiled. "Look at Luke and Grace. They were friends for years before—"

"Before!" Rosemary raised her finger triumphantly into the air. "They were friends *before* they started dating. But I know my son." She began to wag her finger, oddly enough in Anna's direction rather than Jane's. Anna bit back a sigh and swept the crumbs from the counter into her palm, before dusting her hands off over the trash can. "He didn't want to only be friends with Grace. A pretty girl like that? No, no, *no*. He befriended her as a way of getting to know her. To be close to her." She shrugged smugly. "There's always more to it."

Anna snorted, causing Rosemary's smile to immediately fade. She bristled, glancing around her group with an incredulous look, her blue eyes wide with indignation. At least five of the women ducked their heads, pretending to leaf through the pages of their well-thumbed paperbacks. Anna found herself wishing her mother had decided to join the group, but Saturdays were busy for Kathleen's interior design business. Still, a little backup would be nice, and Jane was much too polite to stand up to the likes of Rosemary Hastings, especially as she now worked for her at the ballet studio.

"*Always* is a pretty strong word, Mrs. Hastings. Sometimes friendships do evolve, but sometimes they don't." *And sometimes they shouldn't*, she thought, frowning.

"Well, I'm speaking from personal experience," Rosemary huffed.

"As am I." Anna straightened the baskets of pastries on the counter and untied the strings of her apron. She should have left ten minutes ago, and here she was engaging in an utterly pointless debate.

"Oh?" This bit of news seemed to pique Rosemary's interest.

Refusing to elaborate, Anna handed her apron to Jane, who was taking over the afternoon shift while Grace manned the storefront and register. "Well, it's been lovely, but I'm afraid I have to get to the café. Enjoy your book club, ladies!" She smiled warmly, hoping that would put a gracious end to the conversation, but the expression on Rosemary's face said otherwise.

"Anna Madison, in all the years I have known you, I have never once seen you with a male friend. Romantically or otherwise."

Oh, how little she knew. Anna folded her arms across her chest and looked to Jane for reinforcement, but her sister simply raised her eyebrows and turned back to the coffee machine, adding to Anna's mounting frustration.

"Well, that's not true. I've dated plenty of men." One in particular, but she needn't mention that. Ever. No one in Briar Creek knew about the relationship she'd had in culinary school, and she intended to keep it that way. "Maybe not recently, but there have been men. Lots and lots of men."

From behind her she heard Jane quickly fumble for the tap. The rush of water did little to drown out her soft laughter. Rosemary, however, was not amused. Her lips pinched as she roamed her gaze over Anna's defensive stance. "You work too hard. A pretty girl like you should be married by now."

A gasp escaped from somewhere deep in her gut. Anna gaped at Rosemary's army of hopeless romantics, now nervously staring at their open paperbacks as if cramming for a test, and looked around the room for someone, anyone, who would find Rosemary's opinions as appalling as she did. She turned to Jane, who had decided to keep her back firmly to the room, and tossed her hands in the air before slapping them down at her hips. "This is the twenty-first century. I'm a career girl. It happens to suit me perfectly fine."

"Now, calm down," Rosemary ordered. "You clearly misunderstood me."

"Did I?" Anna glanced at her watch, and her pulse kicked with fresh anxiety. Already noon and the lunch crowd was probably in full swing.

"I meant you're all work and no play. You deserve to have a little fun."

All work and no play. Anna could think of one person in this town to whom the exact opposite applied. None other than Rosemary's own nephew, Mark Hastings. Yet somehow she didn't hear Rosemary complaining about his single status.

Not that Mark was ever single, she corrected herself. More like Mark was never committed.

"Last I checked, Briar Creek wasn't exactly crawling with available men," she pointed out, leaning back against a bookshelf. Oh, how her legs ached from standing so much. She hadn't stopped since she climbed out of bed this morning. At four o'clock. A vision of a steaming bath and good glass of Cabernet brought a faint smile to her lips. It was Saturday after all, and it wasn't like she had any other plans for her evening. By the time the dinner crowd trickled out, and the receipts were looked over, she could be on the couch and in her flannel pajamas by eleven, easy.

She grimaced. Better to keep that thought to herself.

"Oh, I can think of a few available men around here," Rosemary said cryptically, a sly smile playing on her painted lips.

"Well, that's a few more than I can think of," Anna declared. A familiar pang tightened her chest when she thought of Mark, working just down the street at the diner.

Why was she even thinking about him? She knew his reputation, knew it all too well, and she'd decided long ago to stop hoping one day he'd snap out of it. Mark was a flirt. A gorgeous, irresistible flirt. And a cad. Yes, he was a complete cad. And worse was that he knew it. And he had no intention of doing anything about it, either. So really, this had to stop. Right now.

Anna patted her pockets for her sunglasses and realized they were in her bag. Scolding herself for letting her mind wander down paths that should have been long forgotten, she retraced her steps behind the counter and crouched down to collect her belongings from a cabinet.

"Are you going to be all right on your own?" she asked her sister as she stood and gestured with her chin to the increasingly troublesome book club.

Jane gave her a rueful smile. "Don't worry. You're forgetting that Rosemary is my boss for twenty hours a week. If you think this is bad, you haven't seen her at the ballet studio. Trust me, you can never plié low enough for that woman."

Rosemary had a good heart despite her firm exterior, but nevertheless Anna didn't appreciate being on the receiving end of unwanted attention. If anyone deserved to be given the third degree in the romance department, it was Mark.

Mark. There she went again, thinking of the one man she should have put out of her mind years ago. Leave it to Rosemary to stir things up.

From across the room, a murmur arose, followed by what sounded an awful lot like squeals of suppressed glee. Jane's eyes sparked with interest. "Do we want to guess?"

"I don't think I want to even know," Anna groaned, hitching her handbag strap higher on her shoulder. She turned slowly to the group, sensing that Rosemary had one last matter to discuss before she could slip out the door.

"The gals and I have discussed it, and we have an idea." Rosemary paused for dramatic effect. "I am going to find you a man."

"Excuse me?" Anna choked on a burst of laughter, but Rosemary's wide smile did not slip. Her hands remained folded primly on her lap, her back ramrod straight, her gaze locked firmly with Anna's, whose eyes had widened in horror.

"You heard me," she said calmly. "I am going to find you a suitable match."

"Oh... please don't."

"Well, what about me?" Jane interjected, and at that, every woman who had previously been pretending to ignore the conversation snapped to attention. It wasn't like Jane to have an outburst, but the true cause of the prickling silence was the suggestion that Jane should go on a date at all. "Why Anna and not me?" she repeated, setting her hands on her hips.

Rosemary did a poor job of disguising her shock. "My dear... Anna's been unattached for her entire life! Why, she must be coming up on thirty by now!"

Not even twenty-eight and she was already earning a reputation as an old maid. This was getting worse and worse. "I'm the same age as Kara, Mrs. Hastings. And what about her? Why not set up one of your daughters?"

Rosemary waved her hand through the air. "Kara and Molly don't want me meddling in their personal affairs."

And I do? Anna looked past the café to the pedestal tables artfully arranged with books that dotted the storefront, craning her neck to see if another soul could be seen over the tall wooden stacks, but there was no one in sight. Grace was most likely in the back room, going over the inventory lists or joyfully opening the latest shipment of books and planning a new window display, and that left the two younger Madison sisters to keep things afloat. *And my, what a mess of it they were making.*

"What about me?" Jane said again.

Anna stared at her, trying to mask her bewilderment. For a moment she had thought this was Jane's creative way of diverting Rosemary's fixation, but the conviction in her hazel eyes and the pert little tilt of her nose said otherwise, even though it had been only a matter of months since Jane and her husband had filed for divorce. "Don't you think it's a little soon?" Anna asked gently.

"It wasn't too soon for Adam! He got a jump start while we were still married!" Jane retorted with a lift of her chin. Sensing the alarm in Anna's expression, she added, "Oh, please. It's hardly a secret." She looked at Rosemary. "Fair's fair. If you can find someone for Anna, you can find someone for me, too."

"But I don't even want to be set up!" Anna wrapped her arm around Jane's shoulder and announced, "Perfect. Mrs. Hastings, you can call on all these so-called available men in Briar Creek and give them Jane's number."

"Nope." Rosemary made a grand show of shaking her head until her dangling earrings caught on her red cashmere scarf, which was loosely draped around her neck. She winced as she gingerly unhooked it, and frowned as she inspected the snag in the material.

"Jane just told you she needs help getting back out there."

"Oh, I heard," Rosemary mused, dropping her scarf with a sigh of defeat. She smiled at Jane fondly. "And I'm going to help you, my dear. On one condition."

Beside her Jane was beaming, but Anna was no fool when it came to matters of the heart. Once she had been, but that was a long time ago. "What's that?" Anna hedged, her chest heavy with dread.

"You have to let me set you up, too, Anna." Rosemary hid her triumphant smile behind the rim of her mug.

"No way—"

"Oh, come on!" Jane begged, elbowing her gently.

Anna stared into the pleading eyes of her sister, noting the flicker of disappointment she saw pass through them. It was the same look that had been there for months now, a lingering sadness behind that brave smile. Jane was the strong one, the supportive one, not the demanding one. Jane was the one who would hand you the last ten bucks in her wallet and then silently go without herself. Jane never asked for anything. And here she was, asking Anna for the one thing she didn't want to give.

She'd spent how many years avoiding the very thing she was being asked to do: date. Dating led to falling in love, and falling in love led to heartbreak. Jane of all people should have learned that lesson by now, but from the hopeful look in her expression, for some reason it appeared she had not. Somehow, having the father of her child and the man who had vowed to love her 'til death repeatedly cheat on her, lie to her, and then leave her had not destroyed her sister's belief in love.

"Fine," Anna said through gritted teeth, ignoring the whoop that went up from the table of women. She was too busy focusing on Jane's grateful smile. It was the happiest she had seen her younger sister in months, possibly more, she realized. She blinked quickly, never wanting to think of Jane hurting that way again. "And with that, I'm really leaving now."

"Go, go!" Rosemary said over the ruckus. "I don't know how you can expect to run that place if you spend all day chatting with us."

Anna took a deep breath, this time forcing herself to remain silent, and turned to leave. Jane grabbed her by the arm. "Thank you," she said.

"You owe me," Anna warned as she slid her sunglasses

over her nose. She wound her way through the maze of bookshelves and pushed out into the afternoon sunshine, wondering how she could get out of this little promise she had made. There was no time in her life for men or dating or any of that nonsense. There was only time for work. That's how it had to be, and that's how she preferred it. Most of the time.

She lifted her chin, focusing on the sidewalk ahead, on the hours of work that would give her the sense of purpose she craved, when panic stopped her dead in her tracks. There, at the corner of Main Street and Second Avenue, was a gray cloud of smoke. A crowd had gathered opposite the familiar brick storefront, and people along the way had stopped to stare.

A fire truck with sirens blazing whizzed by her, forcing her long blond hair to whip across her face, and it was then that Anna started to run. *Not the café*, she silently begged, *please not the café*. She weaved her way through the shocked onlookers, almost knocking over a small child who was grinning at the trucks rushing by, knowing with each step that her worst nightmare was coming true.

Smoke was billowing out the windows now, and broken glass littered the sidewalk. A team of firefighters was jumping off the truck, clutching a long hose. By the time Anna arrived at the Fireside Café, gasping for breath that felt thick and tight in her lungs, there was so much commotion that she couldn't get a straight answer from anyone. Red lights flashed through the soot that filled the air and caused her to cough. The sheriff was marching forward, barking commands, ordering people to stand back. Firemen stretched their arms wide as they formed a barrier and the mass moved slowly back, gathering Anna into its frantic progression.

She stared at the crowd as she stumbled backward, searching through the blur of her vision for a familiar face, for someone, anyone, to tell her it was all going to be okay, that it was nothing, just a scare.

"Anna, oh God!" Anna whirled around to face her assistant manager, finding some relief in the sight of her friend. Kara's face was stained with tears.

Panic tightened her chest, forcing her out of her haze. "Is anyone in the building?"

"No. No, I don't think so," Kara muttered, shaking her head. She covered her face with both hands as a loud crash split through the town, eliciting a wave of cries from the crowd.

"Probably just a support beam," a gruff voice called out, and Anna felt her knees begin to buckle. Just a support beam. Just a café. No one was hurt—she was safe, she should focus on that. Yet somehow she couldn't. All she could do was stand there, clutching Kara's arm and watching helplessly as everything she had built for herself, everything she depended on, came crashing down around her. Just like everything did in the end.

Fall in Love with Forever Romance

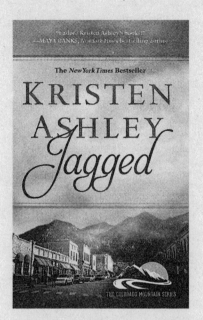

JAGGED

Zara is struggling to make ends meet when her old friend Ham comes back into her life. He wants to help, but a job and a place to live aren't the only things he's offering this time around...Fans of Julie Ann Walker, Lauren Dane, and Julie James will love the fifth book in Kristen Ashley's *New York Times* bestselling Colorado Mountain series, now in print for the first time!

Fall in Love with Forever Romance

ALL FIRED UP

It's a recipe for temptation: Mix a cool-as-a-cucumber event planner with a devastatingly handsome Irish pastry chef. Add sexual chemistry hot enough to start a fire. Let the sparks fly. Fans of Jill Shalvis will flip for the second book in Kate Meader's Hot in the Kitchen series.

Fall in Love with Forever Romance

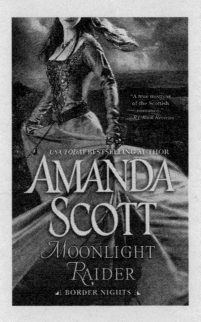

MOONLIGHT RAIDER

USA Today bestselling author Amanda Scott brings to life the history, turmoil, and passion of the Scottish Border as only she can in the first book in her new Border Nights series. Fans of Diana Gabaldon's *Outlander* will be swept away by Scott's tale!

Fall in Love with Forever Romance

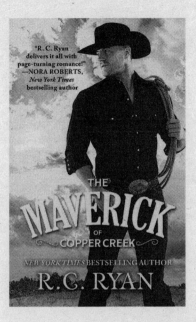

THE MAVERICK OF COPPER CREEK

Fans of Linda Lael Miller, Diana Palmer, and Joan Johnston will love *New York Times* bestselling author R. C. Ryan's THE MAVERICK OF COPPER CREEK, the charming, poignant, and unforgettable first book in her Copper Creek Cowboys series.

Fall in Love with Forever Romance

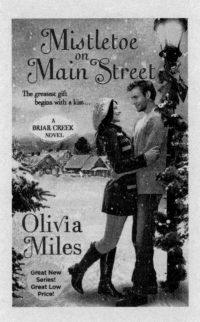

MISTLETOE ON MAIN STREET

Fans of Jill Shalvis, Robyn Carr, and Susan Mallery will love this charming debut from best-selling author Olivia Miles about love, healing, and family at Christmastime.